DARK HALLOWS II

TALES FROM THE WITCHING HOUR

EDITED BY **MARK PARKER**

STORY ILLUSTRATIONS BY **LUKE SPOONER**

SCARLET GALLEON PUBLICATIONS, LLC

DARK HALLOWS II: Tales from the Witching Hour
Copyright © 2016 Mark Parker
Published by Scarlet Galleon Publications, LLC
FIRST EDITION
Edited by Mark Parker
Cover design by David Mickolas
Story Illustrations by Luke Spooner

ISBN – 13: 978-1537639246
ISBN – 10: 1537639242
Printed in the U.S.A.

This publisher acknowledges the copyright holders of the original works as follows:

"The Enchanted Forest" copyright © 2016 by Lisa Morton
"Sugar Skulls" copyright © 2016 by Sean Patrick Traver
"The Witch" copyright © 2016 by Richard Chizmar
"One Bad Apple" copyright © 2016 by J.D. Horn
"The Trespasser" copyright © 2016 by Joshua Rex
"The Minch Lake Tragedy" copyright © 2016 by A.P. Sessler
"Through the Veil" copyright © 2016 by M.L. Roos
"The Jack-O'-Lantern Man" copyright © 2016 Brian Moreland
"Six" copyright © 2016 by Stuart Keane
"Netherlands" copyright © 2016 by JC Braswell
"The Many Hands Inside the Mountain" copyright © 2016 by James Chambers
"The Devil Take the Hindmost" copyright © 2016 by Annie Neugebauer
"The Glad Street Angel" copyright © 2016 by Ronald Malfi

ACKNOWLEDGEMENTS

Sincere thanks go to:

Richard Chizmar and Brian James Freeman for their continued
support and guidance.

David Mickolas for the eye-catching cover design and wonderful
promotional ad he created for *Dark Hallows II: Tales from the
Witching Hour*.

Luke Spooner for his illuminating story illustrations, each of which
really brought the stories to life.

The contributors, whose collective works not only took us to the
'dark holiday' of Halloween, but a step *further*—to the fearsome
realm of the Witching Hour—where magic is said to be at its most
powerful, and the tenuous scrim between the world of the living and
the dead…is *lifted*.

For the readers and followers of Scarlet Galleon Publications. Your continued support means more than you know. Whether through Facebook shares, likes, Twitter tweets, Amazon reviews—or, better still, book purchases—each one of you has helped grow Galleon into a worthy and respected brand. And, for that, we thank you!

CONTENTS

FOREWORD

It's that time again!

As I write this, a light September breeze is blowing in through the window next to my desk, and it has me thinking, once again, of that time of year, when the air grows chill, and the leaves begin their downward spiral, anxious to skitter off like so many brittle, skeletal fingers.

With autumn comes our favorite *dark* holiday—Halloween. Or, if you're a purist, *'Hallows Eve,* that time when neighborhood streets are lined with costumed trick-or-treaters, porches are festooned with jack-o'-lanterns and sundry other decorations dyed black, purple, Day-Glo orange, and bright lime green (the color of freshly opened antifreeze!). And any number of monsters can be found lurking amid the long, unforgiving shadows.

In thinking how this year's *Dark Hallows* could be different from last year's inaugural installment, I found myself thinking... *What if we went* darker? *Perhaps* later *in the evening, long after the little ones have all gone to bed, and the* real *monsters slowly begin to emerge?*

That's how *Dark Hallows II: Tales from the Witching Hour* came to be. In researching lore around the *'Witching Hour,'* it is posited that 3 a.m.—that hour of the night or early morning when no Catholic church is holding prayers—the world is tragically left vulnerable, and thereby *unguarded.* It's also thought that during this time, black magic is at its most potent, and the veil between the living and the dead is ruefully *pulled aside.*

I don't know about you, but that's evidence enough for me!

It is my sincere hope that this year's offerings hold you as entranced as they did me upon first reading them. We have wonderful illustrations by Luke Spooner accompanying each piece, lending some added *fright* to the stories themselves.

Whether it's the fantastical though terrifying world of Lisa Morton's *The Enchanted Forest*, or Richard Chizmar's quizzical hybrid tale—part horror story/part police procedural—or the heady, metaphysical realm encountered with Sean Patrick Traver's *Sugar Skulls*, trust me when I say, you're in for a frightfully good time!

Dark Hallows II: Tales from the Witching Hour is a reading experience filled with all we've come to associate with Halloween, and so much more. For this is the unmistakable time of year, when brightly colored mysteries are only equaled by so many dark, dreaded misgivings.

What will your choice be this year? Trick…or treat?

Mark Parker

Editor

THE ENCHANTED FOREST

Lisa Morton

He stood at the rusting metal gate, heart hammering as he stared into the dark woods beyond. A black cat perched on one of the gate's stone columns, its green eyes glittering with mischief. In a small clearing between the gate and the trees, headstones circled a small fire like campers listening to a ghost story. Beyond the mossy and cracked grave Jeffers, the path that led from the gate into the forest was limned in moonlight, pouring down in a blue cascade between the tall, black-barked trees.

Connor forced himself to examine the surroundings and think. The gate…the cemetery…the forest…something about it was familiar. The forest…

The Enchanted Forest.

The name burst into his consciousness with the force of a physical blow. He staggered back, refiguring, grasping at memories that rushed through his misfiring mind. *The Enchanted Forest.* The beginning… He knew this place. No, he'd *created* this place. He was this place…and it was him.

Drawn now by familiarity that lurked just out of his reach, teasing, Connor leaned forward on his cane and pushed open the gate. The hinges protested, but the cat remained undisturbed, causing Connor to suspect that it wasn't entirely real; but when he poked it with a finger, its fur was soft and its head turned to eye him. He suppressed a shiver as he moved past it. The answers he needed lay farther along the path, deeper in the woods. He hobbled warily past the graves, half-expecting some terrible surprise, a jack-in-the-box specter or paralyzing shriek, but there was nothing.

He knew the real scares waited ahead.

In the meantime, as he made his way along the narrow trail, his cane thumping against hard-packed earth, he tried to remember more about this place. About the day. About the beginning...

***

"Dad, have you been taking your pills?"

Connor looked up at his son, Jeff, whose handsome brow (*when had he gotten that big?*) was furrowed in concern. Beside Jeff stood Terry, the diminutive Guatemalan caregiver.

"Hell, yes, I've been taking my damn pills."

Jeff gestured at Terry, who stood by, impassive. "Terry says she hasn't seen you take them."

"Of course she hasn't. That's because I take them before she gets here in the morning."

Connor wasn't about to confess that he had been opening the little compartments of the huge pill container that Terry made up for him once a week, taking out his morning handful, and flushing them down the toilet. He was sure the pills were making him groggy and tired, and did nothing for him otherwise. But when he'd tried to argue that in the past—with Jeff, with Terry, with doctors and nurses—they'd all told him, "*Oh no, Mr. Carson, you must take your pills...and you can't miss a single day.*"

Bullshit.

"Dad, did you hear me?"

Connor looked up sharply. He didn't want to admit that he hadn't. "I heard you."

"So what day is this?"

Connor tried to gather his thoughts. What day was it? He didn't know, and he didn't care. Days hadn't meant much to him since Margie had died. *Nothing* meant much anymore, even his art. It had taken him a while after she'd gone to realize that everything he'd done—the work at the amusement park, the designs, the paintings—had all been for her. Without her, there was no reason to do it. "What damn difference does it make?"

Jeff tried a smile. "It's Halloween, and I've got a surprise for you."

Halloween. God, he and Margie used to love Halloween. They'd hold grand parties, costume affairs for all of their friends from Merry Mountain, and some years even the great man George Merry himself would turn up, elaborately costumed as a knight or a cartoon Napoleon.

"Halloween…"

Jeff's smile broadened. "Right. The surprise isn't ready yet, but give us another few hours." Jeff and Terry exchanged a conspiratorial look.

"Just don't throw me a party. I haven't had much interest in parties since your mother passed away in May."

The smile on Jeff's face crumpled. "Dad…Mom's been gone for three years. Are you *sure* you've been taking your pills?"

Three years…? Had it really been three years since the cancer had taken Margie, since Connor had picked up a paint brush?

"I'm fine," he lied.

***

Connor pushed into the woods, his way lit not just by the moon's rays but by mysterious glimmerings from behind the trees. Animal voices—bird caws, more distant mournful howls—sounded around him, and Connor felt a shiver that left him both fearful and strangely happy.

At least I know I'm still alive.

He rounded a slight turn in the path, and found himself surrounded by dozens of glowing red eyes. Things were hidden in the branches, in the trunks, small night things that peered out at him curiously, sometimes blinking.

I've been here before. If I'm right, around the next turn I'll see bubble-sized glowing things bobbing overhead, I'll hear tiny voices laughing…

He turned the corner, and was unsurprised to find himself facing an aisle between the trees filled with multi-colored lights floating just out of reach. He approached the first one and saw a humanoid figure, smaller than his fist, with iridescent wings.

Connor nodded and felt a deep sense of homecoming. "The Enchanted Forest," he murmured, as he let the sense of familiarity fill him.

***

"I want to call it 'The Enchanted Forest'," George Merry had said on that day in 1968.

Connor Carson, the latest hire into the design staff for Merry Mountain, tried to stay focused on the boss's words, but he was confused—he had the odd sensation of being two places at once. Part of him whispered, *This is a memory*, but another part was living it now, and he went along with that part.

"Think you're up for the job, Connor?"

Connor nodded vigorously. "Oh, yes, sir, Mr. Merry! If we can't make this the best walk-through attraction ever, I'll eat a dancing skeleton."

Merry chuckled. "That's what I like to hear. Now go draw me some good scares."

***

Connor was staring into the golden eyes of a huge wolf. Its head had pushed out from between the branches next to him, bringing him back to this place, and now he was breathing hard. The wolf's head was as big as an elephant's, its lips were pulled back in a snarl, its mouth filled with lethal white teeth, each as big as a knife blade.

The wolf...how did I forget about the wolf?

The head abruptly withdrew, vanishing back into the shadows behind the trees. Connor's breathing slowed, and he pushed on, trying to remember what came next...

***

Connor was hungry. He was surprised to see it was after 1

p.m. Where had the day gone?

"Terry…?"

His caregiver appeared, unfailingly cheerful. "What you need, Mr. Connor?"

"Food."

"We have some lunch."

Connor saw he was in his bedroom, and he let Terry help him up out of bed, positioning his hand on his cane. "I hate this goddamn thing."

Terry giggled. "Oh, no, no, Mr. Connor, you can't hate the cane."

"I do. I hate the way it squeaks on the tile. I hate the stupid rubber tip on the end. But most of all, I hate having to use it."

Terry gave us his arm a reassuring pat. "I know. I know. C'mon, I get Jeff and Patrick in here and we all have some nice tuna sandwiches, okay?"

"Jeff and Patrick are here…? What are they doing?"

"Something in the front yard—decorating for Halloween."

That's right…today is Halloween. "Terry, did I ever tell you that George Merry himself once told me he thought The Enchanted Forest was the greatest contribution to Halloween since trick or treat?"

Terry smiled. "You did tell me that, Mr. Connor. Many, many people love your Enchanted Forest."

Just then, they passed out of the hallway into the living room and Connor saw—for the millionth time—the huge framed poster for The Enchanted Forest. He'd designed that poster himself for the attraction's opening in 1972. Silk-screened in Day-Glo colors, the art showed a little girl clutching her father's hand tightly as both pulled back, their shoulders tensed, from a gigantic wolf's head thrust out from between menacing dark trees. The bright violet type set against the dark blue background of the overhead sky read "The Enchanted Forest Now Scaring at Merry Mountain". Connor remembered how opening day for the new attraction had broken the park's attendance records, how he and George had stood outside the exit of The Enchanted Forest, disguised in low hats and sunglasses, watching families exhaling and laughing. Finally George had clapped one hand on Connor's shoulder and said, "They love it. Good job, Connor. Good job."

George had walked away, but Margie—who had stood quietly just behind the two men—had stepped forward, taken Connor's hand, and kissed his cheek.

It had been the best day of Connor's life.

***

He couldn't remember what came after the wolf.

Connor stood a few feet from the next twist in the path, leaning heavily on his cane, afraid. The wolf had startled him. What if something even more frightening waited just ahead?

He didn't want to go forward. Should he turn around, go back the way he'd come? But the wolf was behind him, and he didn't relish facing it again. Besides…what if someone was waiting for him outside? How would it look if he'd been unable to complete the trip through his own creation?

He had to go on.

Taking a deep breath, he moved forward, cautiously placing the cane with each stop—it wouldn't do to fall here. It might be days before he was found, alone in this haunted place.

He turned the corner. The route ahead wasn't immediately visible—it narrowed and twisted—but he saw flickers of orange light, heard a low voice muttering.

What IS that?

Connor moved around the last group of trees blocking his vision and saw a clearing, with a house at the back and a figure near the path. The structure was an oversized gingerbread house, with walls and roof made of huge brown slabs of cookie, trimmed in white icing, a smoking chimney was built from red sugar plums, the windows were spun sugar, the trim gum drops and jelly beans. The figure was a wizened crone in a black hooded cape, stirring a huge bubbling cauldron as she softly recited a spell. The clearing was surrounded by a low fence made of candy canes and red licorice cross-beams. Near the witch, the black cat from the entrance sat atop a post, looking at Connor.

Connor was paralyzed with fear. He froze, unable to take his eyes from the witch. She was a fairy tale figure, certainly, but from where he stood she seemed completely real, so real he could almost feel evil rolling off her in waves. What if she looked up and saw him? The path was only a few feet from her—surely there was no way to move past her without being discovered…? And how had the cat moved from the front without him seeing it? Had it run through the forest, a secret trail only it knew about?

Then awareness started to return, and he relaxed: *Of course—how could I have forgotten about The Witch? She became the most famous character in all of Merry Mountain. Even now, in the 21st century, haunters and designers call her the most realistic audioanimatronic character ever.*

But even with the return of his memories—weeks spent over his drafting board, getting every crease in her face and gnarled knuckle just right—Connor was uneasy. For one thing, he could smell the rank odor of whatever she was brewing up in the cauldron, he could feel the heat radiating from the cook-fire…wasn't the fire fake, just a few shreds of fabric and crinkles of foil cleverly lit from below to create the illusion of flames?

He shouldn't be feeling any heat from it. And that smell, like—

"…eye of newt and tongue of frog, a tick from the tail of a diseased dog…" the Witch muttered, as she used a long branch (a broomstick?) to stir the cauldron.

The words, something about the words…a memory of a writer handing Connor a script, a new draft of the Witch's words…

Connor knew that some part of this wasn't real, but which part? Was the Witch nothing but the amazing robot the Merry Mountain technicians had created? Was the cat that watched him even now with a malicious glint in its emerald eyes nothing but gears and metal framework? Or were they not even *that* real, concocted from his memories?

There was only one way to find out.

Connor took a deep breath and moved forward.

"…a mirror's shard and a skin scarred, a potion made for

dear price paid..." The Witch moved slowly, bent over the cauldron, stirring, muttering, stirring, muttering...

And then she looked up at Connor.

He froze, staring back, nerveless, immobilized. There was nothing mechanical about her eyes—hazel green, flecked with red, moist and set in fleshy folds beneath tufted brows. Her mouth twisted up into a grin, and she said, "You haven't taken your pills, have you?"

The absurdity of the question jolted Connor. He looked down, confused—

When he looked back up, the Witch had become Jeff, leaning forward over the kitchen table. His partner Patrick sat beside him, chewing a sandwich. The smell of tuna hit Connor, and he saw he held a forgotten half-sandwich in one hand, tuna salad spilling out of the sides onto the plate.

"I...what?"

Jeff glanced back at Patrick, who set his sandwich down, concerned. "Connor," Patrick said, "you aren't taking your pills in the morning, are you?" Behind Patrick, Terry stood, arms crossed, frowning.

"Look, the goddamn things make me groggy, okay? Yes, I stopped taking them. What's the big deal?"

"Dad, you can't just go cold turkey off some of these medications. That's why you've been so confused lately."

Connor started to utter a denial, but he couldn't do it— he *had* been confused. He felt like a kid busted for underage drinking.

"Look," Jeff said, his tone conciliatory, "I'll make a deal with you: if you take the pills today, we'll get the doctor on the phone on Monday and see if we can't swap them out for something that'll make you less groggy, how about that?" Terry stood now with the white and tan and yellow pills in a napkin and a glass of water.

With all of their eyes on him, he felt the weight of obligation. Silently, Connor reached out, took the pills and water, and downed the handful in a single gulp. "There," he said, rattling the table as he slammed the empty glass down.

Patrick smiled. "Connor, we're just concerned about you. And you know how much we'd love to see you paint again."

Connor shook his head. "That won't happen. Not without Margie."

Jeff patted his father's hand. "Maybe…just think about it." Jeff glanced at Patrick, and they both rose. "We've got a little bit more work out front, so why don't you rest until we're done."

"Fine."

The two younger men rose and headed back out, and Connor let Terry help him to his feet. "I don't want to go back to the bedroom, Terry. I'll stay out here."

"Okay, Mr. Connor." She led him to his favorite couch, the one surrounded by art he'd done for both George Merry and himself. Once he was comfortable, he found himself staring at an oil painting he'd done for Margie ten years ago, one that showed a group of trick-or-treaters at a door, surrounded by glowing jack-o'-lanterns and holding up their treat bags and buckets. Margie had loved Halloween and she'd loved that painting.

No, no more. Not without her.

He closed his eyes and slept.

***

It was dusk when he awoke. Jeff and Patrick were standing over him, both covered in dust and paint. "Dad," Jeff was calling softly, "Dad…"

Connor looked up, awakened from a dream that had left him agitated although he couldn't remember what it had been about. "What?"

"The surprise is finished. Come out front."

Connor groaned as he rose from the couch, knees protesting. Shuffling with the cane, he followed them out the front door and down the walk. He saw children running on the sidewalks, shrieking and swinging orange plastic pumpkins, and it took him a moment to remember:

Today was Halloween.

"Don't look back at the garage yet," Patrick said, trying to walk between Connor and the house. Connor saw tree branches and cables and wires, and he had to admit he was curious. Jeff had vanished, but he called out, "Don't turn around until I tell you to!"

Connor waved over his shoulder. "Okay, okay…"

Across the street, other houses were just setting out lit jack-o'-lanterns and turning on lights and fog machines. From somewhere down the block, Connor heard amplified sound effects—shrieks and moans and jangling chains—and he felt the ghost of his Halloween excitement stir. How he'd loved this day as a child—the freedom, the night, the imagined power—and later, as an adult, he'd understood that the holiday spoke to him on some deep, primordial level. It whispered into his ear with a voice as crackling and rough as tree leaves crunched underfoot; *the seasons change, and death happens, and you can't stop it so you might as well celebrate it.* He'd answered that voice with his own creativity and George Merry's urging, and The Enchanted Forest had been the result.

Connor was still gazing out on the street, drinking in the lit pumpkins and costumed revelers, when he heard an electric buzz behind him, and a glow lit the street. "Turn around, Dad," his son called from behind him.

He turned—and was dumbstruck.

The entrance to The Enchanted Forest now covered his driveway. There was the old iron gate set into the stone pillars; there was the winking black cat perched at one side. Where his front lawn usually was, tombstones circled a reasonably believable fake fire; the interior of the garage had been filled with faux trees and lit artfully from overhead to suggest a full moon lighting a receding path.

Jeff had been bent over an extension cord, having plugged in the lights. He approached his father and Patrick now, smiling tentatively. "What do you think?"

Connor asked, "This is what you were working on all day…?"

"Yep." Jeff put an arm around Patrick. "We've been working on parts of it for the last six months. This is the first time we've set it all up. I think it came together pretty well."

Connor listened, and heard the sounds: crickets, owls hooting, wind in leaves. "You even got the audio..."

Jeff answered, "We called your old friends in the Merry Sound Department, and they got us the original tapes."

Connor took a few steps forward, drinking it all in. "Is it all here?"

Patrick cried, "Oh, gods, no!"

Jeff added, "We couldn't afford to do all of it, but...well, follow the path. I think you'll be surprised by what we *did* manage to pull off."

Without another word, Connor moved forward, and fell into The Enchanted Forest.

***

The path moved on past the Witch, and for an instant Connor glimpsed something else behind her—a normal sliding glass door. Some part of his mind recognized his house, realized that the path had actually wound down the side of his house and into his back yard...but this was The Enchanted Forest, *his* world.

After the Witch came the Pumpkin Village. Sure enough, he turned a corner, and there were dozens of pumpkins all around him, stacked on bales of hay, held under the arms of scarecrows, perched in the crooks of tree branches. He knew this was too small to be the Pumpkin Village from the *real* Enchanted Forest at Merry Mountain—that had *hundreds* of jack-o'-lanterns, not dozens—but some of the pumpkins were animated, singing in chorus. Connor remembered writing some of those lyrics, and as he listened he began to sing along:

Pumpkins glare in the midnight dark,
Watch out for the branches or they'll leave a mark!
The Halloween moon's full and the trees are stark,
Here in The Enchanted Forest.

The pumpkin nearest him screwed up its face into a toothy grin and a wink, and Connor didn't care whether it was real or not, in the past or present. If this was all just some episode of withdrawal-induced dementia, at least it had become a happy one.

Then he remembered what came next, and his happiness snuffed out like a tired candle at the end of Halloween night.

The storm...

The Merry Fantaseers (for such had the designers and engineers of Merry Mountain come to be known) had spent years on the storm. They'd perfected ways to project overhead images of rushing clouds and lightning flashes; they'd figured out how to mimic water in trees, and strong winds, and thunderous sounds. The experience had been so realistic that guests had tried to flee into the trees for shelter, and they'd had to create a waist-high fence to keep them confined to the path. Some laughed when they reached the other side, checked themselves over, and realized they were completely dry.

But tonight, Connor knew something was different; he heard the winds ahead, felt an icy chill rushing down the path, and he knew *this* storm wouldn't be so tame. He was seized by an almost irrational fear of facing it. He remembered this wasn't the real Enchanted Forest, but an elaborate Halloween haunt; he was in his own backyard...wasn't he?

"Jeff...Patrick?" He called out, but his voice sounded weak and hoarse, and no one heard. He couldn't see anything beyond the trees and the pumpkins, only the path leading ahead, into the storm.

Fine, Connor thought. He would swallow back his dread, walk through whatever came, illusion or harsh reality. He would reach the other side and this would all be over.

He set off along the trail, leaving the leering pumpkins behind. The temperature dropped, leaving the old man to shiver. He tried to move faster, but the cane was hard to handle on the dirt. The path grew even smaller, the trees pressing closer, and he saw the faces in the trunks, twisted wooden faces, full of scorn and menace. Were some of the faces moving? He wasn't sure, but the idea terrified him.

The path widened and he was in the storm.

Winds buffeted him, forcing him to lean into them. Thunder was deafening, lightning blinding. He heard voices around him, carried on the air currents, screeching and howling; there were hints of spirits in the air, barely-glimpsed shapes tearing along with the wind. The rain seemed quite real, causing the ground to slicken. The cane slid and Connor went down; he caught himself, though, and wound up on all fours.

He gave in at that point. He put his hands over his ears, squeezed his eyes shut, and screamed.

When he finally ran out of breath, before he could draw in more air to continue screaming, silence descended. Connor moved his hands from his ears, waiting...but the quiet held. He was no longer shivering, the rain had stopped, and when he opened his eyes, he saw something unexpected before him.

There was a small figure now crouched in the center of the opening a few yards away; a boy, maybe eight years old, bent over something, his back to Connor, his hands moving.

Connor's breath caught as he searched his memory: what was this? He couldn't remember it being part of the storm, or any other scene in The Enchanted Forest. At Merry Mountain, the storm had spilled out into the Dance of the Dead, the attraction's grand finale: an open meadow where glowing blue phantoms waltzed to music played by a skeletal band. But this, this kneeling apparition...was it something his son had added? Or was it some bit he'd forgotten, the memory misplaced along with so many others?

Would it be the most frightening thing he'd ever seen? Would it leave him scarred in some way?

He found his cane, painfully got to his feet and inched forward, cautiously, trying to give the figure as wide a berth as possible, never taking his eyes from it. He heard a small sound—high-pitched, musical—and realized the small figure was humming, something familiar.

It was *Monster Mash*. It'd been Connor's favorite song as a child. He'd had a 45 rpm record of it he'd played every Halloween, while he...

Connor suddenly knew.

He no longer walked with fear, but with burgeoning joy. As he rounded the kneeling boy, he saw what he'd realized would be there: a grinning jack-o'-lantern, its face still only half-finished.

The boy had a tiny pocket-knife which he used to saw through the thick orange flesh, up and down as he created the toothy smile. If he saw Connor, he didn't react.

He was Connor. Connor stood over him, watching, recalling...

The joy he'd felt every October, when the plans he'd set up all year long came to fruition. Plans for costumes, for pumpkins, for yard decorations. Plans that had given him his first taste of artistic satisfaction that had paved the way for a life spent pursuing dreams. A successful life, and for the most part a happy life, until...

The boy looked up and he *did* see Connor. He stopped working on the jack-o'-lantern for a moment, screwed his small face into a squint, and said, "You should never have stopped. She didn't want you to."

The boy vanished. Connor saw, clearly now, his house behind the single layer of cardboard trees that Jeff and Patrick had set up, the speakers tucked in among the trunks, the floor fans half-hidden by mossy netting. He pushed past the forest, opened the rear sliding doors, went into the house, and looked at the framed paintings on the walls.

My God, I've wasted three years. Margie would've kicked me in the pants.

"Did you like it, Dad?"

Connor looked up to see Jeff and Patrick standing in the front entry way, eyeing him uncertainly.

He gave them back a smile. "I can't believe how much of it I'd forgotten. You did it real justice."

Jeff's face lit up, while Patrick hugged him with one arm.

"Tomorrow," Connor said, "I'm going to have Terry drive me down to the art store. But tonight..."

Connor marched past them, his gait so strong he barely needed the cane. He picked up a bowl of candy ready for trick or treaters, and marched out the front door. He wasn't sure why he felt so good; maybe his medications had kicked back in, or maybe it was seeing even this reduced version of The Enchanted Forest.

As he made his way down to the beginning of The Enchanted Forest, a black cat ran past his feet. On any other day, Connor might have made a joke about it being bad luck, but tonight it felt like magic, *good* magic.

"Happy Halloween," he called after the cat.

SUGAR SKULLS

Sean Patrick Traver

The neighbors didn't call him the Necromancer, *el Necromantico*. They called him the Catman. But el Necromantico he was, and Dulcé knew it. She'd spent the better part of a year tracking him down.

His modest parcel of land north of Los Angeles was labeled 'Rancho Delgado' in the city records, but the people she'd spoken to all pronounced it *del Gato*. The Cat Ranch. It was no longer a working ranch (not as of today, early in the summer of the year 1900), but merely a sliver of property carved off from one of the massive cattle concerns that had gone belly-up decades earlier, during the drought of 1862, and nostalgically named in honor of that bygone way of life. It lay nestled into the foothills south-east of the Santa Monica Mountains, near an area misspelled on Dulcé's map as 'Los Felis,' which seemed in keeping with the general feline theme. No sign marked the dirt track she found leading off the dusty wagon route between downtown and the strawberry fields up near Tropico, when she coasted to a stop on her fat-wheeled bicycle, but several cats eyed her with calm disinterest from where they lounged in the tall grasses. Dulcé figured that was as clear an indicator as she needed. She gulped the last warm, leathery-tasting water from a Spanish-style wineskin she'd brought along and pushed off across the open field, pedaling toward the copse of trees the track led up to, bouncing over stones and gopher holes and perspiring freely under the famous California sun.

The half-dozen cats who'd been enjoying their midday loll by the side of the road got up, one by one, and silently trotted after her.

***

The Catman knew she was coming. He knew what the cats knew, even across the half-mile of chaparral prairie between his house and the nearest road. That was their bond, revealed by ritual when he was a boy, developed and strengthened in the decades since. Other operators had affinities with other animals, but Tomás Delgado's *nagual*, the beast with the same shape as his soul, was unmistakably the cat. Tigers or tabbies, mousers or mountain lions—it didn't matter. They knew him for a brother, and were always prepared to lend him their ears, or their eyes, or their claws.

He could've dissuaded the woman on wheels, but didn't see a reason to. People came, now and then, with questions they thought he could answer. Sometimes he could, and sometimes he did, especially when the querent agreed to owe him a favor in return. Tom had most of what he needed out here, miles away from the city, but when the realworld had to be met on its own terms, influence could be a valuable commodity.

Still, he always made them work for it, like a Zen abbot turning the same supplicant away from the temple gate day after day, until persistence proved the seeker's merit. Though Tom was no monk, and his brand of enlightenment rarely helped anyone. The dead were easier to stir up than they were to quiet down again, so he liked to know the people who sought him out were firm in their resolve.

He dunked the mouth of an earthenware jug under the spring that burbled from a cleft between two rocks out behind his house until it was full and then carried the cold, heavy vessel back, with his cane tucked under one arm. His hip didn't twinge much in warm weather, but his old habit of carrying the stick ran too deep for him to set it aside.

He'd just settled back into the chair on his porch where he

liked to sit and watch the clouds scud across the sky and poured himself a glass of fresh water when the wheelwoman rolled into view.

She stopped dead at the edge of the clearing, some yards away from the house, and the way she gaped in open astonishment reminded Tom of how overwhelming the presence of *los gatos* could be. He forgot how it looked, he supposed, when it was just him and them out here. A couple dozen animals turning their bright, baleful eyes in a new arrival's direction could be an unnerving sight.

The dark-haired woman in the absurd cycling suit dropped a kickstand on her contraption and dismounted on unsteady legs. She didn't even see Tom, not at first. Not until he stood up, intending to greet her properly, and the fifty or so cats partaking of the relative cool beneath his trees all stood up with him.

The visitor stepped back... but didn't turn and flee.

"Hola," she said uncertainly. Her skirt, Tom noticed, was actually split, more like a pair of wide-legged trousers. The whole ensemble looked cumbersome, far too heavy for the season (though the hems of her skirt-like pant legs did swish prettily around her high-booted ankles). "Hello. I- I'm looking for a Mr. Tomás Delgado. Have I come to the right place?"

Tom tipped his head in a gesture that was not quite a nod. He wore his hat so that the brim concealed his eyes.

"¿Prefiere hablar español?"

"Whatever you like," Tom said. "We're all Americans now."

"Um. Well, yes, I suppose that's so. My name is Dulcé Calavera."

Tom waited.

"I understand you're a man of particular knowledge, Señor Delgado," Dulcé Calavera said, eyeing the cats that watched her from the low branches of the nearest trees. Others stared from the roof or out from under the porch.

"Who told you that?"

"People who call you 'Black Tom'."

Tom tapped his cane on the porch steps and the cats departed, draining away like water. "I think you have been misinformed about me, Mrs. Calavera."

"Miss. Or doctor. Or Dulcé. And I'm quite sure I haven't." The small, determined woman's accent was hard to pin down, like she'd lived in different places during formative years. He might've guessed her for a fellow *Californio*, albeit a well-traveled one. It was part of the reason he was talking to her. "The black magician of los Ángeles," she continued, "whispered of by witches for miles around. They say you walk with a limp because you once fell from a hole in the sky."

Dulcé looked pointedly at Tom's oak-wood walking stick, the one that made him seem older than his years, at first glance.

"A myth," he said.

Dulcé shrugged. "Of course."

"Why did you come here?"

"To see what you can show me, and to know what you can teach me."

"Yes, but *why*?"

Heartbreak and money were the usual reasons. Things left too long unspoken, or valuable secrets taken to the grave.

"I'm writing a book," was what Dulcé Calavera told him.

***

Tom refilled her waterskin so she wouldn't die of heatstroke on the road and sent her away that afternoon without confirming her deductions. He had some regrets on that score, but people's usual reasons were trouble enough, and Dr. Calavera's proposal sounded insane by comparison. Insane and insulting. Tom bristled at the idea of the secrets he'd inherited being recorded as mere 'folklore,' primitivism, though worse still was the idea of the new people, these Americans, actually believing in the stories he might tell. Cooperating in such an endeavor would be a dangerous betrayal of his vows. There'd been trouble enough with interlopers already, in the years since California stopped being Mexico and turned into one of these United States. He didn't want to encourage more.

The enduring mysteries of Mictlantecuhtli, *el Rey de los Muertos*, the funerary god of his ancient Aztec ancestors, were not a fit subject for modern scholarship.

But his idly-conceived comparison to a stern Zen teacher proved more fitting than he could've guessed when the lady anthropologist turned up again a week later, this time carrying a picnic lunch of chopped-chicken sandwiches in a wicker bicycle basket. Tom still didn't tell or promise her anything, but he enjoyed seeing her again. She looked to be in her early forties— ten or twelve years younger than he was—with a few first streaks of silver threaded through her black hair and endearing crinkles around the corners of her very dark eyes, but she had a girlish enthusiasm for the subjects that caught her fancy. She seemed delighted that he shelved *The Picture of Dorian Gray, The Time Machine*, and other silly novels right alongside Darwin and Frazer in his not-so-small library, which had piled up all around the house over a number of years. He may have been a hermit, but he wasn't a hayseed. After lunch he played his guitar for her a bit, like a fool, and sent her on her way again well before dark, but later that night found himself wondering what she thought of him. He'd certainly never known anyone like her.

The next week she brought a bottle of wine along with the sandwiches.

The week after that, she brought two. She didn't go home before dark on that occasion, or before the next night, either.

Dr. Calavera's research focused on magical practices in the modern world, and her methodology consisted of deep immersion in the sub-cultures she studied. She told him about dancing naked with traditional witches in the English countryside, and of seeing a real *zombi* pulled wide-eyed and gibbering from the Louisiana crypt his body had been bricked into a day and a night before. For an academic (hell, for anyone) she led an astonishing life. But she was a local girl, too, as Tom had surmised—born near Pasadena to a once-wealthy Mexican-American family that came through the 'conquest of California' with enough resources intact to let her study abroad.

Her eyes seemed to shine when she described the capitals she'd visited, and Tom found himself envying her wistfully while he listened to her tales. Little of the traveling he'd done in his time had been physical in nature.

Dulcé's increasingly frequent overnight absences from her rooming house in the city began to draw notice, and then commentary. She was given some benefit of the doubt, as she was a respectable scholar working with a grant from the University of Southern California and not some wild young thing, but it was still quite improper for an unmarried woman to sleep where and with whom she pleased—a corrupting influence on the morals of the other boarders, to be certain—and before a month was out her landlady quietly asked her to leave.

That was how Dulcé came to spend the rest of the summer at the Cat Ranch.

Tom hardly felt put out. He didn't worry any more about his hoarded secrets, either. He'd already decided he would tell this woman anything she wanted to know.

***

Not that he didn't have an ulterior motive.

Tom owed his patron another acolyte, a replacement for himself. All of *los Hombres del Rey* did, by tradition. It was the only way to be released from their vows of service after death. No woman had ever joined their ranks, as far as he knew—they didn't call themselves the King's Men for nothing—but perhaps one could, provided she was willing to commit herself.

Dulcé Calavera was the most committed person Tom had ever met. The initiation process wasn't easy, but less qualified applicants had made the grade. That goddam Englishman for one, the newest of the King's Men. The Interloper, as Tom thought of him, though his real name was Winston. Winston Something-or-other. He could never remember and didn't care to. They were never going to be friends.

Replacing himself in the employment of the King wasn't a pressing concern, as he didn't expect to die tomorrow, but the requirement had begun to weigh on him as more gray crept into his beard. Dulcé would inherit the same obligation (if el Rey accepted her), but that only meant she'd have to find a pledge of her own, in due course.

Tom thought she would find the terms of that deal amenable. And he was right.

***

"It's a *real* thing? The hole in the sky?"

Tom nodded. They were lying in bed as a hot afternoon cooled into evening, passing a cigarette he'd rolled back and forth.

"Not a metaphor or a legend or some sort of navel-of-the-world myth? An actual, literal hole in the sky?"

"I don't know another way to say it."

"And it leads to the land of the dead? The *literal* land of the dead? The afterlife?"

"Mictlan. The King of that place is Mictlantecuhtli. He says the first of his priests made the hole with sacrifices. So many sacrifices that the veil between worlds grew thin, and wore through."

"Aztec priests? We're far north from Tenochtitlán."

Tom shrugged. "People migrate. And what we're talking about would have been ancient history already by the time Cortés arrived."

"Why is it in the sky?"

"I asked that once. El Rey told me there was a pyramid. A temple, a 'false mountain,' and those priests made their offerings at the top. But if there ever was, it was *very* long ago. A tree grows there now, right below the hole. An oak that's grown taller than any oak should. You can see it's been there for many hundreds of years."

"And you've gone there? To Mictlan?"

"No. Never. Just to the edge. To Death's waiting room. Once you go over, there's no coming back. But you can talk to the dead at the door. El Rey will bring whoever you want to see. Plato. Cervantes. Shakespeare. Your grandmother who died when you were small. Anybody."

"When can we go?"

"Soon. There are preparations that have to be made. You have to be made ready."

"Tell me what I have to do."

***

They began their work that night.

Tom took Dulcé's hand in his (the one not holding his walking stick), and they set off across the misty fields as the moon came up. Their summer had vanished out from under them. Even though the days were still warm this far into October, the nights cooled off precipitously. *El Dia de los Muertos* was right around the corner, preceded this evening by the Americans' new holiday, which they called 'Halloween.'

By any name, this was a favorable time of year for their operation, when the boundaries between the worlds were at their most ephemeral.

Tom stooped to gather mushrooms as they came across them—the variety known to the old people as 'the flesh of the gods,' *Teonanactl*. (These grew best in grazing pastures, and had been easier to find back in the days when local *rancheros* used cowhides as currency.) He ate a couple straight out of the ground, and handed more to Dulcé so that she might reluctantly do the same.

This was the first invocation.

The Tree Below the Hole in the Sky couldn't be approached directly, Tom explained. There were wards around it, concealments put in place by the first of the King's Men, to guard their secret access to the afterlife and ensure the privilege that it conferred. The age-old hexwork scrambled an unprepared seeker's sense of direction. It deceived eyes that hadn't been adjusted to see the worlds beneath the world. The ritual procedure for locating the Tree despite these effects had been handed down for a millennium amongst el Rey's Men.

Tom could have shown her the route to the Tree (he'd traversed it often enough in the last forty years), but he couldn't show her the *way*. The manner in which they searched counted almost as much as where, in this case. Tom had his cats, but Dulcé needed a guide of her own to help them navigate the wards.

Her task, then, was to meet her beast. Her nagual—the animal that ruled her nature and chaperoned her dreams.

Tom sat down on a handy rock when they reached the bank of the Arroyo Seco. Dulcé stood staring up at the river of stars splashed across the sky. She cocked her head, listening to the wind rustling through the black nighttime trees as though it were music.

"How do we start?" she asked. Her dark eyes were black in the moonlight, like she had no irises at all.

"We already have." Tom tipped his chin, and Dulcé whipped around in time to see a large, tawny mountain lion slink out from the brush behind her. She froze as the cat padded toward her on paws as large as a man's hands, then sat down some feet in front of her, like a trained creature looking for a treat.

"Um, Tom?" Dulcé said, not quite daring to take her eyes off the wildcat.

Don't be afraid, he thought at her, watching her through the cat's flashing eyes. The animal had mentally stepped aside at his unspoken request, allowing him to leave his body and settle into its head. He *was* the big cat now, possessed of new, sharp senses and flexible feline strength. The omnipresent ache in his hip stayed with his human body, distant as a memory, and that was a sensation he always relished. He lay down on the dry river bank and rolled over onto his back, like a tame house pet, to show Dulcé there was nothing to fear.

Now you, Tom thought, and could see from her expression that she was receiving the words, though not exactly hearing them. She took the experience in stride. *Call. Imagine running free across the wild hills. Remember feeling unfettered in your dreams.*

Dulcé nodded, and closed her eyes. She frowned at first, then broke into a smile.

The shadows beneath the willow trees some yards away seemed to congeal into a tall black horse that clopped out from under the low-hanging branches. He shook out his mane and neighed softly. Steaming breath curled from his nostrils. He displayed no agitation whatsoever over the presence of Tom's wildcat.

Look, Tom thought, and Dulcé did. Her eyes welled and she went to tentatively stroke the horse's black velvet muzzle. "Oh, Tom…" she murmured. "Can this be real?"

Do you know him?

Dulcé nodded emphatically. "*El Caballo de la Bruja*," she said. "The Witch's Horse. My aunts told me stories of him when I was little, and I used to ride him in my dreams."

Tom considered. He supposed he'd heard of the Witch's Horse, another local legend, like the Hole in the Sky itself. Why shouldn't more than one of them be true? It was said that the black stallion had haunted the hills and canyons around the Cahuenga Valley for centuries, since before the Spanish even brought horses to this continent, awaiting the return of the powerful sorcerer who'd conjured him from shadows.

"My aunts said he would sometimes come to answer a witch's cry, *el grito de una bruja*, if she needed help. I always thought of him as *Sombra*, Shadow. I used to go out to the fields and call and watch for him when I was sad or upset, like a little ritual. But he only came to me when I fell asleep." Dulcé swiped at her eyes with the backs of her gloved fingers. "I think it was those stories that started my interest in *all* stories. I wouldn't be me today if I hadn't believed them for a while."

Tom paced around the horse on silent paws, examining it from every angle. There might've been something to those tales, because the animal didn't seem entirely real, up close. It smelled like nothing more than dust and rain. *He's saddled,* Tom thought in Dulcé's direction, and she saw that it was so. He wore a bridle as well, and black leather saddlebags, one of which she opened. Inside she found a roll of dark gray fabric that unfurled into a long cloak, very much like the garment Tom had seen Mictlantecuhtli draped in on any number of occasions.

He found this disquieting, but chose to take it as a sign that they were expected.

Ready?

Dulcé looked at the powerful horse. "Really?" Her face was aglow with childlike joy.

Tom tipped his cat's head to the south. Dulcé shook out the cloak and threw it around her shoulders, becoming just another of the night's shadows, and swung herself expertly into the saddle. (Luckily she'd worn her split-skirt cycling suit, which was easier to hike in than most of her other clothing.) She exchanged one more glance with the mountain lion before Tom bounded off in the Tree's direction. Dulcé nudged her mount's sides with her heels and shrieked with delight when the shadow-horse lunged forward, chasing after the fleet-footed cat.

**

The stallion outpaced the lion before they covered the first mile, and gained a substantial lead after that. Tom could still hear peals of laughter echoing back to him even when horse and rider were well out of sight.

His catamount was panting by the time he reached the Tree, but Dulcé had been there for some minutes already. Tom found her standing beside her horse (which didn't look so much as winded), staring up into the monstrous oak's maze of branches. Its overwhelming height left no doubt that they'd come to the right place. Her hair had come loose along the way, and the wind had reddened her cheeks. She grinned at the tired wildcat that came sloping toward her through the yellowed grasses.

"Do we climb up?" she asked when he flopped down beside her. "Do I?"

Tom hesitated. He hadn't expected to climb, not this soon. He hadn't even brought his body, and he could hardly present her to Mictlantecuhtli without it. Who could've expected her to mount up and ride her goddam spirit animal? Tonight's exercise had been meant as a test, but Dulcé was ahead of the learning curve. As she probably had been for most of her life, Tom reflected. And that cloak, so like el Rey's, had been waiting for her. So maybe this decision wasn't his to make.

I'll leave it up to you, he told her. *If you feel ready, climb.*

Dulcé looked up again into the black nighttime foliage as a bank of clouds slid across the moon, casting her face into darkness.

"I'm not sure I am," she said after a moment. "Ready, I mean."

The relief Tom felt surprised him. Now that he'd brought her right to the edge of what he'd promised, he didn't know whether to encourage or dissuade her.

"It changed the course of your life, didn't it? Climbing up there."

This was nothing he could deny. Mictlantecuhtli's patronage had impacted everything about him, down to the way he walked. A crunching fall from the Tree had long ago left him with a permanent limp. The stick he leaned on to this day was one he'd carved down from the treacherous limb that gave way beneath him. It had become a symbol of his contract with el Rey, who'd come to him while he lay unconscious after falling and offered him a second chance to serve. Because he'd thought of fleeing even then and forgetting what he'd seen, after his very first climb. He chose to return to life at that time, and had been the King's Man ever since. El Rey's eyes, his ears, and the instrument of his will, here in the world of the living.

Tom hid none of these thoughts from Dulcé, who experienced them like her own memories. She understood that the weight of his secret knowledge had crippled him in more ways than one. He hadn't shared it with any of the women he'd known in his past, and they'd all drifted away to other proposals or other priorities. Professionally speaking, his necromantic access to el Rey's subjects and all the things they knew had made him a finder of lost objects, a string-puller, and (most profitably) an expert blackmailer—none of them occupations to be especially proud of, even though he'd limited his extortion activities to victims who deserved no better.

He'd never dared to want children, and he'd never once traveled (with body and soul united) more than a day's ride away from the Hole in the Sky. Generations of el Rey's servants had lived similarly, set apart from the world as it evolved around them.

Dulcé was looking down at him (down at *el leon*, that was) with deep sadness in her eyes. Sadness and pity, which he didn't care to see. "This is no life for a lion," she murmured. "To be held captive by a king."

It's mine, and I chose it. But I don't want to put this burden on you, he confessed. *On you or on anyone. Do you understand?*

Dulcé nodded.

I'll serve as I have to after I'm gone, he decided even as he thought it. *That's the deal I made. But I don't want to pass this on. No good has ever come of it.*

"Tom, would you come away with me, if I asked?" Dulcé blurted.

Come away?

"To travel. Wander. To see the world. The *living* world. I've never seen the Orient. We could go, together. And you've never seen Europe. London and Paris and Rome—these are places I know well. Let me show them to you."

But...

"We can get on a train. I have the money; we can just go. Your life doesn't belong to Death, Catman," Dulcé reminded him. "However much of it is left, it's not too late to live."

***

Tom released his panther back to the wild and opened his eyes, alone on the bank of the Arroyo Seco. He walked back to the Cat Ranch, mulling over everything Dulcé had said, and waited for her on the front stoop, as he had on the day he met her. Nearly an hour later she came thundering through the trees on Sombra, the mythical horse of her childhood dreams, and dismounted at the edge of the clearing. Tom stood up. The shadow-stallion dissolved back into night when Dulcé came to him, and he gathered her into his arms, and kissed her.

They kept each other awake almost until dawn that night, exchanging talk and plans and tenderness. He ignored any complaints from his hip. When Tom finally drifted off to sleep it was with one excitable thought in mind:

He and Dulcé Calavera were going to run away together.

***

She didn't have the money. That much was a lie. Her modest inheritance had all but run out before she ever came home to California, and while her scholarly efforts paid most of the bills, they hadn't left her wealthy enough to travel at her leisure.

Yet she knew where she could get money, and she set off on her bicycle the next day, All Saints' Day, with the intention of acquiring it. What she told Tom—that there were arrangements to be made before they could leave—was not at all untrue. But securing travel reservations was only the first of her goals that afternoon.

***

The building on Wilshire Boulevard had been designed in a neoclassical style, Dulcé supposed, to look like a pagan temple from antiquity, but the total effect of all that limestone always struck her as more sepulchral than Vitruvian. The place bore no signage beyond a cornerstone into which the date 1885 had been chiseled, underneath three ovals connected like links in a chain and inlaid with gold leaf.

She knew this to be the symbol of the Ordo Aurea Catena— the Order of the Golden Chain.

The doorman took her name. Moments later she was escorted inside, and upstairs.

***

"Dr. Calavera," Jacobus Vreke said, rising from his club chair to greet her. Members of the Order were supposed to address one another by their ceremonial Latin mottos rather than their proper names, but Vreke flouted formalities whenever it suited him. "It is very good to see you again."

His European diction was crisp, his suit impeccable, his eyes an arresting shade of blue. Much of the blonde in his hair had been displaced by gray, but he cut no less an imposing figure for it.

"Have you met Mr. Watt?" This is Dr. Dulcé Calavera, the eminent anthropologist."

"Winston, please," the tall, balding Englishman who'd been

talking with Vreke said.

"To what do we owe the pleasure?"

"I've seen it," Dulcé said. "That thing we discussed."

Vreke paused. "Have you?" He nodded to Watt, who shuffled away to give them some privacy without a word spoken. Vreke motioned for Dulcé to sit and waited to retake his own seat until she perched herself on the edge of the Englishman's vacated chair. He leaned in. "When was this?"

"Last night."

"And here you are already."

Dulcé made herself sit back as though she were comfortable. This top floor of the Aurea Catena's marble mausoleum was outfitted as a gentlemen's lounge, complete with a bar behind which a bartender stood, quietly polishing glassware. Watt had taken up residence on a stool, with his back turned to them.

A brass plaque on the wall near the elevator read 'The Dashwood Club.'

Dulcé had no idea what Vreke and his coterie of idle rich dilettantes got up to on the other nine floors of their fortress. Access to those lower levels was granted only as initiates progressed through the Order's ten degrees. The idea was that you descended physically as you ascended spiritually, with each grade marked by the presentation of a brass key that let you off the elevator one floor closer to ground level. Dulcé, a mere first-degree Neophyte, could only visit the social club, while Jacobus Vreke—a tenth-degree Ipsissimus as well as the Outer Head of the Inner Order—could go anywhere he damn well pleased. Even down to the basement, presumably, or into the women's water closet. He possessed a whole ring of keys, some ornate, others plain.

"Tell me what it is you've seen."

Dulcé glanced around. She couldn't help it. "The *Tree*," she whispered. "The Cathedral Oak, three times taller than an ordinary tree. Just like in your stories."

Vreke nodded. "Come," he said, rising and offering a hand to help her up as well. "We should not discuss this business here."

***

Winston Watt watched them step onto the elevator, Vreke with a guiding hand placed between the anthropologist's shoulderblades. The liveried lift operator drew an accordion gate closed and started them descending.

Watt knocked back the last of his gin and left a moment later, opting to take the stairs.

Dulcé's stomach sank along with the elevator when it passed the ground floor. They were going down to the basement after all. She should've been excited at the prospect of gaining premature admittance to the Order's privileged spaces, but she dreaded the thought of being buried beneath this tomb of a place.

Vreke said nothing more until they reached the lowest sub-basement.

"Where are we going?" Dulcé asked, trying to sound conversational.

"To the Archive of the Inner Order," he said, leading the way. "You should feel most fortunate. Many of our brethren practice for decades, yet never attain the right to see this place."

And wouldn't this endear her to them, jumping ahead like the teacher's pet. The cattiness these people indulged in despite their spiritual pretentions made Dulcé glad she'd be getting away from them, and from Los Angeles, very soon.

Vreke let them into a hushed gallery of curiosities. Dulcé saw old books with crumbling bindings and an eccentric collection of artifacts. She spotted a skull inlaid with silver and turquoise. An obsidian scrying mirror. A mummified hand that sat under a bell jar, raised in an eternal wave. Vreke saw her staring at it.

"Lurid, yes? You are not the first to feel disconcerted."

He went to a wooden cabinet inset with shallow drawers, of the sort used to store blueprints or drawings, and withdrew a document.

"You mentioned money, when we spoke of this before," Dulcé ventured. "One hundred thousand dollars."

"I would gladly pay this," he said, "to find the Tree Below the Hole in the Sky."

"I can tell you where it is."

"I have been told where it is, by the man from whom I purchased this." Vreke showed her the hand-drawn map he'd pulled from storage. It showed a tall oak tree at its center, with the ocean in the west and the city in the east. It looked accurate enough, at a glance. "And yet it hides behind hexes," Jacobus Vreke said. "It eludes me, even when I follow every direction to the letter. If you have been there, Dr. Calavera, and stood before this Tree, then I would much prefer you to show me."

***

Some hours before Tom expected Dulcé to return, los gatos brought to his attention a two-wheeled gig harnessed to a single horse that pulled off to the side of the wagon road. He recognized the bowler-hatted driver as el Rey's Englishman, Winslow. Or whatever the hell his name was. (Tom was never going to do the usurper the honor of getting it right.) In any case he was already striding up the path, across the field.

Tom came out to the front stoop and was waiting when he emerged through the trees.

"What do you want?"

"To know what in the name of bloody *fuck* you were thinking."

"About...?"

"The *anthropologist*, Tom. The one to whom you showed the Tree. I know it was you—there isn't anyone else left. And do you know where your friend is right now? At the Templi Aurea Catena, selling our secrets to the highest bidder."

Our secrets. That was rich. But the revelation hit Tom like a sucker punch. He knew the OAC, or at least knew of them. They were a cabal of old-world ceremonialists, washed into the city on recent waves of American immigrants. They knew of him, too. Several years ago a fancy importer of patent medicines named Jacobus Vreke had come sniffing around, offering cash for 'initiation,' as he termed it. Tom had turned him down flat. But of course he and his cronies were still out there, titillating themselves with their wickedness in the marble edifice they'd planted on Wilshire Boulevard.

"I know you believe me," the Interloper said, deflating all the arguments Tom was trying to muster. "You must have wondered how I ever found it myself."

In truth, yes. But Tom said nothing.

"They have a map. Bought from one of us, from a man of knowledge. I copied it from the Archive, and I doctored it so that damned Dutch freak would come up short when he tried to match it to the territory. But if your tart knows the whole procedure, then they might be standing at the door to the King's Chamber right now."

***

Vreke drove them west through endless vineyards and citrus groves in his new Daimler auto-mobile until *las cienegas*, the swamps to the south of the mountains, threatened to bog the horseless carriage down. After that they were on foot. Dulcé knew the Tree wasn't far, but Vreke was right—it hid. Following the map, she kept expecting to find it right around the next ridge or over the next foothill, only to be dead-ended by an impassable marsh or an overgrown arroyo.

Dulcé had hoped to exchange a simple list of directions for her thirty pieces of silver, but she could see now why that would never have worked.

Vreke had tempted her into stealing for him what he hadn't been able to buy from the author of his map. Her relationship with the Outer Head had begun professionally enough—he was on the board that oversaw the grant she'd received to research her book. He'd invited her to observe his own order of rich mystics, which could only be done by taking their first-degree initiation. Then he'd dangled the legends of the Hole in the Sky and the necromanticos who guarded it in front of her like a twist of string in front of a cat, knowing full well she'd find her way to Tom. He may even have hired detectives to look into her financial situation, to help choose the best bait.

She felt like a pawn in a game being played on a scale she hadn't properly imagined, and her number of possible moves was running dangerously low.

She no longer believed in the money. Not after catching a glimpse of the pistol Vreke wore in a shoulder-holster underneath his sporting jacket.

One of the instructions written on the back of the map contained a mistake. It called for an *e*vocation of Teonanactl, not an *in*vocation. Dulcé found a sample of the relevant mushroom for Vreke, but he didn't trust her enough to eat it. He insisted she do that, like a royal food taster testing for poison. Now, after more than an hour, Teonanactl still hadn't opened her eyes to the correct path.

"I am beginning to think you have lied to me, Dr. Calavera," Vreke said, taking note of the afternoon's lengthening shadows. "If you can deliver what you promised, I suggest you do so now."

"I told you it might not work for you without the mushroom."

"And I told you I will not eat an unidentified fungus out of the ground. The dangers are immense. Besides which, I believe this excuse is what the Americans call 'horseshit.' So, if you cannot—"

Dulcé saw him reaching under his tweeds, presumably for his gun. But at the same moment she also saw the deepening shadows beneath a copse of trees behind him seem to shift and draw together, and she felt a desperate burst of hope.

"**¡Sombra!**" she cried. "*¡Ayúdame!*"

Vreke whirled to see the ink-black stallion charging toward him. He drew his gun but Dulcé kicked him in the back. She leapt when Sombra feinted around the unbalanced Dutchman, catching a stirrup with one foot and swinging herself into the saddle without the horse having to break stride. It was not a feat she could ever hope to duplicate, but in the moment it almost seemed easy.

She felt something swat her in the lower back seconds before she heard the shots Vreke fired after her, but Sombra never slowed down, racing in the direction of the Tree.

***

Tom didn't expect he'd ever see her again.

He'd been pacing around his living room in a rage since goddam Winthorpe (or whatever) departed amidst a hail of harsh words, but now feelings of general foolishness were taking over. If Dulcé really had sold the key to the wards to the OAC, he didn't know what to do about it. The whole city of Los Angeles might now be fucked in unimaginable new ways.

A sudden clatter of hooves accompanied by a wild neigh caught him off guard. He hurried outside and stopped short at the realization that Sombra had no rider. The bulky horse reared and snorted, pawing at the ground, but Dulcé wasn't on his back. He whinnied again, tossing his mane at Tom. Could she have sent the shadowhorse for help? He had no idea, but Sombra's intentions seemed clear. Tom hauled himself into the saddle. He didn't ride often but he did know how, and still it was all he could do to hold on when the powerful stallion leapt forward.

***

Dulcé was already gone by the time he found her, sitting up beneath the Tree.

From a distance she might've been meditating like a Buddha, but up close her skin was gray. Where it wasn't red with drying blood. It looked like she'd been shot, possibly through the liver, and her blood was everywhere. It had soaked her clothing black. She couldn't have lasted long. Maybe she fled here to hide from Vreke, or maybe this was just where Sombra had carried her.

Who in hell could know, other than el Rey?

Tom closed her glassy eyes, sat down beside her, and cried.

***

He buried her as far from the Tree as he could carry her. Los gatos had followed him out from the Cat Ranch and they ringed around, observing in solemn silence as he assembled a cairn of stones. He balled up the shadow-cloak that hadn't saved her and shoved it back into Sombra's saddlebag before swatting the apparition on the ass to send it back to wherever it came from in the first place.

The cats bled away into the encroaching evening when he

slung his cane across his back on a piece of twine and began the arduous climb up the Tree. The stick was a nuisance, but he'd need it just to stand by the time he reached the Hole in the Sky, and on this night of all nights, Black Tom meant to stand before his King.

If the Aurea Catena wanted to know, he would show them what el Necromantico could do.

***

She was standing beside Mictlantecuhtli when Tom approached, framed in the doorway to the Inner Chamber. Her black hair was the same, and her clothes were like those she died in, but the rest of her was bleached white bone. She looked like one of those political cartoons by José Posada. Los Muertos always did.

The Aztec God of the Dead appeared as he always had—as a skeleton freshly flayed, shrouded beneath a heavy cowl and wearing a garland of glistening human eyes around his collarbones. A bloodcaked altar sat behind him. This was what lay beyond the Hole in the Sky—the sacrificial chambers of an ancient temple. One room in this world and one in the next, with a rough-hewn door between them.

"Vreke?" Tom said to Dulcé, and her ghost or her bones or whatever it was that traveled on to Mictlan nodded sadly.

"Why doesn't she speak?"

"Because I do not wish it, Tomás Delgado," Mictlantecuhtli said. "You sought to abandon your covenant with me, for a second time now." The tall skeleton glanced at Tom's cane. His hip was a bolt of agony. "This I have seen in her memory."

"I changed my mind," Tom said. "And I humbly beg for your forgiveness once again, Mictlantecuhtli."

"Amends must then be made, Tomás Delgado. What will you offer to regain my favor?"

"What you have never known before. A visit to the living world. I offer myself, of my own free will. Walk in my skin, Mictlantecuhtli, when the worlds align tonight. But I do have one condition."

"Yes?"

"I want to kill them all. The people who did this to her. To us."

Dulcé was shaking her skull, pleading with her empty eye sockets for him not to make this deal, but it was already done.

"This I accept," Mictlantecuhtli said.

***

El Rey could let his subjects roam free at this one moment in the year, when holes in the invisible veils converged, but he had never been able to leave his realm himself. Not without a body to occupy, and nobody had ever made an offer like Tom's before.

He was shoved to the back of the brainpan when el Rey crammed into his skull and took over. He felt like an afterthought in his own head, dwarfed by the vast god-consciousness that pried into every secret chamber of his psyche. Even the things he did without doing and knew without knowing came under divine control. The rhythm of the heart, the flow of the hormones, and the replication of cells became conscious acts subordinate to will, like blinking an eye or making a fist. A delighted el Rey chose first to grow, adding two feet of height and many layers of dense muscle, depleting every physiological resource Tom's body had with the effort. Hunger crashed in on them like a breaking wave, but hunger was a feeling the old god knew.

"*¡Muertos!*" Mictlantecuhtli raised Tom's voice to shout, and his skeletal subjects crowded up behind Dulcé's bones at the door between the worlds. "I grant you license this night. Those bearing grievances or grudges, bring me the hearts of your enemies and the children of your enemies, that I may eat and add their strength to mine. Bring me the heads of your enemies and the children of your enemies, that I may rack up their skulls in the name of Mictlan. Do this now, by the command of your King!"

The unquiet dead of Los Angeles responded to this proposition with enthusiasm. A horde of bent and broken bones shoved past Dulcé to follow when el Rey dropped from the Hole in the Sky, and ant-like streams of skeletons scrambled down the Tree's gnarled branches after him.

They spread out across the starlit landscape, marching toward the dim city-glow in the east.

***

The people who named Mictlantecuhtli had sometimes buried their dead with jade beads to offer el Rey when they reached his realm and he demanded their hearts. Dulcé didn't know if this amounted to bribery or deception, but she did know the stories.

She and others of los muertos used the door el Rey left open to visit the dreams of their descendants, reminding them of those old myths, so that they were ready when the angry dead arrived to harvest hearts or heads. She had a feeling Mictlantecuhtli would interpret Tom's directive to 'kill them all' in the broadest possible terms.

The army of the vengeful dead called at every house in the city and extracted sacrifices from everyone they found. *Los vivos* thought they were in a nightmare, but many had been warned. Some gave over gems or silver dollars, and several clever souls evaded death by substituting ticking pocket watches for their own beating hearts.

But sugar skulls saved a great many more. The molded candy death's heads were traditional *ofrendas*, offerings, placed on graves and altars to represent the recently deceased. Confectioners had made more than usual that year, somehow anticipating unprecedented demand, and people who meant to buy just one or two ended up taking home a dozen if not more, to give away to neighbors and acquaintances, without really knowing why. So people had them in their homes, on their countertops and shelves, ready to hand over when those who hadn't deserved their deaths came back on *la Noche de los Muertos*, demanding recompense.

***

Not that everybody was so fortunate. Initiates of the Order

of the Golden Chain were a notable exception. No kindly spirits visited their dreams, and their neighbors tended not to like them, so none of them had sugar skulls to offer in place of the real thing. Mictlantecuhtli ate the wicked hearts his subjects claimed, enlarging himself with every bite. The embodied god stood more than eight feet tall by the time he personally hauled Jacobus Vreke out of bed and dragged him from his mansion high on Bunker Hill, to be hounded through the streets by mobs of jeering skeletons.

They herded him down Wilshire, to the forecourt of his silly temple. A tall brass sundial sat at its center and the Aztec god threw Vreke down upon it, skewering him through the kidney. He howled like a gutshot animal, but stopped when Mictlantecuhtli opened his solar plexus with a hand-chipped obsidian blade and reached up into his chest to rip loose his fibrillating heart.

The skeletons had all fallen silent. They raised the *calaveras* they'd collected when their red-handed King held his prize aloft, completing Tom's revenge. Some of los vivos, the living who thought they were dreaming, had come out to join them in the streets, and they held up more sugar skulls to bear witness with their ancestors.

Every candy skull had the same name written on its brow. By tradition, the offerings always bore the names of the beloved dead, inscribed in sugar icing.

That year, no matter what name the decorators intended, their hands would only write one word—and that was *Dulcé.*

***

Tom awoke on the floor of the First Chamber, with morning sun streaming in through the Hole in the Sky.

He sat up, then stood up without difficulty. The old iron ache in his hip was gone. He was only himself again, but his body's temporary occupant had left it healed.

His arms were still sleeved in flaking blood, though.

"I found myself... overwhelmed, by my experience," el Rey said, and Tom turned to see the King standing framed in the door between worlds. He didn't look like a skeleton now, but rather a tall man with black hair and sharp eyes, dressed in royal Aztec regalia. Reliving the glory days, Tom supposed. The only way he knew for sure this was el Rey was that the god had kept his favorite necklace of gory eyeballs.

"Glad you had fun."

"I would make our arrangement permanent. This will be possible when our worlds align again next year. Will you consider it?"

"Can I be with her? In Mictlan?"

El Rey shrugged. "You will serve until you have replaced yourself."

In other words, no. "Then I want more time. To find a new acolyte."

"Will 'ten years' be enough?"

El Rey had little understanding of time, and why should he? Ten years, ten seconds, and ten centuries were all the same to him. "Should be," Tom said. A decade to figure out a better way to appease the King. Hopefully he wouldn't need as much as that.

"Then it is done," el Rey said. "In ten years' time you will return to my Chambers and we will trade body for soul. What will you do until then?"

"Thought I might travel. I never have, you know."

"As you wish it, Tomás Delgado. I know you won't forget your promises."

Tom gasped when el Rey raised a hand and the old familiar pain bit back into his hip. It buckled under him and he fell, hitting the stone floor hard. The King had rescinded his repairs. He saw his cane lying on the floor some feet away, right at eye level.

"Remember that greater torments await those who disappoint me," el Rey said, and then he was gone, leaving Tom to make a slow, careful climb back down the Tree.

***

Late the next afternoon he was on board a train when it departed from Toluca Station.

He set his cane across the empty seat beside him and watched the sun-drenched chaparral landscape roll past his window for a while. It was probably a good idea to leave town after instigating dozens of grisly killings, so he was going to see the world, even though Dulcé couldn't show it to him now.

She'd deceived him, without a doubt. He'd checked her pocketbook before he buried her, and discovered that she'd cashed out her savings and reserved passage to the east coast the morning before she died.

But, whatever other lies she might've told, at least she bought two tickets.

THE WITCH

Richard Chizmar

"I hate Halloween."

"You hate everything," I said.

"That's not true."

"Name three things you don't—"

"Pizza."

"That's one."

"Fishing."

"Two."

Frank Logan, bald head, double chin, and wrinkled suit, stared out the passenger window of our unmarked patrol car.

"Stuck at two, aren't you?"

"Well, I was gonna say *you're* the third thing I don't hate, but that was before you started with this shit."

I laughed and swung a right onto Pulaski Highway. "So what do you have against Halloween anyway?"

He glanced over at me and I recognized the look immediately: it was his *'Should I really waste my breath explaining this to you?'* look.

After a moment, he decided I was worth the effort and went on. "It's become too damn commercial. I read in the paper last week that Halloween is second only to Christmas when it comes to holiday sales revenue. Christmas, for Chrissake!"

I smiled and changed lanes. Another classic Frank Logan rant coming up.

"When I was a kid, the only thing anyone spent money on was candy, that's it! We made the decorations for our yards and houses. We made our costumes. I was a hobo the first time I went trick or treating. A clown the next year. A baseball player the year after that. All homemade. Didn't spend a penny."

"I can't see you as a clown."

"I was five, Ben. What was your first costume?"

I hesitated. "Umm, I don't remember."

"Sure you do. Everyone remembers their first Halloween costume. It's like a rule, like remembering your first piece of ass."

"I really don't remember."

"Sure you do."

I sighed. "I was Casper, Frank. Good enough?"

"Casper the friendly ghost?"

"No, Casper the angry squirrel."

He arched his eyebrows. "Store bought?"

I turned onto a residential street. Jack-O'-Lanterns grinned their jagged, orange grins at us from front porches. Tombstones poked out of manicured lawns, piles of fallen leaves heaped in front of them in the shapes of corpses. Ghosts and goblins hung from trees. I saw a cluster of police lights in the distance. It was after ten, so the sidewalks were empty of trick-or-treaters, but I could see a good-sized crowd gathered in the middle of the road ahead.

"Store bought?" Frank asked again. Once he got his teeth into something, he didn't let go. It was what made him such a fine detective.

"Yes, Frank, it was store bought. A cheap plastic mask with eyeholes cut out of it, and one of those elastic bands in the back that pinched your ears and neck. I apologize for violating the spirit of Halloween and promise to make up for it next October. Happy?"

He shrugged his shoulders. "Just a question. No need to get touchy."

I pulled to the curb and parked behind a Sheriff's cruiser, opened the driver's door and got out.

"Westerns," Frank said.

I looked at him over the top of our sedan. "What?"

"I don't hate Westerns. You know, movies."

I closed my car door and started toward the scene.

"That's three, Ben," from behind me. "I win."

***

"Whatdya got, Lenny?"

Sheriff Deputy Leonard Perkins looked up from the small notebook he was scribbling in and shook his head. "It's a weird one, fellas."

"That's what we hear," Frank said.

Lenny closed his notebook and looked around at the bystanders, a mix of excited children—many still dressed in costume (all of them store bought, I noticed), masks pushed up off their sweaty faces—and worried, tired adults. "Guess it makes sense. Being Halloween and all."

"Don't get him started on Halloween," I said.

Lenny looked at Frank and back to me again, waiting. When neither of us said anything else, he went on. "Deceased is Harold Torre. Forty-six year old male. Divorced. No kids. Been in the residence for almost fifteen years. Neighbors say he's quiet and polite. Keeps to himself mostly. Doesn't show up at the block parties or cookouts but is friendly enough if you pass him on the street or see him working out on his lawn. Doesn't have many visitors."

"Occupation?" I asked.

"Owns an insurance company right here in town."

Lenny gestured for us to follow and started across the lawn to the front porch of a well-kept rancher. It looked like every light in the house was on.

"This is how one of the neighborhood kids found him."

Mr. Torre was a man of average height and build. I would guess 5'10 and 165 pounds, although it was difficult to accurately gauge since he was presently sprawled face-down on his front porch, one leg tucked beneath the other. He had dark curly hair and wore eyeglasses. The glasses—old fashioned and metal-framed—were lying on the concrete porch amidst a scattering of Halloween candy and an empty dark blue Tupperware bowl.

"No one saw him go down?" Frank asked.

Lenny shook his head. "No one we've talked to." He gestured to a blonde woman and a little boy waiting in the side yard with another police officer. "Kid walked up on him when he was trick-or-treating, found him like that and ran back to his mom crying. She called 911 from her cell."

Frank grunted. "Kid got his trick, I guess."

"Really Frank?" I said.

Lenny ignored us. "Had to be quick, though. Lotta trick-or-treaters in this neighborhood. Can't imagine much of a break between em."

I nodded, remembering my own childhood Halloween nights. "You talk to the mother yet?"

"Emerson did," Lenny said. "And we figured you guys would want to."

"Frank can handle that," I said and held up a hand in Frank's direction to stop what I knew was coming.

"No visible wounds," Lenny continued. "The M.E. had us roll him on his side, but only for a few seconds. Didn't find anything."

"Heart attack?" Frank asked.

"Guess it's possible," Lenny said. "But when you take the note into account, it's...doubtful."

"What note?" I asked.

Lenny looked surprised. "I thought you knew. We found a handwritten note magneted to the refrigerator door."

"A note saying what?" Frank interrupted.

"We bagged it and tagged it. It's in the van right now." He nodded his head in the direction of the crime lab van parked across the street.

"Just give us the short version," Frank said, glancing at me, all business now.

"Note claims that if anything happened to him, his ex-wife was to blame," Lenny said. "Evidently they'd been arguing a lot lately. It's dated a week ago yesterday and signed Harold Torre."

"Interesting," Frank said, a split second before I could mutter the exact same response. I read an article once that claimed police detectives who worked together for long periods of time became almost like twin siblings, reading each other's thoughts and completing each other's sentences. I looked at Frank and really hoped it wasn't true.

Lenny flipped open his notebook and read from it: "Ex-wife is Ramona Ann Torre. Age thirty-nine. Maiden name Ramirez. Residence 237 Tupelo. Over in Aberdeen."

"All that was in the note?" I asked.

"Negative. Just her first name. I dug up the rest waiting on you guys."

Frank slapped him on the shoulder. "That's good work, Deputy."

I backed off the porch and looked at Frank. "You go talk to Mom and I'll track down the M.E. Meet you at the van when we're finished."

Frank gave a nod and started for the side yard.

"There's one more thing, detectives."

Frank and I stopped and looked up at Lenny, who was still standing on the front porch with Mr. Torre's body. The deputy loomed over us, an imposing dark shadow silhouetted in the bright house lights shining behind him.

"What's that?" Frank asked, squinting, impatient now.

"Mr. Torre…in the note…" Lenny lowered his voice to make sure no one else could overhear. "He claims his ex-wife is a witch."

"A witch?" I repeated, unsure I had heard him correctly.

But I had. Lenny nodded his head and said it again, a little louder this time: "A witch."

I looked at Frank. He looked back at me, eyebrows arched. "Happy Halloween, partner," he muttered and walked away to talk to the Mom and little boy waiting in the side yard.

***

"Jesus, please tell me that's not the house," Frank said, staring out the car window at the spilt-level house on the right side of the road.

"That's not the house, Frank."

The home in question was decorated from yard to rooftop like a haunted house from some Grade B horror film. Gargoyles with glowing red eyes stood watch from the second-story roof. Hideously lifelike zombies lurched amongst the grave markers scattered across the front lawn. Fake spider webs drooped from porch railings and tree branches and roof gutters. A blood-splattered corpse, swollen tongue protruding, dangled from a noose hanging from a leaning oak tree. Both sides of the driveway were lined with what had to be at least twenty fat pumpkins, orange flames winking secrets in the cool October breeze and forming a welcoming path for trick-or-treaters earlier in the night. A pair of fog machines hidden behind the shrubbery churned out a hazy backdrop and, even with the car windows closed, we could hear the familiar manic beats of the *Halloween* movie soundtrack.

"Look at that," he scowled as we cruised past. "Must've cost them a thousand bucks. At least!"

"Two-thirty-seven is up here on the left," I said, spotting an unmarked sedan parked at the curb. They had arrived a half-hour earlier, to confirm that Ramona Torres was at home and, in case she was indeed guilty, to make sure she didn't decide to make a run for it before we could get there. The two officers would also serve as back-up in the unlikely event we needed it.

"All that money and for what?" Frank went on. "One stupid night. It doesn't make any sense."

"I figure it makes plenty of sense to them, Frank, or why else would they do it?"

He grunted and shook his head in disgust.

I flipped a wave to the undercover officers parked across the street and pulled over to the curb and shut off the engine. "Ready?"

"To go witch hunting?"

I tried not to smile. "That's what the man said."

Frank looked at the tidy house at 237 Tupelo. The porch light was on, but all the windows were dark. Rose bushes lined the front of the house and a birdbath stood in the middle of the lawn. "Doesn't look like a witch lives here to me."

"Let's hope you're right," I said, getting out of the car.

"Bet you twenty bucks it was a heart attack."

"No bet."

"Chicken."

I laughed. "Let's just wait on the tox report. Remember those kids that spiked their teacher's coffee a few years back and he ended up dead? That happened on Halloween, too, you know."

"I hate Halloween," Frank muttered and slammed the car door.

***

She surprised us by answering the door after the first knock.

Frank and I introduced ourselves and showed her our badges, and she surprised us again by inviting us inside before we could even explain what we were doing there.

We followed her into a candle-lit living room and she motioned for us to take a seat. Frank and I sat side by side on a leather sofa. She settled across from us in a high-backed antique chair. Some kind of incense was burning in the room. It smelled exotic and welcoming. I could almost taste it on my tongue.

Ramona Torres was a big woman, at least two hundred pounds, and she was beautiful. Skin the color of creamy chocolate. Dark lush hair that sparkled in the candlelight and reached halfway down her back. Dark, mysterious eyes that made you want to disappear inside them. She was dressed in a flowing black robe etched with gold border that did nothing to hide her glorious cleavage. I noticed Frank staring and hoped I was being more discreet.

Before either of us could begin to explain our late night appearance at her home, she surprised us a third time. "I've been expecting you."

That woke us both up. I felt Frank shift on the sofa next to me. "And why is that, Mrs. Torre?" he asked.

"You've come to tell me that my ex-husband is dead, have

you not?"

I nodded. "Unfortunately, yes, we have."

"There is nothing unfortunate about it. The man was a pig."

She smiled when she said this, and I felt the temperature in the room drop and icy fingers caress the back of my neck. I shivered. *Jesus, this witch business was getting to me.*

I glanced at Frank, sensing he was feeling the same thing. He sat up on the sofa and leaned forward. "Do you think we could turn on some lights in here, Mrs. Torre?"

"Why not?" She clapped her hands, twice, and an overhead chandelier blinked on, chasing away the shadows in the corners of the room.

"That's better," Frank said, looking around. "Thank you."

I glanced around the room and felt myself relax a little. Mrs. Torre's living room looked exactly like a hundred other living rooms I had sat in before on the job. Shelves lined with books and knick-knacks and framed photographs. A widescreen television attached to the wall above a fancy gas fireplace. A piano in the corner by the window. Big potted plants everywhere.

"So you and Mr. Torre were obviously not on good terms?" Frank asked.

Mrs. Torre laughed. "You could say that. I despised the man."

"If you don't mind me asking," I said. "When and why did you get divorced?"

"I filed for divorce ten months ago. About ten years too late." She crossed her legs, and I noticed that she was wearing sandals. Her toenails were painted bright red. "As for *why*...like I said, Harry was a pig. He lied to me. He cheated on me. He abused me."

"Did you ever report him for abuse, Mrs. Torre?" Frank asked.

"I did not. He never raised a hand to me, detective. The only scars he left were inside my soul."

"But you were happy for a time?" I asked. "In the earlier years of the marriage?"

"Harry was a con man, detective. He made me believe in

a marriage, in a life, that wasn't real. It never existed. It took me awhile to figure that out, but still I remained with him. No, I was never really happy. At best, I guess you could say I was... grateful."

"Grateful?" Frank asked, and I could hear him scribbling in his notebook.

"That's right." Mrs. Torre thought for a moment. "I was always different, detective. I never really fit in anywhere or with anyone. Even when I was young, growing up back in Mexico, because of my family, people often whispered about me. Many were even afraid of me."

"What about your family?" Frank asked before I could.

She uncrossed her legs. "We were very poor when I was a young girl, but my mother was a very powerful woman. Known many villages away as a healer, among other things. There were always stories about my mother and her sisters. As long as I could remember."

"What kind of stories?" I asked, clearly captivated with the beautiful woman sitting across from me. She met my gaze with a direct stare of her own, and the room suddenly felt too bright and too warm. I felt drowsy, almost as if I had been drugged, and I struggled to remember if Mrs. Torre had offered us something to drink upon our arrival.

I looked at Frank and he was staring back at me, and I could tell he was experiencing the same sensation.

"...and of course there were those villagers who accused my mother and her sisters of being *Brujas Negra's*..."

I looked back at Mrs. Torre and she was smiling at me again, a tired, sad smile, and then I wasn't looking at her at all...I was no longer in her living room...I was somehow...

...inside a dusty village in a jungle clearing made up of grass and mud huts and there were chickens running wild and ancient women washing clothes in a filthy creek and a dirty little girl with dark, sweaty skin and wide, beautiful eyes holding the hand of an equally beautiful older woman, standing amidst a crowd of others in front of what looked like a stone altar at the jungle's edge and there was an old man bound to the altar with heavy

ropes and the man was naked and bleeding and sobbing, his toothless mouth gasping for air, and there was another beautiful woman towering above him, arms outstretched to the sky, both hands clutching a roughly-carved stone dagger dripping with blood and plunging it downward...

"...so, yes, you could say I was grateful, detective. Grateful to be accepted by someone from your world. Someone who appeared to be kind and successful and...normal. It was all I ever wanted when I was a little girl growing up in the jungle. It was my fairy tale." Her voice grew harsh. "But it all turned out to be a lie."

I blinked and I was back in Mrs. Torre's candlelit living room. I no longer felt sleepy or drugged. On the contrary, I felt wide awake and alert. I glanced up at the ceiling, looking for the chandelier, but couldn't make it out in the flickering darkness. I listened as Frank's scribbling reached a frenzied pace, and then it abruptly stopped and the room was silent.

After a moment, Mrs. Torre spoke again: "Aren't either of you going to ask if I killed my ex-husband, detectives?"

I felt a single, icy finger trace a path across my neck and down between my shoulder blades, and then it was gone.

Frank got to his feet first, and I was right behind him. I wasn't scared exactly, but I wanted out of that room, out of that house, and far away from that beautiful, mysterious woman.

"Mrs. Torre," Frank said, his voice much softer than I was accustomed to hearing. "Even if you admitted it, I'm pretty damn sure we could never prove it. Not in any crime lab and not in any court of law..."

***

"You think she's a witch?"

"No such thing," I said, merging back onto the interstate. We had been inside Ramona Torre's house for just over a half-hour, but the entire visit was a blur. Exhaustion was to blame; too many cases, too many late nights.

"*Something* was off about her. You see what she was wearing?"

"She was...*different*, that's for sure."

"You liked her, didn't you?"

I looked at Frank. "You were the one staring at her boobs."

"Kinda hard not to," he said, grinning. "Be honest, Ben. What did you think of her?"

I thought about it for a moment before I answered. "I think she's a very beautiful, very sad, very lonely woman."

An SUV suddenly blasted past us in the fast lane, blaring its horn, startling both of us. The driver was laughing and wearing a rubber skeleton mask and his passenger was wearing a Donald Trump mask, complete with fuzzy orange hair. The Donald leaned out the window and flipped us the bird before disappearing down the highway.

"Dumbass kids," I said. "Lucky I don't hit the lights and pull em over."

Frank grunted and stared out the car window at the dark countryside. "God, I hate Halloween."

ONE BAD APPLE

J.D. Horn

"Will McIntosh was a liar and a thief," Gordon said, breaking the silence that had fallen over them. Jonathan shifted his gaze from his smartphone to the man, a boyhood friend to whom time hadn't been kind. Gordon sat, spotted and toad-like, by the hearth, hunched over in a hideous barley twist cane chair, the golden light of the fire making his bulbous, spider-veined nose appear all the more grotesque. His bloodshot and watery blue eyes rested on those same unflattering flames, but his unfocused gaze seemed to be peering beyond it, all the way into their shared past.

"And a dullard, too," added Max, another living relic of Jonathan's childhood. Jonathan turned his attention to Max, recumbent on the claw-foot piece of Victoriana that passed for a sofa in this potpourri hell where Stanley had reserved them four rooms, four days before he blew out his brains.

Dour Timothy completed their quartet. He lurked, silent in a shadowy corner of the room, untouched by the fire's glow, though saved from utter darkness by an anachronistic compact fluorescent bulb shining through a brass table lamp's cranberry glass shade.

The four of them hadn't been together, in the same room, since their high school graduation, each of them having taken to the wind shortly thereafter. Of their group of childhood friends, Stanley, alone, had returned to Maine.

"I swear the boy could only think in stick figures," Max said, chuckling at his own joke. "That's why he was fourteen and still in our class."

"Left behind twice," Gordon said, shaking his head with an air of sorrowed disapproval.

Even though Stanley hadn't given them a choice, they had come for his funeral, not Will's. It chafed Jonathan that they didn't seem capable of coming up with a single warm remembrance of Stanley to share. Maybe it was this void that caused Max and Gordon to ruminate about Will. Still, it seemed wrong to pass the time denigrating a boy, dead and gone for going on…was it six decades now?

A decorous knock at the door announced the arrival of one of the bed and breakfast's two proprietresses, the unprepossessing Mrs. Dempsey. There was no Mr. Dempsey, as far as Jonathan could ascertain. Perhaps there never had been. Though youngish in comparison to Jonathan and his fellows, she might have graduated to the honorific through age without ever having picked up a husband. An odd thing to do in this day, but she seemed a creature of a different age, more Jonathan's mother's contemporary than his own junior. He felt certain the woman would cringe if addressed as "Ms." She bore a non-descript bottle of whiskey, and her expression was one of utmost sympathy. It would not have surprised Jonathan to learn she'd spent the afternoon, which they'd whiled away at the sparsely attended viewing of Stanley's closed, matte-silver casket, preparing a speech for their comfort and perhaps edification. She seemed on the verge of addressing them, but at the last moment appeared to read the mood of the room and kept mum.

Their host cast a quick disappointed glance at the remains of the nearly untouched afternoon tea she'd made the common mistake of referring to as "high tea." An electric stainless steel samovar full of Orange Pekoe loomed over a three-quarters full silver plate coffee pot. Between them sat a ceramic tray lined with wax paper and burdened with tiny finger sandwiches, perfect rectangles of crustless white bread either stuffed with cheese and pickle or some abominable-smelling potted meat. One ruffled-edged plate held an undisturbed mound of fancy jam-filled sugar cookies, the golden preserves peeking out through tiny, five-pointed star cutouts. A second identical plate was filled with small seeded scones, one of which Jonathan had tried with a dollop of clotted cream and a preserve made of the same golden jam used in the cookies. The flavor of the jam reminded him somewhat of passion fruit or perhaps papaya, but didn't really taste like either. Still, it was delicious, though the seeds lent the scones an odd, disagreeable tang.

"Mr. Alexander," she said, for some reason choosing to address herself to Timothy, perhaps because he seemed the most distant, the most in need of being welcomed back into the fold. "You and your friends should have a bit to eat. You'll need your strength for tomorrow."

Jonathan made a show of scooping up a couple of the cookies and biting into one, disappointed to find that they, too, had been impregnated with the disagreeable seeds. He forced a grateful smile to his lips. "Delicious," he said, though he felt an uncomfortable rumbling in his stomach.

"Thank you," she said, opening the bottle of whiskey she carried with her and measuring a stingy splash of the alcohol into Gordon's tumbler. Jonathan took advantage of her distraction to pocket the second cookie. "An old family recipe." She did no more than dampen the bottom of Max's glass with the whiskey before returning the stopper to the bottle. She turned toward the door.

"Leave the bottle," Max moaned, one hand over his eyes. The gesture revealed a faded tattoo of an eagle clutching an anchor, without a doubt a souvenir of Max's Navy career, on his forearm.

Jonathan's gaze passed from Max's time-tonsured pate to the face of Waterhouse's Lady of Shalott, who peered down at them with evident apprehension from over the bow of her boat. She could hardly be blamed—a gilt frame was all that separated her from an unforgiving sea of purple flocked wallpaper.

The bed and breakfast's communal sitting room, where Jonathan and his three surviving boyhood friends had gathered after the closed casket visitation, offered little by way of comfort. His own room, which he'd visited only briefly, had impressed him by achieving the rare feat of feeling both drafty and close at the same time.

As far as Jonathan could, at first, ascertain, their lodging's salient attraction was its two-block proximity to the funeral home where Stanley's corpse now lay awaiting internment. But now, after they'd spent three-quarters of an hour cataloging the innkeepers' cut-rate, if earnest, attempts to resurrect the gilded age, more than enough time for the darkness of the occasion to seep into their souls, Jonathan felt certain neither comfort nor proximity had played any part in the choice of accommodations. No, the bed and breakfast where Stanley had sentenced them to pass the night had been chosen for effect.

Stanley had once been head of the local college's drama department, and he was directing them, even now, through the arrangements he had made for them. This parlor was reminiscent of the cheap set of every tired whodunit ever staged. Timing his exit so they'd arrive on All Hallows' Eve was Stanley's ham-handed coup de grace.

"The bottle," Max said again, this time the words sounding more a plea than a demand.

Mrs. Dempsey stopped in the doorway, clutching the bottle by its neck. She hesitated, casting an eye over each of them, performing, no doubt, a complex bit of calculus that took into account their age—advanced—and current level of inebriation. While Jonathan was stone-cold sober, Max was pissing drunk, and Gordon and Timothy were sliding down the scale toward Max with each touch of glass to lip.

Her lips pursed, and her head had already begun to shake when Gordon spoke up. "It's a wake for God's sake, woman, show some mercy on four tattered old fools."

"I'll keep an eye on them," Jonathan said, doing his best with a single glance to assure her the evening wouldn't end with a claim filed against her insurance policy. After forty-five years of working in contract law, he realized he'd just assumed liability for the others' behavior, but it was better than listening to Max and Gordon's complaining. He crossed the room and clutched the bottle by its heel.

Though she did not exactly hand the bottle to him, she allowed him to tug it from her grasp. "See that you do," she said, her tone maternal, as if she weren't at least thirty years their junior. She ran her now free hand down the front of her olive cardigan. Her expression softened. "Listen. We try to put on a good show each year for the kids coming around to trick-or-treat. Scary noises. Fog machine. Strobe lights. You know, the works. Vera and I like to go all out." Though they hadn't yet been introduced, Jonathan surmised this Vera was Mrs. Dempsey's elusive partner in running the B&B—and perhaps her partner in other areas of life, as well. "It starts out pretty tame for the young children, but as the evening progresses…," she hesitated, "I just mean, don't be alarmed by anything you might hear. The community has come to expect a bit of a production from us. We're always the last stop. The best stop," she added, pride evident in her tone. "Vera is just putting on the final touches now. The first wave of barbarians should hit any time, but it'll all be over by eight." She cast an eye toward the window, apparently estimating the time left before the first little goblins' arrival by the bruising of the sky. She turned her focus back to Jonathan, looking at him as if he were the only other adult in the room. "I'll pop in to check on you afterward."

"Could you bring some of the candy, too?" Max said, his voice turned oddly childlike and plaintive, reinforcing, Jonathan felt sure, the woman's impression of them as puerile, if long past innocent, "if there's any left over, that is."

"Jesus, Max," Timothy spoke up for the first time since returning from the funeral home, "Are you five? Stick to your booze, and leave the sweets to the kids."

"No, no. It's all right," Mrs. Dempsey said, a trace of a smile returning to her lips, if not to her eyes. "I'm sure there will be plenty. We always buy too much." The smile faded, and a line formed between her brows. "I know our festivities may seem frivolous to you," she said, seemingly in response to Timothy's ill humor, "in light of your loss…"

"Don't be ridiculous," Jonathan cut her attempt at apology short. "We couldn't be more pleased that you're entertaining the children." He gazed at his companions. "I know it's probably impossible to believe we were ever young, but once upon a time, back when this house was still a private residence, we four used to come here to do some trick-or-treating ourselves."

"Really?" Mrs. Dempsey said, her expression again brightening, this time with true delight.

"Yes, but the old maid librarian who lived here," Max said, managing to sit up straight, though slurring his words, "only ever gave out those damned soggy popcorn balls. You remember her, don't you, Gordon?"

"Certainly," Gordon said, looking back over his shoulder at their host, "the one who went mad because she couldn't get the children to stop chattering in the library. Loaded each of those popcorn balls of hers with a razor blade, she did, in the hopes of cutting out their little tongues. Back in '56, wasn't it?"

The momentary warmth in Mrs. Dempsey's eyes dissolved in an instant, her expression regaining its previous lacquered politeness. "Bravo. You nearly had me there for a moment," she said, her smile a pantomime of appreciation. "Well then, gentlemen, I'll return as soon as we're done entertaining the children." She stepped back out of the room, pulling the door to with a soft clack.

"The children, indeed," Gordon said as if it were a toast, knocking back his drink, then raising his empty tumbler. Jonathan, whiskey bottle in hand, drew near, opened the bottle and poured his old friend three thick fingers. "Little bastards one and all, if they're anything like the ones still trying to suck at my teat. My eldest just turned forty-five, still trying to find himself. Now he wants to be a writer, he says. I'd say he's having a midlife crisis, but he's never had any kind of life to begin with."

Jonathan didn't really follow what Gordon was saying, struck as he was by the year Gordon had selected for his little tale of horror. The actual events just before Halloween of that very year, 1956, lay at the root of why Stanley lay dead. Now, sixty years later, the four of them were gathered together once again, after a lifetime with little to no contact, for what would certainly be their final meeting this side of hell.

Jonathan tried to remember. Had he gone trick-or-treating that year? No, he had played sick, going as far as to hold a cup of hot tea up to his forehead, so his mother would be convinced he had a fever. He was too old, he'd insisted the following year. His mother had agreed, seeming relieved that she wouldn't have to baste together a last minute costume.

He let his mind drift back even further to the Halloween before the accident, when Jonathan had stood on the porch of this very house wearing an eyepatch and holding a cardboard cutlass. Jonathan could visualize himself, could see the old flowered pillowcase his mother had given him to carry his candy loot—he had complained so about the floral pattern, his mother came within a cat's whisker of calling Halloween off and grounding him. Arriving here today, he had noticed the steps and front door were, except for color, unchanged, so he imagined that he could still see the way they'd appeared on that night. No matter how hard he tried, though, he couldn't bring the image of the woman who lived in this house to his mind's eye. Perhaps the innkeepers had a photo of her tucked away somewhere?

"Hit me, Johnny," Max said, tapping on the side table that held his glass with such force, he nearly tipped it. His hand shot out and righted the tumbler before it could topple and shatter on the inlaid wood floor. Good reflexes, Jonathan thought, for a man of their age and of Max's current blood alcohol level.

He crossed to Max and poured a liberal amount into the tumbler. "Don't be stingy with your old pal," Max said, and Jonathan filled the glass almost to the rim. "There ya go. Didn't cause you too much pain, now did it?" Max reached out with a meaty paw and swiped the glass up to his lips. He nodded at Jonathan, then proceeded to drain a third of the whiskey in a single draft.

"Timothy?" Jonathan held the bottle up in offering.

"None for me," he said, his tone softened. "I've had enough."

"Ah, come on," Max said, his tone jeering. He never did know when to quit poking. "Can't have a wake without a toast to the dearly departed." He lifted his glass, sloshing a bit onto the sofa. He didn't seem to take notice. "To the dearly departed Mr. Crofton."

"A toast, my ass," Gordon said, then fell silent, holding his tumbler up, examining the amber liquid backlit by the fire. "I lied to den mother Dempsey. This isn't a wake. As far as I'm concerned this is a forced abduction, and we're the abductees." He knocked back its contents, then held the glass up to Jonathan. Jonathan filled the tumbler once more, then left the bottle on the coffee table, central to both Gordon and Max's reach. It was bad enough he'd volunteered to act as chaperone. He'd be damned if he'd spend the evening bartending, too.

What Gordon said was true enough. They'd each received the same letter, sent via one of the large overnight delivery services that offered nearly instant confirmation of delivery. The letters contained the reminder of an ancient shared sin, as if they needed to be reminded, and a threat to reach out from beyond the grave—with the unwitting assistance of his will's executor—to expose the crime unless they each attended Stanley's funeral. Stanley must have pulled the trigger within moments of learning the final letter had been received.

"I'm not drinking to that sonofabitch extortionist," Gordon said, his voice coming out in a near growl.

"True enough," Max said. "He took the coward's way out, but not before laying a plan to take the rest of us down with him. To us, then. To men who have something to live for."

Gordon snorted, but he took another sip of the whiskey. "A bit too briny for my tastes," he said and licked his lips.

Jonathan would have choked had he tried to join in the toast. He no longer counted himself among those who had something to live for.

With the world outside passing into darkness, each of the window's panes had transformed into a mirror, reflecting the interior of the room. Jonathan caught sight of his own haggard expression, the deepening lines in his face, the receding hairline. The grayness of his very being. Helen had left him ten years back, claiming he'd grown old before his time, although she meant he'd grown old before her time. Their daughter Meg had shown such an unwavering commitment in choosing her mother's side in the divorce, anyone would have believed Jonathan had committed a grave sin against Helen, when in truth he'd only been guilty of slowing down.

Seventy is the new fifty. That was the message he'd received from a colleague on his last birthday. For God's sake. Back when he was growing up, right here in Waterville, most folk had the sense to realize that even fifty was old. Not now, though, when it seemed that even a nonagenarian was meant to win the match, then leap over the net to land with athletic grace in his well-manicured grave. "Alcoholic hepatitis," his doctor had nearly sung the words. "Not too late to turn it around, John, if you'll lay off the sauce." He could just about hear the whiskey bottle calling his name. Maybe he didn't care if his condition developed into full-blown cirrhosis.

"Miss Tanner," Timothy spoke up, the non sequitur causing Jonathan and the others to turn toward him. "That was her name," he said, then, perhaps realizing that none of them had the slightest clue what he was talking about, added, "the spinster librarian who lived here. I spent a miserable summer taking piano lessons from her." Timothy moved closer to the fire. "She wasn't even that old, really. She just seemed it at the time." He took hold of the poker, adjusting the logs so the dwindling flames shot higher. "I didn't have to take lessons the following year. She'd moved away. North. Presque Isle, I think." He stood still before the hearth, seemingly frozen, staring into the fire. "I didn't come here because I was afraid of being arrested." He roused himself and returned the poker to its stand.

"Nor did I," Max said. "It's been sixty years now. We were kids. And then there's the matter of proof. No D.A. would ever dream of attempting to prosecute."

"No," Timothy said, his eyes widening as he leaned in toward them. "That's not what I mean. I don't care about any legal ramifications. And," he added quickly, seemingly intent on cutting off the next argument, "I'm not worried about a public shaming, either." He clasped his hands together and held them out before him. Jonathan had actually never witnessed anyone wring their hands before, but now his old buddy looked like he was auditioning for the role of Lady Macbeth. "I've been dreaming about him…about Will. For around three months now. Not sleeping more than a couple of hours a night."

Well, that explained his sallow skin and dark-ringed eyes.

"More than once," Timothy continued, his voice now barely audible, "I've been at the point of doing the same thing Stanley's done, only I'm afraid it wouldn't end it. That I'd find myself stuck for all eternity with Will McIntosh by my side."

"You need to pull yourself together," Gordon said, turning, red-faced, to glower at them. "It was an accident. An accident that happened before the moon landing, before the Kennedy assassination. Before the Beatles, for God's sake." His shoulders relaxed, and his face softened. "And besides, McIntosh was not blameless in the incident." He turned back to face the fire.

"He was a petty thief, and a liar," Max said almost if by rote, reaching anew for the tumbler. "If he hadn't died when he did, he would have undoubtedly graduated to more serious offenses. Perhaps it's uncharitable to say, but maybe it was for the best. Maybe the world was done a favor."

Jonathan bit his tongue, refusing to give in to the urge to defame the long dead boy. They were cataloguing the reasons they themselves should be held blameless for what had happened, and he wouldn't take part in that. Not when the boy's darkest sin had been stealing a slew of knick-knacks. Jonathan did the calculation. It was precisely sixty years and one week since the day that the four of them—five, if you counted Stanley—had met to try, then execute old Will. Of course, they'd only intended to threaten the execution, never carry it out, but as often happens with a group of adolescent boys, matters got carried too far. Someone had pushed where they ought not have, or perhaps one of them had just tripped, and the charade of the execution had become real. It nettled him that Gordon seemed to feel that the fact that Will's death occurred six decades ago was a strong enough defense in and of itself. As if their collective sin could be washed away by the stream of time.

"That boy was born to meet a premature end," Max mumbled from behind his drink, giving Jonathan a look that resembled defiance. Jonathan wondered if Max had read his thoughts from his expression. "It was only a matter of time."

Now, Jonathan realized Max was merely parroting words they'd all heard spoken by callous adults long ago. The whole of Waterville had agreed that Will was a troubled boy. It'd been no secret the McIntoshes had adopted him, and when you take on a stranger's child, well, you never knew what you were going to get. There was never a question that his death could've been anything other than suicide, even though as an adult, Jonathan had reflected how the police must have noticed several sets of child-sized shoe prints, a diagram for the panic dance, in the barn's dirt floor. At the time, Timothy's dad had been a bigwig in city politics, and perhaps that was why no suspicions were ever voiced.

Sure, Mrs. McIntosh refused to believe Will could've taken his own life, but then she went away. To rest, everyone said, though the whole town knew she'd had a breakdown. She'd been the one to find him, after all. Still, after she returned home, she, too, seemed to have accepted Will's hanging as a suicide.

"I saw him," Timothy said under his breath. "I saw him," he said more clearly. "Will. For real. Today." His voice trembled, and his face flushed. "Not in a dream. Here. Outside. I was upstairs, looking out my window, and I saw him, just like he was…"

A shrill cry sounded from a tinny speaker somewhere near the front of the house, followed by a loud snap. Jonathan knew that in their collective mind's eye, they'd each had a flash of the hayloft, of the beam, of the rope jerking tight. Of Will McIntosh swinging like a pendulum, his bladder letting loose a stream of urine that traced an ellipse onto the barn's dirt floor. One of them had laughed. Laughed that Will had pissed himself. Laughed before the full horror of what had happened settled on them. Jonathan couldn't remember which of them it had been. Maybe he'd never known.

Max turned ashen and sat his still half-full glass on the table.

Jonathan, fearing his companion was about to be sick, scooped up the room's scallop-edged, floral decoupage waste bin and hurried to Max's side. His old friend stared up at him as if he'd lost his mind.

Gordon's throaty laughter punched its way into their consciousness. "Good God, you've turned into a bunch of superstitious, jumpy old women." A cruel glee covered his own shakiness. "It was only some sound effect meant to spook the trick-or-treaters." He narrowed his focus on Timothy, who was visibly shaking. "And you. You looked out your window, and you saw a boy. A normal living child who just happened to be passing by…"

"But his eyes were fixed on me. He was staring at me."

"Probably wondering what kind of old perv was looking down at him. Must've thought you had your dick in your hand." Gordon said and snorted, seeming pleased with himself for having set aside his own disquiet. "Did you, Timothy? Were you up there watching the boy and polishing your pecker?"

"Stop it, Gordon," Jonathan said, disgusted by the snipe. It would seem that weakness still prompted Gordon's cruelty.

"Jesus," Gordon said, looking struck. "Just trying to lighten things up here. Diffuse the—" He held up his hands and wiggled his fingers, "Wooooooooo."

"His neck was broken," Timothy insisted. "The boy. His head lolled to the side." Timothy paled as he lost himself in the telling. "He reached down and used his hair to draw his head up straight," he said, reaching up over his head and grabbing a handful of his own hair, still thick but silvered with age. "Maybe there's still time for the three of you. If you haven't seen him. You should go. Just get up and walk out of here now. Together…"

The door swung open, and a distraught Mrs. Dempsey poked in her head. "There's been an accident. Vera was in the tree adjusting a speaker, and the limb snapped. I think her arm's broken. I've got to take her into the emergency room." Her eyes shot to Jonathan. "Listen. I hate to ask, but the children will begin arriving at any moment. Would you mind passing out the candy as they come?"

"Be a shame if the little pissers egged your lovely establishment," Gordon said, "wouldn't it?" Jonathan was struck by the feeling that Gordon had been anticipating some form of calamity, and was now greeting its arrival with glee.

"Of course," Jonathan spoke up over Gordon and placed a hand on Mrs. Dempsey's shoulder, easing her back out of the room before Gordon could upset her any further. "Not to worry. We'll hold down the fort for you."

She fixed him with a somewhat grateful, but mostly nervous stare. "Thank you…"

"Cora." She turned at the sound of the other woman's bellow. "Come on. My arm hurts like a…"

"I'm coming." She spun on her heel and rushed down the hall. Jonathan caught a glance of Vera, her back at least, as she stood hunched over by the open door, a man's leather bomber jacket draped over her broad shoulders. *Good farm stock.* That's how his father had always referred to this sturdy type of female. It was odd, but something about her voice seemed familiar. Jonathan hesitated, curious to see her face, or at least catch a glimpse of her profile. It struck him that the women had no personal photos anywhere in the house, at least not in any of the public spaces. Mrs. Dempsey, Cora, snatched a set of keys from the hall table, and followed Vera over the threshold. She pulled the door shut with a bang.

Jonathan took a step back into the sitting room. Gordon sat there, looking in his general direction, though with an unfocused gaze. "Jesus, Gordon." He fought the urge to spit. "When did you become such a bastard?"

Gordon's eyes sharpened in a tic. "Always was."

"It's true," Max said. "You've just forgotten."

Timothy now stood by the window. Leaning toward the pane, his face just half an inch or so from the glass, he said, "They're coming. The little ones."

Jonathan could hear children's voices. Squeals and shouts and laughter. Distant but coming closer. Excited. A witch's screech came from the direction of the front door. A moment's silence, then the harpy called out again. The innkeepers had evidently replaced the doorbell with a novelty buzzer. Tiny fists began pounding on the door.

"Take care of him," Jonathan said, addressing Gordon and nodding toward Timothy's back. "Don't torment him."

The logs in the fire settled, causing flames to shoot up amid a shower of sparks.

"'...the enjoyments of Genius...'" Gordon said, making one of his trademark obscure references. He had picked up the habit of searching out and regurgitating the words of others back in middle school, a youthful tendency he appeared to have cultivated rather than quashed. Having delivered his quote with pompous theatricalism, Gordon nodded to acknowledge his charge and dismissed Jonathan with a single imperious wave.

The cry of the witch repeated itself several times in quick succession. Jonathan shut the door to the parlor and hurried down the long, narrow hall, glad to find five large bowls filled with sweets lined up on the hall table. He scooped up the one nearest the door, then swung the door open. Eyes widened and one child cried out when the gaggle of trick or treaters at the door caught sight of the strange old man in the severe black suit towering over them. They began backing up, the vocal one turning and flying back to his mother's side. Only one girl, the smallest of the bunch, held her ground. She gazed up at him with unimpressed blue eyes.

"You're not that scary," she said, then quickly added, "trick or treat." She held out her plastic pumpkin, already heaped with treats.

"I didn't mean to be scary at all," Jonathan said, and held the bowl down within her reach. "Here, take as much as you want."

"Excuse me," a young—well, younger—man's voice called out as the man himself mounted the steps. Jonathan glanced up. "Where're Vera and Cora? The owners?" the man added, his voice thick with unwarranted suspicion. "Are you a friend?"

"A guest." Jonathan smiled in an attempt to seem less a threat. "A paying guest," he felt the need to clarify. "I'm afraid there's been an accident. The ladies are at the emergency room having Vera's arm set. Mrs. Dempsey asked us, well, me, to see to it the children's fun isn't ruined."

"Oh, wow. Shame," the young man said, his tone making it plain that as long as Jonathan hadn't chopped the women to bits with a hatchet so that he could pass out poisoned treats to the children, he wasn't all that concerned with the details. He turned and appeared ready to wave the all clear, but rather than walk away, he whirled around. "Listen. I know it's Halloween and all, and you're just trying to get in the spirit of things, but it's a bit too early for that. At least while the young kids are out. Maybe you should…" He didn't finish his sentence, he just wagged a finger at Jonathan's face. "That…that's just not cool, okay?"

Jonathan felt his brow furrow. "Here," he said, forcing the bowl into the man's hands. "You do the honors." The guy nodded at him, but never took his eyes off Jonathan's forehead.

Jonathan left the front door wide open and, passing by the closed door to the sitting room, walked to the claustrophobic powder room at the far end of the hall. He patted his hand along the wall until it found the light switch. He flipped it on, and peered into the antiqued mirror. At first he thought he was imagining things. There, in reversed script, were the words "Kid Killer" on his forehead. He blinked. Leaned in. Blinked again. He turned on the tap, grabbed one of the ridiculous rosette guest soaps, and spread its lather across the black-blue ink. But when he rinsed the soap out of his eyes and focused again on the mirror, the message remained clear and dark above his eyes.

"Goddamn it, guys," he called out. How had they managed it? *When* had they managed it? Sure, he could see Gordon and Max fighting to hold back their snickers, but certainly Timothy would have intervened. Then again, Timothy had spent most of the last hour staring at the fire or out the window, talking about ghosts. He grabbed a hand towel and held it under the water. He scrubbed his forehead, but the ink was indelible.

He threw the towel to the floor, stopped the tap, and stomped off toward the sitting room. He flung the door open, the sound of it hitting the wall, causing Gordon and Max to look up at him with half-startled, half-amused expressions. "Very funny. Now how the hell am I going to get this off?" There was no way he'd get through airport security tomorrow. The thought of tomorrow jolted him; he had a sick and sinking feeling that it would never arrive, that he'd be trapped here forever. He knew the thought was irrational, but it stuck with him. Like he'd finally, after all these years, been caught.

Gordon tilted his head. "The pressure of rotting children's teeth too much for you?"

Jonathan tramped up to Gordon and bent over him. He felt his angry pulse in his neck. "What am I supposed to do about this?" He leaned in closer and jabbed his finger at his forehead.

Gordon pushed back into the chair, then flashed Max a look of confusion. He turned back to face Jonathan. "I don't know. Take it to see a psychiatrist."

Max gave a single snort.

Jonathan stood erect, turning now on Max. "To hell with you, too. Whose idea was it? Not yours, I bet. When we were kids, you couldn't even piss unless Gordon put you up to it."

The look of amusement fled Max's face. "Jonathan. Get a grip. What's wrong with you?"

"What's wrong with me?" Jonathan's voice roared in his own ears. He pointed at the words on his forehead. "This is what's wrong with me. How could you guys do this?"

Timothy drew closer, his haunted expression replaced by one of concern. "Do what?"

"Ah, dammit. Not you, too, Tim."

The light in the room seemed to dim and then brighten in pulses. Jonathan felt a cold sweat form between his shoulder blades. His breath was labored. He knew he had to relax. "You'll die of apoplexy," he heard his long dead mother's voice as clearly as if she stood beside him.

"There's nothing wrong with you," Timothy said.

Max forced himself up and stumbled over to get a better look at him. "He's right, buddy. There's nothing wrong." His voice rang with sincerity this time.

Jonathan couldn't believe they were still trying to have him on. His eyes landed on the previously ignored gilt-framed mirror hanging over the fireplace. He pushed past Max with almost enough force to push him down. He leaned in, ignoring the heat of the fire on his pant legs, and stared into his own wide eyes.

The writing was gone. Not smudged. Not smeared. Completely gone.

Disappearing ink of some kind? Maybe some form of suggestion? The young father. Had he pulled some kind of street magic to amuse himself by shocking an old man on Halloween?

"Maybe you should sit down," Max said. Timothy was already by Jonathan's side, guiding him to the tasteless settee Max had only just abandoned.

The witch cried once more.

The three other men looked at each other, then turned in unison toward him. Max held up his hand. "You stay put. I'll see to the little shits."

Max shuffled out of the room, his heavy, whiskey-burdened steps thumping down the hall. The shrill cackle sounded again. "I'm coming. I'm coming." He heard Max call out, his tone churlish. "You goddamned little piranhas."

Gordon turned toward him. "Are you sure you couldn't do with a stiff one?"

"No," Jonathan said, his refusal too staunch, too much of a protest. "No," he said again, cooler, calmer.

Gordon snorted. "Too bad. Sitting by this fire has given me a boner."

Jonathan closed his eyes. Shook his head. "You are a pig. A total pig."

"True," Gordon said, "but I just got you to relax." Jonathan opened his eyes to find a look of genuine concern peering back at him. "Listen. We just have to get through the funeral. The executor of Stanley's will is going to meet us there. He'll hand each of us our damned envelope. We'll shred what's in them, burn what's left. Slather it in mustard, swallow it, and shit it back out. This time tomorrow, we'll be on planes out of here."

Jonathan drew a breath. Felt himself nodding, grasping on to this glimmer of hope. Yes, they would leave this place. They would go back to the lives they'd formed.

Max shuffled back into the room. "Door was open," he said. "So I turned on the porch light." He crossed to the settee. "And I sat the whole damned candy store out on the porch," he said, seemingly exhausted from his efforts. Jonathan noticed beads of sweat had risen on Max's forehead, and damp rings had formed under his arms. Max turned and collapsed onto the seat, shoving Jonathan over as he did.

"I ripped down that damned trick doorbell," he continued. Then paused and nodded at the bottle, as if he'd sobered up some and didn't much like it. Gordon held it out to him, and he snatched it from his grasp. "And then I locked the goddamned door. Problem solved." He opened the bottle and freshened up his drink. Clutching the tumbler of whiskey, he leaned back. "There was one little freak out there. Creepy kid with one of those plastic pumpkins. Said you'd given her some candy already, but she wanted to know if she could have some more to give to a boy who was too shy to come to the door."

He leaned back and glanced sideways at Jonathan. "I told her if the little pussy wanted candy, he could come himself or do without." He paused. "How you doin', buddy?" He reached out and squeezed Jonathan's shoulder.

"He's fine," Gordon spoke for him. "We're all fine. Isn't that right, Timothy?" Then he raised his hand to his mouth, stifling a yawn.

"We're all fine," Max echoed him, seemingly indifferent to any objection Timothy himself might have. "Maybe it's just the relief of getting this whole mess with Will off my chest, but truth is, I've never felt better." Max swiped at his forehead with the back of his hand. "Let the fire die down a bit, will you?" He tugged on the front of his damp shirt. "I'm sweating like a jailed frat boy with a pretty mouth."

Jonathan startled when a phone started ringing somewhere in the house. A ringing of the kind he hadn't heard in more than thirty years, a clapper striking a metal bell. The sound continued for a full minute or longer, but the four sat in silence, staring at each other, none willing to seek out the source of the din. The ringing stopped, only to start anew a few moments later.

"It's probably our innkeepers reporting back on the business line," Jonathan said, collecting himself. "They wouldn't know our numbers, would they?" Max shrugged. He didn't seem to give a damn who was calling or why. Gordon turned and raised an eyebrow, a silent confirmation that he could wait the ringing out. Ignore it till it went away. Having silently conveyed that message, Gordon closed his eyes and rested his head on the tatted headrest cover. Max, too, seemed to be giving out for the night. He began soughing.

Timothy had returned to his lookout by the window, his shoulders stooped, his face nearly resting on the glass. One of the Dempsey's strobe lights started to pulse beyond the glass, triggered by an errant visitor or perhaps an animal. The frenetic flashing seemed to increase the urgency of the antique phone bell.

Jonathan sighed, and placing his hands on his knees, forced himself up. He followed the ringing out into the hall, then turned left toward the back part of the house. He passed the powder room, the furthest boundary of *terra cognita*, and carried on along the darkened corridor. The hall, which struck him as being too long to fit within the footprint of the house, led toward a space he felt certain, in usual circumstances, was kept off-limits to paying guests. He shuddered as he passed through a nearly palpable boundary between the ordained and the forbidden, asking himself twice if he should stop, turn around, return to his fellow inmates, and let the bells clang for all eternity. But the incessant ringing compelled him, and with every step it grew louder.

At the end of the hall, he pushed through a swinging door and reached in, patting the wall for a light switch. His fingers found it, and flicked on the overhead light.

With the first flash, it was obvious that their innkeepers had put all their resources into updating those areas reserved for guests. Though spotless, the kitchen's decor hadn't been touched in years, maybe not since before Jonathan had left Waterville for university. The walls were a sad, faded institutional yellow. An ancient avocado refrigerator hummed a love song to its mate, a range of the same color and vintage. They had probably come into this kitchen together, and would undoubtedly be carted out to the dump together when their time came. He pushed past an irrational sense of jealousy, and focused on the source of the din, a phone colored a deeper yellow than the wall to which it clung. It was somewhat more modern than the rest of the room's appliances, but still a refugee of a different era. Jonathan staggered across the checkerboard—and undoubtedly asbestos-lined—linoleum tiles to snatch up the receiver and hold it to his ear. His eyes focused on the phone's gray push buttons.

"Hello," he said, then thought to add, "Vera and Cora's line." He wondered if he should've used the bed and breakfast's name instead, but what the hell, he didn't work for these people.

He waited for a response, but there was only a static-fleeced silence on the other end. "Hello," he repeated himself, jumping to the conclusion that it was a Halloween crank call, then with the next breath wondering if kids still made crank calls now that everyone had caller ID and cell phones. "Hello," he said a third, and he was determined, final time. If there were no response, he'd slam the receiver down. A good, old-fashioned hang up that would cause the bells inside the phone to clang, not the anemic smartphone click you had to settle for today.

"You gotta get out of there, Johnny," a voice cut through the static. "Run."

Jonathan felt his pulse quicken and his mouth go dry.

"Who?" Jonathan held the receiver out, staring at it out of habit, expecting it to betray the identity of the caller. He shook his head, angry with himself. He put the receiver back to his ear. "Who is this?"

"Ah, Johnny, you know who it is." Another blast of static caused him to yank the receiver away. "It's Stanley." It sure sounded like Stanley, or at least the way Jonathan assumed Stanley would sound after so many years, well, decades really. The lights around him dimmed. His heart beat in painful thuds.

Jonathan dropped the receiver, and it struck the wall, falling and swinging on its curled bungee of a cord. The memory of Will hanging in that barn, the figure eight he'd scrawled in piss beneath him, rose again before his mind's eye, and Jonathan suddenly couldn't bear the sight of the receiver, dangling inches above the ground. Stanley's words, now a distant, tinny gabble, continued to hiss through the earpiece. "You have to listen to me, Johnny. It's too late for the others. Just go." He bent and caught hold of the receiver, lifting it, dropping it back into its cradle with a click.

Jonathan felt sick to his stomach. Beads of sweat formed on his forehead. This type of joke was too dark even for the combined forces of Max and Gordon. Stanley was dead, sealed for eternity in a midrange metal casket.

Or was he?

Jonathan forced his breathing to slow. Forced himself to remember who he was. What he believed. First and foremost, he was a realist. He couldn't reconcile calls from the great beyond with the everyday brick and mortar world in which he lived. If the voice on the other end of the line was Stanley's, that meant Stanley was still alive. And then it came to him in a flash. The summons. The closed coffin. The setting. Nothing but amateur theatrics. The whole thing had to be some kind of sick hoax.

Acting on a hunch, he pulled his smartphone from his jacket pocket and opened a search. Stanley Crofton. Cora Dempsey. Waterville Theatre. The first article that appeared was headlined, "Crofton Leads Local Cast in Comedic Production," so he clicked on the link. Eighteen months ago the Waterville Players had staged a comedic adaption of an old Hitchcock film, featuring multiple characters, but only four actors to play them. The female lead, Cora Dempsey, had played all of the female roles. Max tapped on the photo that accompanied the article, using his thumb and forefinger to enlarge the woman's face. She didn't resemble the Mrs. Dempsey he had met—not at all—but the actress was in heavy makeup, and her hair appeared to be a wig. It could be her. *It has to be her. Doesn't it?*

Jonathan reached up and wiped the perspiration from his brow. Inspiration struck him. He turned back to his phone, this time searching for Stanley's obituary, then for news stories about his suicide. He found none.

There would be no funeral tomorrow, as there had been no death.

Had Stanley's conscience led him to seek catharsis through this little melodrama they were producing? Did he plan to pop out of that matte-silver casket tomorrow like some avenging Jack- in-the-box angel? How much did Cora and Vera know? Or the handful of mourners manning the folding chairs at the viewing? Did they consider this gambit an elaborate piece of performance art, or were they merely humoring Stanley by participating in an elaborate trick on his old friends, who hadn't cared enough to stay in touch, who had done everything possible to leave the past in the past—leaving Stanley there with it?

He turned, intending to rush back to the parlor, but Timothy stood in the doorway, blocking his way. "This hasn't changed," he said, glancing around the kitchen. "She used to bring me back here sometimes. After lessons, while I waited on my mother."

"Stanley. He isn't..." Jonathan began, but Timothy wasn't listening.

He moved deeper into the room, and as if on cue, the phone began to ring again as he passed it. He lifted the receiver. "Yes. It was Jonathan. Yes. See you soon," he spoke into the mouthpiece, then returned it to its cradle. "Mrs. Dempsey asked if you're okay. She said she was sure you could hear her, but you wouldn't respond."

"No," Jonathan said. He shook his head with certainty, though that certainty faded with each shake. Timothy might be losing it, but he was not. Then his mind flashed back to the disappearing ink, with its damning accusation. Maybe he was going mad, too. Could madness be contagious? Could one bad apple...? No, he couldn't accept that. "That wasn't Mrs. Dempsey..."

"I used to sneak in here sometimes," Timothy interrupted him, a smile twisting his lips. "When I knew Miss Tanner would be out. I found all her hiding places. And made a few of my own. I wonder..." He pointed toward the ceiling, a gesture signaling a found memory, then crossed the kitchen to the doorway to the old servants' stairs. Jonathan felt compelled to follow, but they didn't go very far. Timothy knelt at the base of the stairway, and began pulling out the riser of the third step from its stringers with his bare fingers. The nails securing it in place acquiesced in silence and came out with a single smooth gesture. Timothy leaned the riser against the wall and then looked back over his shoulder with a delighted gleam in his eye. "It's still here. Right where I left it."

Timothy reached into the space and produced an antique tin with the words "Irradiated Coffee" in proud calligraphy above the promise of "MILLION DOLLAR FLAVOR." He turned and sat on the second step, then pried off the tin's lid, tilting it in Jonathan's direction so he could see its shifting contents. A tin whistling yoyo, just like the one Jonathan had lost as a child. Bits of brightly-colored cardboard—baseball cards, he realized in a flash. The glint of a coin. A few cat's eye marbles. A clear blue shooter, pontil facing up. A time capsule treasure trove of boyhood belongings, the inventory of which needled his memory. Timothy tilted the can back, reached in and pulled out a Swiss Army knife. Without examining its accessories, Jonathan recognized it as the Fisherman model, simply because this, along with the can's other contents, completed the list of the smaller items they'd accused Will of stealing.

"You? You took these things?"

"Will was my half-brother, you know." Timothy said, ignoring his question and setting the can aside. "No, of course you didn't. I didn't know it either. Not till the summer before he died." He dropped the knife back into the can before sealing it and returning it to the space where it had spent the past six decades. "The idiot was my own flesh and blood brother. Well, half." He looked up at Jonathan. "Back before we were born, Miss Tanner left town for a year, supposedly to attend a piano conservatory in Chicago. Mrs. McIntosh, her cousin, couldn't have children, so the McIntoshes agreed to adopt her son and raise him as their own. My dad's son. Of course, everyone knew Will was adopted, but no one had any idea Miss Tanner was his mother. And no one, certainly not my mother, could've guessed the identity of his father. Or at least my father thought so. But my mother knew. That's why she insisted that I take piano lessons from the woman."

His gaze seemed to turn inward. "Miss Tanner told me where she hid her key, supposedly so I could let myself in if she were running late. My mother assured her that I wouldn't be able to resist snooping. They *wanted* me to snoop. They wanted me to know that Will and I were brothers." He laughed. "They must have thought they were doing me a kindness. That I could embrace that dull mouth-breather as my brother. One rainy day, when I had a lesson scheduled, but Miss Tanner was nowhere around, I found a letter my father had written her." Timothy seemed to jolt back to the present, focusing on him. "He told her he didn't want a thing to do with her or 'her' kid. Recommended she use a crochet hook or May-apple to deal with the situation."

"You know of the May-apple, don't you?" Jonathan's eyes shot to the head of the stairs, where Mrs. Dempsey stood with one hand on the railing, the other behind her back. "It grows wild all around here. Women used to use the green fruit to induce miscarriages. Ripe May-apple is delicious. You had some of the jam on your scone. The green fruit is toxic, though. So are the other parts of the plant, including its seeds." He steadied himself against the wall. "You had some of those today, too. Just not enough to kill you. A shame, really. It would've been such a poetic end." She took a few steps down. "Really, though, you could've made this so much easier on all of us if you'd just shared the whiskey with the others the way we'd planned." She gave him a wink. "There was a generous dash of GHB mixed in." She paused. "I'm not a purist. I have nothing against modern chemistry when it proves efficacious. Your friends never even felt it when you slit their throats. Did they, Tim?" She held the still bloody serrated hunting knife out where Jonathan could see it. Jonathan startled. "They just drifted off to sleep and justice was done. Now it's your turn, though I'm afraid you'll be awake to know what's happening."

"Justice?" he said in disbelief, his heart pounding. He focused on Timothy. How had he not noticed the red sheen on Timothy's hands, the crimson stains on his cuffs that were now so plain? "But you had a hand in his death. You convinced the rest of us he was stealing." Jonathan's mind reeled through the memories of the day, adrenaline sharpening details he'd long sought to repress. "Up in the loft. You were the one standing closest to Will." The memories slowed, and Jonathan turned them to examine each facet. "Will didn't stumble back off the loft. You pushed him."

Timothy nodded. "Yes, I did," he said, his features relaxing as he acknowledged this truth. "You have no idea how much I hated him. I was ashamed that he was my brother. I wanted him dead, so I killed him."

"But the rest of us were innocent," Jonathan said. "I'm innocent…"

"Innocent?" Timothy said. "You laughed as he died." Timothy's words cut through his denial, brought the full memory back to him in sharp detail. The laughter he had heard, as Willy swayed in an arc, had been his own. "We were all guilty to a degree. Stanley, Max, Gordon, and you, too. Though it's true I'm the guiltiest by far." Timothy looked at him through calm, accepting eyes. "I'll be remembered forever as a murderer. A madman. You. You're lucky. You'll escape any stain on your memory." He reached up and took the knife from Mrs. Dempsey's hand. "There's a noose. The one outside in the tree. It looks like a decoration, but it's real, and it's waiting for me. I'm gonna write my confession about what happened here tonight, about what happened all those years ago with Will. And then I'm going to put that noose around my neck. I won't die from a swift break like Will did. I'll go slowly, kicking and struggling, the rope rubbing my skin raw as it chokes the life out of me. But they're going to make me kill you first. Just like they made me kill Max and Gordon. Just like they made me kill Stanley, then lure you all here. Just like they made me kill the women who owned this place."

"Made you? How can they make you do anything?"

The woman who'd masqueraded as Mrs. Dempsey laughed and raised one hand. The riser that had been leaning against the wall flew toward Jonathan's face, the pointed end of a nail stopping a hairsbreadth from his eye before the board fell and clattered to the floor.

Jonathan spun and lunged through the doorway into the kitchen. He bounded toward the kitchen's back door in three steps, a distant part of his mind telling him that maybe he did have something to live for. That he hadn't felt so vital in years. But another voice, riding on the first one's coattails, wailed in mourning that his life would soon be ended.

Timothy gained on him, then flung himself forward, reaching out to grab his ankle and trip him, but Jonathan avoided his grasp and brought the heel of his dress shoe down on the other man's fingers. A loud crack was followed by an enraged howl. "You're making this easier for me now," Timothy growled. "I'm going to make it hurt."

Jonathan grasped the doorknob and tore open the door. He was moving with such force that he rebounded off the leather-jacketed woman's sturdy frame. His whirling mind pointed out she wouldn't be able to wear that jacket over a cast. He tumbled back into the room, only just managing to keep his balance. The woman stepped over the threshold and into the kitchen. "Where you off to, Kid Killer?" There was something about her, her large gray eyes, the sound of her voice. *It's impossible*, he thought, realizing that he was staring into Mrs. McIntosh's face, unchanged by the decades. But no, it was her. He felt certain of it. Guilt had burned her features into his memory.

She grabbed Jonathan's upper arms in a steely, bruising grip and spun him around. Timothy stood before him, his left hand held close to his chest, its fingers bloodied and broken. The knife was clutched in his right hand. He took a step closer, then another, bringing the blade within striking distance.

Mrs. Dempsey—no, the woman who had called herself Mrs. Dempsey—glided up to Timothy's side and laid a hand on his forearm to stay him. "I remember you, boy," she said, addressing Jonathan. "Unlike your friends, I can still see *you* behind that wrinkled mask you wear. And the only thing that can make this moment more perfect would be for you to remember me. Think back. Back to the Halloweens you stood out on this house's front porch—that year you came with a pirate's hat on your head, or the one before, when you came dressed as that ridiculous cartoon duck. Think back to the woman at the door. That loveless spinster librarian."

"Miss Tanner," he said, his own voice sounding distant, alien.

Her eyes widened in delight. "Yes, that's right. Now you know. And the look on your face in this moment makes it worth all the terrible things I've done—" she glanced first over his shoulder at Mrs. McIntosh, "—all we've done to avenge Will. The son you and your friends took from us. The son my poor cousin here sold her immortal soul to bring back."

From behind him, Jonathan heard a shuffling movement. Dread washed over him, followed by a horrible certainty. The corner of his eye caught a shadow, and then a boy circled around to face him. The Tanner woman went to the boy, and took his face between both hands. She leaned in and placed a mother's kiss on his brow. She released him with care, and his head drooped to the side. The boy reached up to right it, and dead eyes, so appallingly familiar, stared at Jonathan. *What did they do to him?*

He flinched in Mrs. McIntosh's grasp as she laughed, a wild, high-pitched screech that reminded him of the holiday door buzzer. "What can I say?" she snarled into his ear. "If you ever come across a man dressed all in black out in the forest, make sure you've ironed out the details before you sign his damned book."

"When our plans to resurrect Will fell short," Ms. Tanner added, "I made a deal of my own, to see to it that you little bastards would pay for your complicity, and this one—" she shook a quivering finger at Timothy, "—would finally be known for the murderer he is." She was shaking with anger now, her limbs trembling, her words spewed out in a hate-filled staccato. "No. This moment won't go wasted," she said, taking a moment to gather herself. "I'm going to allow myself to enjoy this."

Ms. Tanner traced a finger along Timothy's arm, along his hand, down the blade. She touched its sharp tip, then raised her hand so Jonathan could see the drop of blood forming on her finger. "You're a lucky boy, you are," she said. "This day would've come much sooner if we'd had our way, but it pleased Him to wait until He considered the lot of you ripe for sacrifice." She stood before him, taking him in from head to toe. "A bit overripe by my estimation. But now your time's drawn to a close." She turned to Timothy. "Tick tock."

Mrs. McIntosh tightened her grip as Timothy stepped forward and pushed the blade, serrated edge up, into Jonathan's navel. At first it felt like being punched, then Timothy jerked the blade up toward his sternum. The pain seared through him. His arms still held securely at his sides, Jonathan could only watch as his blood and viscera spilled out before him. His knees began to buckle, and his childhood friend gave him a rough shove to the side. He landed, falling on his back. The room around him pulsed alternatively between a bright light and total darkness. His brain told him that his body couldn't move. Wouldn't move. Still it did, pushing backwards with his elbows and feet, trying to aim itself toward the doorway, trying to escape but slipping on his own fluids.

Another flash of light, and he saw Miss Tanner's solemn face bent over him. Her features shimmered, then reassembled themselves into that of the trick-or-treater who'd looked up over her plastic pumpkin at him. "See? I told you that you weren't so scary." A glacial chill fell over him. The girl's face gave way to blackness, an utter absence of light.

Jonathan's first thought upon being immersed in darkness was that he must be dead. But no, the sensation of icy agony continued. He could still feel the slippery tile floor beneath his hands. He jumped to the conclusion that as his body gave out, as the synapses of his brain died, his sight had failed him before his other senses. But then he sensed movement in the darkness; the lightless world around him condensed, reorganized itself into a man's lusterless face. The kitchen, once again visible, dissolved around them, leaving just this man woven from shadow and Jonathan, still supine on what now felt to be a bed of moss, alone in a murky wood. The sound of running water caused Jonathan to turn his head. A wide stream, a near river, of liquid onyx flowed beside him.

Jonathan felt the weight of the watcher's stare on him, and he turned back to find the creature had drawn near. "Yes," he answered its silent question without even moving his lips. "I was the one who laughed."

The shadow came another step closer. He tried to close his eyes, to ready himself for his end, but he could not. The being knelt beside him, and out of nothingness, produced a large book, bound in what appeared to be leather and filled with ancient vellum sheets. The man fanned the sheets of the book, each page covered with line after line of signatures, some in Roman script, some in foreign characters, though most of them were nothing more than simple Xs scrawled by uncertain, illiterate hands. The man stopped at a fresh, uninscribed sheet, marred only by the seal of an anchor clutched in an eagle's claws. Although there was only silence between them, Jonathan began the most intense, painstaking contract negotiation of his life. It might have taken a millisecond. It might have taken a millennium. But he came to an understanding with the living shadow, and when he did, he dipped his finger into his own blood and traced his name on the page.

THE TRESPASSER

Joshua Rex

How had they gotten so lost?

Todd certainly didn't know. This was *Jed's* neighborhood, after all. *He* was supposed to know where he was going. Todd had, as usual, just been following the big kids, trailing behind his cousin and older brother from house to house, dressed in his Sergeant Surge costume and glorying in the fistfuls of candy filling his bag a little fuller with each block.

Spencer and Jed were collecting candy as well, though with much less enthusiasm. They were going about this whole Halloween thing rather lackadaisically, Todd thought. Both were costumeless except for monster masks they wore up on their heads, the grisly faces pointed skyward (Jed a grinning werewolf with a mane of bright orange hair, and Spencer a white-faced goblin with black-rimmed eyes, red teeth, and pointy ears) carrying their sacks of Halloween loot synched in their fists like bank robbers.

Todd understood what was happening. Spencer and Jed, both recently thirteen, were doing the unthinkable; they were *outgrowing* trick-or-treating. Todd had observed this brand of indifference before in adults, whose Christmases didn't seem to revolve around the getting of presents any longer. The two older boys were much more interested in locating a spot in which they could set off the fireworks Jed had acquired on the blacktopped black market of his junior high parking lot, than they were in gathering free sweets. Earlier that day, Jed had spread the explosive contraband out on his bedroom floor, the red and yellow rockets and firecrackers brilliant against the drab, threadbare carpet. His eyes had lit up as he gazed upon them, already imagining their crackling blasts and stellar flares.

"There's an abandoned school down the street. It burned when our parents were kids. We can shoot them off after we're done taking *him* around," Jed said with a tick of the head in Todd's direction, making Todd feel in that moment like the world's smallest third wheel.

This had been the first thing their father and mother had warned them about on the ride up to the city from the affluent suburb in which they lived. Their parents were leaving them, reluctantly it had seemed, for the weekend while their mother attended a business conference downtown. *Don't wander off from the neighborhood. And don't, for any reason, go into any abandoned places,* their father had said. He'd grown up in the city—in the very same house, in fact, where Spencer and Todd would be staying. Aunt Jennet, their father's sister, being the last to live at home (as her brother was already established and quite wealthy) had inherited the homestead by default after the boys' grandmother had died. Their aunt had had Jed when she was sixteen, and their cousin had grown up there, though during decidedly less prosperous times than when their father was a boy.

Their father had used the adjectives "rough" and "overrun" to describe the declining place he hailed from. The latter designation had perplexed Todd. Overrun by what? He'd pictured hordes of Grim Ghouls, the enemies of Sergeant Surge and his Interstellar League, roaming through the streets in search of Star Elixir—that highly coveted astral booty. But then the thought of anyone raiding and pillaging *these* houses for anything that could be deemed "highly coveted" seemed ridiculous. Most of them appeared to have been raided and pillaged long ago, and if they were anything like his aunt's house, with its outdated appliances and stuffy, stinky furniture, the thieves would hardly be lining up with their ski masks and pry bars.

"They're disadvantaged," their mother had said about the people who lived in their father's former neighborhood, a statement that made their father scoff in the leather driver's seat of the family luxury sedan.

Regardless of the semantics, it was obvious to both brothers as they drove past the rows of run down bungalows with their unkempt yards hedged in by mangled, rusting chain-link fences that something had gone awry here. Compared to their townhouse in White Lane Commons, with its freshly paved and track-lit sidewalks, neatly groomed lawns dotted with beds of seasonal flora, and gates that rose and closed automatically behind your car when you came home, this place seemed almost third-world. But these differences also held some allure for Spencer and Todd; the decay and lack of order was appealing. There were no security cameras bolted to the buildings, no security guards keeping watch, no neighbors shaking their fists at you if you cut through their identical square of green grass. But, most enticing of all, there would be little or no adult supervision for the entire weekend. Aunt Jennet worked twelve hour shifts at a factory, and during the few hours she *was* home, she smoked and sipped wine coolers and insisted that the boys *play outside,* even after dusk. They would get to go on adventures and explorations led by their tough, streetwise cousin Jed.

Which is how they'd ended up lost.

"The school's down here. Not far," Jed had said at the threshold of a road whose street sign hung bent and crooked from a leaning telephone pole that resembled the rotted mast of a sunken flagship. Spencer threw a long, apprehensive gaze down the dodgy looking road while Todd regarded Spencer, waiting, as he always did in such instances, for his older brother's decision.

"I don't know…"

Jed rolled his eyes. "Oh, come *on*, man. Halloween only comes once a year!"

Todd didn't know what this had to do with anything, but he knew it carried with it the implication of risk. "Our dad said we weren't supposed to wander off from the neighborhood," Todd offered, in solidarity with his brother.

"Why, cause it's *dangerous* here? Cause we're *poor*?"

"No, I didn't mean…" Todd stammered, "That's not what I…"

"Your *dad* thinks he's so great living in his fancy house, driving his fancy car. But *he's* one of us." Jed paused, looked them up and down. "You're not, though."

"What's that supposed to mean?" Spencer said.

"You're yuppies. You live in a safe little world with mommy and daddy who give you whatever you want. You ain't got no *grit*."

"I have *grit*," Spencer said, rather unconvincingly.

Jed looked at them a moment, chuckling, then spat on the sidewalk and started down the road. Spencer watched him go, and Todd saw the change in his brother's expression at Jed's challenge, noticed the way his eyes narrowed and twitched at the corners.

"He said it's not far," Spencer said without taking his eyes off Jed.

"But it's almost *dark*, Spencer."

"It'll be fine. Just stick close to me, okay?" Spencer said. He had their mother's eyes—same shape, same color, and thus, for Todd, offered the same instinctual comfort. He supposed this was part of the reason he trusted his brother implicitly. When he nodded, Spencer slapped him on the back—a rare "one of the guys" gesture—that made Todd grin. In that moment he would have followed his brother anywhere.

***

Todd hadn't thought it was possible, but the area through which Jed now led them was even sketchier than their father's old neighborhood. The roads were especially bad, the asphalt looking like it had been struck by a meteor shower, loaded with cracks and crevices and shoddily patched—or not patched— chuckholes. The houses were sparser along this stretch. Those that remained were clad in sun-faded siding and vine snarl, or wore the blackened scars of arson. Most, however, were gone; leveled or burned, their concrete stoops, leading nowhere, standing like grave markers in the overgrown lots.

Eyeing the charred bones of one of the houses, Spencer said, "Why would we want to go to this school if it's burned down?"

"It didn't burn *down*, just burned up," Jed corrected.

Todd tugged Spencer's sleeve. "What's that mean?" he whispered.

"The building's still standing but it's just a shell now."

Todd nodded. As usual, he had more questions, but knew he was running the risk of being the annoying little kid, so he kept quiet and fished in his bag of sugary loot for a piece of sour apple Atomic Taffy. When he found one, he popped it in his mouth and dropped the wrapper on the ground. He knew this was littering—he would never have dared do anything of the kind at White Lane Commons—but he didn't want the wrappers cluttering up his bag. And besides, it seemed to be what everyone else did around here. There was trash *everywhere*. Plastic bags, snagged in shrubs, flapped like battle-shredded standards in the chilly late-October gusts. Soda cans rattled bone songs along the crumbling pavement. The shards of shattered, multi-colored glass bottles formed abstract mosaics in the street.

As he chewed, Todd regarded all of this as if it were the setting of one of those late night horror movies he and Spencer watched on the weekends after their parents had gone to bed— movies in which scary things happened, but at a distance, safely on the other side of the glowing screen. Like most kids his age, Halloween gave him that same spooky feeling, as if he were actually in one of those films, though still *safe* in his costume as he went about his gathering of free candy. On this one night of the year, everything seemed more ominously symbolic, loaded with supernatural innuendo; the huge moon shrouded behind a murky cataract of cloud, the high wind making the brittle autumn leaves cackle, the hint of pagan wood smoke on air already beginning to smell of snow. Every rattle and bang was of ghostly origin, every dark place a *haunted* place, every creak and groan was some unthinkable inescapable monster shambling toward you from out of the shadows.

Jed stopped at a corner, looked up the road they were on,

then down the intersecting road, from which came shouting and thumping music. "It's this way," he said with a tick of the head in the direction of the noise.

Spencer hesitated, glanced back over his shoulder and then at Jed. "How much *further*?"

Jed either didn't hear, or was pretending not to hear as he started off. Spencer gave Todd a pained smile before continuing on.

Eyes peered at them from the shadows of sagging porches, behind bucking screen doors, through the windows of parked cars. *The Disadvantaged*, Todd thought. For some reason when his mother had said this, he'd pictured beggars with no teeth waggling tin cans at passersby for spare change. But these were not hapless, clichéd vagabonds ingratiating themselves for a random dime. There were no cordial nods or little smiles like people gave one another at White Lane. These were hostile faces, threatening, territorial, and despite it being a public street, Todd felt very much a trespasser here. Even Jed seemed uncomfortable, walking quickly, head down and mumbling for the others to do the same.

Todd shrieked as something struck him in the arm. He looked down at the half eaten chicken leg at his feet, and then up at the boy who had thrown it. He was around Todd's age, wearing a torn black-hooded sweatshirt and bleach-stained jeans, instead of a Halloween costume. One of his blown out shoes gaped at the toe like a slit throat. A little chorus of laughter from the porches and the cars then, accompanied by more bones, a volley of them as the voices grew loud again, taunting.

Spencer, Todd and Jed broke into a run, pelted by an array of random trash, which escalated to bottles shattering at their heels by the time they reached the end of the road and rounded the corner. They ran another five blocks until collectively winded, they stopped, heaving breaths. Jed was laughing.

Spencer, cheeks mottled red, said, "What's so funny?"

"That was awesome! That's one of the *worst* streets in the whole city."

"And you took us down there?"

"I should have thrown one of the smoke bombs!" Jed mused. "*Damn…*"

"What the hell is your problem? You could have gotten us killed!"

"Come on man, I thought you had *grit*?"

Spencer clenched his teeth. "So where is this school?"

"This way—" Jed said, with a vague wave in no particular direction.

"You've been saying that for the past hour."

"What are *you* trying to say?"

"It's eleven thirty! We were supposed to be home an hour ago!"

"Then *go home*," Jed said with a smirk. The smirk faded suddenly when he saw the group of kids, led by the boy in the black sweatshirt, coming toward them. They were shouting, and Todd saw something gleam silver in one of their hands.

"*Run!*" Jed shouted, taking off without waiting for Spencer or Todd. Behind them, Todd heard a war cry, and then Spencer was pulling him. "*Go, go, go!*"

Together, they sprinted down a side road that dead-ended at a shallow patch of scrub grass, and, beyond that, a black wall of trees. Todd lagged behind the older boys, slow in his baggy green Sergeant Surge pants, which turned out not to be so super-hero-ific in the face of real danger. His eyes widened as a rock whizzed by his head. Glancing over his shoulder, he saw the boy in the black hooded sweatshirt not fifty paces back.

"Throw your candy!" Jed screamed.

Todd hugged his bag to his chest and shook his head.

Spencer turned and fired his bag at the kids, striking the leader in the gut, and buying him just enough time to scoop Todd up. From his view over his brother's shoulder, Todd saw that most of the kids had given up the pursuit and were now fighting amongst themselves like hyenas on a carcass over the contents of Spencer's trick-or-treat sack. Some of them kept following right up to the line where the pavement gave way to field and trees. But here, they unexpectedly stopped.

Todd regarded them curiously. *Maybe they're afraid of the*

dark? He knew that *he* certainly was, let alone the *woods* in the dark. But then another thought occurred to him, this one much more disturbing. What if they were afraid not of the dark itself, but something they knew to be *in* it?

Jed, squatting behind a massive deadfall which had been rotting in-situ for a generation, waved them over. For several minutes they huddled there in silence, listening.

"Alright. I think we're okay," Jed said after some time.

"*Okay?*" Spencer said. "Where are we?"

"The south woods."

"Where's *that?*"

"*South* of the city," Jed snapped.

Spencer stood. "Take us home. Right now!"

Jed got up. "What a bunch of sissies. One night away from home and you're crying for your mommies!"

"You know, I'm getting a little tired of your smart ass mouth," Spencer said.

"Yeah? What are you gonna do about it?"

The two glared at one another, Todd looking from Spencer to Jed, Jed to Spencer, waiting to see who would be the first to strike. Or blink.

It was Spencer. He checked his watch, pressing a button which made the screen glow. Todd was envious of this watch because it was the same sort of device and the exact shade of green that Sergeant Surge used to summon the Interstellar Gang. Spencer glanced around at the woods, then looked at Todd and said: "This way."

"*This way?*" Jed scoffed. "Where do you think *you're* going?"

"Home."

"You don't even know where you are!"

"Neither do you," Spencer said flatly.

"So you're just going to walk off into the woods?"

"Well we can't go back *that* way," Spencer said pointing toward the dead end.

Jed opened his mouth and closed it.

"So? What do you suggest?" Spencer asked.

"There's a path here that is supposed to lead back to my block, though I don't know that for sure."

"Great. Is there anything you *do* know for sure?"

"Yeah, you can either follow me or go your own way and…" Jed paused to pull his mask down, "…get eaten by the wolves."

Todd could see Jed grinning madly at them through the mouth hole in the gaping rubber werewolf jaws, his teeth slick and grey as old bone in the moonlight.

***

Of course there were no wolves. Still, it took several reassurances from Spencer before Todd felt confident that he wasn't about to be devoured whole, costume and all. They followed Jed along the moonlit trail, their progress slow and tedious, until arriving at a place where the trail unexpectedly forked. Jed chose the left tine and the three boys walked silently for the better part of an hour, until Todd, exhausted and half paralyzed with terror, sunk down onto a large stone just off from the path. The further they'd gone, the more his behavior had reverted to that of a small child, refusing to let go of his brother's hand, and whimpering at the slightest noise, of which there were plenty.

What *were* all those cracking and clambering sounds? Todd was beginning to wonder if those kids really were following them after all, corralling them deep in the woods where no one would hear their screams. And what of the perpetual movement in the dark, always glimpsed out of the corner of his eye? During one such glance, he was sure he'd seen a pair of faces peering back at him, their eyes bright, their countenances slick like oiled ebony, before receding back into the darkness. Now he sat hugging his bag of candy to his chest, his Sergeant Surge outfit in tatters, the mask lost long ago (a tree branch had snagged the cheap rubber band, ripping it off his head). He no longer had that singular Halloween feeling. There was nothing hauntingly enigmatic or mystically furtive about the gravestone-grey clouds against the black, starless sky—or the cold wind murmuring like breath through the lips of the dead.

This is what happens to little boys, he thought, *who don't listen and wander off on their own. They find themselves outside of safety, far beyond protection.*

Spencer sat down beside him on the rock. "You're right, we should take a little break."

"What the hell are you two doing? I thought you wanted to get out of here?" Jed said.

Todd picked up on the tinge of worry in his cousin's tone, which made him feel even more frightened.

"I have a very important job for you, Toddy," Spencer said, removing his wrist watch. He put it in Todd's hand. Todd looked up at him with confused wonder. "I need you to be the time keeper while I help Jed get us out of here. I can't do both, and I think it's really slowing us down."

"Fine. I'm leaving! You two have fun on your faggot rock," Jed said as he tromped off through the brush.

Todd looked down at the watch resting in his palm. It was his brother's most prized possession; the one thing he was allowed to see but never touch. He knew that Spencer was just trying to cheer him up by letting him hold on to it...to get him back on his feet and moving again. And it worked. Being entrusted with the stewardship of the watch, in addition to the prospect of helping them get out of the woods by keeping time—even if only in some ceremonial way—changed his mood in an instant. He looped the watchband around his wrist and slipped the notch finder three holes past Spencer's usual spot.

"Press the lower left button to make it light up," Spencer said.

Todd did this, and for a second his trepidation evaporated. But then he saw what time it was. Dread tunneled through his chest like a long black root, as he gawped at the digital numbers. Could it really be *2:56 a.m.*? He couldn't recall ever having been awake at that time before in his life. It was a place unfamiliar as a foreign country.

"If we get separated, just press that button, and I'll come find you, okay?" Spencer said, his face half illumined in the absinthe green glow.

Not for the last time that night, Todd marveled at his brother's composure. There wasn't a trace of fear in his expression. In fact, he was *smiling*.

Suddenly, Jed was shouting for them to "*Come quick!*"

The two brothers got up together and made their way down the rambling path. Jed stood at the top of a rise in a breech in the trees.

Home, Todd thought. *Home is just ahead...*

But as they came up alongside Jed, it wasn't their cousin's poorly lit street they saw, but a massive ruined building leering back at them like a blackened skull through the tangle of trees. Jed, Todd noticed, was gazing at the school with an expression of palpable wonder, like an archaeologist discovering a place long fabled to exist.

Grinning wickedly, he gripped each of his cousins by a shoulder. "You guys ready to have some *real* fun?"

"What are you talking about?" Spencer said gravely.

"Now we can see if there really *are* any skeletons!"

"Skeletons?" Todd whispered.

"The ones of the kids who burned up in the fire."

"I want to go *home...*" Todd moaned, soon beginning to cry. He'd held out as long as he could. Being lost was one thing, but lost with the potential of skeletons was too much.

"We *are* going home, okay?" Spencer reassured him. "There are no skeletons, just like there aren't any *werewolves.*" Spencer glared at Jed, who was sniggering against a tree.

"Give me those fireworks..."

"No."

"Come *on*, give me them!"

"Why?"

"I'm going to shoot them off from the roof, so that people will see that we're here!"

"You're actually going to go *in* there?" Jed said.

"No...!" Todd shrieked.

"*Give me the god damned fireworks!*"

Jed flinched, regarded Spencer with a raised eyebrow, then reached in his coat and came out with three arrow-shaped rockets.

Spencer grabbed them and immediately started off in the direction of the school.

Todd was right behind him, hands reaching, and then clenching, at the back of his brother's windbreaker.

"I'm coming with you!" the boy said.

"No, Toddy. You have to stay here with Jed."

"I don't *want* to!"

"You remember what dad said? Abandoned places can be very dangerous."

"Then why are you going?"

"Because, I'm the oldest. And, because if anything happens to you, my ass is grass."

This expression had always made Todd laugh. '*Your ass is grass...and I'm the mower,*' their father said on occasion, when he was really angry. It never failed to make them laugh. Even their father would crack up, the threat of punishment momentarily averted. But Todd didn't find it humorous now. "I don't *care*," he whined. "Please let me come too!"

Spencer crouched before his little brother and lifted Todd's left arm, the one on which he wore the watch. "Flash me a signal in fifteen minutes, so I know where you are. This is very important Todd. Do you understand? You are my compass now. Without you, I won't know how to get back."

"Alright," Todd said reluctantly, swiping at his tears with one of his tattered plastic sleeves.

"Good," Spencer said, pressing his lips into a tight smile. Then he turned and hurried off through the snag of trees.

Todd watched his progress until he disappeared into the school's shadow, cast by the back-lit blazing moon. It seemed to swallow Spencer, this shadow, a void deep and tenebrous as a plague pit.

***

Todd would remember that night for two reasons. It was the last time he trick-or-treated on Halloween. And it was the last time he ever saw his brother.

He'd checked Spencer's watch diligently, counting down the tense minutes one by one. When 3:15 a.m. arrived, Todd flashed the green light. He did this over the next several minutes. But as 3:25 approached, without a single red rocket blast, Todd's anxiety reached a crescendo.

"We have to go look for him."

"I'm not going in there," Jed said, picking his nose and wiping his finger on a nearby tree.

"Something's *wrong*, Jed."

"He's probably just messing with us."

"But what if he tripped or fell down the stairs? It's so *dark* in there…"

"He's the tough guy that wanted to go in by himself. He'll find his way out." Jed shrugged. "Or, he won't."

Todd bit his lip and turned back to look at the school, where something was changing. There was a vast internal movement now, as if the dark itself was shifting en masse from room to room. Jed was looking at the school too now, the wolf mask hanging slack off the side of his head.

"See?" Todd said, "Someone's *in there!*"

"It's just bats," Jed said, without taking his eyes off the place. Sounds accompanied the movement, a clatter like hundreds of footfalls eagerly racing along the blind halls as if it were the last day of school before summer break. But it wasn't a sultry afternoon in late May. It was the middle of the night on the last day of October. And there were no kids, of course, unless—

"It's just *rats*," Jed said again, his voice barely audible.

A charcoal grey cloud slid away from the moon, and by its light they saw a small figure standing under the school's arched main entrance, wearing Spencer's goblin mask. Todd knew right away that this was not his brother. The figure was too short, too slouch-shouldered. It beckoned to them in a voice sifted through ash—a cindery reed—its cracked and blackened arms extended. Other lights began to appear behind it, a hundred pairs burning moonlight-bright.

Todd didn't remember fleeing, nor could he recall screaming his throat raw, though he did have a vague recollection of kicking and clawing and biting Jed's face, as his cousin carried him out of the woods. He guessed that he must have passed out; either that or Jed had knocked him out, as his left temple was sore to the touch for a week after.

The next thing Todd knew, they were back on Jed's street, and there were red and blue flashing lights out front of his aunt's house, and his father's car was there parked behind the cruisers. A throng crowded around them; his mother and father were asking about Spencer. *Where's Spencer, Todd? Where's your brother?*

Todd, drool running from his mouth down his battered Halloween outfit, could only stammer about white eyes in the dark as he pressed the button on Spencer's watch, sending out that green signal over and over and over again.

But Spencer never came.

***

Twenty years passed.

Todd, a senior financial consultant and acquisitions assessor for Resurrection Foundations Development Corporation, found himself back in the old neighborhood for the first time since his brother's disappearance. He was on assignment to evaluate a parcel of foreclosed properties his company had recently snatched up.

At first he'd declined the task, having no interest in revisiting what was buried under two decades of scar tissue. But his intractable project supervisor insisted that, ostensibly, Todd was the only team member who possessed the proper credentials. He'd told himself on the drive up that he would do his job and go home. But after inspecting the derelict plots and ramshackle houses, most of which would feel the wrecking ball's kiss, he found himself driving down that pitted road where he'd last trick-or-treated.

He spotted his aunt's house, pulled up in front of it and put the car in park. The place was a shambles—roof sagging, gutters hanging like rusticles on a long-sunken ship, the grass so tall a lion could hide utterly unseen amid its blades. This was no surprise, of course. Aunt Jennet had died (cervical cancer) the year Todd got his driver's license and Jed began serving his first prison sentence. They hadn't gone to the funeral. Neither Todd nor his mother and father ever spoke to his aunt or cousin again, after that fateful Halloween. Todd's father had blamed Aunt Jennet for Spencer's disappearance—so brother and sister had never reconciled. Todd had always felt some degree of guilt for this. It was, after all, Jed's and Spencer's, and even his own fault, for not doing as they were told. But adults, he'd learned after his own failed marriage, had a predilection for blaming each other for life's inexorable incidents.

He wanted to go in, *should* go in, he thought, if for no other reason than to make sure there were no personal family relics left behind to be claimed by squatters or vandals.

Todd opened the car door, got out and was just about to shut it behind him when he noticed the man sitting in a rusting patio chair beneath the drooping porch roof. He was fat, bald, and shirtless, clutching a dented tallboy beer can between his flabby tits. He rose with surprising speed though, and made his way toward the stoop, flexing and unflexing a fist as he scowled at Todd's luxury sport sedan. Todd only recognized Jed by the half-crescent bite scar on his cousin's right cheek. Whether or not Jed recognized him he couldn't be sure, though if Jed's gimlet stare was any indication, this was decidedly *not* the occasion for a family reunion.

"Sorry…wrong house," Todd said. He got back in his car, put it in drive, and didn't look back as he punched the pedal.

He turned left at the next road and followed it down a hill toward another cluster of houses, these newer, with hay still strewn in the front lawns where sprinklers waved lazy arcs under the late afternoon sun. It gradually began to dawn on him where he was. The *Disadvantaged*, as his mother had so saccharinely referred to them as, had become the *Displaced* as companies like his snatched up the derelict properties en bloc and immediately hiked up the rents. This was no surprise to Todd. It was what he did, and good riddance, too. Once the undesirables were cleared out and the dilapidated bungalows had been razed, they would be replaced with modern renditions and anomalous geometrical shaped townhouses which could then be sold at ten times the value of the latter.

The street had been freshly paved. No chicken bones or shattered glass crunched beneath his tires as he retraced that inauspicious route, steering left again when he reached the corner and again five blocks down where the dead end and that wall of woods stood beyond.

He parked along the curb and stared into the trees while fingering the buttons of Spencer's watch, worn now with the notch finder furthest from the timepiece.

He took out his phone and searched for a satellite map of the area. Locating the woods, he zoomed in. He saw the path right away—a slender line snaking through the forest and forking near the center. Todd could see now how they'd gone awry that night. The right tine led back up to higher ground, toward Jed's neighborhood and safety, while the left, the one they'd taken that night, led to a solid black square hedged in on all sides by leafy treetops. Todd squinted at this, frowning. Why would the search engine blot out the area? He zoomed in further, scanning for detail, but it was as if his screen had burned out in that spot, the edges hazy and indistinct.

For a solid month after Spencer's disappearance police had scanned the vicinity, in addition to the school, inch by inch for any sign of him. Todd had heard they'd come up with nothing, not even a single piece of candy. Was the school still there? If so, there was the chance, however small, of finding some spec relating to his brother—something, anything, which might suggest Spencer hadn't simply walked into its black maw and vanished without a trace.

There was only one way to find out. Todd popped the trunk, grabbed his boots and put them on in place of his imported leather shoes. He found himself replaying the events of that night as he started off into the woods. Details he hadn't thought about in years disconcertingly overlapped with the present. The tombstone clouds…the way his cheap plastic mask had pinched his face…the slimy surface of the deadfall they'd squatted behind while hiding from the rabble of kids. When he reached the fork in the path, he kept left, pushing through the encroaching brush, until he reached the school fifteen minutes later.

He'd half expected to see phantoms, ghouls, great billows of black smoke pouring from its empty orifices, but there was only the silence of an un-thought of place; intentionally forgotten perhaps. A place where tragedy was seared into the walls. Nevertheless, there was an unforeseen tranquility to the slowly crumbling ruin, an immemorial peace suggested by the sun dappled masonry and the birds traipsing along the scorched window frames. Yet for Todd, it was a false semblance of peace, and as he gazed upon it bitterly, the idea began to take shape in his brain.

He would pull some strings, confer with the CFO—who owed him one—and his company would buy the school, and then Todd would spearhead its demolition. They would level the fucking dump, clear the land and put up some sylvan oasis in the form of high priced condos in its place, and Todd himself would be the one to light the fucking dynamite.

The thought made him smile, despite his tears, as he made his way toward the arched entrance through which his brother had gone all those years ago, and had never come out. The smile soon wilted, and tightened into a grimace, when he saw what was waiting for him just over the threshold.

The goblin mask...

Heart beating triple time, he crouched and picked it up, turning it over and over in his hands, noting the black stains on the inside. From the corner of his eye he saw something shift in the shadows.

"Spencer?" his own voice sounded thin and whiney, as if his nine year old self had spoken the name. Todd rose and walked down the central corridor, and as he did, the dark followed him, receding from the walls and the debris-littered floors, the black scorch stains creeping like hordes of bats or rats or...

Little figures with moonlight for eyes.

He stopped, threw a look over his shoulder. The passageway was gone, replaced by an impervious wall of blackness. The dark was condensing all around him in this perpetual dominion of night, arching over his head like the ceiling of a cave. There was movement and sound on all sides, yet he could see nothing substantial, no shapes in the thickening gloom. There was only stillness and a nervous, loaded silence.

Todd looked down at the mask, pulled it on, and lined up his eyes with the holes at its front. Then he looked up. The blackened figures stood all around him, sculpted from soot and ash and charred matter. They jutted from the walls like flying buttresses, hung upside down from the scorched ceiling, gazed up at him like effigies from the floor, their white eyes blazing.

Shuddering, Todd held up his wrist and pressed the watch button. The green light emanated like a spectral beacon.

"Spencer..." he said dryly. "Come and find me."

At the end of the hall, the vast curtain of shadows parted, and there emerged a figure cast from early morning Halloween moonlight. It moved toward Todd determinedly, implacably, and with it came ashen figures, their blackened arms outstretched, groping for the trespasser.

THE MINCH LAKE TRAGEDY

A.P. Sessler

The October breeze chased the children into the long, empty hall while Miss Mowry held the playground door. Fallen leaves nipped at their ankles, along with all the unseen things that arise when a child's back is turned.

"Let's keep moving, single file. That's it," Miss Mowry droned, her eyes off somewhere else.

Giggling girls and boys poured inside, fleeing from playtime fantasies to the quiet classroom ahead, where they would find shelter from the irrational and imagined. Without looking, Miss Mowry halfheartedly counted the heads breezing past.

"And don't let go of your leaves. We didn't just spend a half hour outside to drop them on the floor," she said.

She let the door close slowly when she was sure the last student had entered the hall.

"Miss Mowwee, wait for me," the tiny voice came from outside.

With an exasperated sigh she pushed the door back open and waited for Landon, who came bounding up the sandy path from the playground.

"Hurry, Landon. You should have been in here already," she whined.

Landon passed by at the same carefree pace. "Wook at my weaf, Miss Mowwee," he said, holding the crisp oak leaf up for her to see.

"Yes, I see your weaf wooks wiwwy wow," she mocked his speech impediment.

The observant boy stopped in his tracks and turned to offer a scowl, to which Miss Mowry replied with an unconvincing smile.

He turned and hurried to the classroom, looking back once more with the same scowl.

***

"Alright class, does everyone have their leaves? If not, raise your hand," said Miss Mowry.

She stood with ankles crossed, half-seated on the front of her desk, scanning the room through glasses that hung on the tip of her nose. The children clutched their plucked or freshly fallen leaves, anxiously waiting at activity tables with construction paper, paint and brush.

"No one was a butter-finger, very good," she said. "Now you've all been assigned a partner, so make sure you help each other out. If you absolutely cannot figure out how to make your leaf print then raise your hand and I'll help if I absolutely have to.

"Now when you've finished your leaf print, use our Leaf Identification Chart next to the chalkboard to identify which leaf you've chosen," she said and motioned toward the green chalkboard. "When you're finished with your painting, write the name of the leaf next to your name. And everyone who collects the same kind of leaf you chose today on our approaching field trip will each receive a special prize."

The class bubbled with enthusiasm.

"Alright. Everyone get started."

She immediately returned to her chair and found the place she had left off in her book. The dust jacket cover of the yellow-paged tome read Center of the Circle: The Magick Radius.

Landon and William sat in front of the large window to Miss Mowry's right, their backs growing warm in the morning sun. Landon covered his oak leaf in a coat of green and pressed it on the sheet of gray construction paper.

"What are you making?" asked William, seated to his right.

"Miss Mowwee," he said with a laugh. He pressed the painted leaf to the page repeatedly until a mass of jagged edges surrounded the negative shape of a faceless head. "That's her hair."

"Why's it green?"

"'Cause you have the gway."

"Here. You can use it," William said and slid the small can of silver paint over.

"It would wook wong on my paper."

William noticed the color. "You're right," he said, and after looking at the green-haired likeness he whispered, "She's ugly."

"Not wike Mawwowee."

"You mean Mallory?"

Landon scowled at his partner. "That's what I said."

William held his peace and continued with his silver-leaf airplane on sky-blue construction paper.

"I need some wed," said Landon.

"Go see if Mallory has some," William egged his friend on.

Landon accepted the challenge. "Okay."

He stood and walked to the next activity table, where Mallory sat with partner Samantha. "Mawwowee?" he asked with all the confidence a nine-year-old boy could possess, until he noticed how the sun turned her blond hair into a golden halo of angelic beauty. Now he was afraid to look in her eyes.

"Yes?" she asked.

"Do you have any wed I can bowwow?"

She placed her leaf down. "Here," she said, handing him the can of paint. "Don't spill it, and bring it right back."

"Thank you," he said and returned to his table.

He covered the oak leaf in a layer of red and nearly pressed it to the page when he stopped. "This is too big. Can you use your weaf?"

William looked over. "You're only supposed to use yours," he said.

"It's just for her wips," said Landon.

William laughed. "Okay," he said and dipped his narrow,

elm leaf in the red paint. He pressed it down, horizontally, leaving a red mark near the bottom of Miss Mowry's "face."

The two laughed.

"I wiww be wight back," said Landon and took the can of red paint to Mallory's table.

"Here you go, Mawwowee," he said, placing the can in front of her. "I didn't spiw any and I bwought it wight back."

"Thank you, Landon," she said and smiled at him.

When the sun sparkled in her green eyes he couldn't help himself. He didn't even bother to see if Miss Mowry was watching. He simply stooped over and kissed Mallory on the cheek, then turned as fast as he could and jumped in his chair.

"Miss Mowry!" she called out.

The teacher placed her book down. "What is it, Mallory?" she asked.

"Landon kissed me."

Miss Mowry stood from her desk. "Landon what?"

"He kissed me. On the face."

Miss Mowry marched to Landon's table and towered over the cowering boy. "Landon Larson!" she barked.

"I'm sowwy, Miss Mowwee," he said, afraid to look up.

"Don't apologize to me. It's Mallory you owe an apology to."

"I'm sowwy, Mawwowee," he said, still facing his painting.

"Don't look down when you're apologizing to her. Stand up and look her in the eye and tell her that you're sorry."

"Miss Mowwee," he whimpered for mercy.

"Don't `Miss Mowwee' me. Do as I say."

He looked at her with his familiar scowl, only now his eyes were red with tears.

"You better wipe that look off your face and do as I say," she said.

He turned to William for some sign of support, solidarity, sympathy, anything. He looked to all his classmates for the same, but found only unblinking surprise on every face. His angry scowl melted into a frown. He stood, his bottom lip quivering when he turned to the golden angel whose divinity he dared defile.

"I'm sorry, Mawwowee," he cried and began to take a seat.

"Not so fast. Sorry for what, Landon?" said Miss Mowry.

He sobbed and looked to his fallen angel again. "For kissing you," he said.

"Now take your chair and sit in the corner of the class," ordered Miss Mowry.

Landon half-dragged the chair to the far left corner of the class, where he sat with his back turned in shame.

Miss Mowry approached the embarrassed girl, who began to cry. The teacher embraced the child in her arms. "There, there. It wasn't your fault," she whispered.

***

Miss Mowry was enjoying her drive home from school as she did every day. It was her decompression time—when she was allowed to shed her school teacher persona with all its demands and just be everyday Christina Mowry.

She drove her purple Prius alongside the army of evergreens, nodding her head occasionally at anyone that stood out among the others. With her window down she greeted them.

"Merry meet," she said in a monotone that matched her nearly monochrome persona.

She looked like something in a colorized black and white film. Deprived of such interference, the white woman's burgundy lips would surely be dark gray (and on late-night excursions off the clock, they in fact were), and the hint of olive hue in her cheeks would most definitely translate to light gray. She complimented her palette by wearing her favorite colors—black with gray and purple.

None of the trees replied to her greeting, but it didn't bother her. She was used to silence and the solitude that usually accompanied. But once, just once, she would give anything to truly hear nature speak.

"Merry meet," she said to another.

Ahead, a white car drove at a Sunday pace, and the distance between them was quickly closing. She exhaled an impatient sigh and reduced her speed until the gap between them was a steady one.

She saw another tree ahead worthy of greeting.

"Merry meet," she said with a glance toward the tree.

When her eyes returned to the road, a dark shape bolted across the grassy shoulder out in front of her car.

"Oh Goddess!" she blurted out and stomped the brake.

When the car came to a screeching halt in the right lane, she threw the gear in PARK, popped her seat belt, flung the door open and jumped out.

"Please don't be dead. O Goddess, please. Are you okay, whatever you were—I mean, are?"

She circled the car, paying special attention to the grill and undercarriage, but found no sign of the thing, dead or alive. She looked for a trail of blood (or worse) behind the car, then across the highway to see if the critter had made it there safely.

A car horn honked loud and long.

"Pull off the road, freak!" a voice yelled.

As the car passed she recognized the high school student, his head hanging through the passenger side window. She mumbled a curse under her breath when the speeding car swerved dangerously around her own and raced ahead past the white car down the road.

When she saw other vehicles coming up the long, country road she hurried to hers and buckled up. She adjusted the rear-view mirror and bid the anonymous animal farewell.

"Merry part," she said with a frown.

She laid a heavy foot on the gas to put distance between her and the approaching vehicles, but it wasn't long before she had caught up with the white car in front of her.

When she looked to her right she observed the last of the emerald sea of evergreens. No more trees to greet or imagine responding. Instead of ents, dryads and wood elementals, she found herself surrounded by cold, brick buildings, chain stores and mom & pop shops. Her melancholy resumed.

Meow.

The cry interrupted her pity party with the same unwelcome

surprise a balloon popping in one's ear might bring. She felt it brush against her leg. The animal had obviously climbed inside her car when she went looking for its carcass.

She involuntarily raised her foot and sure enough the small cat took an assumed cue to climb over her brake and gas pedal.

The car naturally decelerated but when Christina returned her attention to the road, she saw the white car with its right blinker on at a near-full stop, executing a turn.

She lowered her foot to hit the brake but felt the fragile feline beneath her shoe. She played an untimely game of footsies to shove the cat to any side it would go, but when she finally won the round and placed her foot squarely on the brake, she nicked the tail end of the white car. It spun and shot forward like a cue ball nearly 20 feet. When it came to a stop it faced the oncoming traffic.

"Oh Goddess!" she screamed, clearing the intersection before her car halted.

She gripped the wheel, hyperventilating. When she caught her breath, she reeled about to catch her bearings. Her stiff fingers opened, releasing the wheel to adjust her rear-view mirror. Reflected inside was the immobile vehicle behind her. A steady, indiscernible stream of smoke or steam poured from its hood.

A tapping sounded to her right, someone rapping on her window.

"Hey, you! You in there! Roll down your window!" an old voice wheezed.

"Hello?" she called to the outsider while searching the floorboard for the mischievous cat.

"Hey!" the man called.

She faced the stiff-legged senior in turtleneck and lavender jacket. A comb-over with lazy-fingered strands relaxed limply atop his balding head like the "brain-suckers" those jerks from high school had so often placed upon her head.

He circled from the passenger side of the car, placing his heavy-handed left palm on her hood with each hurried step.

"Do you know what you did to my car? Get out here and

look!" he wheezed.

"I'm sorry. I didn't see—"

"No kidding. I hope you're not one of those freeloading hippies who don't pay their insurance."

"I'm insured—"

"Then I hope you're fully insured. With good insurance. Not that barely legal crap!" he said, waving his finger at her.

"Don't put your finger in my face," she said and rolled her window up.

"Don't you roll your window up on me! You get out here and look what you did to my car," he said, pulling on her door handle.

Her heart raced. "Hey! Don't touch my car!"

"You're worried about me touching your car when you just ran into mine? I ought to kick in your headlight and break your window, you freeloading hippie."

"What did you call me?"

"You heard me, you freeloading hippie! Now get out here!" he gurgled on a throat full of phlegm and pulled on her door handle again.

"Quit touching my car!"

"Get out here!"

"You're crazy, old man!"

"Whadidyou call me?"

"You heard me, you senile octogenarian," she said and hit the gas.

"Come back here, you hippie!" he yelled and slapped her car as she sped off—off past the ugly, cold world of brick and mortar and black hearts that reminded her why she preferred the silence and solitude of nature and all its denizens, even when at their most disagreeable.

"Goddess! Stupid old people," she complained aloud. "Why don't they just all just die? Especially you, you senile freak in your loud clothes! Just die, old man. A slow, horrible death."

Meow.

The cat startled her from the passenger seat.

"Jesus Christ!" she shouted.

The black thing hissed at her with raised fur.

"Well, quit jumping out and scaring me, already!" she said to it and stared back at the road. "You nearly got me killed."

It continued hissing, the fur on its back like a black, serrated blade.

"Calm down, already. Goddess!"

She faced the irritated cat with a forced smile.

"Let's try this…Merry meet."

The hissing ceased. The erect fur lowered.

"Merry meet?"

Meow.

"Much better."

She relaxed and set her eyes on the road ahead.

***

"So this is my place," said Christina.

She closed the door behind her, the cat cuddled in one arm.

Meow.

It looked into her eyes.

"Okay, *our* place," she corrected herself and let it down on the hardwood floor.

It stood on its hind legs to climb her burgundy couch. The piece's pattern was a purple diamond outlined in orange inside one in purple, next to one in orange outlined in purple in one in orange, all repeated across the fabric.

"Not your place," she scolded the curious cat.

Meow.

It dropped its front paws on the floor and looked about the room for a more suitable spot.

A rectangle of inviting sunlight from the only uncovered window surrounded a stone pedestal in the center of the living room. Beneath the pedestal sat a round braided rug, its alternating rings in indigo and gray.

The cat approached the pedestal and gazed up at the white, plaster bust atop. From the animal's view it was firm breasts covered in toga folds, a relatively undefined chin, pouty Greek lips and large, but delicately flared, nostrils.

"Kitty, meet Diana. Diana, meet Kitty," said Christina.

The cat's head bobbed side to side while it observed the bust's ventriloquist act.

"That wasn't the statue talking, silly. It was me."

The cat gazed at the bust, only to scurry away when Christina's unseen hand came down upon the nape of its neck.

"I'm sorry, Kitty. I didn't mean to scare you," she said, pulling the cat into her arms and petting it. "This is the goddess Diana, one of the deities I serve. Do you serve, Diana?"

Meow.

"I thought so. Go ahead. You can have this spot, it's all yours," she said and placed the cat in the rectangle of light.

The cat gazed at the bust again before laying down in the sun's satisfying warmth.

"Good kitty."

***

Christina sat with her back to the hand-carved headboard of her bed. She took a sweet spoonful of Rice Dream from the wood bowl in her lap while watching the evening news on her dresser-top TV set. The black cat lay at her feet.

After a story about a local drug rehabilitation program, a video clip of a familiar intersection was shown. There was the corner drug store she drove past every day, and between the east and westbound lanes there was a white car turned diagonal.

On the blue bar at the bottom, bold white text read "HIT & RUN TURNS DEADLY." When Christina recognized the car as the one she had clipped, her heartbeat skipped.

She placed the spoon in the bowl and turned the volume up with the remote from her nightstand.

"Eyewitnesses say the dark-colored vehicle that struck Arthur Watts' white Ford Focus fled the scene, leaving a distraught Watts in the middle of the intersection, exposed to oncoming traffic," the journalist narrated.

The next clip featured a young fair-skinned girl with her orange hair pulled into a ponytail, her black Saturn in the background.

"I didn't see him at all. It's like he just jumped out of nowhere," the trembling teen said, wiping tears from her eyes.

"That's when this vehicle, driven by Tern Point senior Elizabeth McDowell, ran into Watts, trapping him beneath," the journalist continued as the video clip changed. "Emergency personnel arrived soon after, but faced difficulty when trying to remove the former insurance salesman of 45 years from between the street and the Saturn's still-hot exhaust system.

"When he was recovered he had third-degree burns on his chest and face and is believed to have expired from carbon monoxide poisoning. An investigation is now underway. Anyone with information regarding the vehicle that struck Watts is instructed to contact the police."

Christina sat open-mouthed with the remote in her hand still aimed at the TV.

Meow.

"Did you see that?" she asked the cat, who raised its head.

Meow.

It walked across the gray blanket that covered her crossed legs.

"If they think I'm turning myself in over some senile man who physically threatened me, they've got another think coming. He got what he deserved. Senile, old man."

When Christina looked down, she caught it licking from the bowl in her lap.

"Hey…that was mine."

The cat ignored her.

"Go ahead, you can finish it. Not like I need it anyhow," she said, eyeing her slender frame with disdain.

When the bowl was emptied, Christina placed it on her nightstand and turned off the TV and lamp.

"Good night."

The cat squirmed about in the dark until it found a comfortable spot on her bed.

***

Meow.

Christina jumped awake from a deep sleep. Her pounding-heart reminded her she had forgotten something. Something black. Cat. Black cat.

She looked at the alarm clock. 5:29 am. She closed her eyes and fell back into her pillow.

"I still had a—"

The alarm clock rang.

"—minute," she finished. She swatted blindly at the clock until she found the OFF button.

"Okay. Where are you?"

Meow.

Christina opened her eyes and looked to her feet, then rolled to the side of the bed.

"There you are."

***

The last step of her short morning routine and Christina would be ready to hit the road. She nibbled on a lightly toasted slice of gluten-free bread smothered in orange marmalade.

Meow.

"What?" she asked with her mouth full.

Meow. It looked at Christina's breakfast and pawed at her leg.

"I'm sorry. I guess I forgot little guys like you need to eat, too. Let me get you some milk."

She placed the piece of toast on the plate and ventured to the fridge. She removed the carton of soy milk and placed it on the counter, then found a terracotta bowl in the dish drainer.

Meow. Its head bobbed side to side curiously.

"Just wait. I'm getting it right now."

Meow.

A paw brushed at her foot.

"I heard you. Be quiet."

Meow.

"Okay, okay. Here you go. Shut up, already."

Christina placed the red-orange bowl on the floor by the

counter. The cat lowered its head, and after a sniff and a quick lick, raised its sad, hungry eyes back to its mistress.

Meow.

"What? It's milk. Or soy milk. Same thing."

Meow.

Christina sighed impatiently. "Okay, have some water then."

She took the bowl, emptied it in the sink, filled it with cold water from the tap and placed it back on the floor. "On the way home I'll stop by the store and get some *real* milk."

The cat looked at her, then at the bowl. After a moment it lapped up the cool water. Christina finished her piece of toast and dropped the plate and knife in the sink.

She took her purse and went to the door. "Don't crap anywhere."

Not being fluent in feline just yet, and for the sake of her house, she returned to the cat, took it one arm, yesterday's newspaper from the coffee table in the other, and carried them to the utility room connecting to the kitchen. She let the cat down and unfolded the paper on the floor.

"Okay, you can crap here, and *only* here; nowhere else."

Meow.

"Okay. I hope you understood that, because I have to go. Be a good kitty. Bye."

The cat watched its hostess pull the door shut and disappear from view. Within a minute a car door shut, an engine started, and the car that almost killed the cat drove off.

When the silence had settled in the small house, the cat crossed the floor to the round braided rug beneath Diana's bust. It gazed up at the towering image.

***

Christina ascended the concrete stair to the double-door entrance of Beagle Elementary. In her dark clothing she was a rain cloud against the school's yellow cinder block facade. She entered and soon passed the quiet library, her footsteps echoing through the high hall. When she neared the bend, a door opened and a head peaked through.

"Chris, Mr. Brickman would like to see you," said Mrs. Robins and retreated back into her classroom.

"Thanks, Drew," Christina said and continued toward the bustling cafeteria ahead to her left. When the smell of buttered yeast rolls and sausage hit her, she was reminded how much she once loved them, before she committed to her vegan lifestyle.

She passed the cafeteria and entered Mr. Brickman's office to her right. She immediately cringed when she saw the mounted deer head on the wall, its giant, arching antlers like the top of a bare, autumn tree. Donald Brickman sat at his heavy, oak desk, his affects spread across the top behind an engraved nameplate that served to remind visitors of his position: PRINCIPAL D. BRICKMAN.

He was white, fat, and, judging by the framed photos and taxidermist's tokens scattered about his office, a gun-owner wealthy enough to go on hunting trips and exotic safaris. In essence, everything she could possibly hate with every ounce of her being.

"Chris," he greeted her informally, neither standing nor extending a hand.

"Don," she said, her hand not leaving the purse strap on her shoulder.

"We need to have a talk."

"About what?"

"Just have a seat."

While she placed her purse on the floor and took her seat, he approached the gray, metal filing cabinet and found the M-N drawer. He pulled the silver steel handle and after sifting through several folders, removed one labeled Mowry.

"This morning I received a phone call from an irate mother about your handling of a situation involving her son yesterday," he said gravely.

"Is that what this is about?"

"I think it goes deeper than that."

With a hand on the bottom to keep the contents from falling out, he sat at the desk and removed a pair of glasses from his shirt pocket.

"We're all aware why you left your position at Tern Point," he said.

"And what does that have to do with anything?" she asked.

"Just let me finish, Chris."

She squirmed in her seat when he opened the folder and adjusted his glasses. He ran his finger down a page.

"In your resignation you listed repeated sexual harassment as your reason for leaving, which seems to be general knowledge, so don't get bent out of shape for bringing this up—" he said with eyes raised, "—but you alleged that one of your male students was responsible."

"*Alleged,* nothing. He was guilty as charged."

"My point is that you appear to be transferring your dislike or distrust of male students to a nine-year-old boy who kissed a girl on the cheek. Does that seem reasonable to you?"

"Does it seem reasonable that I'm upset a male student is again expressing dominance over a female student; that a male student expects a female to just surrender her consent while he takes advantage of her? Yes. Does it seem reasonable that you and everyone else thinks that is acceptable? Absolutely not."

"So you *are* basing your judgment of a nine-year-old boy on your previous experience with a hormone-driven teenager?"

"Because he has hormones he can't control, it's my—" she corrected herself, "—or Mallory's fault?"

"He's a boy with a puppy crush, not a serial rapist."

"Not today anyhow." Her eyes shot left a moment before returning to his face.

"Chris, are you hearing yourself speak?"

"Yes, I think my hearing is fine," she said. She stood from the chair and took her purse from the floor. "And I think I'm hearing myself say at this very moment, right now, *you'll* be hearing from my lawyer."

"Chris, do you really want to put your career at jeopardy over a presumed wrong, not to mention putting this school and its faculty in the spotlight of a media circus?"

"Is it *your* hearing that's not working? I said you can talk to my lawyer."

She turned and exited the office, slamming the door behind her. She hadn't made it to the next bend when she heard his office door open.

"Where do you think you're going, Chris?" Mr. Brickman yelled.

"To my class," she said without stopping. "Is that okay with you?"

"As of this moment you're on administrative leave."

She turned around. "I'm what?"

"You need to go home. I'll contact you when this whole thing is sorted out."

She approached him. "What about my field trip?"

"I'm afraid you won't be going on any field trip."

"But I've been talking this field trip up for a month. It's not fair to the children."

He sighed. "*They'll* be going, Chris. *You* won't."

Her jaw and shoulders dropped. She stood there in disbelief.

"You know what? Fine. Take everything this school was supposed to stand for and hang it on your wall next to everything else you've killed," she said, and stomped out of the building.

***

Christina pushed the front door open with the gallon of milk in her left hand.

"I'm home," she called to her new roommate in hopes of a merry meeting after her horrible day. "Hello?"

She stepped inside and locked the door before turning around to face the disaster left for her.

"No! Not that!" she said, slamming the plastic gallon jug on the kitchen counter.

She laid her purse down on the floor and rushed to the jagged chunks of her broken Diana spread across the floor. "Kitty? What did you do?"

A foolish question.

"Get out here, now!"

There was no response. She searched the bedroom, bathroom and finally the utility room before she found the cat lying on the opened newspaper.

"You know, if it wasn't bad enough I have to deal with some mush-mouth kid's mom and my gun-toting boss holding my job over my head, I go out of my way to buy you *real* milk some poor, defenseless cow had to get manhandled for, and now I come home to you breaking the one, solitary thing in this world I hold dear?"

The cat looked at its mistress and gave a decidedly mocking, or else ill timed, yawn.

"Excuse me? Did you just yawn while I was talking?"

While the cat remained unaffected, Christina's eyes turned wild, unreasoning. There was a surging of blood in her neck and throbbing of temples, and immediately her face was red with fury.

She took up the cat in both hands and squeezed it until a sound like a smashed, broken accordion came out. When a flurry of swiping claws came tearing at her breast she threw the cat into the kitchen.

"Ow, you bastard! I should have run over you when I had the chance!" she yelled and stomped toward the cat.

It scurried across the tiled kitchen floor and eluded her pounding shoes.

"That's alright. Run away. You know that milk I just bought? Say goodbye!" she shouted.

She took the jug to the sink and removed the cap. When she turned the jug over and poured its contents out, a mass of white clumps plopped into the sink. Her brow furrowed when the spoiled milk began to squirm. She leaned over the sink and stared in disgust at the mass of writhing maggots.

When the stench of sour milk hit her, her stomach convulsed. She placed her hand over her mouth until her stomach settled.

"I just bought this," she grumbled to herself and reread the jug's eventual expiration date. By that unreasonable and involuntary habit, she put her nose to the lip of the carton and sniffed. "Goddess, that's disgusting."

She put the cap on the carton and dropped it in the trashcan under the sink. She ran the water and washed the foul mess down the drain. She turned around to find the cat at her feet.

"You did this, didn't you?"

The cat raised its eyes to her and opened its mouth to meow.

"Yes," its masculine voice spoke.

Utterly horrified, Christina stumbled back into the kitchen counter, her hands fumbling for a flat surface to steady her balance. Her hand came across the wooden rack of kitchen knives. She blindly took hold of the largest blade's handle and removed it from the rack, pointing its tip at the cat with trembling hands.

"What are you?" she asked.

Meow.

She stared at the black shape in confused terror. She heard it speak. Or had she? First she had lost her temper and now she would lose her mind. Maybe it was the start of a psychotic break. She had read about them plenty of times.

A normal or not-quite-normal person who had way too much thrown at them, or the same troubles piled on their plate higher and higher until they snapped—the straw that broke the camel's psyche. Surely she must be going insane.

Meow.

She gasped. Only it was just a meow now. Not words. If she was going insane shouldn't the cat still be talking? Or did madness come and go like a diseased organ or broken bone that sends its painful throbs throughout the body in waves?

She laid the knife on the counter.

"Oh, Goddess," she said and went to the bathroom and locked herself inside.

She stared at her own red eyes in the mirror. She ran cool water over her face, and looked into her eyes again. She closed her eyes and breathed deeply. When she was satisfied she had returned to her senses, she exited the bathroom and called the cat.

"Here, Kitty, Kitty, Kitty."

Meow.

It came running.

She picked the cat up.

"I'm so sorry. Please forgive me. I'll never do it again," she promised and held him to her bleeding breast. "Oh Goddess, I hope you forgive me."

Meow.

She almost expected it to answer, "Yes, I forgive you," but it didn't. She wished it had, not because it would mean she was mad—it might just mean she was gifted in the craft of magic that she had devoted her life to thus far in vain.

***

She lay in her bed, a novel opened facedown over her waist. Above her, the crescent moon face carved in her headboard look down while she rest.

She heard soft snoring; she presumed it was the cat's. When she looked at the foot of her bed she saw a solid black figure of pure shadow, darker than the darkness of the room itself. It stood six feet tall.

Her heart raced. She held her breath to avoid telegraphing her fear. Her hands fumbled around the bed and nightstand for anything that could constitute a weapon. The thing's head turned, its unseen eyes surely fixed upon her movement.

Her hands recoiled, and doing so discovered the book on her belly. She threw the novel at the thing, but it passed through the shape as if a dark cloud, hitting the dresser behind it.

An unseen object on her dresser top fell to the floor with a thud and crack of glass. She flinched at the sound, but the thing moved not a muscle. Whatever intruder stood in her room she was completely vulnerable to.

The lamp!

She reached for the touch lamp and pulled it to her chest, forgetting the light would activate the moment her skin came in contact. Her eyes dilated too fast, rendering her momentarily blind. Instead of taking the potential projectile she covered her closed eyes from the harsh light.

When her eyes adjusted she saw the thing, still standing there, unmoved, at the foot of her bed.

It looked like a man, mostly. It was black and gangly, but not without muscle. Its eyes were yellow, luminescent, absorbing and reflecting the light of the lamp. A transparent, sagging sack clung to its neck where a chin should be.

Like a toad's vocal sack, the loose folds of flesh swelled and shrank while it hummed each measure of a mostly monotone tune. The depth of its vocalizations vibrated within her nerves.

The thing placed its palms flat beside Christina's feet, then scaled the length of the bed over her until the two lay eye to eye.

She swallowed hard. "Who are you?" her voice trembled. "How did you get in here?"

"Barter for the magic owed," it said in a voice so deeply soothing she was lulled to a sleep within sleep—the deepest place of human consciousness. She felt its arms, its body, all descend down the bed a short distance, then its bony hand pulled at the collar of her purple nightshirt and exposed her flesh to the cool night air.

When she opened her eyes she saw only the bald crown bowed over her breast. Its pursed lips pulled and pressed, pulled and pressed, at first painful, then pleasure, until she felt a welling surge from within her bosom. Her heart fluttered, now weakened while some strange, warm essence rushed from her body into the thing's sucking, swallowing mouth. Her head flung from side to side in ecstasy while it drank.

When she felt the thing stop, she heard it exhale a satiated breath. She raised her head and found it gazing at her with black ellipses on yellow irises.

She awoke. She stared at the crescent moon face that watched guardian above, for there was no man-thing hanging over her, staring into her face. It had been a dream, but still, she felt a weight upon her chest, and her nightshirt grew damp over her breast.

She raised her head and stared into the piercing yellow eyes of the cat, lying on top of her. It licked the gray-white droplet from its lip. She lowered her eyes to see the wet spot over her heart, right where the cat then laid its head.

Fear seized her. What did she bring into her home?

The cat's eyes opened halfway.

"Was that you?" she dared to ask.

There was silence while the cat examined her, as if she was speaking a foreign language, or with the voice of an unknown animal. She sighed, chalking it up as another experience due to her overactive, or else disintegrating, imagination.

"I'm tired," said the cat, in the same throbbing voice the man-thing had, and closed his eyes.

"No, wait!" she said, sitting up so fast the cat leaped off the bed in fear.

"I'm sorry," she said and searched the dim room with squinted eyes. "Come back, please."

"It's rude to wake someone so abruptly," the voice came from somewhere.

She turned quickly to find the cat peeking over the side of the bed, standing on his hind legs. She patted the empty spot on the bed beside her.

"Come here," she said.

He leaped with just enough strength to make it onto the bed, then crawled slowly beside her and lay down.

"You can talk?" she asked.

He didn't answer.

"That goes without saying," she corrected herself. "What else can you do?"

He yawned and stretched to wake up for their conversation.

"With the proper ritual in the proper mind, whatever you will," he said.

"Can you come to me again in my dreams, like you did before?"

"Why do in a dream what we can do now?" said the black shape as it changed form and took her form into its arms.

***

In the morning she awoke. She looked to her side. There was no demon lover. She looked to her feet, where the cat lay at the end of the bed.

"Kitty?" she called.

His eyes opened slowly.

"You don't have to call me that anymore," the large voice came from the tiny mouth.

"What would you like me to call you?"

"You will think of a name shortly, and I will take it as my own," he said with a long yawn then began to stretch.

"How about Jim?"

"I said shortly, not the first thing that comes to mind. When the time is right you will know and I will take that name."

She swung her legs out of bed and placed them on the floor by her black lace underwear and frog-faced slippers—being green, they were the most cheerfully-colored things she owned.

"So, you're like my familiar?" she asked, pulling the underwear up her legs beneath her nightshirt.

"Precisely. And I will be the medium between you and my kind. Whatever belongs to my realm will be at your disposal. I will even transmute your will into substance, as I did with the old man."

"What happened to him?" she asked, placing her feet into her slippers.

"Didn't you listen to the television?"

Her shoulders dropped. "I mean—after," she said. "Is there, you know, a heaven and a hell?"

"He was not long for this world, and has been prime for the reaping for quite some time. What my brethren are doing to him right now pales to your worst nightmares."

"So...there *is* a hell."

"You have said so."

She looked at the floor as she approached her dresser. She was sure she had thrown her book at her lover the night before, but when she turned and saw it closed and bookmarked on her nightstand she wondered what all had been a dream and what, reality.

She found the antique family heirloom not broken on the floor but whole, still on the dresser beside the analog TV. She had been asleep during their first encounter—a dream within a dream. She took the oval mirror brush and ran it through her black, barely shoulder-length hair several times.

"And God?" she asked.

"Mother, daughter, sister, lover...do not speak of Him. You are now servant to that forsaken legion who abandoned their former estate long, long ago. Those who dwell in darkness and rule the heavens above."

"But if there's a God—"

"You turned your back on that One as a child, and that day you were betrothed to Evil. Your soul was the dowry and now you have consummated the union. We are one—mother, daughter, sister, lover—and ever shall be."

"You're not going to keep calling me that, are you? It's so wordy," she said.

"Do you prefer Tina?"

"I prefer *Chris* or *Christina*."

"On the contrary, a simple Tina will suffice, for hopefully obvious reasons."

"Tina it is. So, I don't have to sell my soul to Satan or something?"

"Do you believe as the Christians do? That there is some androgynous fellow named Lucifer? Heaven's high priest of worship? Satan is not one. He is Legion. All who oppose the Holy One are Satan. I, you, Simon Bar Jonah at his worst, Iscariot at his best, the world."

"I see," she said, her gaze fixed on her slippered feet. She looked up. "You're saying it's my destiny to be evil? Do I have a choice?"

"Do you want a choice?"

She was silent.

"Tina, you were not made to serve the institutions of men. You are to exert authority over them, and not as a teacher of children. You are a witch—not in that small, earthy religion you've observed your whole life. You are a black witch in the blackest of all Crafts. And before you think otherwise, know that I don't enter this world to serve foolish women in cloaks that please themselves with brooms as they summon fairy folk. I come for one purpose. *Havoc.* Total destruction. Pain to all who oppose. Do you understand?"

"You mentioned a ritual. What kind of ritual?"

"The kind you wish to perform."

"I don't know what I want to perform."

He laughed. "It's been on your mind since that boy first laid hands on you."

"That was a long time before I met you."

"I know all about you, Tina."

She turned the mirror brush over and stared at her own image.

"Principal *Brickhead* said I was transferring my anger to Landon Larson," she said. "I can't help they were both perverts. I'd clip all their balls off if I could. The principal included."

"Very good. You're not holding back. Revenge is a good place to start, but it's still far beneath your full potential."

"Why's that?" she asked, placing the mirror brush glass down on the dresser-top.

"You're a bride of Evil, Tina…not human nature."

There was anger in his voice. It terrified her. Not his anger, but her desire to please him.

"The desire for revenge is a natural one. But you're no longer of the natural order. You must dig deep into the kingdom of Hell within you," he said.

"All of them…" she said with a trembling voice.

"All what?"

"Dead."

"Who, Tina?"

"The whole school."

"Now, that's more like it. But small steps first, my dear."

"My whole class, then."

"Why?" he asked, not because he didn't know.

She thought for a moment. "Because children are a waste of space. They're a waste of time and attention. They have nothing to offer the world but crying and begging and taking everything they can. Then they complain that it's not enough; they always want more. They bankrupt entire societies. They force us to be examples of moral perfection, and when we fail to live up to their expectations, we chastise one another. Who are they to tell us what to do with our time, our money—or our lives? They…"

"That's quite enough. In fact it's perfect. You possess the proper mind. Now all that is required is the ritual. The day has dawned. Prepare yourself. This is a good day to do something wicked."

***

She sat on the couch with her legs folded to one side, her steaming, herbal tea on the coffee table in front her. She'd dressed for the occasion—a black knee-length dress with frilly sleeves and purple-gray striped thigh-high socks and black shoes with silver buckles.

"How do I perform the ritual if I don't have anything that belongs to them?" she asked and took her cup. She blew on it several times before taking a sip.

"Think, Tina. Perhaps you already do."

"It's not like I get to cut their hair and fingernails and save the clippings."

The cat jumped from the braided rug to the coffee table and sat on a small pile of manila folders.

"Get off the table!" she demanded.

A hellish fire flashed in his eyes and all the curtains whipped upon their rods throughout the windless room. "Excuse me?"

She swallowed hard. "I don't like when you sit on the table. You shed," she said, much softer.

The curtains lowered and the room was calm once more.

He yawned. "Well, then. I'll just lay here until you figure it out."

He sprawled out on the folders and closed his eyes. While she looked at him half in anger and half in fear, an eye opened. He waited for her to speak.

"You're sitting on their homework," she said.

"Am I?"

"Yes, you are. And I have to grade—"

He closed his eye.

"The *homework*," she said, a hellish spark in her own eyes.

"What about the homework?"

"It has their writing on it. Their names. Is that enough to perform the ritual?"

"You're getting closer. What else might there be?"

She thought a moment. "Nothing. Just a few spelling tests and an artwork assignment."

"And?" he asked, opening his eyes again.

"Nothing."

"Tina, what do you know of expression?"

"Can you be more specific?"

"Melody, prose, the portrayal of positive and negative in any medium."

"Artistic expression?"

"It is as much a part of their being as their flesh...and *blood*," he said, his eyes dilating when he said the word.

She touched the folders. "May I?" she asked.

He stood on all fours and arched his back. After another yawn he leaped onto the floor and returned to the braided rug.

She sifted through the folders until she found the collection of crayon drawings. She fanned the stack of pages, noticing her students' name on each corner.

"They're all in here," she said with a wicked giggle.

"Good. Let us begin."

***

In the flickering light of the black candle, Tina tied the stack of drawings together with a coarse strand of grapevine. Her familiar sat on his hind legs atop the couch just behind her left shoulder. His titanic shadow stretched across the living room wall; it seemed an entity itself.

At her feet, between the couch and coffee table, lay a steel tub half full of water.

She took the stack of drawings from the coffee table and lowered it into the tub. The water parted to receive its victims, and just as quickly enveloped them. Then, quite oddly, the drawings became remarkably buoyant, so much so that Tina had to lean the majority of her weight into it.

The edges of paper folded up around her hands and rose

above the water's surface.

"It's not sinking," she complained.

"Tina, what are you holding beneath you?" he asked.

"A pile of drawings."

"They're *souls*, Tina! *Human* souls. Did you think they were just going to lie down and die?"

She fought to keep the drawings submerged. "They're too strong. I can't keep them down," her voice broke.

"You are stronger, Tina! You are their mistress! You will not be outdone by a brood of unbaptized children!"

She looked at the topmost drawing—happy stick-people of varied sizes played in a field of green grass and smiling violets beneath a corner-mounted sun, with its visible rays emanating as squiggled lines.

Tears streamed down her face.

"I can't do it..." she cried.

"You can't or won't?"

"I want to. I just can't."

"Be stronger, Tina. Stronger!"

Her quivering lips tightened over clenched teeth. Still pressing the drawings under the water, she dried the tears from her eyes with each shoulder. Her frown became a scowl, and then with a grunt it turned into an insane smile with wide, matching eyes.

There was a scream. A child's scream. Was it her fragile state of mind that caused her to imagine it? Too many things had happened for her to second-guess herself anymore. Another child's scream joined it. And another. More and more screams followed.

The small curves that formed smiles upon the faces of the happy stick-people slowly inverted into frowns. Crayon clouds in dark gray floated onto the paper left and right until they filled the sky and eclipsed the lemon-yellow sun. A wavy, blue line spanning the width of the drawing floated from the bottom to the top and disappeared again.

Bubbles erupted from the bottom of the steel tub and floated on the water's surface. The tub shook violently. Water sloshed over the sides onto the hardwood floor. Finally, the last bubble surfaced, floated about for but a moment, and popped.

***

The children stood in line by the white charter bus. The driver, a black man with freckled, beige skin, stood by the open door in blue pants and silver company windbreaker, welcoming his pint-sized passengers. The rectangular, plastic name tag over his heart read James Gerard.

Parents bid their sons and daughters farewell with a kiss or a loving pat. Boys' hair was tousled, and backpacks were checked for necessities and secured. Children slowly boarded the bus and with waves from anxious parents they departed for Cornerstone National Park.

Within the hour, groups of girls were chatting, some boys played games of Hot Hands, while others stared serenely through windows at the diminishing city that turned to rolling countryside.

Mrs. Brillo, the plump white woman in her fifties with graying hair and red cheeks, knee-high dress and hat, sat in the front right seat, occasionally glancing in the mirror or turning around in order to catch some unruly child in an unacceptable act.

The bus soon approached the quarter-mile bridge that spanned Minch Lake.

"Not so hard, Wiwwiam!" said Landon, shaking both of his hands, one much redder than the other.

"Don't be such a girl," said William.

"Landon, William, I saw that," said Mrs. Brillo. "No Hot Hands!"

The boys sank silently in their seats to avoid her burning stare.

The bus neared the peak of the bridge when a loud blast sounded, like the firing of a shotgun. James gripped the spinning steering wheel with both hands and stomped the brake. The bus veered into the left lane and toward the concrete railing, causing the children to scream.

Mrs. Brillo took hold of the pole by the door to avoid falling into the aisle. Those seated on the left side of the bus were thrown into closed windows. Those on the right attempted to mimic their substitute teacher, but their tiny hands slid off slippery, leather seats, sending them into the aisle and on top of one another.

James fought to gain control of the steering wheel, turning hard right. He released the brake but the overcompensation brought the bus back to the right lane and into the bridge's opposite concrete rail.

Children were flung to the right of the bus, screaming as concrete met steel in a screeching display of sparks.

"It's okay children! Be calm!" the scared teacher pleaded.

With a grunt, James turned the wheel to the left, bringing the bus out of the concrete rail. The flashing sparks ceased but the terrified children were again thrown into the aisle.

The bus straightened, yet continued to bounce like a runaway horse galloping madly away, the children's voices rising and falling with each leaping motion.

James depressed the brake again until the bus decelerated to nearly 10 miles an hour. The tempo of his heartbeat matched every pounding jolt.

"Is it over?" Mrs. Brillo asked.

"I think so," he answered, with his hands still tight on the wheel.

Several children were crying. Others looked about the bus as if some attacker lay in waiting to strike again.

"It's all right, children," said Mrs. Brillo. "Everyone is safe. Now get back into your seats."

The bus continued to bounce ahead as it neared the end of the bridge. The teacher stood to walk toward the children, but could only take a step or two before falling into a nearby seat.

"Can't you stop now?" she asked James.

"Not in the middle of the bridge. I need to find a spot to pull over," he said.

The bus cleared the bridge, still rattling as if driving on square wheels.

"Okay. We're off the bridge. Pull over, already," she insisted.

"Do you see that guardrail?"

He pointed to the metal railing out of habit, but immediately returned his hand to the wheel.

"Okay. I just hope we don't all end up with rattle-head syndrome," she said.

"Your head got rattled a long time ago," he mumbled and turned the wheel left.

The quaking bus left the hard asphalt and pulled onto the soft, grassy shoulder, just past the guard railing. It slowed to a halt and ceased from its violent trembling. James put the bus in PARK, removed his seatbelt and opened the door.

"What was that?" she asked.

"A blowout. I have to change the tire."

"Should we get the children off the bus?" Mrs. Brillo asked.

"They can't stand in the middle of the street. They'll just have to stay seated," he said, exiting the bus.

"Okay, class. Mr. Gerard is going to change the tire so we can continue our trip to the park. While he is doing so, you must remain absolutely still. No moving about. Is that understood?"

"Yes, Mrs. Brillo," came the relieved children's chorus.

"Very good. Now I'm going to step off the bus so I can assist Mr. Gerard, so please be on your best behavior. If I have to come back and speak to any of you, then no one will be going to the park gift shop. Is that understood?"

"Yes, Mrs. Brillo," they said, not nearly in unison as before.

"Very good. Remember, I'll be watching and listening."

As she stepped off the bus, the more obedient students turned a watchful eye on the lesser. Mrs. Brillo didn't have to see their interaction for a malicious smile to creep across her face.

"You can't be getting on and off the whole time I'm doing this," said James.

"That's why I'm out here," she said, half offended.

"They better not be squirming about either."

"I've given them reason enough to stay put," she assured.

"I sure hope so," he said, kneeling onto his silver windbreaker atop the damp grass. He placed the jack beneath the axle by the blown-out tire.

"Come on," said William.

"We can't. Not untiw we start dwiving again," said Landon.

"Not untiw we start dwiving again," William mocked him.

Landon scowled at his cruel friend. "Okay, but me first," he said, holding his hands palm's up.

William placed his palms flat against Landon's. He noticed the anger still seething in the boy's face. His fear of retaliation made him flinch with every pulse of blood through Landon's hands.

"Scawed?" Landon asked.

"No," William lied, flinching again as he stared at their hands.

"Aw you suwe?"

"Yeah I'm—OW!"

Landon swatted with a viscous speed William was unprepared for. Before William could start shaking the sting out of his right hand, Landon struck his left with even more intent.

"OW! Stop it!" William shouted and jumped to his feet, out of harm's way.

"That's what you get!" said Landon.

"Be quiet in there!" Mrs. Brillo yelled and swatted the side of the bus.

The tinny thud echoed through the valley and the jack fell flat.

"Don't!" James shouted, jumping back to avoid the crushing tires.

He dropped the iron and leaped to his feet to take hold of the open door but it slipped out of his grasp. He fell flat on the ground but quickly scrambled to his feet, grass stains across the knees and chest of his uniform.

The children, oblivious for all but a moment, observed Mrs. Brillo's angry countenance turn into pure horror as they rolled down the slick, grassy hill. James ran alongside the bus, trying to grab the door. He managed to lay his right foot on the first step of the entrance while hopping on the other. He proceeded to pull himself halfway inside with the handrail when the bus came to the steeper part of the hill.

The children watched his face twist into terror as Mrs. Brillo's had, when he fell out of the door and landed on his back. They were thrown from their seats and down the aisle to the back of the accelerating bus.

Their screams escaped through the open door all the way down the hill until the bus broke the glassy surface of Minch Lake. The door swung shut of its own accord, trapping the children inside, as the bus began to sink beneath the cold, blue water.

Fingers, palms, and cheeks turned bloodless white as hands and faces pressed against glass. Boys and girls struggled to open stubborn windows that would not budge.

James slid down the hill, half way on his butt and half on his belly, to catch up with the runaway bus, while Mrs. Brillo babbled and screamed from the roadside above. She waved her arms at passing cars, which began to gather along the slippery shoulder.

James found a small earthen landing where the grass ceased and dirt turned into mountainside. It was from this limbo he heard the muffled cries of children beneath and the reverberating lament of adults above; a halfway hell where neither side offered refuge or escape.

He broke into a numbness—a hopeless inaction. The children were lost. There was no salvation, no rescue. He watched the water swallow the vehicle up to its very rooftop. A chilling wind began to blow. It stirred the lake until small waves lapped against the metal roof. The doomed children trapped inside were drowning in the frigid waters that flooded through every crack and crevice of the vehicle's structure.

Two men had slid down the hill to join James on the dirt ledge. One was selfless enough to disregard his own physical limitations in the form of age and excess weight. The moment their feet touched the flat bit of earth, they felt the same sudden despair overcome them, that any effort to save the children was futile.

The three strangers cried and pleaded for mercy, for divine

deliverance. But there would be none.

***

"It's like a crystal ball," she said, gazing at the delightfully horrible incident in the steel tub. "Or a magic mirror."

"Choose," said the cat, peering over her shoulder from atop the couch.

The image portrayed on the surface of the water looked as if cast by a movie projector. She saw the blue faces, the gaping mouths and bulging eyes, their bloated bodies. Some had already begun to float. Like bobbing apples, they rolled along the ceiling of the bus. Others, like balloons running out of air, bumped into each other when their weight occasionally shifted. One boy's arms flailed in slow-motion, an aquatic marionette.

To Tina he appeared to fondle every girl who floated nearby.

"*Him,*" she said, pointing at the dead body of Landon Larson, his brown hair flickering like wet flames.

"Take him," said her familiar.

She looked at the cat over her shoulder. He nodded at her.

She reached into the watery image inside the steel tub and strained to take hold of the boy.

"He's heavy," she said.

"He's full of water, like a sponge," said the cat.

She got on her knees to give herself leverage, and then struggled to stand. Slowly, she rose to her feed and pulled the waterlogged body from the image out of the steel tub. She held Landon Larson's dripping corpse over her hardwood floor. Water pooled beneath his feet.

"Are you ready to fly?" asked the cat.

"Yes?" she intoned, as if a question.

The water inside the steel tub began to boil, until steam rose. It filled the room.

"Lower him into the tub," said the cat, hidden in the steamy mist.

She obeyed.

***

From high above the bridge, it resembled a white metal raft floating atop the lake's choppy surface. Tina hovered among the graying clouds with the broom between her thighs and the black cat nestled in her lap.

"Today was the perfect day," she said.

He craned his neck to behold the site without moving from his comfortable spot.

"Indeed," he said. "I think it should be commemorated."

"I think you're right. What is today?"

"It's the Sabbath."

Her eyes raised and lips puckered in thought. "I think I found your name," she said.

He waited quietly with the sort of curious smile only a cat can express.

"You shall be called *Saturday*," she said.

His eyes flashed, save the black pupils that narrowed to a hairline.

"You have named me well—mother, daughter, sister, lover—" he said, purring while he bunted her waist. "Now let us together rule the air."

Leaving the disaster and anguish far beneath them, the two soared over treetop and steeple, until the small town and all its little people they despised were nothing but a distant memory.

THROUGH THE VEIL

M. L. Roos

Mama wandered around the house lighting candles and laying sprigs of mugwort on the windowsills. The ritual started every October 30th and ended on November 1st. By that time, the cloying scent of dried mugwort filled the rooms, and any article of clothing you had lying around.

"Mama?"

"Yes, Sweet Pea?"

"What happens if we miss a window, or don't put out any herbs? I mean, isn't this just an old wives' tale about mugwort keeping the evil away?"

I looked up from my drawing because I wanted to see if she actually told me the truth. I could tell when she was saying something just to get me to be quiet, and when she really meant it. It was one of my gifts. I could read anyone and know what the truth was.

"Well, Lilly, this ritual has been in our family for generations. I learned it from my mother and grandmother, and they passed it down from theirs. I guess I really don't know if it works, but your Nana always did it, and we ain't never had any problems. So if it isn't real, there's no harm done. And if it is, we're safe."

"Did Nana do lots of magic?" I asked.

"Yes she did. Way more than I do, I s'ppose."

"And I still do baby girl," Nana said. "Cause I have seen and heard things you ain't never known could have lived in this world. Your mama grew up too comfortable around this town, but I came from Louisiana. And, child, the things that go on when no one is looking would scare the pants off you."

Nana sat at the kitchen table and looked at my drawing.

"I like what you've done there with the pumpkins and the lights. Really pretty, baby girl."

"Can you tell me something from the olden days, something that scared you real bad?" I asked with a sly grin. I knew my mother was a New Age witch, where everything was circles of bright light and rainbows. But Nana was a *real* witch. The kind that did things in the woods late at night that no one talked about.

Mama's face blanched and she wrapped her arms around her skinny torso. I could see the hairs standing on end. "I don't think that is a good idea, Lilly. You're not ready for that kind of talk. When you are older you can decide which path to follow." She glared over at my nana. "But while you are young, I need you to follow my path, understand?"

"Yes ma'am." The blood ran across my cheeks and I bowed my head. I knew I was pushing it, but I had to try. I was tired of all the Law of Three. I wanted to see what magic could really do, not just all the blah about helping the planet and praising the Goddess. That was so boring. I think Nana knew. She looked at me and winked when Mama turned her back.

"Lilly, please go wash up for supper." The look on her face told me I had better not question her command.

"Yes, ma'am." I gathered my papers and pencils and went to my bedroom.

I could hear Mama and Nana whispering loudly. Mama was giving Nana a hard time. And it was all my fault.

I sat on my bed picking at the blankets, wishing I hadn't asked the question. Or at least, had just asked Nana. *Too late now, Lilly, you big dummy,* I thought.

I hoped Nana wouldn't be mad at me. But I needed to know more than what Mama taught me.

I sighed and walked to the bathroom. But, as I did, I saw that stinky mugwort sitting on my sill. I looked quickly over my shoulder to make sure no one was there, grabbed that mess of green, and flushed it down the toilet. If Mama asked, I could say the cat must've snatched it. He was always on my window sill.

"Supper smells great, Mama." I smiled at her. She smiled back. And I knew then that everything was fine.

We all sat around the table passing food, laughing and talking. It was a great evening.

I went to bed that night and had the best sleep ever, Timber sleeping and purring softly beside me.

***

"We'll, Miss Lilly, I see you are ready for school. Get home straight away, so we can get ready for Halloween Night. There is a lot more we need to do tonight before the dark hits."

Mama looked a little twitchy to me. I saw the muscle in her right cheek hammer away like it was keeping time with her heartbeat. Halloween spooked Mama. Weird for a witch to be spooked by Halloween, but Mama was spooked by a lot of things that I didn't understand—darkness, mirrors, windows, and a whole lot more.

I know it was bad, but I kind of giggled a little thinking of being afraid of windows. Heck, even Timber sat on the sill in my room every night.

***

The house smelled of cookies and cakes and warmth when I returned home from school. I loved Mama for that. She always baked up a storm on Halloween. Each Holy-Day was wrapped in warmth, fire, magic, and sweet things.

Mama was singing a song in the kitchen, and Nana was helping by arranging treats on platters. They both giggled like kids when I walked in.

Nana wrapped her arms around me. "Hey, baby girl! Come here and give me a big old hug." She smelled like cinnamon and sugar.

"Okay…now go upstairs, and change out of your school clothes. We need to get the fires lit in all the fireplaces. And that will be your job this evening." She glanced at Mama, whose back was turned. "I'm gonna chop up some more mugwort," she said. "And then I think we're about done."

I grinned and ran upstairs as fast as I could. Nana was up to something. How exciting! My first real Halloween as a witch, instead of a little kid.

***

I hiked up my jeans and pulled on a grey school sweatshirt. Fire smell always soaked into the fabric and it lingered now, but not as bad as mugwort. I gathered the logs for the fires, cleaned out each grate, and swept all the old year's ashes away. I even hand-washed each fireplace before placing the new logs inside. In the living room, I placed a few drops of essential oil of black pepper on the top log, and in the family room I used birch essential oil. And in the basement, wintermint. The house was going to smell amazing when all the fires were lit. Best of all, it would be protected.

I raced back upstairs to look for Nana. I needed to know what was going to happen tonight. My entire body felt like it was filled with an electric current, humming and vibrating with excitement. This was way better than Winter Solstice. This was a night for magic.

Nana was in the backyard clearing a circle and placing salt all around the edges.

"Hey, Nana. So, you going to let me in on the secret"?

"What secret, love?"

"Oh, come on. I saw the way you glanced at Mama when you said you were chopping mugwort. Don't make me wait. I don't think my heart can take it."

"You're here. You're twelve. Your heart's shinier than a newborn's butt. Jeez girl." Nana smiled. "I just thought you should know that tonight on all the most sacred of nights, that I have a gift for you. Now," she looked at me sternly, "your Mama does not know, because if she did she would fly off the handle faster than white off rice. So keep your lip zipped and pay attention."

I stepped back but made sure to stay within the circle. Nana sprinkled the mugwort into the salt. She raised her arms and whispered a prayer to the Goddess, but I could not hear a word. I bowed my head and ended the prayer with 'So mote it be' in time with Nana.

"Come, child. You've done been blessed. Now we can start on the festivities."

We walked into the house and Mama was still in the kitchen acting all jittery. "Something's not right here. I can feel it. Something's off. Mother," she looked at Nana, "did you do something?"

"Sweetheart, of course not. I was just helping Lilly with the fireplaces. I think we should light them now. And, Janey, you should see what your girl has done. Those grates are gleaming!"

Mama looked at me and tried to smile, but she knew. Maybe she had the knowing gift, too. She looked at the clock and a frown creased her forehead, and the corners of her mouth. It was 11:00 p.m.

Nana and I went downstairs and lit the basement fire. The room exploded with the fragrance of wintermint. The clean, medicinal scent filled the entire space. "Oh, child, you do have a gift, don't you?"

We walked up together and lit the other two. Within minutes none of the nasty mugwort was in the air. All we could smell was a savory odor of black pepper mixed with birch and wintermint. Mama looked so proud, like I passed a test. I guess in a way I did.

"Come, love. Sit with me. I want to tell you a story."

"*No!*" Mama said.

"Oh, what could it hurt?" Nana asked. "We have the mugwort, and she knew which were the most powerful oils to use to keep evil away. We did a blessing, so I think we're safe."

Mama did not say a word. She just dropped onto the couch and folded her arms. The set of her face would scare off a preacher, but Nana ignored her.

"Okay," Nana started. "I was about your age when I learned my first spell. It was about this time of night and my mother—your great grandmother—Martha, was puttering in the kitchen, getting ready to set out the harvest. Earlier that day, I was rummaging through the attic and came across this thick, smelly book. It said *Revelare Viventium*. I didn't know what it was, but I was drawn to it like a moth to a flame. The cover was thick, lined and wrinkled, and was brown with age. I was flipping through the pages, looking at all the neat hand-drawn pictures of different things—like objects, people, clouds, spices, and such—and knew right away it was a book of spells. But, it was written in this weird language. I stumbled over a few words here and there, but this one phrase jumped out at me over and over again. *'Sit vivorum ingredi.'* I said it a few times and thought nothing of it."

A rumbling sound came from upstairs.

"Mother!" yelled Mama. "I thought you said we were safe. "What in the name of all that is holy have you done."

There was the sound of glass braking and then heavy footsteps pounding across the upstairs floor.

"Oh, sweet Goddess," Mama said, running to the bottom of the stairs. "Lilly, you stay back, ya hear!" Mama raced upstairs, yelling and screeching at the top of her lungs. I could hear her yell, *"NO*...you do not belong on this side of the veil. You are alive, ya hear. Alive! DO NOT ENTER HERE. You are not welcome! In the name of the Goddess, I cast you back to Earth!"

A ghastly scream filled the house, and then with a roar, whatever it was, was snuffed out like a light.

Mama walked down the stairs rubbing her hands. "Mother, you may think I'm a flighty witch, who deals more with the calming of the Worlds, but that is what I do best. Please, from now on, no more stories..."

Nana apologized. And I asked, "So what was the name of the book and what did you say?"

Without hesitation, Nana continued on. "I realized later, much, much later, that the book was called *Revel the Living,* and so I muttered a spell to allow the living to enter. That's how we ended up with Timber. He's around 80 years old now, but will be here forever. A *cat* heard my spell that time."

"What was up there tonight, Mama?" I asked.

"A *human*. And we don't need none of their kind here."

THE JACK-O'-LANTERN MAN

Brian Moreland

At ten o'clock on Halloween night, Corey Wilkes and his little sister, Paige, sat on the den floor, sorting their piles of candy after an evening of trick-or-treating. Corey, age ten, still wore his Darth Vader costume, all but the mask, which sat on the floor. Paige, age six, was dressed as a pink fairy with silver wings.

Thunder roared above, making both kids flinch. Heavy rain clapped against the roof. Wind howled like a ghoulish voice, and cracks of lightning brightened the dark windows.

Corey and Paige sat wide-eyed as Dad topped off their night with a story that sent chills creeping up their spines. "Then out of the foggy night came the Jack-O'-Lantern Man, with a tall, dark body, hands made of twisted roots, and a head shaped like...what?"

"A pumpkin!" the kids said in unison, having heard the story many times before.

Their dad smiled. "That's right, with a monstrous face carved into it."

Corey thought of all the glowing jack-o'-lanterns he'd seen around the neighborhood tonight. Some had silly faces, but others, like the one he and Dad had carved, contained evil expressions with wicked eyes and jagged teeth. Corey pictured the Jack-O'-Lantern Man with the face of the pumpkin on their front porch. The boy imagined its glowing eyes staring down as a dark hand reached for the victim's throat.

As the story got to the good part, Paige squeezed her brother's arm.

Dad leaned close to them. "To this day, they've never caught the Jack-O'-Lantern Man. Every Halloween someone reports seeing him creeping around their barn or in the cemetery or even in neighborhoods like ours. And every few years, on stormy nights like this, children and their families mysteriously disappear. Because whenever he finds small children sleeping in their beds, he sneaks into their rooms, lifts back their covers, and gobbles them up."

Dad lurched at Corey and Paige. The kids screamed and giggled as he tickled them.

Their Uncle Malcolm, who lived with them, sat on the sofa and stared with drool dripping off his bottom lip. Their Dad's older brother was what their parents called "special." He never talked and rarely looked you in the eye. He just stared. Tonight, Uncle Malcolm wore the same goofy costume he wore every year, a clown suit, because clowns were the only thing that made Malcolm smile, or show any emotion at all for that matter. Dad said their uncle was always aware, though, always listening. Malcolm just didn't know how to express himself like normal people. Corey thought it was a little weird that a grown man still dressed up for trick-or-treating, but Dad said their uncle would always be a kid inside.

Dad continued to laugh and tickle Corey and Paige. Their mother entered the living room. "Okay, little monsters, time for bed. You still have school tomorrow."

Paige stood. "Aw, Mom. We were having fun."

"Yeah," Corey said. "Dad was telling us a really scary story about this bogeyman who eats children."

She shot their father a look. "Well, I'm so glad your father could give you two the willies so you have nightmares all night." Their mother checked all the locks on the windows and sliding-glass door like she did every night.

"Mommy, I'm too scared to sleep alone tonight," Paige said. "Can I sleep with you and Daddy?"

Mom said, "Sweetie, you know that once you got into first

grade it was time you slept in your own bed. You're a big girl now. If you want, you can sleep with the closet light on. Do you want yours on, too, Corey?"

"Would Darth Vader be afraid of the dark?" he said, posing like a dark knight who feared nothing. He swung his lightsaber and made swishing sounds.

"I guess not," Mom said, walking his sister into the hallway. "I'm going to tuck Paige in. I'll be back for you in a minute."

Dad wiped a tissue across Malcolm's chin and then sat on the couch next to Corey. Father, son, and uncle watched the storm through the sliding-glass door. Another flash brightened their backyard. Beyond their two-acre lot stretched the old pumpkin patch that bordered their rural neighborhood.

The pumpkin patch had belonged to Corey's grandfather and was passed down to his parents, who harvested pumpkins for the local stores that sold them. His mother made scented candles and baked the best pumpkin pies. Corey and his father worked these fields until their hands were raw. Uncle Malcolm helped out too. Even though he couldn't talk, he was still able to do simple chores around the farm.

After watching the thunderstorm a minute, Dad said, "It was on a night just like this that we saw him once."

Corey's eyes widened. "The Jack-O'-Lantern Man?"

"In the orange flesh."

"I thought that was just a story Grandpa told you when you were a kid."

"It's been a legend that the people of Millcreek have passed down from generation to generation, usually told as a story on Halloween, but it's based on something that really happened." Corey's father looked at him with serious eyes. "Back in the 1950s, our town's founding fathers were at war with a coven of witches who lived in a wooded area just beyond the edge of town. They were battling over the very land our neighborhood was later built upon. The coven refused to move.

"One night some townsmen with white hooded masks and guns came into the commune to scare the witches off, but they wouldn't leave without a fight. The night turned violent and three women ended up shot in cold blood. Then the masked men took the coven's leader, a man named Hector Ravencroft, and hung him from an oak tree. The hooded townsmen warned that if the men, women, and children of the coven didn't vacate the land immediately, soon every branch of that tree was going to be hanging bodies. The witches were gone by dawn. As a reminder of the threat, Hector's corpse remained hanging for weeks, rotting away in the sun, pecked by crows, and ravaged by insects."

Dad stood and walked to the sliding-glass door that faced the backyard. "Then a few weeks later, on the night of Samhain—what we call Halloween—the witches gathered in the pumpkin patch, the very one behind our house. According to the legend, they buried Hector Ravencroft in that patch and performed a ritual to put a curse on Millcreek." Dad turned around and looked back at Corey and Uncle Malcolm. "Hector's corpse rose from the dead to become the Jack-O'-Lantern Man. And he still lives in the patch today, somewhere underground. Every few years he rises on Halloween to seek revenge, sometimes snatching a child, sometimes butchering an entire family."

"You mean he's *real?*" Corey felt the hairs lift on his neck and arms, thinking that such a creature could actually be out there prowling the night.

Dad nodded. "I've seen him with my own eyes. I was about your age and couldn't sleep because of a bad thunderstorm. I noticed that Malcolm had gotten out of bed and was at the window in our room. Back then, he was normal, like you and me."

Corey looked at his catatonic uncle. "He wasn't always like this?"

"No, he wasn't born this way. That Halloween night changed him forever."

"What happened?" Corey asked.

"I got out of bed and joined Malcolm at our bedroom window, watching the lightning streak the sky. I was afraid of storms and panicked every time the thunder shook the roof. He told me to be quiet—that he thought he saw someone moving outside. Our window faced the houses across the street, like yours does, and it was then that I saw *him* or *it*—just like I described, with a huge pumpkin head and a face that looked like it had a hunger for vengeance. His skeletal body was covered in roots and vines. He still wore the clothes that Hector had been buried in and a pair of workman's boots. He was prowling on the dark porch of the neighbors across the street. I remember my heart racing when I saw him enter their house."

Corey gasped. "Did you call the police?"

"Malcolm and I were too scared to do anything, so we just sat and watched the house for what seemed like an hour. The lights never came on. Then finally he came back out again, a tall grotesque shadow, carrying something long and sharp in his hand. A machete. He crossed the street through the rain, entered our front yard."

As Dad was talking, Corey's mother came back into the den and leaned against the wall behind his father, listening.

"The Jack-O'-Lantern Man came right up to our window," Dad continued, "stared down at us. I backed away with terror, thinking he was going to break through the glass and kill us. His eyes were hollow black sockets and he held the machete dripping red. He pressed a bloody palm against the window, and Malcolm matched his hand against the killer's. They stayed like that for a long time, just staring at each other. Then the Jack-O'-Lantern Man disappeared into the night. After that, Malcolm never spoke another word."

For a brief second Corey thought his uncle's eyes glanced sideways at him. It happened so fast Corey wondered if it happened at all. In a blink, Malcolm was back to staring out the window.

"What happened to the people across the street?" Corey asked.

"The whole family was found murdered, their faces carved like jack-o'-lanterns."

"Okay, that's enough, Robert," Corey's mother said. "You've got Paige too scared to sleep by herself."

Dad said, "My dad told me these stories and they didn't kill me."

"No more vampires or pumpkin creatures. Corey, give your Dad a hug, and then get ready for bed."

Dad squeezed Corey tightly. "Goodnight, Darth Vader. May the force be with you."

Corey smiled." 'Night, Dad."

While his father walked Uncle Malcolm to his bedroom, Corey gathered all the uneaten candy and put it back in his trick-or-treat bucket. When Mom wasn't looking, he couldn't help but toss a couple of candy corns in his mouth and secretly stash a Reese's peanut butter cup for later. He purposefully took his time, wanting to make his favorite night of the year last as long as possible.

Mom stood with her hands on her hips. "Corey, you need to brush your teeth and change out of that costume. Halloween's over."

"It's not over till midnight."

"It's over for you. Now get into your pajamas."

"I want to sleep in my costume, *please?*"

"Won't you be uncomfortable?"

"No, ma'am. I can dream I'm Darth Vader, leader of the Galactic Empire, master of the dark force." Corey didn't want to admit he felt safer in his costume. In the *Star Wars* movies, Darth Vader wasn't afraid of anybody. He ruled the galaxy.

Corey quickly brushed his teeth, then climbed into bed, black costume and all. Mom tucked him in and kissed him on the forehead. "Sure you don't want to leave on your nightlight?"

"I don't need it anymore."

"You are growing up fast. Well, goodnight, my little man."

"Wait, Mom?"

She stopped at the door. "Yes, honey?"

"Do you believe in the Jack-O'-Lantern Man?"

"That's just a ghost story."

"But Dad says the legend is true."

"Your father was just having fun with you. Bogeymen aren't real. Now, go to sleep." She turned off his light and closed the door. The room got so dark Corey couldn't see anything, except when lightning flashed outside the windows.

After an hour of listening to thunder hammer the sky and rain hitting the roof and windows, he finally dozed off. But instead of having dreams of leading storm troopers into battle against Jedi Knights and rebel soldiers, Corey dreamed of dripping pumpkin fangs and black shadows creeping all around. He heard rain slapping against his windows, the moaning wind, and—were those screams coming from the house across the street? The cries seemed to echo in the storm, penetrating his dreams. Then he was at his window, and a rain-drenched woman ran across his yard and up to his window. Blood covered her white nightgown. Her face was a mask of terror. Her bloody hand smeared his window pane. "Let me inside, please, please!" she screamed, looking over her shoulder. That's when Corey spotted the tall, pumpkin-headed shadow walking behind her. Lightning flashed, shining on half its horrid face, and the bloody machete as it rose over the woman's head.

Hands tugging at Corey's feet woke him.

He sat up and screamed.

The tugging stopped, and he stared at the darkness at the end of the bed. "Who's there?"

No one made a sound, but he had the strangest feeling that he wasn't alone in his bedroom, that someone or something was huddled in the black corner at the end of his bed. It wasn't Paige, because she was deathly afraid of the dark. Besides, the tugging hands had been too big and strong. His uncle was a chronic sleepwalker, and sometimes Corey woke up to see him standing over his bed.

"U-Uncle Malcolm, is that you?"

He imagined his uncle standing in the darkness, still wearing his clown suit, strings of drool dripping off his grinning face. But it was too dark to see if anybody was there. From beyond the foot of his bed he swore he smelled mud and roots, the same odor as when he and his sister explored the creek after it rained. There was another scent too. Earlier that evening Corey and his father had gutted a pumpkin, pulling out all the stringy innards and seeds so they could carve it. The room was now ripe with that smell.

Shivering, Corey yanked the covers over his head, hoping that whatever intruder was in his room wouldn't be able to penetrate the shield of his *Star Wars* blanket.

The storm created a din inside the room that washed out any sounds of movement. But Corey still felt a presence. He lay in a ball under his covers, wondering why his parents hadn't come to his rescue yet. They always came in when he woke up screaming from a nightmare. He yearned for the comforting touch of his mother's hand on his shoulder, the reassurance of his father's voice that always seemed to chase the bogeymen away. Corey kept waiting for the hall light to turn on, but it never did.

The storm, he thought. *They couldn't hear me because of the storm.* He wanted to yell for them to come in here, but didn't know if he should chance it. Whoever or whatever was in the corner might yank back the covers and…

If I lay here long enough, he's going to get me.

His ankles still felt the phantom touch from when the hands had grabbed them and tugged him awake. That sensation had been too real to be part of his dream.

I've got to make a run for it. I'll jump out of bed, turn on all the lights, then sleep in Mom and Dad's room, or with Paige, just until morning. Then Halloween'll be over and everything'll be okay.

Taking a deep breath, Corey counted backwards in his head, *5, 4, 3, 2, 1!* He threw back the covers, leaped off his bed, and raced for the light switch. When he hit it, no light came on. He felt for the door, but it was already open, even though he remembered his mother closing it. Feeling the air of someone moving behind him, he darted into the hallway, hit the light switch.

Again, no light.

The power must be out. His heart pounded. Running through the hall, he turned into his parents' room, approached the bed.

"Mom…Dad…I'm scared."

Shadows cast across their bed. Two dark lumps lay in the faint light of the windows.

Corey walked to his mother's side. "Mom, wake up. I can't sleep. *Mom?*"

He shook her arm, but the dark lump didn't move. His father wasn't snoring either. And his mother's arm felt...cold.

"Mom!"

Outside, the night lit up in a bright flash that illuminated the room. The boy reeled. Blood splatters covered the pillows and headboard. His father's head was missing, a carved pumpkin in its place. When the room flashed a second time, he saw his mother's head was still attached but looked all wrong. Her eyes were wide open, staring at nothing. Her face had been carved to look like she was grinning from ear to ear, all her teeth visible along the jawbone.

Corey backed against a dresser and froze, again feeling a strange presence with him in the darkness. The muddy creek smell returned. He studied the large windows at the far end of the room. Through cracks in the curtains, storm light crept in, but there were also sections of the curtains where shadows prevailed.

When the lightning flashed again, he saw movement in the corner of his eye by those curtains. He watched the surrounding darkness, praying his black costume camouflaged him enough to stay hidden. But then in another bright flash he saw a tall silhouette standing on the opposite side of the bed. The killer had a pumpkin-shaped head and gripped a machete.

Corey gasped and its head turned toward him. The shadow pointed the blade at him. Then the killer began to advance around the bed just as the room turned dark again.

Corey bolted out of the room and down the hall, knocking off family pictures as his flailing arms brushed the wall. He dashed into his sister's room and closed the door.

"Paige! Paige!" he whispered. "We gotta get outta here. Wake up!"

He shook her body, which was stiff and lifeless in her bed. The lightning confirmed his biggest fear. On his sister's pillow, staring at him, was a pumpkin engraved with her face. Blood covered the blankets. Corey clamped a hand over his mouth to stifle a scream.

"They're all dead," he whimpered, trying to hold in the tears. *"I'm alone."*

A hand lurched from beneath the bed and grabbed his ankle. He yelped and fell to the floor, kicking his legs in panic.

"Shh…it's me," whispered Paige.

He crawled on his stomach over to his sister.

"I'm scared," she said. "A monster came into my room."

"Mine too."

Paige sniffled. "I want Mommy and Daddy."

Corey didn't have the heart to tell her their parents were dead. He still couldn't believe it himself. He did his best to shove the image of his mother's jack-o'-lantern face to the back of his mind. All that mattered now was protecting his baby sister. He gripped her hands and whispered, "It's going to be okay. I need you to be really, really quiet."

He tried to open the window beside her bed, but it was double-locked. His parents had recently installed storm windows and it was impossible to open them.

The floorboards creaked in the hallway. Footsteps echoed closer and closer.

Corey squirmed under the bed with his sister. She was trembling and sobbing, and he had to cover her mouth to keep her quiet. They lay side by side for several seconds, peering out from beneath the bed. The relentless storm put on a flickering light show in Paige's bedroom, flashing on the faces of dolls and teddy bears. Corey's heart kept hammering his chest. He held his breath as the bedroom door creaked open. Again came the smell of mud and roots.

A pair of muddy workman's boots clumped across the floor, inches from where Corey and Paige hid. He felt a warm puddle pooling around his leg. His sister had wet herself. Corey held onto her tight, praying she didn't make a sound. Praying the killer didn't crouch down and peer under the bed.

The legs that were clothed with dark green trousers moved away from the bed and vanished into the walk-in closet. Corey could hear the sound of wire hangers being moved from side to side as the killer searched for them. Then came angry whacking, as if the machete was stabbing into the wall. A few seconds later the boots stepped back into the room, walked toward them.

Don't look under the bed, don't look under the bed...

A sound echoed from another part of the house and the killer turned and hurried out of the room.

Corey let out his breath and pulled his hand from Paige's mouth. He whispered, "We have to sneak out of here."

She nodded.

They both crawled out from beneath the bed. Corey picked up Paige's baton for a weapon. Holding his sister's hand, he led her into the hallway. To the left was his bedroom and beyond a long tunnel of darkness, his parents' room. There was no way he was going back in there. He didn't want his sister to see their butchered bodies. He pulled Paige toward the other end of the house. They quickly ran past a study and den to the foyer. Corey tried to open the front door, but it was dead-bolted and the lock required a key.

"What now?" Paige asked.

Corey put a finger over his mouth, signaling to stay quiet.

He considered their options. Another escape route was through the sliding-glass door in the den. Corey had the strongest sensation the killer was in there. The den was cluttered with furniture, Mom's boxes of jarred candles from her side business, and Dad's collection of taxidermy animals. Too many places in that room for a killer to hide.

Then Corey remembered Uncle Malcolm's room led to the garage. Maybe the Jack-O'-Lantern Man hadn't gotten him yet. His room was at the far end of the house. Corey and his sister would have to make it all the way through the living room and dining room, kitchen and breakfast area before reaching the back bedroom. He had never realized what a maze their one-story house was until he had to navigate it in the dark with a killer looking for them.

He and his sister hurried through the gloom-shrouded living room and dining room to the kitchen. The drapes to the window above the sink were open, so enough flickering storm light leaked in to see parts of the kitchen. Water streaming down the window made the gray light dance like specters among the shadows.

Corey and Paige crouched behind a butcher's block. He traded the baton for a butcher knife, liking the feel of a blade in his hand a whole lot better. He heard a scraping sound coming from the den, like a blade dragging across wood. Ushering his sister into the walk-in pantry, he said, "Stay here and keep really, really quiet. I'll come back for you."

"Don't leave me."

"I'll be back for you, I promise. I have to find us a safe way out."

Paige nodded and crawled under one of the shelves. He placed a few bags of flour and cereal boxes in front of her. He hated leaving her, but he felt vulnerable moving through the house with her. He'd rather lure the creature away from her and confront it alone.

Squeezing his knife handle, he drew upon the courage of the superheroes he'd read about in comic books. They always confronted danger with bravery. It took every ounce of will to push down the voice that reminded him he was just a ten-year-old kid, no match for a killer.

Corey needed to get to the garage where he could escape out the backyard and run to a neighbor's house. First he had to get past the breakfast area which faced the second entrance into the den. Creeping around a kitchen counter, he counted to three then ran past the den and breakfast table. He half-expected hands to grab him, but none did.

The sliding-glass door was open, the curtains billowing like ghosts, and rain pouring into the den. Had the killer left? Gone to a neighbor's house to slaughter another family?

Corey thought of getting Paige and running out the open back door, but was stopped by a cold rash of fear. What if this was a trap, the killer crouched and waiting for them to make a run for it?

Whenever the family had gone deer hunting, Corey's dad had taught him to always follow his gut instincts. Now, checking his gut, the garage felt like a safer route.

The door to Malcolm's room was closed. Corey opened it, the hinges creaking, and moved through the blackness toward the bed. He whispered, "Uncle Malcolm?"

Normally, his uncle was a loud snorer. Tonight, he made no sound at all. Corey dreaded reaching for his uncle. His mind conjured images of a blood-soaked body, a face carved with a permanent clown's grimace. When Corey felt the bed, terror ripped through him. The mattress was empty. He stumbled back away from the bed.

Where had Malcolm gone? Was he sleepwalking again? Then a more disturbing thought struck Corey. Had his uncle murdered his parents?

Most of the time Malcolm sat and stared at nothing, but there were moments when he would turn his head and stare at Corey. *Your Uncle Malcolm may not talk,* Corey's dad had told him, *but he's always aware, always listening.*

Corey ran for the doorway but was stopped when he ran into something that hadn't been there a minute ago. He tumbled to the floor.

An unseen thing breathed heavily at the doorway. Metal scraped against the wood, splintering it. Corey scooted back into the deeper gloom of a corner. He imagined his catatonic uncle wearing a jack-o'-lantern over his head, peering out the triangles with those flicking eyes; only Malcolm was completely aware of what he was doing.

Corey sweated beneath his costume. He tried to remain as quiet and still as his nerves would allow him.

The scraping-breathing thing at the doorway moved into the bedroom. Corey could hear it by the bed, ripping the mattress and tearing pillows. The scraping blade moved down the wall, toward the corner in which Corey huddled. Just as he felt the machete dragging above his head, he tore from the corner. He banged his shoulder against the door as he ran back through the den and into his dad's office. *I've got to do something. I can't let Malcolm kill us.*

Picking up the phone, he dialed 911 but the line was dead. Feeling the urge to break down and cry, Corey hung up the phone and hid under the desk. He tried to think of what to do next. Maybe he and his sister were better off just staying put. *I'll wait here till morning,* he thought. *Then Halloween'll be over and everything'll be okay.*

Then he heard his sister's high-pitched scream.

Paige! Corey crawled out from beneath the desk and ran toward the sound. When he reached the den, her voice squealed outside. The sliding-glass door remained wide open.

Still holding the butcher knife, Corey raced out of the house and into the pouring rain. A crackling vein of lightning lit up the backyard and field behind their house. A hundred yards ahead, the killer marched into the pumpkin patch, carrying Paige. She had fallen silent.

Corey scolded himself as he ran through the pelting rain. *I should have hidden in the pantry with her. I should have protected her.* He prayed he could get to her before it was too late.

At the center of the field stood a two-story barn. The killer opened the double doors and stepped inside.

Corey entered the patch, weaving around pumpkins that were rotten and misshapen, the rejects of the harvest. The clinging vines and sucking mud made his efforts difficult. A couple times he tripped and fell, crushing pumpkins beneath him. When he finally reached the barn, a light was emanating from inside. He slipped between a crack in the double doors. Inside, the barn was warm and dry and smelled of dust, old wood, metal tools and, dominating all smells, the orange fruit of the patch.

Growing up on a pumpkin farm, Corey had explored this barn many times. He'd learned every nook and cranny of the ground level and the second-story loft. But for all the times he had spent inside this barn, he never knew that it had a basement.

A trap door in the floor was now open, and flickering candlelight glowed from beneath the wood floor. The last thing he wanted to do was to go down there, but the killer had his sister. Corey would die before he'd abandon her. His sweaty palm gripped the knife. His heart beat wildly as he followed a set of wooden steps underground. Built of flaking concrete walls, the basement was damp and covered with mildew. Spider webs clung from the rafters. At the bottom, candlelight danced in the carved eyes and mouths of a dozen jack-o'-lanterns perched on crates and metal shelves.

Corey rounded a corner and wasn't surprised to find Uncle Malcolm sitting in a chair. He was dressed in wet, muddy farm clothes. His eyes held Corey's gaze a few seconds before going catatonic. Paige sat in another chair, soaked to the bone and frozen in a state of shock. Corey ran over and hugged her tight. "Thank God, you're alive!"

Furious, he spun and faced his uncle, holding out the knife. "You...you killed Mom and Dad." Corey raised the knife, ready to drive it down into Malcolm's chest.

"Don't hurt him!"

Corey stopped and turned when he heard the voice.

From the shadows stepped his father, wearing green trousers and muddy workman's boots. He removed a pumpkin mask from his head.

Next to Dad stood Mom, her face and nightgown covered in blood. "We're not dead, Corey. See?" She peeled prosthetic knife wounds off her cheeks. "Mommy's all right."

The knife fell from Corey's hand as he stared at his parents with shock and disbelief. Everything that had happened tonight, all the adrenaline and terror, hit him all at once and he started crying. His mother placed a hand on his cheek. "It's okay, honey. It's okay." She looked back at Dad in anger. "Robert, I told you the kids are too young for this. We should have waited another year."

"They're old enough," Dad said. "You and I were their ages when we found out."

Corey didn't understand. "Found out what? Why did you scare us? I thought we were gonna die." He felt ashamed that he was crying so hard, but this Halloween prank was the cruelest thing his parents had ever done.

"Tonight was your initiation," his father said. "Every member of the coven goes through it. Boys at around age ten, and girls when they turn six or seven. Come with us." Dad took Corey's hand and Mom took Paige's. Corey felt numb as he was guided around a stone wall toward the back side of the basement. The room had a musty, rotting stink to it. Paige hid behind Mom's leg and Corey squeezed Dad's hand at the sight of what met them in the room. Sitting against three walls were skeletons dressed in tattered farm clothes. At least a dozen of them.

"These are some of our elders," Dad explained. "Coven members who used to farm the patch. That one over there was your grandfather. You two were probably too young to remember him, but Grandpa was a hard-working man who loved his family and would do anything to protect us. The night that Malcolm and I saw the Jack-O'-Lantern Man slaughter the family across the street, it was our father wearing the pumpkin head. That night was our initiation into the legacy of our coven.

"And this man over here..." He led the kids and Mom to a wall where one corpse sat off the ground on a platform. The skeleton was tall with long bones wrapped in roots and vines, some of them still green with ivy. Its bony arms, supported with sticks and baling wire, were raised as if it were blessing the long-dead followers. Its hands were massive, the root-entwined fingers resembling claws. A large pumpkin atop its shoulders had blackened and molded around an enormous skull.

Mom and Dad got down on their knees and encouraged the kids to do the same. With deep emotion in his voice, Dad said, "This is the Jack-O'-Lantern Man, the original leader of our coven, Hector Ravencroft."

Corey stared in awe at the legendary monster. Mason jars with candles burned around the skeleton's feet. There were dried flowers there, too, and other little offerings. Corey spotted a blue rubber ball that he'd been missing since he was five, jars full of baby teeth, and one of Paige's dolls, its pink dress and plastic face covered in dust.

Mom said, "The Jack-O'-Lantern Man makes sure that every year we have a good harvest, and he protects our family from the evil people of Millcreek." She pulled both kids into her arms. "We expect you kids to always respect our protector and to never, ever mention him or this place to anyone. This is our family secret."

Dad knelt beside Corey. "In order to keep receiving his protection, we must make blood sacrifices. As children of his coven, it is our duty to carry on the curse against this town."

Corey swallowed hard as he looked at his father. "What do you mean, Dad?"

Dad smiled. "It means you never have to fear the dark or the bogeyman again." He pulled a freshly-carved jack-o'-lantern from the platform and placed it over Corey's head. He stared through the triangle eyes as Dad handed him a machete and gave him the look of a proud and loving father. "Son, from this night forth, you and I *are* the bogeymen."

SIX

Stuart Keane

Katrina Beckett stared through the windshield, her weary gaze oblivious to the patter of light rainfall that bounced and trickled down the exterior of the misted glass. The thrumming sound was subtle on the humid air, almost rhythmic in its candor, and added an improvised, natural soundtrack to the sinister thoughts spiralling around inside her head.

But her gaze wasn't on the heavy rain, or the toughened glass as it sparkled in the vivid beam of a nearby streetlight—or even on the flickering shapes that passed the car in eerie silence, their almost-spectral activity drowned out by the savage downpour.

No, her eyes were on the vast, dark shadow that stood before her, central behind the windshield, dominant with its array of obtuse angles and contours. She couldn't see the entirety of the horizon right now, a familiar scene that greeted her during the dawn of every morning, but she knew it was there, and the shape was splicing a large silhouette into it, signalling its ever-foreboding presence.

Even now, Katrina could see the high, steady curve of the rollercoaster, the spindly eye of the Ferris wheel and a tall structure constructed of metal girders she knew to be the Whisper Plunge, the infamous drop tower. In her mind's eye she pictured stalls and amusements, lavish games designed to take your money with little reward for your eager participation.

She imagined the greasy smell of fresh doughnuts, the sugary tang of cotton candy, the cool essence of Mr Whippy ice cream, all fond memories from her childhood that were now tainted with abject terror. Beyond the wide strip of food stalls and game tents stood the plethora of deserted rides, structures that would remain abandoned for the evening, quiet and isolated, backlit by the white moon beyond.

Katrina swallowed.

She hated this place.

The theme park that haunted her dreams.

Whisper World.

Katrina chewed her bottom lip.

She didn't want to go back there, to return to the lights and laughter of *Whisper World*. She wanted to start the car, turn around, and get out of Dodge. Katrina didn't want to walk across the multi-colored threshold, or nod to the familiar cashier with that eerie lopsided face, or feel the cold steel turnstile caress her exposed hip as she entered the grounds. She didn't want to look at the plethora of rides within, or feel a sudden familiarity as she wandered its empty paths. She didn't want to remember the tragic past, one that risked putting a smile of fond remembrance on her face.

Not again, she thought.

Please, don't make me do this…

She glanced down and sighed, and noticed that she was inappropriately dressed in a revealing blue tank top and white jean shorts. She tugged at the base of the flimsy material, but it pinged back up, leaving a strip of bare, toned stomach. She felt the uncomfortable dampness on her thin shoulders, the slicked hair on the nape of her lithe neck, and the prickle of goose flesh on her forearms. She hadn't escaped the rainfall when climbing into the car, one that continued to drum repeatedly on the roof, and for some reason, she never could escape it. She always wore the same clothes, always parked in the same spot outside *Whisper World*, and always forgot the seventeen minute journey that brought her here.

She never remembered the downpour.

But then, she never remembered climbing into the car, either.

Never, on five separate occasions. Thus far, anyway.

This was the sixth time, the third in October alone.

And, in her eyes, the final time.

Today. Today was the day.

Halloween. The date seemed apt.

This couldn't continue.

She had to face her fear.

And deep in her terrified eyes, two wide orbs flecked with the color of beautiful emerald, she made the difficult decision. The green may have ebbed and faded away over the years with the tragedy and pain of it all, but she didn't care anymore. She was finally in a place to do something about it. The mysterious, amnesiac excursions from her home had to stop.

She knew what she had to do.

You will get Abby back.

Now. Tonight. Somehow.

And no one will stop you.

***

Moments later, Katrina climbed from the car and shut the door slowly, forcing it closed with her palm. For some reason, slamming the door filled her with a queasy dread, and the thought of hearing it *thunk* in the silence of the eerie evening terrified her.

The air was chilled, still fresh and cool from the heavy downpour. She could still hear the pitter-patter of rainwater running off rooftops and splashing down unseen guttering. It eased her a little to know that normal natural sounds still existed in this strange world. She shook her head while rubbing her temple, and for a second, the image of *Whisper World* blurred, distorted, and scratched back and forth across her hazy view, like an old VHS tape on pause.

She looked around.

The flickering shapes, no longer silent and blurred by the drenched glass, were people—couples and parents and children exiting the theme park after an exciting day, their exhausting experience all but over. She watched as children reluctantly climbed into vehicles, observed as parents partook in the routine theatre that had probably interrupted their lives on numerous occasions. One child refused to climb into the vehicle until his father scooped him up underarm and thrust him into the backseat. Katrina heard his whining cries as the door slammed shut. One guy on his lonesome walked to the back of his car and forced several bobbing balloons into the trunk of his Vauxhall. After a battle that saw the rubber ovals bop him in the face several times, he came out the winner.

Katrina jumped, then shivered. She rubbed her arms, and felt the gooseflesh pimple.

And was knocked aside by someone.

"Oh, dear God. I'm so sorry!"

Katrina stumbled and regained her balance, leaning against the car. She looked up and came eye to eye with a thin, excitable woman. Her pale face was lined by fluffy brown hair, her expression youthful but tired, the skin smooth but pocked with the odd line here and there. As Katrina straightened up and took a small step back into her own personal space, she realized the woman had her arms wrapped around a little girl. The girl was hiding her face behind her gloved hands, shy, the obvious culprit of the unexpected collision.

"I'm so sorry," the older woman repeated. "It's been a fun but long day. The kiddo is a little excited."

Katrina smiled and nodded, an expression which required all of her effort. For a moment, she took her eyes off the theme park, losing focus. "It's no bother, really."

"My little girl does enjoy coming to *Whisper World*."

"Well, it's a great place. Lots of fun and rides," Katrina said, her contempt barely hidden.

The little girl lowered her hands, and said nothing.

"Seven-year-olds, eh? The woman continued. "I made the mistake of giving her a Pepsi this morning. Amateur hour, am I right?"

Katrina nodded, looking at the mother. *I always get them, don't I? Stop talking to me.*

After a second, she nodded again. "Yes," she answered. "My little...yes, it's not good for the kids. I bet she tried the cotton candy too, right?"

The woman smiled, her brow furrowing. "Yes, how did you know?"

You said it yourself, amateur hour. Plus, Whisper World *makes their own, it's the best for miles around, you'd be a fucking numbskull to pass it up.* Katrina coughed. "Educated guess," she said.

The woman smiled. "I'm so sorry for the intrusion. Amy, say sorry to the lady."

"Amy?" Katrina continued to smile, and dropped to one knee. She didn't want the kid to be scared of the mean old lady in the parking lot; she had enough to cope with in her mother. "That's a nice name."

Amy nodded. Said nothing.

"It's okay, you don't need to be sorry," Katrina said. She started in on another sentence, and then fell silent. Her gaze looked at Amy for a little too long, and her eyes began to wobble.

The mother took the hint. "Well, we'd better be going. Looks like the rains coming in. That cloud there sure looks like a doozy. Say goodbye to the lady, Amy."

"Bye," the little girl uttered.

The two of them began to walk away. Katrina opened her mouth, thought about it, and then refrained. She nodded. "Take care."

Rains coming in? You just missed it, love.

Katrina wiped her shoulder, the trembling fingertips caressing the collar bone, and felt the slick wetness there. The skin felt slippery beneath her gentle touch. She brushed the back of her hand against her sodden hair and groaned. Then, she remembered the woman's hair had been dry, fluffy, untouched by any foul weather. She narrowed her eyes, confused. She watched the woman go, Amy trundling along beside her, and realized that the concrete around her was bone dry.

But I was just...

She scuffed her shoe on the concrete. The crunching sound

of dry, dusty asphalt rattled in the air, obvious for all to hear. Katrina looked at several nearby trees. No water dripped from the leaves or branches; there was nothing to suggest that a heavy shower had just passed. She strained to hear the water sluicing off rooftops and down guttering, as before, but heard nothing.

What is going on?

Was I imagining it?

Katrina placed her small hands on the roof of her vehicle, realized the roof was also dry, and pushed. She felt the muscles of her back flex, pushing against her tank top, and the tendons in her forearms erupted on the tanned skin, bulging beneath the surface. She groaned, forcing her tired gaze down to the dry concrete.

This is one of its tricks...her tricks.

Another one. You should be used to this now.

I'll never get used to it.

If you're going to come out of this alive, you need to get used to it yesterday.

"I know," she said aloud. "I *know*."

She pushed away from the car, pulling her tank top down over her stomach. She adjusted her waistline and rubbed her arms one more time.

I wish I'd brought a jacket, and put on some actual jeans.

That's not how this works, you don't make the rules.

You wear what you wore that day, and nothing else.

And you never remember getting here.

But, on the other five occasions, you never climbed out of the car either.

She might not like that. You're meant to spectate, to suffer.

You know this.

She might not like it.

"Who gives a fuck what she likes," she said, speaking to herself. "It's time to finish this."

Katrina walked to the trunk of her car, opened it, and retrieved the green gym bag that sat there. She hefted it, the contents clonking against one another, its weight reassuring. After the fourth episode of travel, she thought it might come in handy, and had packed it just in case.

I don't make the rules, but I can sure bend them.

Let's see what you make of this, bitch.

Closing the trunk, Katrina walked past her car and headed toward the entrance of *Whisper World.*

***

The first thing Katrina noticed was the complete isolation.

Mere moments ago, before the small girl had bumped into her, the car park had been thriving with the bustle of people and moving vehicles, alive with the constant thrum of departing activity. She remembered the bizarre balloon man, the impatient father, the multiple families who looked exhausted from their days exploits.

Now, the parking lot was empty, deserted.

An eerie silence settled on proceedings. Katrina spun on the spot, the gym bag arcing out a little, and she realized that not one vehicle shared the vast space with her own. She saw rows of seemingly endless pale lines stretching out before her, each indicating an empty space, the occasional tire mark piercing the faded whiteness. The daunting outline of *Whisper World's* gates loomed ahead, high and wide in the silent evening, the gloom adding an air of menace to the protective structure. Katrina walked toward it, her bare thighs swishing against one another.

Off to the left sat World Motel, the attached establishment for customers who travelled from afar. The eighteen-room motel was also deserted. Not one light shone in any of its multiple windows. The reception door was firmly closed, all of the curtains were pulled shut, and even the Pepsi machine at the edge of the building was turned off, the rectangular monstrosity almost lost in the deepening shadows.

Is this really happening, or is it part of her tricks, her games?

Katrina kept silent, milling the prospect over inside her mind. Seconds later she passed the motel, paused to compose herself, and slipped through the open gates. Taking a few steps and staring ahead, she saw six ticket booths, all lined up and exact, each the replica of the next.

All of them were empty.

Her weary eyes fell to the metal turnstiles, and she realized that her hand was automatically rubbing her stomach through her damp tank top. Again, her memory failed her as she took a tentative step forward, but she had an inclination.

Was this part of that day? Did I bump my hip before the shit hit the fan?

Is she trying to remind me in her own sick way?

Glancing at the empty booths, Katrina hopped the barrier, avoiding the cold metal bars altogether. She landed gently on her feet, the gym bag slapping her side with a clunk. She couldn't help but smile at the small victory, yet couldn't pry her eyes from the empty, shadowy booths. They seemed vast, almost, larger and sharper at the edges, and their appearance made her wince, like a simple touch of the wooden huts could separate flesh from bone with ease. It reminded her of that menacing hesitation when seeing a wicked blade or something so sharp it forced your common sense to approach with extreme caution.

Then, she wasn't looking at the edges or the shapes. She was gazing through the misted glass at the shadows within, murky recesses that contained high leaflet holders and a small locker and a key holder. They remained still and silent, almost grey behind the protective glass.

At any second, she expected the man with the grotesque lopsided face to appear and smile at her, an action that only lifted the right-side of his face, a movement that merely tweaked the shiny, puffy scar tissue, like some hideous fleshy mask. His smile was innocent, she was sure of that, but nothing filled her with more dread at that exact moment, not in recent memory anyway. She shivered and blinked her wide eyes as they ricocheted in their sockets.

But he didn't appear, unlike her nightmares. There, in the never-ending misery of her fractured dream state, he was a constant figment of the confusion, the demonic gatekeeper to this unknowing hellhole. Katrina swallowed and realized she was sweating, the perspiration dripping off her warm chin despite the cool evening breeze and her state of minimal dress.

Ironically, she rubbed her thighs to usher the goose flesh away.

Backing away from the booths, she prepared to enter Whisper World.

"This is where is all began," she said to herself, the sound of her voice a little comforting.

As she took her first steps forward, she saw a triangular sign embedded in a small patch of manicured grass. Wooden slats pointed in several directions, and Katrina lifted her eyes to gain her bearings, despite recalling every inch of the theme park in her mind. Her sense of direction was usually inept at best, and mostly controlled by satellite navigation, but *Whisper World…*it was as if she created it, designed it. She knew every single path, every nook and cranny, every entrance and exit. She couldn't get lost, and she wasn't entirely sure why, but she knew her way around the attraction with the utmost certainty.

Another one of her games? Likely.

Still, despite her mysterious knowledge of the park's layout, Katrina located the sign that read RIDES and followed it, veering off to the left. For some reason, right at that moment, she didn't trust anything that her fragile mind told her.

But why trust the park? Any of it could be an illusion.

Her games and tricks will guarantee that.

The better of two evils. Either way, she wants me to come. I'll find her, I'm sure of it.

Katrina followed the looping path, the rides rising up before her as the pavement dipped into a recess lined with pristine flowerbeds. Red and blue and pink petals caught her eye and made her feel serene in the muted madness of the park itself. She noticed the occasional expired jack-o'-lantern embedded between the plants, the orange pumpkin faces staring like corpses. Halloween decorations tied to lampposts and furniture whipped and whistled on the slight breeze. Being alone in this place was truly awe-inspiring and wonderful, yet creepy at the same time. She spun on the spot, taking in the empty surroundings, and felt a hard shiver crawl up her spine.

The rides stood still. No twirling of the carousel, no spinning of the teacups, no roar of a rollercoaster. The drop tower was nothing but a tall metal stick, the seats that slide up and down rooted to its base, itself hidden behind some clown-shaped hedges. Everything was silent, stoic, unattended. The silence was deafening.

Katrina rubbed her arms and moved on.

The path ascended again, and within seconds she was in the center of the park, a huge circular hub of concrete painted with colorful patterns. Katrina narrowed her eyes and pictured droves of people milling around—children laughing, adults instructing, families enjoying themselves, park employees going about their business. She imagined the smells of cotton candy and sweat, the sounds of annoyance and frustration combined with pure exhilaration and joy. The usual theme park soundtrack.

Katrina closed her eyes, and for a second she could hear those noises, could feel the atmosphere of the park. She remembered that fateful day, the day that seemed to haunt her dreams, the day that had, in her own mind, brought her back here. The slivers of memory from that day were everywhere, from her clothes and the weather, to remembering certain people and the rides she partook in.

To remembering *Abby*.

She opened her eyes, and wiped away a tear. Nothing had changed.

And then the dodgems behind her sparked to life, the music grinding from dead to excitable within seconds, the lights flickering on and illuminating the dull space before her. Katrina glanced up and realized the sun was now setting. Darkness would soon fall.

The rectangular ride lit up, displaying the white floor marked with thousands of almost invisible scratches. The bumper cars—a mixture of red, gold and blue—were placed around the edge of the structure, their seats level with the entrance of the ride. Katrina imagined a queue that rolled around it, hundreds of people long. She'd seen one before, every time she attended the park, so the complete isolation of the ride was a small shock.

She almost missed it when a dodgem shot forward and crashed into the siding, inches from her shivering frame.

CRASH.

Katrina stumbled backward as a second car followed suit. *CRASH.* And another. *CRASH.* Composing herself, she noticed that all of the cars were now throbbing with electricity, ready to drive forward at any given moment. She distanced herself from the ride and backed away.

Which is when the carousel started up.

And the rollercoaster, its cars empty as they climbed the steep slope at the beginning of the ride. The spiking ratchet of the wheels felt like knives piercing her eardrums. She clapped her hands to them, and felt her sanity slip.

What do you want?!

I can't hear you, came the reply, a ghostly voice that danced across the chaos of the now active theme park. It wasn't a voice, no, it was inside her mind, like a conversation remembered from years gone by. But she remembered the voice, no, the internal speech, and it wasn't anything she recognized. She shook her head.

No. There's no way...

It wasn't Abby, it couldn't be, but she knew in her thumping heart that it was.

What do—?

Katrina breathed in and swallowed, realizing her internal thoughts weren't strong enough. She took one step forward. "What do you want?"

The rides ceased. The lights and music remained, playing on an incessant loop that usually became an afterthought as you perused the park with your family on an average day out, but was the only single noise that now wrapped itself around Katrina's world. Confident that her question had worked, or attained the attention of whatever was doing this to her, she repeated herself.

"What do you want?" she said, her eyes flicking to the suddenly stoic rides.

"You," came the ghostly reply, a voice that hummed and throbbed through the music, a voice that didn't sound human, but couldn't possibly come from any other species. "You."

The rides started up again, stuttering to life after their brief respite.

Katrina swallowed, and swiped her slick forehead with the back of her hand. She was about to speak once more, but found that she couldn't—a primitive fear prevented her from uttering a word. She backed up a step and turned around.

And stumbled over something in her path.

Katrina regained her balance quickly, her shoes scuffing at the concrete as she straightened up. Quickly glancing left and right, to confirm she was alone, she knelt down and placed her fingertips on the cool walkway.

A sodden teddy bear lay on the scratched concrete, and Katrina stared, a tickle of familiarity stroking at the base of her brain. It was Pepsi, Abby's beloved friend, so called because of his dark-brown fur and, according to Abby in one of her many mature moments, his bubbly personality. A smile of remembrance touched her chapped lips; Abby took him everywhere, usually carrying him by the left arm, smiling as she did so. They were inseparable—once, anyway.

Abby *used* to take him everywhere…before. *Before.*

Before what?

This?

Yes, before everything.

Which is why she gasped when she finally broke through the cloud of memory and noticed the condition of the beloved toy.

Pepsi's left arm was torn from its drenched body, discarded a few feet to its side. As Katrina moved in, she groaned. Dark blood leaked from the tattered hole, the white fluff usually associated with such a toy mishap replaced by actual sinew and torn muscle. The blood pumped from within, weak and slow, onto the concrete.

No way. You're imagining this.

She noticed the bear's chest was moving slowly, breathing. Hesitant and stupefied, she placed a fingertip onto the pulsating fur and felt it move, felt its slickness push against her minimal resistance.

In the early days of motherhood, Abby used to sleep on

her mother's bosom, a part of the bonding experience between mother and daughter, and this reminded her of that, took her back to that moment. Katrina recalled the slow rise and fall of Abby's young chest, the innocence of such a beautiful act that was now frowned upon in the over-PC society of today. Her eyes widened as she realized what she was watching, and tried to consider the impossibility of such a thing.

There's no way...

And then Pepsi's head turned to look at her, the beady eyes dead and lifeless, yet foreboding and terrifying all at once. There was a swilling darkness in those beads, not unlike the soft drink of its namesake, an empty abyss of futile despair and humility, shadows etched through utter torment and tragedy. Katrina thought she saw the toy smile, saw the fur on its face rip and stretch into a grimace of pain or misery or sadistic joy, or all of the above.

She closed her eyes and rubbed her eyelids, putting pressure on the orbs beneath.

It's another one of her tricks, just another one of her tricks.

Katrina opened her eyes and looked at the bear.

It no longer breathed, and Pepsi simply stared off into the distance. The drenched toy remained still, one limb missing as before, its white fluff now spewing onto the concrete, and wobbling on the humid breeze. There was no blood, no torn muscle, and no smile.

Wait a minute...

Katrina narrowed her eyes and looked at the pavement beside it. An elongated arrow was etched in pink chalk, a color that appeared bright considering the surroundings. It pointed off to the right. Katrina looked up and located the path that followed. Finding another triangular sign for reference, the indicator stated ARCADES.

Katrina smiled.

Huh. Abby's favorite part of the park.

Fancy that.

Katrina straightened up and wiped her fingertips on her rump. She winced as one of her knees clicked back into place.

It had been a while since her daily treadmill routine, months in fact. It seemed her body was now suffering for her negligence.

The weary woman started toward the arcades, her fragile mind a mixture of raw emotions. She rubbed her temple, hoping her sanity would hold out, hoping it would stay firm until she finished this…whatever this was. Katrina glanced up at the moving rides and tuned into the melodic hypnotism of their musical call, and found herself captivated by the majestic aura of it all. Her eyes wobbled as the roaming lights flecked across their shiny surface, her lips trembled against the stifling air, and her brain pushed at a door of remembrance once more, a memory that fought to stay hidden in the depths of her mind for some unknown reason. Protection of her sanity, perhaps? Or was the memory so devastating it could derail her completely?

She looked back at Pepsi, and frowned when she noticed the bear was gone.

Katrina continued her walk and entered a triangular courtyard flanked by colorful buildings. The arcade, a wide blue building with red and white stripes on its slanted roof and a circular yaw of an entrance, was lit up by hundreds of arcade machines. Some lined the exterior, mostly claw and prize machines—50p a go, or three attempts for £1—that enticed the unfortunate and gullible. Within, Katrina saw hundreds of popular gaming machines including *Super Mario Kart*, *Mortal Kombat* and *Guitar Hero*. Each colorrful screen danced in silence, their movements designed to tempt the go-lucky punter. Tonight, their luck was out. She was neither a gamer, nor feeling go-lucky. She sneered at the building and turned to the right.

A replica building stood off to the left, albeit with slightly different games and amusements, but it wasn't these buildings she had come for. Abby had been a sensible child, not one easily distracted by the lure of a screen, like most children of her generation.

No, Katrina walked over to the Hook-a-Duck stand, a circular tent-like monstrosity lined with all manner of fluffy toys and tempting prizes. Within, she saw a circular pool with yellow ducks, their heads bobbing and wobbling on the false current beneath.

She passed the stand, a little disorientated. *I'm sure it was... Ah, there it is.*

Passing the tent with little focus, and skipping around some overgrown weeds that blocked her way, she emerged on an open pathway that branched into four, a staggered cross of possibilities. Several attractions lined a high piece of fence that backed onto the Ferris wheel, with two paths either side, and although these games were her initial destination, her eyes wandered.

Katrina frowned and noticed that the path was now cracked in multiple places. Wild green intruders were protruding from beneath the concrete, spiking up into her path. The faint whiff of decay and age tickled her nostrils. She looked back at the arcade building and saw faded flaking paint, chipped wood, broken arcade machines devoid of toys, and a hole in the roof that wasn't there before. The Hook-a-Duck tent was now closed, the metal shutters battered with neglect and faded graffiti.

As if the park was changing around her, aging before her very eyes.

Katrina swallowed. *That's not good.*

She stepped in front of the Test Your Strength machine, a fond favorite of Abby's. The young girl had been an eager fan of science, so this game had been particularly interesting to her. Abby had been convinced that she could win with minimal strength, it was all about the positioning of the strike, something to do with force equals mass times acceleration...something or another. Katrina wasn't sure, but smiled; she'd never been one for complex talk like that.

Abby, though? She was something else. A child prodigy, she was sure of it.

Out of curiosity, Katrina pushed the red button. The machine dinged, its lights circled above her, and the red leather punch bag lowered into position. Breathing out and relaxing, Katrina swung a punch and landed dead center, smashing the bag back into the machine with a *thunk*. The scale behind it lit up until it was two-thirds to the top, through the red and orange and tipping toward the green. The lights subsided, and a heinous clown laugh erupted from the machine, making her jump, a sound that indicated she'd failed.

Despite the situation, Katrina smiled.

She'd spent hours on this machine with Abby. The girl had never won in her attempts, but every time she tried, she improved, notching the scale slightly higher. Maybe there was something to her scientific belief, after all.

One more go? Punch that clown's lights out.

Maybe this is what Abby wants?

Katrina pushed the button again, and this time stood prepared in a boxer's stance. The machine dinged, the lights circled.

C'mon, you piece of shit, she thought.

The decapitated human head that lowered from the machine made her scream.

Katrina fell backward, landed on her rump, and scuffed the backs of her thighs against the concrete. She winced, hissing through her teeth. She couldn't take her eyes off the mutilation before her.

Then, she recognized the severed head, its bloated, pasty skin and bloodied stump vibrant in the dancing lights of the machine. The eyes were closed, the lips parted in a macabre death squeal. A huge gash in the forehead showed some slick skull and a little brain. A creamy maggot writhed in the hole and slipped out, hitting the pavement below. More followed, dropping from the savage hole in a rhythmic pattern. *Thud. Thud. Thud.*

Katrina slapped a hand to her mouth. Tears streamed down her face.

"B-B-Ben?"

The woman climbed to her feet again, ignoring the abrasions on the backs of her thighs. She took one step closer, scrutinized the severed head of her late husband, and shook her head in disbelief. She reached out a hand, stopped inches from the dead flesh, and then retracted it. She sobbed, and wiped her eyes with a trembling hand.

"You always were a snivelling bitch."

Katrina flinched, looking for the source of the sudden voice. She spun on the spot, her hands out in front of her as a weak defense. Completing a full circle, she stared at the head again.

Ben's dead eyes were open. As was his mouth.

"Stop fucking crying. You've been nothing but a disappointment to me."

"B-B-Ben. What?"

"You heard me. A failure as a wife, that's what you were. I wanted to get close to you, tried getting you to open up, but you never did. There was always something hidden between us, something more that you wouldn't share, and it ate away at us. Our marriage was a three-way split; me, you, and whatever you were hiding beneath that cold exterior of yours. You made my life miserable because you were always hiding something. Katrina, you're a pathetic excuse for a human being. No wonder I went to the fucking grave early."

Katrina said nothing.

This is one of her tricks. Has to be. Ben died in a car crash, nothing more.

He never spoke to me like this.

Did he?

No longer trusting her fragile memory, or any thought that crossed her ravaged brain, Katrina backed up. She wouldn't engage with the severed head of her dead husband—*what a ridiculous sentence that was*, she thought—and turned away, running to the left. She thought she was heading toward the exit, having had enough of Abby's sickening games, but had she noticed the sign, she would have discovered she was wrong.

Dead wrong.

Katrina entered the ride area, a vast hub lined with payment booths and attendant stands; this part of the venue required tickets and cash payment, and acted as the activity center of the park itself. This is where the real money was made, the reason people came to *Whisper World* in the first place. Katrina herself had spent hours in this area, usually with a smile on her face.

But when the gates slammed shut behind her, and the music and lights died, leaving her in a dark space flanked by the demonic shadows of the silent rides, she knew something was amiss.

However, the moonlight provided a brief respite. She closed her eyes, preparing them to adjust to the darkness. She sniffed, and soon regretted that decision.

The smell of decay was back, and stronger than before. Katrina actually gagged when she breathed deep, and opened her mouth. It reminded her of dank alleyways back in the town, small narrow spaces filled with moldy food and all manners of rubbish. The smell of rusted metal was strong too, a wet, slippery smell tinged with a coppery tang, the essence of extreme neglect.

Was it metal? Or was is blood?

Katrina swallowed and looked around. She stood in front of the Ferris wheel, its circular structure towering high above her. On closer inspection, she noticed three of the cars were missing on the wheel itself, replaced by nothing but broken clasps and dangling cables. Aware of her surroundings, she glanced down at the access platform to the ride. The corrugated metal steps were drenched in a slimy liquid, with flecks of red rust floating in it. The metal itself was darkened from age, and bent in several places.

She shook her head. *This is impossible. People were just here, riding the rides, having fun.*

Yet, closing her eyes provided no redemption. The decay remained, nothing disappeared. She wasn't imagining this, although she still held out hope that she was losing her mind and the darkness and decay would soon disappear. Stepping away from the Ferris wheel, she saw the rollercoaster, its track bent and broken. Parts of the track were missing, leaving gaps in the looping runway, and several parts had collapsed to the ground, buried amongst the unfathomably long grass there. Off to her left, she noticed a red rollercoaster car laying on its side in the pathway, broken and smashed from what she could only assume was a high fall above. She slowly roamed her eyes from the car to the track, and back again. Katrina caught her breath.

The pink, heart-shaped entrance to the Tunnel of Love loomed on the horizon, and Katrina knew that walking past this ride took her to the busiest part of the theme park. She'd tried the arcade and failed, so if Abby wasn't waiting by her favorite part of the park, maybe she was waiting by her least favorite.

Which means...

Oh, God.

Katrina gulped, and for the first time on this mysterious quest, she found she couldn't move.

She didn't want to go any further.

Walking to the side, Katrina placed her hand on a bent metal fence. A rustle of plastic caught her attention, and she quickly retracted her hand. Glancing down, she saw a plastic sign attached to the metal criss-cross, and on closer inspection, she noticed a piece of paper within the plastic, and realized it was hung there intentionally. A sign. A warning. Taking advantage of the beautiful moonlight, she lifted the paper out of the plastic and began to read.

THE AMUSEMENT DEVICE SAFETY COUNCIL (ADSC)
The British Association for Leisure Parks, Piers and Attractions
Inspection Date: November 2, 2015
Inspector: James Rogers
Inspection Results/Findings: FAIL – PARK TO BE CONDEMNED

Katrina wiped her brow once more, but her hand slid off the flesh with little traction. She groaned and continued reading. Skipping the mandated part of the report, she skimmed to the crux of the document. She shook her head, and a drop of hot sweat hit the paper with a tiny thud.

There's no way, this can't be happening.

Blinking, she continued to read.

A list of the fatalities and accidents that have occurred in the park since it's opening in 2014.

Two women drowned in the Tunnel of Love. A third man survived, but with severe brain damage. He refused to press charges.

A child lost an eye when a pellet ricocheted in the Shooting Gallery.

Three separate incidents of suspected suicide; two victims jumped from the Ferris wheel, one from the top of the rollercoaster. Six people witnessed this. No charges were pressed.

An empty rollercoaster car derailed during testing and killed a family of four on landing.

A man in a wheelchair was electrocuted when he rolled over an exposed power cable.

Seventeen children have been reported missing during park hours. None were found or located. No parents pressed charges.

Katrina released her grip on the notice. It fluttered on the breeze and lightly slapped the concrete. She rubbed her temples, groaning in the silence of the night.

No. This can't be. The park is still open, has always remained open. It's never been condemned, it's always been one of the safer places to visit in Lake Whisper.

Hasn't it?

I just saw people exiting the park, people leaving after a fun day. People leaving, exhausted by their escapades within.

Like I did with Abby.

Six times, no, five. The sixth...that didn't happen.

I left alone on the sixth time.

Katrina stared at the paper on the ground, remembered its tragic listing.

I left alone...

Now, I remember.

Abby.

She's still here. She never left.

Neither did the other children. Whisper World *claimed them all.*

I have to find her.

Breathing in, Katrina started to walk forward, her gait unsteady in the wake of the latest revelation, and headed for the Tunnel of Love. Out of the shadows of the Ferris wheel, the crumbled path became clearer in the stark moonlight, and Katrina suddenly wondered how the moon had come up so quickly. She estimated she'd been in the park less than an hour, and the sun was setting just after she entered. What had happened?

Nothing is what it seems. You know that.

Katrina nodded to her own statement.

The sloshing water of the Tunnel ride prickled at her ears. The sound was usually soothing, relaxing, especially during a warm summer's day. Katrina observed the six Cupid-shaped boats as they bobbed on the water, and found herself wandering closer, to sate her curiosity. The paint was flaking from the boats in multiple places, and one Cupid had lost an eye, revealing the wooden texture beneath. It reminded her of *The Terminator*, with skin missing from half of its face. Looking down at the murky depths of the water, she felt her stomach spin and coil. She gagged and vomited, splattering the overgrown grass with her lunch. *Wait, had she eaten lunch today?*

The water was dark and rich in color, but as it lapped at the base of the pale boats, the gentle waves were deep crimson in color—blood red. On the surface, Katrina noticed several corpses lying face down, some complete and some not so much, floating and bobbing along. A head, still intact with blonde matted hair and sickly bloated skin, clonked against the bottom of the nearest boat and rolled off to continue its unending journey. An outstretched hand complete with a silver wedding band drifted along on its lonesome, its curled, withered fingers arcing skyward.

Katrina backed off, now terrified and on the verge, on the edge of losing it.

She returned to the cracked path and headed to her destination.

The Tunnel of Love disappeared behind her as she walked. The humidity in the air was disappearing now, giving way to a cooler, colder temperature. She rubbed her arms and felt the rigid gooseflesh there. For the first time, her outfit was becoming a hindrance.

Stepping beneath the wooden arch for Whisper World Central, she came face to face with the remainder of the rides. The entrance to the incomplete rollercoaster, its broken skeleton backlit by the moon, the spinning Tea Cups, the Log Flume, The

Whisper Plunge, the Ghost Train and the Whispering House of Horrors all stretched out before her. A narrow path between the two horror attractions reminded her that so much more of the park was yet to be seen.

But that didn't matter. She'd found her place and didn't need to explore further.

She knew she was in the right place, was certain of it.

And that's because Abby was standing at the entrance to the House of Horrors.

"Abby?" Katrina uttered, her strength suddenly sapped at the sight of the young girl.

Instead of disappearing into the derelict building that housed one of the spookier rides of the park, as Katrina expected, Abby walked forward, and approached her.

Katrina fell to her knees, the smooth skin flaying on the rough concrete, her journey almost complete. The strenuous horror and toil of the previous—*hour, hours?*—finally crushed her inner spirit, and rendered her useless. Abby walked over in silence, her eyes hidden beneath her long brown hair, her footing assured and confident, especially so for a six-year-old. The young girl stopped a few feet from the kneeling woman, but said nothing.

"Well, I'm here. I came," Katrina uttered, exhausted. "What do you want?"

"You," came the hissing whisper, but it came from the chilled air, not from the figure standing before her.

"Well, you…you have me," she said, defeated.

"It's been too long," the voice replied.

"Yes…yes, I believe it has," Katrina said, playing along.

"Are you ready to return?"

"Return?"

"You don't remember, do you?"

"I don't. I remember this place, I remember…it's a part of me, I can feel it in my blood for some reason, but I don't know why."

"You don't remember because you're one of the lucky…no, scratch that, you're the *only* lucky one to have escaped its hellish gates, to have walked free in the aftermath."

Katrina bit her lip, confused and a little concerned. *Do I want to remember?*

Haven't you had enough? Your vivid dreams and nightmares—both of which combine on a regular basis—that sap the very soul from you, your many insecurities, the death of your beloved husband? How much can one woman take? You deserve better. You deserve to walk away pain-free, without knowing. Leave this be, leave this alone, let this one thing be left mysterious.

But I must. It's been eating at me for years.

Swallowing, and breathing through her nose, she went for it. "Aftermath of what?"

Abby looked up and smiled, revealing her battered face and her gapped grin, and that's when Katrina remembered. Years of her life disappeared in a savage instant and whipped her back to her childhood. She finally felt her sanity slip and vanish, washed away like a pesky spider in the tub. The memory came crashing back, violent and forceful, the door in her mind that had protected her to this very moment obliterated like mere matchsticks in a hurricane.

The sounds of the rides started up once again and exploded in her ears, rocking Katrina to her very core. The rollercoaster roared like a demonic dragon, the Ferris wheel creaked and groaned like rusty bolts inside her very skull, screeching deep inside her ear canals. She slapped her hands to her head and screamed, trying to block out the stunted joy and the innocence of such music, but she heard nothing aside from the drone of the theme park as it returned to normalcy. The decaying rides once again found strange new life in the mysterious new world, one where small girls somehow managed to survive in an abandoned—*no, it's not abandoned, its alive*—theme park.

A bolt of rigid lightning severed the night sky with a vicious crack, making Katrina jump. The light patter of rain began once more.

But it wasn't a small girl, was it?

It was you. You were the small girl.

No, it's impossible. Abby is my daugh...my daugh...

You can't even say the words, and that's because you never had a daughter.

I did. Abby was...

No.

You didn't.

Katrina stood up, but immediately flopped to the ground, sweat pouring off her exposed flesh; her clothes sodden through from the heavy rain that now fell. She suddenly remembered with utmost clarity, a starkness that blinded her for mere seconds.

I'm *Abby.*

No.

Yes.

Katrina forced her eyes open, fighting against the pain, and after a blinding white flash, Abby was wearing a blue tank top and white jean shorts, a pair of white trainers, and had her hair tied back—a replica of her outfit on that day. The small girl stood in the rain, drenched, her clothes crinkled and transparent from the downpour, hugging her tiny frame. Katrina reached out for her, and fell forward, her face splashing in a muddy puddle on the concrete. She gazed up at Abby, who began to cry.

The metal turnstile poking her hip...

The rainfall that no one else noticed, and never seemed to stop...

The man with the grotesque, lopsided face...

Memories that pained and scared a grown woman, but totally petrified a young girl.

Of course!

Katrina crawled forward, her hands sinking in the water and finding slopping mud where the grass verge was seconds before, the puddles forming around her hindering her progress. The rain thrashed her back and sides, pushed her to her knees, and whipped her to the ground with no mercy. The deluge prevented her from mounting a suitable stance. She needed to reach Abby—although she wasn't sure why. She just knew that reaching the young girl was the sole reason for her coming here, the only reason she was beckoned.

"You survived this once. But I didn't," Abby mused, her words tinged with sadness.

Katrina shook her head, water sluicing off her face. "You did," she gasped, breathing heavily. "*We* did."

"No, *you* survived. I didn't escape. I'm trapped here for eternity."

"We both escaped," Katrina uttered. She screamed in defiance, punching the soaked ground, splashing water into the soggy air. "*We both did.* And we can do so once again. *Now.*"

Abby shook her tiny head, her soaked hair slicked to her pale face. She was holding Pepsi's sodden left arm in her hand now. The rest of the bear was nowhere in sight. She held out her other hand, inches from Katrina, water dripping from the fingertips.

Then, she was feet away.

And seconds later, Abby grew smaller as she vanished into the distance. Katrina screamed, an animalistic howl, the roar lost on the cacophony of heavy rain that now slapped her, beat her, and abused her. Every inch of her bare flesh stung from the rapport of raindrops, but she couldn't stop. Wouldn't stop.

But that wasn't her choice anymore…

Katrina felt her strength ebbing, and lowered her slick face to the sodden ground. It dropped into a shallow puddle and she panicked, fearing that she was drowning. Despite this, she closed her eyes, coming to terms with her inevitable defeat.

The memory became clear as crystal in her mind's eye.

Twenty-four years ago…women drowning in the Tunnel of Love…missing children…a wheelchair user electrocuted. Aside from those tragedies, suicide and murder forever changed the innocence of *Whisper World*.

But people and their families didn't care. The deaths were urban legends, myths, surely. Some even suggested that the stories were mere creation, to drive people through the gates, to promote the horror aspect of the park, the Ghost Train and the Whispering House of Horror. After all, worse PR had been documented in the past.

No one in his or her right mind would keep a theme park

open following such tragedy, right?

Right?

Katrina remembered reading the condemnation notice only moments ago, and recalled her confusion at the date on the document. 2015. She didn't recall the park being condemned or recommended for closure.

And then she realized why.

No, it was 1991. That's when the inspection took place, and the unsafe park recommended for closure. That's when I came here for the sixth time in my life. The final time in my life—my young life anyway.

Because for all of the drowned women and disappearing kids and suicidal patrons, no one ever mentioned the fatal tragedy that occurred in the Whispering House of Horrors. It never gained exposure, never made the news, and never surfaced as part of popular folklore. It never had the chance to become an urban legend because no one knew about it. Compared to the other deaths, most of which happened with witnesses or in public, it was possible to cover this one up. And in the wake of the bad publicity, she was certain that's what the park owners had done.

Only three people saw it happen.

Abby, and her parents.

None of them walked away from that ride. None of them had survived.

After all, you can't reveal the truth when you're dead, can you?

But Abby isn't dead. You're *Abby.*

No, I'm Katrina. Abby was me in a former life.

You're claiming you're the subject of reincarnation?

No…I mean…I don't think so.

Abby mentioned it herself, I was the only lucky one to survive in the aftermath.

But what does that mean?

And suddenly, Katrina was no longer in the water. Her drenched body became weightless, lifted into the air, as if nothing but a sodden feather. She gazed down and shrieked, her fear of heights suddenly becoming a problem, ironic considering she loved riding the rollercoaster.

Wait, no, you don't have a fear of heights.

Abby *does*.

After floating for a moment, the theme park disappeared silently behind vast curtains, and as they closed, the velvet folds solidified into something tangible. They became a colorful tapestry of terror, decorated with flesh-eating zombies and evil demons and blood-soaked vampires.

Katrina narrowed her eyes before recognizing the vulgar display before her. She gazed downward and found a curving metal track placed on a narrow wooden walkway. Below the track was a shallow stream of water. Typical horror memorabilia flanked each side of the rails, including cheap Halloween decorations, which made the place seem cluttered yet terrifying. Candles flickered, cheap bunting waved on the breeze, and mechanical screams filled the air. As she watched, a cloud of blue smoke started to rise, hiding the track from sight.

Katrina recognized the interior of the Whispering House of Horrors.

Oh no… she thought.

As if reading her mind in some macabre way, the image flickered, and a small car slowly rolled into sight. The round device squeaked on its rusted wheels, its bodywork painted with the portrait of a screaming woman. Katrina felt hot tears prickling at the back of her eyes. She smiled, unable to move, a mere sightseer in this particular memory.

Mum.

Dad.

Abby…that's me. Yes, it is.

The small family sat huddled in the car, enjoying the theatrics. The adults smiled nervously as they watched the ride unfold, her father with his arm around her mother, and Abby cowered behind the fluffy shape of Pepsi, her beloved teddy bear.

Abby… she's… I'm scared. I never did like this place.

Mother. Father.

Can you even remember their names?

No…

Your dad was called Paul.

Ah, yes, I do remember. Fragments of my memory are slowly returning.

Her father gently kissed her mother on the lips, blissfully happy. They both smiled. He turned to his daughter, placed a hand on Abby's head and rubbed her tousled hair, causing her to yelp. Katrina smiled. *He said there was a spider in my hair. I was terrified at that prospect.*

And that's why you dropped Pepsi onto the tracks...

As if following her exact thoughts, Pepsi toppled from the car and bounced on the tracks with a substantial thud, one that echoed around the room, just as it had for Abby that day. Katrina knew that was a trick of the startled imagination. The mind plays tricks when you're sad or unhappy, or when you just lost your favorite toy.

It's funny how the mind works for a child, huh?

Her mother, seeing the distress of the child, began to climb from the car, gingerly placing her foot on the track. Paul helped his wife, holding her right arm to give her some balance as she searched for the unseen toy, which had disappeared into the smoky depths below.

Which is when things started to go wrong...

Katrina reached out, helpless to prevent her mother's violent death. She knew it was coming.

And your mother was called?

Katrina. Of course.

Katrina walked forward on the invisible track, slipped, lost her footing and fell, her arm snapping at the elbow as it bent across the rim of the car, a crack that sounded horrendous in the playback of the devastating memory. The woman screamed and fell forward, disappearing into the smoke. Seconds later, there was a small splash.

She drowned, didn't she? Broken arm, no way of pushing up, her face in the water.

I didn't know it then, but I do now. Shit.

Her father panicked at the sudden disappearance of his wife, and stood up in a hurry. He lost his footing too, danced for a long second like a marionette with its strings cut, and slipped backward into his seat. His neck cracked on the rim of the car. After that, he didn't move again.

Abby remained, alone and frightened. Six seconds of unexpected violence had left her an orphan, all because of her love and adoration for a stupid teddy bear.

Six-years-old.

Six instances of this mysterious, amnesiac journey.

Six…there was something else.

I did this, Katrina thought. *I killed my parents.*

This is my fault.

She struggled against the tears, but the remembrance was now breaking her, shifting her sanity to a dark, irretrievable place in her mind, a small locker that, once sealed, would remain so. She felt her mind, as she knew it, shutting down.

I did this…

Yes. And you walked out of Whisper World *in 1991 without a care in the world, a traumatized child with no one to care for her, the tragedy of that day changing you forever. Your childhood remained in this park, trapped for eternity by the horror that claimed it. No one ever knew about your parents because they condemned the park, refurbished and rebuilt it soon after. Their corpses are probably buried deep in the foundations of the new Whispering House of Horrors.*

But you walked free of Whisper World *alone, a survivor, the only child involved in the parks continuous violence to ever emerge alive. You walked back to town and began to live, your mind shutting down on you. You had no ID and no birth certificate. A generous family took you in. It took you six months to utter your first word. Soon after, your memories repressed by the violent death of your parents, you became someone else. You became* Katrina.

Katrina. The last word your father ever uttered.

1991 was a different time. They didn't have big computers back then, no digital records. For all intents and purposes, you didn't exist. Abby did, of course, but you didn't go by that name anymore. Katrina, or not, no one was any the wiser. No one ever knew. Apart from you.

You forgot everything that happened that day, and the tragedy helped you to forget. In a way it protected you. Until now.

Until now…

***

The lobby was cool and brisk. A large jack o' lantern sat on a desk in the corner, the candle flickering behind neat triangular eyes and a zigzag grin. A cartoon witch on a broom hung from the left hand wall, while a trio of zombies joined at the arm hung from the right. The seasonal decoration was minimal for Halloween, but she expected nothing less from the government building.

Katrina wrapped her arms around herself, rubbing the gooseflesh from her bare arms. Her dingy tank top and jean shorts—both soaked and wrinkled from the events of the revealing evening—were no longer of any use. She was freezing. Her skin was pale and clammy, and shivers made her shudder as if an electrical current was coursing through her veins. Her teeth clacked as she walked forward.

This has gone on long enough, she thought. *I need to do what's right.*

A young woman with bunched blonde hair and glasses looked up from behind the reception desk. She smiled, a practiced expression that should have made any visitor feel at ease. Katrina felt immediately violated, as if the woman was judging her on sight. She paused, stopping short of the desk in doubt, wondering if this was the right decision to make, before finishing her short walk. She leaned on the wooden top, flinching as the slick surface tickled her arm. Only then did she notice the woman's gold badge pinned to her lapel.

"May I help you?" the police officer asked.

Abby nodded. "Yes, I'm here to confess to the murders of Paul and Katrina Six.

NETHERLANDS

JC Braswell

The toy figurines—a special line created by famed video game designer Greg Dawson—lined the computer desk, all casting their forlorn gazes toward Tyler, who pounded away on his tortilla chip-covered keyboard. Each of the twisted figurines, some with ebony horns, others with skin-shredding claws, represented a demonic clan from the online video game *Netherlands*. Tyler preferred playing as a demon rather than a human. They were wicked and misunderstood, just like he considered himself as a high school sophomore.

But tonight they proved his adversary, their plastic grins mocking his efforts as he ventured with his friends across the electronic Midnight Plains—one of the more difficult sections of the night elf kingdom leading to the anticipated expansion pack to be launched at midnight Pacific time.

The latest adventure had been an obstacle for his clan (which he proudly proclaimed himself leader) over the course of the past week. Night after night, he defied his parents' wishes with stinging eyes and a refusal to shower in an effort to thwart the human advances. And each night proved as futile as the last, ending with his demon wizard dying by some idiot's hands, likely some hardcore player halfway across the country.

"Damn it!" Tyler slammed his fist across his keyboard as another magical arrow found its way into his character's heart, ending the journey, which always began as soon as he got home from school. The screen faded to black as his Osorno demon—a mixture of a ram and a human with fiery red skin, black leather wings, and a single tusk curling up from its forehead—exploded in a pyre of smoke.

"Shit on me. You guys still there? What the hell happened?" He barked into his headgear's microphone, expecting an explanation from his "teammates."

"Sorry, dude. Told you we were still too weak." Jared's high-pitched voice cracking with puberty answered first. Tyler immediately imagined wringing Jared's pencil neck, watching as his freckled face turned as red as a Christmas light.

"Too weak? Come on, man. The guide says we're the right level." Tyler flipped through the pages of *Netherland's* official guide—chock full of hints and maps of the game world. Pizza stained fingerprints and faded brown soda spills covered half of the pages. "We need to be the first into the expansion pack lands if we're going to make the clan more powerful."

"Then maybe we should've healed up first." Roger—a kid from Minnesota, who Tyler only knew from the game—came to Jared's defense.

"We didn't have time, or the gold. I mean, how are we going to buy potions if we don't have any gold?"

"Go back to the Westerfield Dungeons," Jared dared speak.

"Westerfield Dungeons? Are you kidding me? I'm tired of fighting vampires and their stupid hypnotic spells. No, we're going to find out what's in *The Witching Hour* expansion. I hear there's a new spell book with blood magic." Tyler rested back on his chair, the armrests worn and frayed from years of abuse from his slightly overweight frame. They were better than fighting vampires.

"We don't stand a chance if we don't have any gold to buy potions, and Westerfield Dungeons is the easiest to find more gold…" Roger pleaded.

"Maybe if you didn't buy that stupid sword—"

"We needed the sword."

"Yeah, a lot of good that sword did tonight." Tyler tossed the guidebook aside, as he'd done many times before, and cursed with words his parents would punish him for saying. If only his figurines could come alive and convince them it wasn't time to quit. "No, it doesn't matter. We have the team. You guys just need to cast healing when you're supposed to. I did my part."

"Whatever…I'm out," Roger said.

"Out? What do you mean you're out? It's only seven o'clock." Tyler glanced at the digital clock his parents gave him for Christmas, the type that projected up on the ceiling.

"Dude, it's Halloween. Only have a little more time to trick-or-treat."

"Aren't you a little old for that?"

"I have to take my little brother before it gets too late. See ya." Roger logged off without another word, his name disappearing from the chat menu.

"Man," Tyler whined.

"It's ok, man. It *is* Halloween," Jared said. "Maybe we should take a break and go trick-or- treating. Scare some middle schoolers."

"No. We need to get across the Plains and make it to the mining camp. We've been trying all week. Can't stop now."

"I'm too tired. Can't we just hang out and watch a movie or something."

"I'm still game," Darren's ominous voice interrupted. He was one of the new recruits to the clan that Tyler was outvoted on allowing to join.

"No, no, that's ok. We kinda need Jared's thief for backstabbing. If he isn't playing, we don't have a shot." Tyler said, part of him thankful for avoiding Darren. The kid didn't seem right, especially with his weird ramblings about the occult. "You know, Jared, we'll hang out tonight. Parents are going to some stupid costume party for work. Might as well take advantage of the peace and quiet."

"Cool, I'll ride my bike over. Give me like ten minutes. Shouldn't take me long."

"Yeah, yeah." Tyler watched as Jared's name disappeared from the chat room's list. He only lived three streets away, but he was sure that Jared's irritable bowel syndrome accounted for the delay.

"Sure you don't want to play?" Darren asked, his voice half-teasing.

"No, man."

"Well, I'll be here when you want to come home."

"Wonderful." Tyler answered, turning off his microphone. "Weirdo."

Tyler glanced at his abandoned notebooks in the corner, a disheveled pile with folders filled with unfinished homework. His abandoned backpack rested next to the pile, buried within a string of mediocre report cards from the fancy private school where his parents enrolled him. For a moment, he felt ashamed.

His attention wandered to his chest-of-drawers, where his "family" portrait rested behind another line of *Netherlands* figurines. Just like his demon figurines, his parents, both of whom were high-powered executives in the telecom industry, mocked him with their smiles. They pretended to be a family, Tyler being the only child, his parents more proud of their promotions and luxury sports cars from some name brand he didn't care about.

He wiped his hands across his shirt, clearing the tortilla grease from his fingers, thinking back to when his parents were proud of him. Those were the days when he was an honor roll student, with a regular hair cut at the five-dollar barber, and un-ironed clothes fit for a king. His online friends were his family now.

"Ty-Ty," his mother's voice called in a teasing melody. She entered his bedroom without as much as the courtesy of knocking, wearing a stupid cat costume she'd been displaying throughout October. Her blonde locks cascaded down to her personal trainer-infused shoulders. Not an ounce of body fat was found on her, a far cry from her "frumpy" son, or so she told her friends.

He was sure his mother was having an affair with Brett—the twenty-something pretty boy trainer she hired once to "whip Tyler into shape," which had failed miserably.

"Yeah?" Tyler said, not daring to look at his mom, especially with the ridiculous whiskers extending out of her nose.

"Ty-man," his father's authoritative voice followed, causing Tyler to straighten up in his chair. One stuffed horn extended up from behind his mom's head, followed by another. His father's slim frame was wrapped in faux-fur, accentuating his Viking costume. "Don't tell me you're going to stay here alone in your room all night. You need to get off that thing."

He looked back at the computer screen, remembering his middle school days when his dad would take him out to a movie and to play pool every Friday. He missed those days.

"Well, no." The warm rush of embarrassment filled his cheeks as he thought about his predicament. "Jared is coming over."

"Jared?" his father asked.

"Yeah, Jared Haney. Red-headed boy," his mother said.

"Oh, *that* kid." His father's disdain couldn't have been any more obvious. "Hey, why don't you hang out with Ms. Lorraine's kids? I know she's been asking about you."

Ms. Lorraine's kids—Nick and Shawn—were bigger pricks than some of the kids he met online. Unlike his other friends, Nick and Shawn physically developed faster, and therefore, became athletes who the girls in school worshipped. Tyler had been on the receiving end of several wedgies because of those two.

"Maybe I'll give them a call. Maybe..." his voice drifted.

"Ok, bud. Well, listen, Mom and I have this party tonight. We're going to be a little late getting home. We left some pizza money on the kitchen counter. You and Jacob—"

"Jared."

"Sure, Jared, can have some pizza. Maybe you guys can go trick-or-treating or something. Better than, you know, your dolls." His father picked up his Osorno demon figure—his prized possession—and wiggled it around. His father's eyes rolled as he placed it back down with a sigh.

"Stop it," his mother said, half-pretending to protect him.

"Just try to get out. It's a nice night." And with that, his father and the ridiculous Viking costume left.

"It's ok, Ty-Ty. Your father just wants the best for you."

With a kiss on the cheek, his mother scuffed his hair and left. As she closed the door behind her, the bedroom lights blinked once then twice.

"Mom?" Startled, Tyler jumped up and opened his door, only to hear a jingle of keys, the automatic engine of his parent's Lexus, and the closing of the front door. "Damn." He looked down then over to his Netherlands figures.

"Hey…where's Muerte? Mom, did Dad take Muerte?" Tyler yelled down the hallway, realizing his prized Osorno figure, the same one his dad had played with, was gone.

***

Jared plopped down on the couch, kicking his shoes off and hugging an overflowing bowl. The ginger shoveled a handful of popcorn into his mouth and flipped on the ridiculously sized television.

"Feel like watching one of these Halloween marathons? Maybe a slasher?" Jared asked with a mouthful of popcorn, gnashing down like a horse eating grass. Part of Tyler wished he'd just called it a night after their unsuccessful attempt at trick-or-treating.

"No, man, too tired," Tyler collapsed in his father's chair, sipping on his Dash-N-Go cherry cola, welcoming the cool sugar-infused carbonation. He blew down the inside of his collar, across his sweat-slicked chest. "Still can't believe how humid it was. Felt like soup outside."

"We did just ride up to the store." Jared turned up the volume as the news came on. "What time did you say your parents were coming home?"

Great, Tyler thought, *that question could only mean Jared planned on trying to stay the night.* He'd have to find a way out.

"Early. We have to head out at like nine tomorrow morning or something. Going shopping."

"Oh." Jared woofed down another two handfuls. Tyler cringed at the thought of Jared wiping his hands across his parent's sofa. "It's, like, 11:20 already. How early are you thinking?"

"Dude, I don't know," Tyler snapped. *Shit. How was it so late already?*

"I was just asking. What's up your butt anyway? You've been in a bad mood all week. Is it because of Chemistry? Don't mind Mr. Murdock, he's—"

"It's not because of that old buffoon." Tyler looked down the hallway, toward his bedroom door. Muerte's absence continued to make his stomach turn. He'd spent hours painting and repainting the Osorno demon. His dad must've taken it to prove a point.

"Then it's something—"

"Don't worry about it." Tyler turned his attention back to the living room. "You sure it's that late?"

"Positive."

Outside the bay window, a white light pulsated, bringing the dark sky to life. A low rumble followed, shaking his mom's wind chimes with a *tinkle.* The branches of the oak tree on the front lawn bowed with a sudden gust of wind, taking with it the faded oranges and reds of the autumn leaves.

"And in a bit of odd news perfect for this Halloween night, Greg Dawson, CEO of DarkStorms Entertainment, the company behind the multi-million dollar video game enterprise known as Netherlands, was arrested earlier today in his Silicon Valley home, in connection with a bizarre string of animal sacrifices that were apparently tied to rituals that other members of Silicon Valley's elite..." Rob Boblin, Channel 11's graying newscaster, said as the screen flipped to a video of Greg Dawson—clad in a black suit, sunglasses, and hair slicked back into a ponytail—being escorted out of his mansion, a gothic-styled home with two brick towers built into the façade.

"What? Ain't no way." Jared jumped off the couch, spilling the remnants of his popcorn across the hardwood floor.

"Be careful," Tyler said, knowing his parents would kill him if they found popcorn grease on the floor.

"Man, I'm sorry. It's just this," Jared whined, immediately falling to his knees to scoop up the snack.

"Animal sacrifice and rituals? Can you believe it? I mean,

the guy is creepy and all." Tyler watched as the officers led Dawson, whose face adorned a blank expression, to their police cruiser. A sudden smirk crossed Dawson's lips as he disappeared into the backseat.

Tyler had to admit part of him was intrigued at the news.

"Actually, I can kind of believe it. I read his autobiography and watch his YouTube channel. Guy is bizarre. He talks about the occult and these witches and old pagan things. Mom hates it when I watch it. Have to wait for her to go to sleep."

"Why do you think he did it?" Tyler remained transfixed on the screen as the police cruiser drove off, the broadcast ending in a basketball graphic as the goofy sports reporter appeared.

"How am I supposed to know that?" Jared huffed as he stood up, clutching the popcorn bowl and pulling down on his Goblin Army t-shirt. "He's just rich and weird."

"You looked at his YouTube channel. Was it some kind of demon ritual? Kind of ironic that he did it tonight of all nights," Tyler said, finding himself intrigued by the news. Another flash of lightning illuminated the cul-de-sac, once again outlining the skeletal tree.

"I already told you, just goofy stuff about Satan and Lucifer and all. Stuff you shouldn't mess with," Jared's voice trailed off slightly. "Don't tell me you really want to know about it."

"The guy's a genius. He's made a lot of money with the game. Just curious if you think there's more to it."

"No. He's just a sicko. Lots of sickos are rich." Jared flipped the channels until an overplayed horror movie captured his attention. It was the same one they watched year after year, the one with the resurrected pirate demon. "Let's just ignore all that."

"Ain't no ignoring what we just saw. I want to know more," Tyler insisted, picking up the remote and turning off the television as the walls shook from another bout of thunder. "Something tells me you know more."

"Are you kidding me?" Jared threw up his arms and slapped them back down at his sides.

"No, I'm not." He stared into Jared's eyes, taking two

steps toward his best friend. His mind wandered elsewhere, somewhere he never felt before. "Tell me."

"You're acting weird…"

"No, I'm not." The depths of his imagination manifested with anger. "I just don't like it when my best friend lies to me."

"I'm not lying. Trust me, you don't want to know."

"Tell me—or leave." His arms tingled, the hair on his forearms standing on end.

"You're obsessed."

"Screw you." Without another thought, Tyler shoved Jared's bird chest, causing him to fall to the floor with a *thud*. Jared whimpered as he clutched his arms. Tyler's anger subsided as his muscles relaxed.

"Asshole," Jared said, still holding his elbow, while struggling to his feet. His face turned to a scowl. The two had been friends since kindergarten. Sure there'd been fights, but this felt different to Tyler.

"Dude, I'm sorry. I didn't mean to…" Tyler said, remembering the one time he saved Jared from Nick's scorn.

"It hurts." Jared pulled his arm closer to his body, keeping his head down, almost ashamed of his presence. His elbow had already swelled to the size of a golf ball. "I think I need to get to the doctor."

"Listen, I'll get some ice. Then we can play some Netherlands or—"

"No, I'm just going to go home." Without another word, Jared headed for the front door, not bothering to look back at his friend.

"Bye…" Guilt set in as Tyler watched Jared disappear into the coming storm.

***

"It's got to be around here somewhere." Tyler shuffled through his army of demonic figures, searching for Muerte. He'd already been through the collection once since Jared left, looking under his dresser, bed, and computer desk. The practice seemed a little more morbid considering Dawson's arrest, the images haunting him as he studied each figure, reciting their stats, special attacks, and uses.

"It's not freaking here!" Tyler plopped onto his computer chair, his tail sinking deep into the almost non-existent cushion. He buried his face in his hands and leaned forward. Like earlier in the evening, his demon army stared at him, mocking his efforts. Somehow, each twisted face appeared more diabolical than he last remembered. "Damn it, Dad."

Just as he uttered his father's name, his smartphone lit up with a vibration, revealing the word "Dad" on the screen. Tyler immediately jumped at the chance to solve the mystery.

"Dad?" He asked, feeling a slight hint of relief, knowing his parents were on the other end.

"Ty-Ty," his mom's words slurred through a cloud of static.

"Mom?"

"Yes…honey. I'm here."

"Where's Dad? I have to ask him…"

"Dad's driving, honey. We're heading…there soon. Bad… with lightning." His mother's voice continued to cut in and out, not that she would make sense anyway.

"Can I talk to Dad?"

Another boom of thunder, this one loud enough to rattle the dining room's chandelier down the hallway, shook the house. Then there was nothing.

"Damn it."

Tyler attempted to call back several times, each time receiving a dial tone for his efforts. For once, he actually wanted his father home, or even for Jared to have stayed, which reminded Tyler he needed to find out how he was doing. He knew damned well Jared's parents wouldn't take him to the hospital this late, not with his little brother and sister at home.

He spun on his chair and stared at his computer's blank screen, brushing his pinky finger along the mouse to awaken his monitor. The Netherlands welcome screen popped on, complete with the window of his clan's chat list. He recognized a couple names, but none he regularly accompanied.

Then there was Darren, who always seemed to be logged on.

"Good to have you back!" Darren's voice spoke through the computer's speakers. "Care to join us?"

"What?" Tyler whispered to himself, remembering that he'd turned off both his headset's microphone and the computer speakers. He formed the habit after his dad yelled at him for waking him up several times during work nights.

"I said, care to join us," Darren's monotone voice—deader than usual—answered.

"Where?" Tyler looked out his bedroom window, hoping to see his parents' familiar headlights barreling down the cul-de-sac.

"I'm on the Plains. I found a way to beat the invasion." Darren's words immediately dissipated the fear creeping into Tyler's subconscious. He forgot about Muerte, Jared, and his parents. Maybe Darren had a use after all.

"How?" Tyler placed on his headset and rolled his chair closer to the computer desk.

"Meet me by the Red Oak. I have some items I can give to you, but know that it's going to require a sacrifice."

"Sure, sure," he answered without thinking of the words.
***

Tyler's electronic journey to the symbolic Red Oak—the marker for the entrance to the Midnight Plains—took a short time from his respawn point. He made sure to spend the last of his paltry gold on healing potions before venturing out. And, as he expected, much of the online chatter revolved around Dawson and his arrest.

Tyler attempted to query about what'd happened. He received answers ranging from Dawson being a Satan worshipper to using it as a promotional tool for the launch of The Witching Hour expansion—which had completely escaped Tyler's mind. Most people didn't seem to care, rather, focusing their attention on gathering to open the portal at midnight.

Tyler looked at his digital clock as he spotted the tip of the Red Oak. 1:30 a.m. *Late.*

"Where are you guys?" He muttered, looking out the window again in hopes of seeing his parents drive up. The windowpane welcomed his attention by rattling with a gust of wind. Dark clouds rolled forward, expanding outward like Jared's popcorn, capturing the energy of the unseasonable lightning storm.

"Over here," Darren said, pulling Tyler's attention back to the screen.

"Where?" he asked, as he spotted a lone figure—an unrecognizable race—standing beneath the glowing amber leaves of the Red Oak. "That you?"

"Yes."

"I thought you were an orc?"

"You made it faster than I would've imagined, even for a devout player like yourself." Darren skipped over Tyler's question.

As Tyler approached Darren's new character, he realized he'd seen the race before. He immediately looked down at The Witching Hour expansion box and spied the tall, gaunt features of the creature painted on the front of the box. A slight pinch of jealousy caused Tyler to wince. He'd wanted to be the first.

"Wait, how did you become a Nether Creature already?"

"I was resurrected in the darkness."

"How?"

"By my resurrection, of course."

"No, that's not what I mean. The expansion doesn't go live for another hour. How did you pull that off?"

"Jared's online." Again, Darren ignored the question.

"What?"

"He's online. I'm sure he's already made it halfway across the Plains, but I fear he's too weak, not devoted enough to the cause, unlike yourself."

"How? I don't see his name." Tyler scrolled through the clan list. Sure enough, Jared's name popped up. "I knew it. Hey, Jared." Tyler half-yelled into the microphone, only to see a cross icon next to Jared's name. Jared had muted him. "Son of a bitch."

"You're going to need more powerful magic if you intend to succeed tonight."

"Like what?" He made a mental note to yell at Jared the next time he saw him.

"Blood magic."

"Blood magic? But I'm not a high enough level."

"Not if you are willing to sacrifice…"

"Sacrifice? Like what?"

"Your loved ones. Those who you cherish the most will be able to give you blood magic."

"Dude, you're sounding weird."

"Then you won't be necessary. We won't go."

"No, no, no. I want to go!"

"Then maybe we could start with Jared? If we catch up to him, perhaps, we can sacrifice him?"

"Are you serious?" Tyler crossed his arms, thinking of the proposition. "He's going to be pissed if I loot his character."

"It's the only way to be granted blood magic and open the portal."

"Sure, whatever, fine. He'll just respawn."

"Oh, no, this is quite permanent." Darren laughed. "They can't come back from this. No one will."

"You know…whatever. I hate the fact that he's a thief, always sneaking around in the shadows, while we do all the work. Maybe he can come back as a new race with the expansion. It's a weird night anyway, with what happened to Dawson and all."

"Yes, he was indeed the first to cross over, the first to realize the sacrifice."

"Whatever you say, boss," Tyler answered, dismissing Darren's ramblings as par for the course.

***

With the help of Darren's Nether Creature, the two advanced farther across the Midnight Plains than their entire party had throughout the entire week, slicing through barbarians and two villages Tyler had never encountered before. He had to admit, the graphics were phenomenal, almost lifelike, and the towns were eerily familiar.

He made sure his Osorno demon drank enough blood to prepare for whatever blood magic Darren talked about during their journey, which was in itself weird.

Darren proved a fount of knowledge about Dawson, even

down to knowing Dawson's graduation year. Through the flurry of mouse-clicks and manufactured computer screams, Darren sounded like a zealot of Dawson, praising the video game creator's efforts to open up a new way of thinking through the Netherlands. He claimed it would help humans "evolve" into a greater species—and opening the "portals" through the game, would usher in a new era for humankind.

Tyler dismissed the monotone explanation as nonsense, too intent on watching his Osorno demon gain strength as the two sacked the next human town, killing off most of its inhabitants. He was engrossed with the new towns, his attention pulling away from the computer screen only when the lightning storm outside flashed again, or the wind howled, snapping a tree branch outside his bedroom window.

They climbed a hill where a pulsating red portal extended across the horizon and throughout the forlorn landscape, revealing a foreign land that Tyler did not know. Other players gathered to their left and right, waiting for The Witching Hour's grand reveal.

"We're here," Darren said, his tone slightly escalated, as if he'd run down the stairs on Christmas morning.

"We are?" Tyler rubbed his eyes clear of sleep and looked over at his smartphone. 3:00 a.m. *How is it already three o'clock? Where's Mom and Dad?* He chugged his second energy drink of the night, wondering why it wasn't working.

"It's open...It's time." Darren's Nether Creature extended its branch-like arm toward the foot of the hill, where a gathering of stone homes flickered with candlelight.

"That's right!" Tyler shouted, remembering the 3 o'clock launch. His parents' whereabouts and his need for sleep were suddenly a distant memory.

The streetlight outside Tyler's window sparked with a flash of electricity, and then faded to black, sending their entire cul-de-sac into total darkness. One by one, his neighbor's homes mirrored the streetlamp's fate, until the entire street was eclipsed by the Halloween night.

With a click and sputter, the rumble of an engine vibrated to life across from Tyler's house. Fortunately they had a generator. There would be no loss of power once he fired it up.

A smile of satisfaction crept across his face, knowing that all of his friends at school would be far behind in the expansion because of the power outage.

"Are you prepared?" Darren's robotic voice asked.

"You're damned straight I am."

"We need to find Tyler's thief. He's hiding in the town somewhere." Darren's character started down the hill, where some of the stone houses went dark.

"Wait...wait..." a hint of uncertainty crept into Tyler's voice.

"What is it!?" Darren growled.

"Are you sure we have to kill him, I mean his character? He's worked pretty hard for it. He's at Level 26, you know."

"Then you are unwilling? What fun would that be?"

"I mean, can I still become a Nether Beast?"

"Not without sacrifice. Dawson would have it so."

"Dawson..." Tyler muttered. "Ok. Sure. Fine. He already said he doesn't need that annoying thief. Maybe he'll create a better character next time."

"Good, then follow me." Darren's Nether Beast took off like a hyena, bounding down the side of the hill, along with the other eager characters who'd ventured across the Midnight Plains, their reward to be the first to explore the heralded Witching Hour expansion.

The demon horde spread throughout the dirt roads of the unnamed town, overpowering the wayward humans who'd found themselves a target of evil's onslaught. They, too, would become Nether Beasts—at least according to Darren, because of their sacrifices.

"Down, this way!" Darren instructed, flying through an alleyway that led to another part of town the other characters had yet to plunder. Again, the layout seemed somewhat familiar, but at 3:00 a.m. Tyler's imagination had grown wild. "Tyler should be in there." Darren's beast pointed toward the house at the end of the dirt road. "How had he'd gotten to this part?

Never mind..."

The two characters approached the wooden doorway where the sounds of footsteps echoed through the computer's speakers. Tyler was indeed inside. *Maybe I should call and tease him?* Tyler laughed to himself. *Get him back for spilling popcorn and calling me obsessed.*

"Are you prepared?" Darren asked, his Nether Beast backing away from the door. "It should be locked. Use the blood magic I gave you to open it."

"I can't believe he signed on without telling me. Prick."

"He is. The human deserves this," Darren prompted.

"Whatever. Watch this. Used this when we finished off that one Viking guy." With a click of the cursor, Tyler summoned his newly acquired blood magic fireball. He savored the aftermath of the spell, as it blew apart the door to the hideout, exposing Jared's leather armor-clad thief.

"You will be rewarded for this," Darren said.

"I'd tell you sorry if you didn't have me on mute!" Tyler yelled. His entire body tingled as he clicked over the spell's golden icon once more, casting a crimson ball of light from the Osorno demon's ebony claws, toward Jared's thief. In an instant, blood red flames engulfed the character.

Somewhere in the distance, Tyler thought he heard a scream.

"Nice effects." Tyler smiled, watching Jared's thief stumble backward, his digital skin charred from the attack. And just like that, the mute icon next to Jared's name clicked off.

"Ty...Ty...stop it! Stop it!" Jared half-yelled, half-cried, causing Tyler's eardrums to explode through the headset. Tyler tore it off and threw it down, rubbing at his ringing ears.

"Damn it!" Now he had a reason to kill him.

"Evolve!" Darren commanded.

Regrouping, Tyler moved his cursor back over the blood magic fireball, ready to finish the job. And he did.

With a flash of light, Jared's character flew against the wall and collapsed into a pile of smoking flesh. Tyler pumped his fists in the air as a sign of victory, knowing he would be rewarded for his efforts.

Another, more desperate scream, bellowed out of the computer speakers as Jared announced his defeat. Again, the sound effects made it all seem too real. Tyler knew Dawson, regardless of his personal tastes, he'd created a winner with the expansion.

"Excellent," Darren said, accentuated by a crack of lightning outside. "We are almost ready."

"Almost? What are you talking about?" The sound of the generator's engine sputtered, then stopped. Light faded to darkness inside the house, except for the computer screen, which remained powered on...somehow. "What the—?"

Tyler jumped out of his chair and looked around. The walls of his bedroom seemed a little closer, his ceiling a little lower. Then he noticed the recognizable silhouettes of his demon army. Or lack thereof.

"I suggest you sit down," Darren instructed from the computer speakers, overtaking Jared's last screams, even though Tyler's headsets remained on the ground.

"What?"

"You must complete the last part of the ritual so we can evolve."

"What are you talking about?" Tyler swallowed hard. Something was off. Something was *very* off.

"You agreed to the sacrifice!" Darren shouted. It is needed to move Master Dawson's vision forward."

"*Vision?* What—no. You've lost your mind."

"No, I've quite moved on from my mind."

"You know, I'm going to find out just what's going on." Tyler didn't hesitate. His trembling hand grabbed for his smartphone to call and apologize to Jared. But before he could press the buttons on the screen, he saw his parents' names glowing there. There'd been *six* missed calls from them in the past two hours.

How hadn't he seen this? He scrolled down until he found Jared's name.

Two rings became four, and then four turned into Jared's stupid recorded voice message.

"Come on." Tyler paced across the floor.

"He won't answer…" Darren said. "Now turn your attention back to the computer where it belongs. You have one last sacrifice to make before you can evolve."

"No!" Tyler exhaled, watching his breath frost in the chilled air of the room. He noticed the steady rumble of lightning outside had stopped—replaced by a sickening silence.

He tried to look outside, but a thin film of frost etched like spider webs across the windowpane, blocking his view.

"What's happening?" His heart thumped heavily against his chest, as he tried to open the window.

"If you don't fulfill your promise, a different sacrifice will be required," Darren said. He won't wait forever. You are either part of this or not."

"Who won't?" Tyler groaned, as he pulled on the window, his muscles engorging with lactic acid.

"Dawson," Darren said.

"This is bullshit!" With one final tug, the window flew open, welcoming in a steady breeze of the coldest air Tyler had felt since last winter.

Poking his head through the open window frame, out into the chilled October night, he hoped he wouldn't empty his stomach. A frozen landscape reminiscent of late December welcomed him. It was a far cry from the muggy air from just a few hours ago. In the distance, he thought he saw the makings of a blood red horizon.

"He'll give you one more opportunity," Darren said. "And then he will have your avatar take matters into its own hands."

"And then what?" Tyler ducked back inside and looked over at his computer screen. His character, along with Darren's Nether Beast, stare in his direction.

"I suggest you finish the ritual, Tyler," Darren said, his words not merely a suggestion, but a command.

"This…this isn't right." Tyler focused back outside, where the sound of heavy footfalls reverberated from the opposite side of the street. They were followed by a shadow that seemed to grow along the frosted grass, before fading to nothing. Then, he heard the *unknown's* growl. It was the same growl he'd heard when he pressed the F4 key with his Osorno demon. "Shit!"

"Sit back down, or know that he will find you. The portal is open. Fulfill your obligation!"

"No! I'm not fulfilling anything."

Tyler darted for the door, and then stumbled out into the hallway. He attempted to fill his lungs, cursing his lack of physical activity as he turned the corner into the foyer.

"Dad!" Tyler shouted when he spotted the silhouette of a horn against the front door's window. He was never more excited to call out for his father, or to see the ridiculous outline of his Viking costume. The doorknob, cold and covered with a half-frozen film, slipped in his palm at first, before he managed to turn it and pull back, revealing the ominous figure.

"No!" Tyler backpedaled into his mom's decorative side table, spilling its contents, including pictures of their family, onto the floor. His eyes grew wide as he swallowed hard.

The beast's onyx skin was as black as the sky itself. Blacker than any of Dawson's pixels in Netherlands. The Osorno demon's muscular figure enveloped the front doorway, its crimson eyes casting an ominous, iridescent glow along the wooden floor. The beast's chest expanded, then contracted, its terrible purpose suddenly cast upon Tyler.

"Help!" Tyler screamed, scrambling to his feet, as he let his instincts take over. He ran toward the kitchen, and out the back sliding glass door.

The night air was crisp and captured in silence, biting at his exposed skin. Frost covered the reds and browns of the late autumn leaves. Frozen blades of grass glistened in what little light the moon provided. With each stride, he felt the ground beneath his feat crunch. He knew he was alone, but didn't want to accept it.

As he rounded the front of the cul-de-sac, his attention was pulled to the road, where he saw the silver outline of his parent's SUV.

"Dad!" he cried through shallow breaths, glancing over his shoulder to see Muerte's hulking shadow prowling around the outside of his home.

Has to be my mind, Tyler thought.

He pushed past the pain, past his stunted breaths, and ran toward his parent's parked vehicle.

"Dad!" Tyler barely got the word out of his mouth, as he approached the driver's side door. In the distance, a distinct holler—blood-curdling and desperate—followed the screeching of brakes and the crunch of metal.

"Dad! Mom!" Tyler slapped frantically at the SUV's side window. Inside the car, his father's Viking helmet fell forward, onto his face. And his mother, on the opposite side of the car, slumped against the moonlit dashboard.

Neither of them responded.

"Please, please, open the door. Open the door!" Tyler begged, his tears cold against his cheeks. His parents remained silent. The thin film of frost covering the windows made them both look statuesque.

Then something shifted further down the cul-de-sac. Muerte's wild eyes lit up fiery red, focusing on Tyler. Feeling the thing's presence closing in upon him, Tyler ran around the back of the SUV, and saw that the rear hatch had been decimated. Glass shards scattered across the pavement, crunching beneath his tennis shoes. The entire back of the SUV looked like an enormous party favor, but instead of colorful streamers fluttering into the wind, shredded ribbons of metal exploding outward, as if something big had tried to escape its confines.

"No!" Tyler gasped, transfixed on his parents' silhouettes in the front seats. His imagination seized him, with visions of the Osorno demon extinguishing the flames of his parents. They were both gone. "Mom…? Dad…?"

The red sky vibrated with electricity again—a horrid energy that seemed to cast the world around him into a terrible stillness.

"What did I do?" Tyler backed away, closing his eyes, hoping it was just one of his horrible childhood nightmares. He felt the beast closer now—its unrelenting purpose of blood magic immanent—as it swiftly approached from his home.

"No…" Tyler, still taking in heavy breaths, abandoned his parents and continued his escape, sprinting as fast as he'd ever sprinted before, wondering where he would go. Tyler rounded the corner onto Lake Maple Street, where the corner signpost had been cast to the ground in a contorted mess.

He kept going...

Up ahead, Ms. Lorraine's monolithic house remained quiet, like the other homes along the powerless street. Its windows reflected candlelight, keeping the darkness at bay. There would be no refuge there, either, he knew, noticing the white BMW parked diagonal across the usually immaculately groomed front lawn, its hood folded upward like an accordion against the cherry tree, the front door of the car wide open with a motionless body spilling out.

Tyler recognized the damned Ravens' jersey, the same one Nick wore every Friday at school to show his "team spirit." The jackass was wearing an appropriate Halloween costume—the last one he'd ever wear.

Nick's listless body didn't move, and Tyler wasn't about to stop to check on him.

Shit...shit...shit, he thought. His knees throbbed. His chest constricted, begging for oxygen.

"Help! Help!" A voice called from the house's second floor. Tyler wanted to ignore it, before looking up and spotting Shawn waving his arms out like a maniac from his bedroom window. "They're gone! They're all gone..."

"What?" Tyler looked behind him, seeing the Osorno's shadow growing closer.

"I'm trapped. I don't know if it's going to come back," Shawn cried.

"I...I can't." Tyler couldn't stay, not with the demon trailing him.

Woodberry Lane.

Tyler nearly toppled forward, as momentum carried him through his turn, spying Jared's house, dark as well, up ahead.

Something suddenly broke the silence. A guttural roar emanated from every direction, bounding down every street, echoing forth from every house.

Warmth spread throughout his crotch, drenching his gym

shorts.

Tyler stumbled across Jared's lawn, his lungs nearly empty. He bent over, sucking in air, his arms shaking as he braced himself against his knees. He didn't want to look up at the impossible scene all around him.

The earthy smell of burnt grass and timber clung to the back of his nostrils, as he was bathed in the tainted air around him. Splintered pieces of painted wood covered Jared's porch, its frame charred with soot. It looked like a damned missile had hit the front door—but he knew it was no missile. He remembered the blood magic fireball that he himself had thrown. He remembered the massacre that followed, at the urging of Darren.

"Why?" Tyler whimpered.

He didn't want to explore the house. He didn't want to see his best friend, a friend he'd played t-ball with, a friend he'd explored imaginary dungeons and killed fairytale dragons with. A friend he stayed up late on Saturday nights eating pizza with, talking about their future plans as video game designers.

He had no other choice, though. He needed to know.

The remnants of the front door grinded along the hallway, as he set off toward Jared's bedroom. The room's entrance had suffered the same fate as the front door—a door torn from its hinges, a white light flashing against the unmade bed.

Looking inside, he saw his friend's lifeless body sprawled across the floor, still smoking and barely recognizable.

"Jared?" Tyler's voice cracked as visions of his Osorno demon burned Jared's thief from Netherlands into his mind.

Sacrifice?

Another growl. Closer. Stronger.

"Sacrifice…" The word squeaked out of him. Could this really be happening? Could he have really killed his friend though the game they both loved so much?

The closer he inched forward, the more the smell turned from firewood to something more pungent—far more taboo.

He looked down to see Jared's familiar freckled skin blistered and blackened. His eyes were two craters devoid of a soul. His computer headphone had melted onto his skull.

"Jared!" Tyler screamed before vomiting onto the carpet. "I'm…so sorry." He began sobbing, covering his face in horror.

"The time has come," a familiar voice called out to him. It was sinister but purposeful in its command. "To those who will join," Darren's voice said, "I applaud you."

Tyler looked up, still hiding behind the curtain of his fingers, opening just enough to see Jared's computer screen spring to life, the man broadcasting through it. It wasn't Darren, but rather Dawson. His face appeared distorted, seemingly covered by some sort of dark matter.

A wide grin—almost too wide to be human—painted his face. "Do not worry. Our coven shall hold total power by sunrise," Dawson said, flanked by cinderblock walls and iron bars, meant to cage a human to his right, a body dressed in a blue uniform by his feet.

Two heavy footfalls, followed by labored breathing, rebounded down the scorched halls of the game. The Osorno demon had found him.

"It's been too long. Way too long for us. We've been scorned since Salem, our kind punished for our beliefs." Dawson paced his computerized cell, not bothering to look at the "camera," if one even existed. "You have all made sacrifices for our purpose, as The Witching Hour is now upon us all. You have harnessed the power of sloth through this digital world that I have created. We have evolved."

Hypnotized by Dawson's words, Tyler heard two more footfalls reverberate behind him, as the presence of Muerte weighed in upon him.

The video game creator stopped speaking, then continued on.

"I ask you for one more sacrifice before this night is over… for they will all know not to mock us any longer. You each have a *familiar*, a creature you've been cultivating for some time through Netherlands."

The doorframe cracked loudly behind Tyler as the Osorno beast's body busted through the doorframe. Tyler didn't move. He *couldn't*.

"You must feed it more blood tonight, more during our festival of Samhain. But be warned, these creatures will only obey as long as you feed them—with the blood of those who have humiliated us. Do not cross them. They are fickle and need only to feed. You have until sunrise..." With that, Dawson's voice faded to nothing.

Fear almost having escaped him altogether, Tyler slowly lifted his head. The Osorno demon made no motion forward, but rather remained next to him, standing sentry, awaiting a command, as a dog would from its master.

"Finally—" Tyler whispered, thinking of Shawn waving desperately out of the second floor window of Mrs. Lorraine's house.

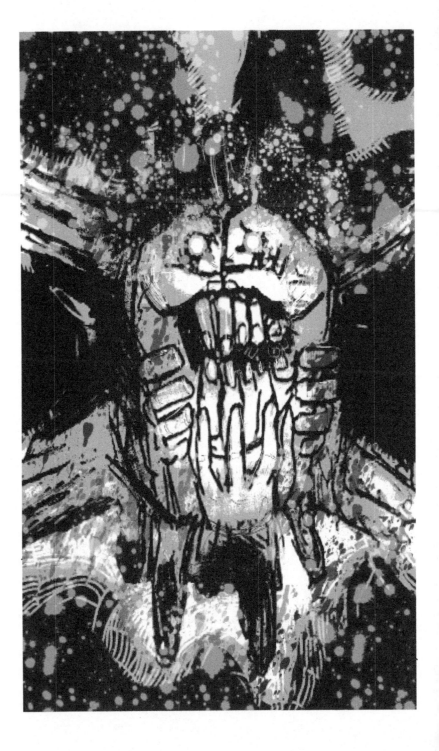

THE MANY HANDS INSIDE THE MOUNTAIN

James Chambers

Whatever guilt Zach Reynolds felt as Tamara Porter's warm, naked flesh slid against his disintegrated when he opened his eyes to his ramshackle bedroom. Tamara kissed and caressed all his cautions away, but his dingy room behind the auto garage left him by his father reminded him of what justified all they did behind Katrina Van Bollin's back. Grasping Tamara's waist, he pulled her heat tight to his, and released his body to the rhythms of pleasure. Neither spoke. The time for talk lay well behind them, and after this last secret tryst, each would have their heart's deepest desire.

Later, sweat drying on their skin and the setting sun impelling golden bars through the blinds, Zach slid from the sheets and assembled his Halloween costume. Tamara followed suit with a sigh, pausing with her shimmering, translucent gown around her waist to pepper kisses down Zach's bare back. Then, dressed and ready, Zach saw her to the door and shut it without looking back.

Outside, the two shared a lingering, last kiss, ended with reluctance.

"Tell Cord not to foul this up," Zach said.

Rolling her eyes, Tamara said, "Cord will do what I tell him. You do your part."

"You can count on me."

"I know." Tamara slid one hand down Zach's back to his

butt and pressed him against her. "You could still come with me."

"I'm pretty sure Cord would have a problem with that."

Tamara snorted. "I can dump Cord here, or when I get to New York City. No difference to me, especially if I get you in the bargain."

"Nah. I owe this town too much, and I'd like to own it one day."

"You think too small."

"That's the first time you ever accused me of being small."

Tamara laughed, slapped Zach's rear, and then pushed him away.

"Suit yourself. Is Bollin's Creek the only thing you love?"

Zach blushed.

"You're *really* in love with Kat?"

"It's not her fault who her father is."

"Promise me you won't have a change of heart before we do this."

"Kat had nothing to do with what Arthur Van Bollin did to my father, but she and I can't have a life until I settle scores with him. Do it how we said, everyone gets what they want."

"Mostly." Tamara ran a fingertip down the side of Zach's neck. "Have a nice life with that fancy bitch and her ice queen aunt. Maybe I'll send you a postcard from the city."

Zach watched Tamara walk away in her opalescent faerie gown. Silk and cellophane wings bobbed on her back. Where the path through his oil-stained yard hooked right out the gate, she looked back and blew him a kiss. Her smell still lingered in his nostrils, her taste on his tongue. A high price, losing her, but he deemed it fair trade for obtaining what he'd longed for since third grade. For half a heartbeat he considered accepting her offer to shuck his past and all its burdens in exchange for a fresh start far away. But he *did* love Bollin's Creek. After Arthur Van Bollin ruined his father's business and drove him to suicide, the people here took care of Zach like one of their own children. They fed and clothed him and hired him to repair their cars when he reopened his father's garage. He owed them, and breaking the

Van Bollin's hold over the town and its people would settle the debt.

No one knew exactly how the Van Bollin family earned their money, but nor did anyone object to them spending a fair chunk of it on the annual Bollin's Creek Halloween Masquerade Festival. A town tradition dating back to the Depression, Zach had joined in the party as long as he could remember, starting with the children's Trick-or-Treat March before graduating to the Haunted Horse and Buggy rides through the graveyard, then moving on to the Corpse and Corn Maze, and the bonfire behind the high school football field.

Now, only a few years out of school, he'd devised his best costume ever and been invited to the Festival's exclusive last hurrah at the Van Bollin house—the Midnight Masque. Hell or high water, he intended to make it a night to remember. Katrina Van Bollin deserved no less.

Her father deserved no better.

* * *

"Oh my god, Zach, it's brilliant!"

Katrina squealed as she grabbed his shoulders and planted a kiss on his lips, tickling them with the tip of her tongue. She stepped back for a better view of his costume, which consisted of a navy blue silk shirt bought from the consignment shop and a breastplate hammered from sheet metal scrap and painted with a unicorn head sigil. Snug, black pants and battered, leather boots completed the overall look, to which he'd added a low-slung belt strapped with a short sword at his left hip, and a blaster at his right—the prop weapons fashioned from odds and ends around his shop. On his sleeves he'd sewn gold bands of his rank as Prince Vinn Northstar, Commander of the Algernon Rift Fleet, meticulously designed from descriptions in Katrina's favorite series of fantasy novels, *The Northstar Saga*. His touch of genius, though, lay in his shirt's collar, which projected color sequences onto his face and torso. Reflected by the polished breastplate, they created a cloud of light that mimicked the personal auras essential to the saga's characters.

"How'd you do the aura?" Katrina said.

"Tiny lights sewed into my collar, controlled with an app on my phone."

"I *love* it! Promise you'll do one for me next year, okay? We can go as the King and Queen of House Northstar with the brightest, most perfect auras."

"You bet."

Katrina spun to show off her red-and-black gown, slits rising to her waist, accentuating her long, lithe legs. A ring mail shawl draped across her shoulders hid much of what the gown's plunging neckline revealed yet exposed a temporary tattoo centered below her breasts, a thorny vine twined into a heart shape topped with a black rose.

"What do you think?" she said.

"Absolutely stunning," Zach said. "Lady Asanander, right? Aren't she and Prince Vinn enemies?"

Katrina replied with a salacious grin. "You haven't read book four yet."

"Maybe I should jump ahead."

Katrina laughed then pulled Zach by the hand. "Come on! See the costumes. Everyone looks wonderful. This will be the best Halloween ever."

She led him through the house, every room decorated. The parlor resembled an enchanted woodland, the den a spaceship command bridge, the dining room a tableau of grinning corpses set to feast. Clever wall hangings and projected light transformed the halls into torch-lit tunnels. In the kitchen, cooks and waiters in skimpy, gothic outfits worked among black-and-white tiles with serving dishes smeared with faux blood. Zach had grown up like everyone in town listening to rumors of the Midnight Masque's excesses but the rumors fell far short of the reality.

They stepped out onto the back veranda, overlooking a yard where the party's heart beat to a four-piece band playing on a skull-shaped stage surrounded by a dancing crowd. Guitars, drums, and voices filled the air with a rockabilly cover of "The Monster Mash." Tables alongside offered heaps of food lit by candelabrum draped with cobwebs, and at each corner, bartenders in skin-tight, black-and-white skeleton suits served drinks from behind gravestone bars. Candles, bonfire barrels, and wrought-iron braziers provided the only light. Beyond that, stars glimmered above the dead-black peaks of the Nasquaiga Mountains. The partygoers all wore masks, some integral to their costume, others ornate leather sculptures tied on with decorative silks.

Katrina handed such a mask to Zach, House Northstar blue and gold, the eyeholes cut in the peculiar, trapezoidal shape of the Northstar race.

"Daddy insists."

Zach let Katrina tie the ribbons around his head and then he did the same for her, a blood-red mask with cat's-eye tips.

"You're supposed to put it on before you come, but I wanted you to see me," Katrina whispered. "I hated the idea of you dancing with other girls all night trying to find me. Go fetch us drinks. I'll tell Daddy you're here."

Katrina hurried off and submerged into the crowd.

Zach worked his way to the nearest bar, where he discovered the bartender wore body paint, not a skin-tight suit. Goosebumps rippled her flesh, and he pitied her working in the chill night, but if the cold or her nakedness gave her any serious discomfort, he saw no sign of it. He ordered a pumpkin spice beer and a glass of Malbec for Katrina then crowd-watched while he waited for her to return.

A text from Tamara buzzed his phone: *We're here.*

Setting down the drinks, he texted back: *Don't c u.*

U will.

He glanced around for Tamara's faerie outfit amidst a living collage of pirates, wizards, football players, werewolves, nurses, and super-heroes.

Cord's a gladiator. Rog and Kevin took the pickup up the service road. Everything's set.

All good here.

U sure u don't want to come with?

I'm sure.

Ur loss. U really love her that much?

I do.
More than me?
I never loved you.
Jerk.

Before Zach could reply, Katrina gripped his arm. Startled, he tried to shove his phone into his pocket, but his blaster blocked it. Katrina turned him to face a burly man in a tuxedo of forest green and a porcelain jack-o'-lantern mask engraved with scrolls of fine, archaic writing, secured by flame-colored ribbons.

"I'm truly happy to see you here, son," Arthur Van Bollin said.

Shaking the man's hand, Zach nodded. "I'm honored you'd have me. Everyone in town dreams of getting an invitation here."

"People here and pretty much anywhere else they've heard of our Festival. Folks come from all over these days. The Festival has become quite the tourist attraction. Good for business, good for the town. Lots of money coming in. The bad old days are far behind us. Of course, no tourists ever score invitations to the Midnight Masque. Can't have that. This is only for those of us who call the mountains home. You should see the emails we get, begging and pleading. Make no mistake, Zach, you're right to be honored, but the invitation is only icing on the cake. The true honor is you'll be family soon. Family outshines everything. We don't bring young men into the Bollin fold idly. But you make Katrina happy. I know I could ever fill your father's shoes, of course, but I hope I can fill an empty part of your life."

Zach swallowed then stammered, "My father…" but only angry words and accusations came to mind, so he held his tongue.

"He'd be proud of how you've made his business a success. A less stubborn man might be here celebrating with you, I suppose. I hear folks come up all the way from Albany for your custom car services. That true?"

"Bollin's Creek is so out of the way, those customers are few and far between. I do a lot more oil changes and brake jobs to pay the bills."

"Why not take your talent elsewhere? Get yourself a reality

TV show. I've seen that Jeep you made over like a *Star Wars* fighter ship for Force Insurance in Hackett. It's good enough for the bigtime."

"Leave Bollin's Creek? No, doesn't feel right."

The changeless expression of Van Bollin's pumpkin mask rattled Zach; he couldn't tell if Katrina's father smiled or sneered behind it. "Wise words. And, believe me, we'll be glad to put your creativity and skills to work for the Halloween Festival. Here, let me snap a picture of you and Kat."

Zach's heart jumped as Van Bollin took the phone from his hand, and Katrina sidled in close to him. Every last drop of moisture in his throat dried up. He prayed the text window had closed. Then the camera flash blinded him while Katrina rubbed the back of his neck, and her father returned his phone.

"You kids have fun. I've got people to entertain. See you at midnight for the unmasking."

"Daddy likes you a lot," Katrina said.

She sipped her wine, while Zach downed half his beer to soothe his dry throat.

"Guess I'm lucky," he said.

"We make our own luck. I see how much you love this town. You'll fit in perfectly with our family. You'll hardly remember all the years you spent without one."

Zach withdrew from Katrina, too reflexively to stop himself.

"I'm sorry," she said. "What a dumb thing for me to say."

"Forget it."

"No. Growing up alone is part of what made you the man I love. So is what happened between our fathers. I don't want to ever forget that, but I want you to be happy with us."

Finishing off his beer, Zach tossed the bottle into a recycling bin and took Katrina's hand.

"I can't imagine why I wouldn't be," he said, pulling her toward the music.

They eased through the crowd, close to the band, now rocking through Screaming Lord Sutch's "Jack the Ripper," and they danced.

* * *

As the night grew long, Zach spied Tamara in her iridescent gown, always with Cord in tow, and she ignoring the lascivious looks men cast her way when the light caught her right and gave glimpses of her body within her wispy costume. She ignored Zach, even when they passed close on the dancefloor, and her indifference chilled him. She had planned tonight for more than two years, from before she and Zach ever spoke, before she introduced him to Katrina, maybe even longer.

The band finished off Michael Jackson's "Thriller" then announced a short break.

Katrina seized Tamara in a manic hug. Zach caught up and gave Cord a nod.

"Can you believe we're all here together?" Katrina said.

"It's like a dream come true," said Tamara.

Katrina pulled Zach to her side.

"Cord, take a picture of me with my best friend and my fiancé."

Cord dug out his phone and snapped a shot.

"Take one with mine," Tamara said, digging into the folds of her dress.

Katrina play-swatted her arm. "Forget it. Cord can send it to all of us, right, Cord?"

"You bet," said Cord as he hit send. He put his arm around Zach's shoulders. "Hey, amigo, let's grab a fresh round."

They walked to the nearest bar and ordered. While the bartender poured, Cord leaned in close and said, "You better be ready, Reynolds. That pussy costume of yours doesn't give me a lot of confidence. A fucking unicorn? That's some *My Little Pony* shit."

"Kiss my ass, Cord. We wouldn't even be here if not for me."

"If not for Tamara, you mean."

Zach put his hands around two drinks, but Cord squeezed his wrist, hard.

"As long as it plays out how Tam said, everything will go

fine."

Cord squeezed harder.

"I mean it, Reynolds. Kat's told Tam stories about this since her first sleepover here in the second grade. No one outside the Van Bollin family knows more about the mountain vault or the Many Hands inside the Mountain."

"You really believe they killed the men who built the vault then slaughtered and buried them up there to keep the secret?"

"Why not? The family goes up there once a year to pay homage or some bullshit. This year, we're going too. We got one shot at this so when Rog and Kevin arrive you do your part. Understand?"

"Fuck off. This isn't high school," Zach said. "I'll convince Van Bollin to go along about the vault. *You* make sure whatever you do to him looks like an accident so I don't catch any blame. And *don't* hurt Katrina, or I promise I'll rip you in two."

Cord snorted. "Like you could take me."

Zach held his gaze steady on Cord's eyes until the flicker of doubt he desired appeared. "You really got a thing for Katrina, huh. How sweet. Hasn't stopped you from boning Tamara behind my back, but sweet. Yeah, I know all about you two—and I don't care. She's using you, she's using me, she's using Kat, and I'm using her, and so are you. We're all using each other, because that's just how things get done, ain't it?"

Cord took his and Tamara's drinks.

Zach watched him shoulder a path through the crowd. His phone pinged. The picture from Cord popped up onscreen, Zach between two smiling women dressed like things that didn't exist.

He downed a long swallow of beer then rejoined the party.

* * *

The effigy heralded the unmasking.

Part piñata, part balloon, part latex foam, it stood twenty feet high, swaying like a parade float, all flowers, crepe paper, and colored streamers. At midnight, servants in orange and black robes wheeled it out from the woods on a rolling platform. The crowd fell silent. All eyes turned to the towering figure, which featured an exaggerated phallus and prominent breasts. An almond-shaped orifice tapered from its cleavage to its waist, sealed with a translucent membrane bulging with piles of jewelry, watches, gold and silver chains, boxes wrapped in orange foil, bags of gold coins, and even rubber-banded stacks of cash. A massive jack-o'-lantern, etched with obscure writing, like Van Bollin's mask, bobbed on its shoulders. Fires flickered in its eyes and mouth, streaming aromatic smoke.

The party staff cleared the skull stage and the party debris, damping the candles and braziers, leaving only the bonfire barrels lit. Their black body paint blending into the dark and their white bones reddened by the firelight, the bartenders passed out sticks, each about six feet long and tipped with an iron bulb. Workers hurried a five-foot-high platform with stairs on either side in front of the effigy. When preparations ceased, for a moment the night existed only as wind, shadows, fire, and the crowd's collective, withheld breath.

Van Bollin ascended the platform and raised his arms.

"Thank you for celebrating this special time with us!" His voice resonated from behind his mask. "Your presence means a great deal to my family, but more importantly, to Bollin's Creek. We have a wonderful town here. May it never change, and our traditions keep us forever prosperous. Tonight we share the wealth!"

The crowd applauded. Van Bollin waved them quiet.

"Soon, we'll play that special music we hear but once a year, on this very evening. When the first notes sound, all who wish to may don a blindfold, and take three swings." Van Bollin gestured to the effigy. "Three strikes only. The first to break the seal gets pick of prizes. When all are taken and the music ends, we'll light this on fire and the unmasking will commence. If no one breaks the seal before the music stops, all this treasure goes up in smoke. Remember to kiss the person next to you when you remove your mask. If it's not your boyfriend, your girlfriend, your wife, or your husband—well, I hope they're the understanding type."

An outburst of laughter and applause covered his descent.

Hidden speakers played organ music, dolorous and low, a pulsing rhythm for a melody of reedy pipes and discordant strings. The tempo lumbered. The notes wove a hypnotic sound web as the partyers lined up. The effigy's membrane vibrated to the music. A woman in a black cat-suit tried first, blindfolded, spun three times, and ushered up the steps by a robed servant. She hit the figure's arm, leg, and phallus, which shook up and down, eliciting laughter, but missed the membrane with all three swings. Loose bits of paper, flowers, and embers showered down. Next, a man in a knight's costume tried, and a Mad Hatter waited his turn, along with dozens of others. Kristina took Zach's arm.

"Time to go," she said.

They slipped away, scooping Tamara and Cord out of the crowd, then joining Van Bollin on the edge of the woods.

"Everyone here? Good," he said. "Let's go."

They walked a gravel path among the trees. While the voices from the party faded, the music traveled along, replaying itself in Zach's mind. The gravel glowed faintly, especially when Zach looked at it sidewise. Eventually, the path ended at a hard-packed dirt road and a Jeep.

"Get in!" said Van Bollin. "Zach, sit up front with me."

Katrina climbed in the back with Tamara and Cord. The engine growled. Van Bollin hit the gas. The Jeep shuddered then rolled into the night. Its headlights revealed the service road up the nearest of the Nasquaiga Mountains, then reduced the woods to a shadowy blur as the vehicle accelerated. A sharp turn sent them up a steep incline. The lights in Zach's collar played across the dashboard. After a time, when the ground leveled again, the mountain range lay splayed out in every direction beneath stars twinkling high in a cloudless sky. On each peak, a pillar of flame burned, overlooking the valley behind the Van Bollin land.

"What is all this?" Zach asked.

"We aren't the only ones who celebrate tonight," said Van Bollin.

The Jeep lurched as it renewed its ascent.

Bonfires came in and out of view on the far peaks. Shadowy figures passed in front of them, some dancing, others jumping, some playing with what Zach took for dogs. He swiveled to check Katrina and spotted headlights lurching far down the rough service road, sticking steady behind them. Soon the Jeep stopped in a clearing at the base of a sheer rock face. With child-like excitement, Van Bollin dashed out and lifted a branch with rags coiled around one end. He took a lighter from his pocket, touched fire to cloth, and the rags erupted in flames.

Zach and the others exited the Jeep. The aroma of kerosene lingered in the air,

Van Bollin lit the wood pile with his torch. An abrupt conflagration swallowed the logs and boards. The night chill fled and heat licked at their faces. Van Bollin mounted his torch in an iron brace on a tree beside a stone ring, eight feet in diameter and two-feet high, surrounding a pool of utter darkness. He glanced over the low wall.

"What's in there?" Zach said.

Katrina touched his lip. "Ssshhh."

Van Bollin dragged a footlocker from the brush, opened it, and pulled out gear. Soon the dreary music for the effigy played on a portable speaker linked to his iPhone. He dropped two bulging burlap sacks from the chest at Zach's feet, then handed him a leather case the size of a book.

He winked. "Don't open that yet."

"Katrina, what's going on?" Zach said.

Ignoring him, Katrina tapped on her phone. Zach's pocket buzzed. He checked his alerts and found a text from Tamara's number.

Ur not really a jerk. I love u 2.

Zach stared at empty-handed Tamara, but Katrina waved a phone, sheathed in Tamara's familiar pink, leather case. She keyed in a new message. Zach's phone vibrated, another text from Tamara's number.

Trick or Treat!

"Why does Katrina have your phone, Tam?" Zach said.

"What are you talking about? My phone's right here." Tamara reached into her pocket. Her face crinkled with surprise then worry. "Where the hell did it go?"

Katrina giggled.

An engine's low grumble echoed from the valley. Zach scanned the mountains, the fires too distant for him to see much besides the ecstatic shapes gathered by them. The crunch of dirt and rocks beneath tires joined the engine noise. Brightness sprang from the road as Rog's pickup truck jolted to the edge of the clearing and then squealed to a stop, headlight beams pale against the flames.

Cord drew his Roman short sword, exposing it as a long hunting knife, grabbed Katrina by the waist, and pressed the blade to her throat.

"Cord! What the hell are you doing?" said Van Bollin.

"Shut up, you old prick! Do what I say, or I'll cut Katrina."

"Shit, that's Rog's truck," Zach said.

Van Bollin smirked at Cord. "What's this about?"

"You and Zach are going to open your mountain vault for me."

"Shit. That's all? Do you believe every half-assed rumor you hear around town, Cord? There's no cave. There's no vault. Why would I stash a fortune out here in the mountains? You think the 'Many Hands inside the Mountain' would watch over it? The ghosts of a bunch a dead workers who never existed?"

"Don't fuck with me, old man. Rog and Kevin will wait with Katrina. You and Captain Unicorn open the vault. Then I'm out of here with the money and Tam. Either of you pulls any shit, Kat dies." Cord jerked Katrina against his chest, creasing her neck with his blade. "I've got your daughter, and I've got backup."

"No, you don't." Prudence Van Bollin, Katrina's aunt, stepped out from the driver's side of the pickup. "Unless you mean me. But I don't help douchebags who threaten my niece."

Dressed in a blood-soaked wedding gown, hair matted, face streaked deep red, Prudence reached into the truck and pulled out an axe, its blade dripping. Firelight turned the blood nearly black. She wiped at it with the back of one hand, only smudging it around.

"Trying to scare me?" Cord said. "I don't fucking scare!"

"What's Halloween without a few good scares?" Van Bollin said.

"Rog, Kevin! Get your asses out here *now*!" Cord shouted.

"Don't waste your breath. Pru, show Tamara how her boyfriends are doing." Van Bollin nudged Tamara. "Go on. It'll clear things up."

Reluctantly, Tamara followed Prudence, a woman half her brother's age, around back of the truck. Prudence lowered the tailgate then yanked off a canvas sheet. Tamara screamed and recoiled then bumped Prudence and fell to the ground. Struggling to rise, she landed on her knees, shivering, and then threw up.

"What? What is it?" Cord asked.

Blade tight to Katrina's throat, he dragged her to the truck.

When he glanced into the bed, all the color and bravado fled his face, and his knife hand drifted from Katrina. Prudence's face lit up, and she swung her axe. A spray of blood flew off the blade before the flat of it thumped Cord's head, snapping it sideways and silencing the cry he'd opened his mouth to release. He dropped the knife then toppled, missing Katrina by inches.

"What did you do to them?" Zach asked.

Van Bollin's hand came to a fatherly rest on his shoulder.

"Only what's needed. Understand, Zach, marrying my daughter is all or nothing. We do this for the good of Bollin's Creek. My great-grandfather started it in the Depression to keep the whole town from dying. We've kept the tradition ever since, so we take the lion's share of the profit. I believe you love this town. I believe you love my daughter. Her little game with Tam's phone was a test—you passed. Now you have to pass one for me. Go and look."

Stomach clenched and churning, Zach inched toward the truck, hoping what he imagined proved far worse than the reality only to feel his hopes shattered when he saw Rog and Kevin's mutilated bodies. Naked, side by side, hacked dozens of times, throats cut, and skulls opened—and from chest to groin, they lay split apart, with piles of candy stuffed in among their organs. Plastic wrappers and colorful logos glistened with blood. Hershey's bars. Skittles. M&Ms. Laffy Taffy. Life Savers. Twix.

Bubble Yum. Rog and Kevin looked as if they'd fallen into a thresher alongside a candy counter. The stench of their innards flooded Zach's nostrils. He felt a quiver in the mountain, and the sky swirled, the stars becoming fiery, golden streaks spiraling toward the flames on the other peaks. Multi-colored flashes sparked before his eyes. He switched off the lights in his collar and steadied himself against the pickup.

Prudence and her father carried Rog's body to the pit.

Katrina, clutching Cord by the armpits, dragged him there.

Wind swirled the dirt, and the dour, oppressive music flowing from the portable speaker resonated in Zach's mind, awakening his senses in an unfamiliar way. He took a step and almost tripped over Tamara lying in a fetal ball beside him. Katrina came back, helped her onto her feet, and walked her to the pit. She tried to break free, but Prudence whacked her with the flat of the axe, and they laid her out stunned beside Cord.

"Bring those sacks over here, would you, Zach, sweetie?" Katrina asked.

Zach did. The music made him want to comply. He looked inside one sack, filled with brightly wrapped candy, and then dropped both by Katrina.

Gradations of shadow whirlpooled within the darkness of the pit.

An enormous hand emerged, bony fingers tipped with crimson talons on an arm at least nine feet long. The hand scrabbled in the dirt until one talon sank into Rog's throat and dragged the candy-stuffed corpse to the wall. Three similar hands came to pull Rog up and over the stone ring into the pit. Looking at them hurt Zach's head. One second they all looked bony and hairy, and then scaly and plump the next, then fur-covered and cat-clawed, then charred, rotten, and tipped with bone-needles, then chitinous and coated with sharp bristles, then....

Zach shook his head and looked away.

"Hurts the eyes. You get used to it," Van Bollin said. "We have to break the membrane to earn the treasure. This one night of the year it weakens enough for us to breach it as long as we follow tradition."

"Tradition?" Zach said.

"Five sacrifices and all the candy they want. Satisfy the Many Hands inside the Mountain and they'll fill our real vault, safe in the basement of my house, with riches by morning."

"We have to do this together so we can be married, Zach," Katrina said.

"I… I don't know what to do."

The music tamped down Zach's rising hysteria and eased his rejection of the impossible. Its elegiac melody erased his fear.

"We prepare the offering. I'll do Cord. You do Tamara."

"How…?"

Katrina unwrapped a Jawbreaker and popped it in her mouth. With a smile, she rammed Cord's knife into his chest below the neck and carved downward.

Blood sprayed her face and ring mail shawl.

"Inside that case, Zach, is the blade of my great-grandfather," Van Bollin said.

Zach undid the snap, revealing a silver knife.

"You want me to…to do this to Tamara?"

"Not like she doesn't have it coming," Katrina said, still sawing at Cord. "Little hussy's been plotting against me ever since I screwed her brothers in the eighth grade."

"You did what?" Zach asked, but Katrina only shook her head.

"Let it go, sweetie. *You* get to marry me," Katrina said.

More hands reached from the pit, each with a changing number of joints, their skin and features in constant flux as if unable to comprehend their reality. Zach's mind shuffled possibilities like a deck of cards. He looked away when they clutched at Kevin's body.

"You said five sacrifices. Who…?" he said.

"You don't mean you didn't know?" said Van Bollin.

Katrina chuckled. "You and Tam have been boning like rabbits for months. What'd you think would happen? We were worried she might be barren the way you two went at it, and her as regular as can be. It was such a relief when she told me a few months ago, not that she said who the father was. But I know it's you."

Zach sank to his knees beside Tamara, placed his free hand on her belly, and watched her chest rise and fall as she breathed.

"She meant to get rid of it in New York, I'm sure. Bitch never could keep a secret worth a damn." Sticky sweetness touched Zach's lips, a caramel Katrina pushed into his mouth, her fingers leaving salty blood on his lips. "Here, it's easier with a piece of candy."

A grasping muddle of hands emerged from the pit. A dozen. Twenty. Forty. *More.* Zach couldn't count unless he looked at them, and he couldn't bear the pain of looking. The sight of the effigy filled his mind, its burning pumpkin eyes enmeshed by ancient writing, its engorged sex aspects, its treasure-bloated womb, and the earthy scent of the smoke from its eyes.

Break the membrane.

The music rode him. Katrina smiled. Even bloody and deranged, her smile made his heart race. She had shown him the real Bollin's Creek as only the few who knew it could understand.

Her great-great-grandfather's knife weighed heavy in his grip.

Giant, inhuman hands bristled from the pit like horrid flowers writhing in a vase.

Zach bit the caramel, releasing a creamy center tinged with woody bitterness.

He swallowed and it filled him with sweetness and light.

THE DEVIL TAKE THE HINDMOST

Annie Neugebauer

For three nights the dream had been nothing but memory replaying itself inside Hellen's mind, restless and aware she slept but unable to wake. Helpless, she stood at the front of the crowd, refusing her father's attempts to draw her under his arm, staring instead up at her mother's stoic face with her own jaw clenched tight, shoulders stiff, arms wrapping her cloak about her. The morning smelled of wet wool and animal dung.

The magistrate intoned in a low, hollow voice, "On this day of the twenty-third of October on the year of our Lord, 1596, under the power vested in me by Fyvie court and condoned by the Royal Scottish commission, I hereby condemn Marjorie Urquhart to death by burning." He lowered his torch and lit the fagots piled around her mother's feet. They caught in a hungry billow.

The villagers had refused to mix in green wood like she asked. The younger wood smoked more, and might have sucked her mother away from misery sooner. This wood was all dry, carefully gathered.

Hellen stared into her mother's eyes—so piercing and green. When Hellen was a lass she'd asked her father to tell her the story of how those eyes had made him fall in love with her mother, over and over. *Like a living emerald*, he used to say, smiling at Marjorie over Hellen's head. *Like the grass in the highlands after the spring rain. They cast a cantrip over me, those eyes. They held me enchanted. Kind she was not. She stabbed me through the heart and I loved it.*

The wording no longer seemed romantic. Not after Giles had testified against his wife. Not after he had betrayed her, innocent, to prove his innocence.

Hellen shrugged off his arm, looking into those beautiful eyes.

"I love you," Marjorie said, panic singing the edges of her tone, but still it carried the tenderness it always carried when she spoke to her only daughter. The crowd murmured, but Marjorie said again, louder, "I love you." She could have been speaking to her husband or sons, but Hellen knew she spoke to her.

I love you too, Hellen mouthed. Her heart had never beaten so hard. Her mother was over fifty, aye, but still in good health and too young to die. She'd yearned to see Hellen married with children of her own, and with Hellen over twenty and betrothed, surely she would not have had long to bide.

The flames rose to catch the plain white robe they'd draped on her. That's when her mother started to scream.

Perhaps it was the screams that drove the crowd back. They were the worst Hellen had ever heard, and she'd witnessed her mother midwife countless births. These screams were deeper, from a place of pure abandon. In long, rapid succession her mother screamed, drawing breath as fast as she could for the next, finally breaking her gaze with Hellen to toss her head back against the stake that held her.

Or perhaps it was the smell of burning flesh that drove the crowd back. Through the amazing orange flames her mother's skin melted and crisped and sloughed off her legs, but still she screamed.

Hellen didn't know if the beads of liquid dripping down her own face were sweat or tears. The heat grew fierce. The flames leaped higher. The fagots snapped with sharp pops. Her cloak dropped to the mud. Sobs shook her chest but she refused to let them out. She stared up at the underside of her mother's throat as the screams ripped from her.

Her father tried to pull her back and she brushed him off

again. He gripped her by the arm and dragged her backwards, away from the flames now wide enough to lick her. She stumbled, a shoe sticking in the shin-high muck, but she regained her balance and kept watching.

Marjorie began thrashing. Her head whipped side to side, the scream fading in and out, her arms jerking as much as her bonds would allow, and the flames climbed higher. Higher. Higher like the pitch of her relentless screams. Living agony, those shrieking wails. Someone in the back yelled out, "Mercy!" but it was far too late.

"Mercy," another woman cried, weeping, but no one moved except her mother until, finally, she didn't. The screams stopped, and the air was infused with the overpowering smell of burning hair, thick and sharp. "Mercy," the woman sobbed.

Her father turned away, and the villagers followed. Her brothers followed. Everyone followed except Hellen, staying until the blackened skeleton collapsed in feathery pieces, until the flames died, until the wood and stake itself were but a pile of ashes and all that remained were the echoes of the screaming and the lingering taste of burning hair clinging in a bitter film at the back of her throat.

Three times, Hellen had dreamed this. Every night she'd slept since it happened exactly that way, five nights ago.

This night, it was different.

This night, when she stared into her mother's jewel-green eyes as the flames caught and billowed, dancing up her clothes and skin, her mother winked at her.

A trill of fear flipped in Hellen—not fear for her mother, but for herself—and she started, looking to see if any of the villagers had seen the gesture and what they might suppose, but she was alone. No one had come. In real life, the entirety of Fyvie, their small village north of Aberdeen, had turned out to watch the purification of Marjorie Urquhart. But now Hellen stood alone in the gray sludge.

"I'm dreaming," Hellen muttered.

When she looked up at her mother, those sharp green eyes still stared. This was where Marjorie said, *I love you*. Twice, she'd said it.

Marjorie remained silent.

"I love you," Hellen said, prompting the dream. She wanted that part.

Her mother did not scream, did not blink. Her mouth remained closed, her eyes staring into Hellen's.

"Mother?"

The fire grew, eating away the skirt, the legs, the flesh. The smell of healthy wood smoke thickened into the aroma of cooking meat, then the tang of burning hair assaulted the air.

Her mother didn't break the gaze, didn't fight the pain.

The flames lapped the air, searching for new tinder. One caught the cloak over Hellen's chest. Still she couldn't pull her eyes away from her mother's stare. Her silence was terrible. Hellen had thought nothing on this Earth could be worse than her mother's screams, but surely this silence was.

Hellen was hot. Even hotter than she had been in real life. No one pulled her back this time. She must be burning. The wool smoldered over her chest, scalding her in a sharp bite.

She shrieked, gasping, but choked.

Tears streaming from her eyes, she looked back at her mother. Marjorie's hair was on fire, the skin on her face pitting like spoiled cheese, but still her eyes remained, watching motionlessly from inside the blaze, appraising her daughter as the flames ate her alive.

The smoke crawled down Hellen's throat, rushed into her lungs and sank there. Heavy, thick, warm. So warm. Smothering.

She woke up.

Two otherworldly green eyes stared into hers from inches away, piercing her soul. They floated in the blackness of her room, and Hellen was still burning, still choking, but she couldn't move, couldn't breathe for the terror those eyes filled her with.

"Mother?" she coughed out, and before the word was finished she hated herself for saying it, for thinking it, for attaching it to the fear.

The eyes blinked over vertically slit pupils. The cat.

The eyes stared. The fear lingered.

Hellen sucked in a deep breath—possible. Harder with Mery's warm weight on her, but possible. Not the deadly suffocation of smoke.

"Mery-bell," Hellen whispered, swallowing another cough. "You frightened me."

Hellen's hand trembled as she worked it from beneath the cover to stroke Mery's silken fur. The green eyes closed in bliss, a deep purr emanating from her small body. The delicate chin rested beneath her own, balanced on her neck so the rhythmic breath coated her flesh.

Did Mery sense something was wrong? Did she know Hellen needed comfort? Or did she simply seek the warmth the nightmare brought?

Closing her eyes, Hellen floated down through the darkness back into sleep, hoping the memory was done for the night. She sought comfort in the cat's warmth. The last thing she felt was the concentrated lick of Mery's rough tongue on the soft, sensitive skin of her throat.

***

Hellen woke to the vague sensation of dreams fleeing, feeling a heavy weight on her chest, but when she opened her eyes, Mery was no longer on her. Nothing was on her but the cover.

The morning was cold. Mery had left her sometime during the night and her father and brothers had never started the fires before leaving for the field. As the woman of the house now, Hellen would be expected to rise the earliest and ready breakfast, but so far her father had said nothing. The men hadn't touched the cold bread sitting on the table, growing hard with blue-and-green spots. Had her father not lit the fires because he, too, could think only of the flames? Did he dream? Did it still seem better her than him?

Hellen stared at the leaking thatched roof. Her limbs felt heavy as the cauldron they boiled water in, heavier than the stones that made the walls of this low, squat house, heavy like the weight of her future holding her down.

She lifted herself wordlessly beneath the covers, sliding her bare feet onto the cool, packed dirt floor, and shuffled toward the dead coals, debating whether the warmth was worth the pain. Her foot landed on something soft and round, pressing into her arch.

Hellen cringed, closing her eyes and lifting her foot away. Mery often left her hunted treats, anything from mice to birds and once even a hare, some still struggling. At least this felt dead. Bracing herself, Hellen glanced to see what she'd stepped on.

It was small, pale gray, and doughy, slightly curved. She looked away with revulsion. A slow-worm tail. Mery often caught those snake-like, legless lizards, and they were notorious for dropping their tails as a diversion. She shuddered, hoping the rest of the creature wasn't sliming around somewhere she might step on it, too.

Why did Mery bring her such things? Was it an offering? A game, warning, or threat? An attempt at mothering? The disconnect between people and cats had always struck her when she looked into Mery's nearly featureless black face. Even her whiskers and nose were black. The only color besides her green eyes came when she yawned or hissed and Hellen caught a glimpse of her bright white teeth or long pink tongue. They bonded, aye, but they did not speak the same language. Any communication was subject to misinterpretation.

Whatever the reason, she couldn't bear to touch the tail. After slipping on her shoes, Hellen took the broom from its hook and swept the grotesque wee thing toward the open doorway at the front of the dwelling. She shoved it with the stiff bristles, trying to send it far with each swipe but not squish it. Glancing only from the corner of her eye, she got it to the threshold, but it caught on the straw layered there to stiffen the slick mud outside. The smell of the outdoor fire wafted to her, low and smoky beside the midden.

Hellen swept at the stuck appendage furiously, trying to thrust it up and over the edges of the straw, but it wedged in.

Feeling eyes on her, she looked up.

Across the street their neighbor, Euphemia Prat, who her mother had called Old Effy, watched her with a sneer, her pock-ridden nose curled in disdain.

Confused, Hellen looked down, wondering if her skirt was up, then realized she held her mother's broom. The very broom Euphemia, Jonet, and the others had claimed her mother rode to the revels. Her cheeks burned. Such lies.

Hellen lifted her chin. She would not be shamed. "Good morning, Euphemia."

"'Tis a good morning, with the village free of evil once again."

Hellen held herself still, but her body trembled with rage. "I do not believe sending an innocent woman to burn is a good deed. I should beg the Lord for forgiveness had I been involved in such happenings."

Euphemia smiled. She had three teeth left. "Marjorie Urquhart confessed. Only the guilty confess."

The heat in Hellen's cheeks melted down her neck, spreading wide across her chest. "Anyone would confess when put to the rack long enough."

"Aye, but she confessed to more than was asked of her, didn't she? She admitted to seeing the Devil himself traipsing through the woods."

Hellen nearly burst forth a reply, but bit her tongue. Finally, she said, "She said she saw him leading others. I should hope none of it was true, for if so our village isn't free of evil yet." She hoped Euphemia thought about that. She'd been close with her mother. Marjorie had refused to list names, but should any others be accused, surely Euphemia would be amongst them.

"Is it not? The mothers and fathers of Fyvie have slept soundly since Marjorie was taken in, knowing their babes are safe. And who can see the Devil?" Euphemia asked, jaw wagging. "Who can see Old Scratch save for witches, eh? I never seen him. I never walked with him. 'Twas your mother who admitted to what she was by claiming to see others follow."

"My mother was a good woman."

Euphemia sent a pointed glance to the broom Hellen now

grasped like a bludgeon. "If you like. And did you ever see him, Hellen Guthrie? Did your mother introduce you to his pact?"

It was a threat, as surely as Hellen's, but far more likely. The village was already suspicious of her, wondering how much mother passed to daughter. She couldn't afford to play these games. "Of course not," she demurred, ducking her head. "I have never seen him." *But neither did my mother.*

She leaned the broom against the wall, knelt, and grasped the dead thing between her thumb and forefinger, letting emotion override revulsion. She carried it toward the midden, the dunghill where they piled their refuse.

Euphemia gave a delighted scoff before retreating into her dwelling. Hellen turned her back, staring at the rotting waste, panting, trying to calm herself. Finally, she raised her hand to toss the thing.

She paused, drawing it closer to her face instead. She eyed it, freshly calm in her curiosity. It wasn't smooth enough to be a slow-worm tail as she'd thought. It had two puffy creases in it.

Hellen cocked her head. There were no scales either. It was smooth gray. Not a lizard part.

She set it on the flat of her other hand, turning it with a finger. At one end, tiny and delicate and shockingly familiar, she recognized it: a nail. A fingernail.

It was a finger. Small.

A baby's.

Swallowing a gasp, Hellen studied the opposite end, where it had been detached. Indeed, there was a bone in the center. Her stomach heaved a great lurch. It was an infant's finger, drained entirely of blood and going gray.

She hurled it into the fire beside the midden. The flames continued on unhurried, growing slightly at the new tinder. With a glance to be sure Euphemia hadn't seen, Hellen darted back inside.

***

Over and over she punched the dough's firm, tacky mass into the use-smoothed wood of the family table, folding it onto itself. Her mind turned endless revolutions with the kneading.

A baby's finger. From whence had it come? If anyone but her should have seen it, they'd have thought it damning evidence. But it hadn't been in their house. Mery had brought it from elsewhere.

Hellen had no doubt there were those who practiced witchcraft, but not in Fyvie. Theirs was a small village of good people. Maybe in Aberdeen where the market was large and the officials corrupt, but not here. Not her mother.

Her mother. Those burned at the stake never received proper death rites. Where did her mother's soul go then?

"'Twas only because they were babies," Hellen whispered. As soon as the words left her she felt spied upon. She looked up, searching the dimness. A twitching motion caught her eye. Mery perched in an open window, sitting on the wall. Her tail swayed back and forth, brushing against the stone. With her dark fur and the gray of the day outside only slightly brighter than the gray inside, she was but a silhouette.

"Oh, Mery-bell," Hellen sighed, kneading in a gentler rhythm. "I thought someone was here."

The cat stayed motionless but for her tail, and though Hellen couldn't see them, she felt those green eyes on her.

"You brought the… thing to me." Hellen always spoke to the cat when she was alone. She had since she was a lass; it eased her loneliness. "You left it for me where you always leave your treats. Where did you find it?"

Mery turned her head, showing Hellen her delicate feline profile.

Hellen shifted the dough to spread more flour beneath it. "You ken that's why they burned her? They accused her of using them in her flying ointment. The midwife is simply the easiest to blame when babies go missing."

Mery jumped from the sill in a graceful fall, onyx fur gleaming as she prowled past Hellen's feet to sprawl between the table and the ashes of the cooking fire. It was unheard of for the Guthrie family to let it go out, but Hellen thought it right. Something should change. It wasn't right for life to go on as usual, and the quiet coldness of the house seemed better suited than any other change.

"And those babies didn't go missing." Hellen continued, keeping her voice low. "They died. Their parents killed them through neglect or meagerness or bad luck and they felt guilty, grew feart, and they hid them. Buried the bodies so no one would—"

Hellen stopped, fingers sunk into the dough. That was it! Mery had dug up one of the bodies that could prove her mother's innocence. If the child were buried in the dirt, it couldn't have been used in an evil concoction. Hellen turned to the cat. Mery was sitting up, her tail wrapped neatly around her two front paws, and staring at her with those wide green eyes, her head cocked ever so slightly to the side, as if listening. The look on her pointed, alien face was so alert, so alive, so seemingly intelligent that Hellen froze.

Mery dipped her head and began cleaning the fur on her chest with great, limber licks of her tongue. Hellen let out a breathless chuckle. She placed the dough in the pan, covering it with a cloth and setting it to rise.

"That is it, though," she said. Mery continued her bath. "Maybe I can gain my mother's death rites and set her soul to rest. Will you lead me to the bodies?"

Mery's ear twitched to the side. Goose bumps rose on Hellen's arms.

"Tonight when you go out to find your dinner, I will follow you," Hellen whispered, bending to scratch Mery between her velvety ears. "And see if we can prove them wrong." A gentle purr rose in the air.

Hellen leaned over the cat to gather fresh peat blocks to set in the ashes.

Mery let forth a vicious hiss.

Hellen jerked back, shocked. "Mery-bell," she exclaimed. "I didn't mean to startle you. I just need to start the fire."

Mery stood, arching her back, and hissed again, flashing fangs.

Hellen was so surprised that her feelings were hurt. "What's gotten into you, lass?"

When she stepped forward again, Mery swatted at her ankle. This time Hellen brushed past her, letting her skirts force the cat out of the way. Mery meowed, fluffed her fur, and ran out the door, tail standing.

Hellen piled the peat blocks with a deep sigh. There went her company for the rest of the day. She grabbed the molded bread off the table and tossed it to the far edge of the midden where the goats could pick it off. 'Twas every man, woman, child, and beast for himself in this world. Hellen was learning that faster than any, but even goats had to eat.

***

Hellen sat at the table with her father and two brothers. She had made a large batch of stew with boiling fowl, leeks, rice, and prunes, seasoned with sugar, pepper, bay leaf, and thyme. The remains still steamed in the bronze cauldron, but the portions in their wooden bowls had already begun to cool. The men dipped bread into the stew and slurped. Behind them, the cooking fire smoldered, the smoke rising in a ghostly column to drift out the hole in the ceiling.

Her father drank the bottom of his stew and leaned back, the old wooden bench creaking with his shifted weight. "The Meldrum lad has called off the betrothal," Giles said.

Hellen dropped her bread into her bowl, pulse quickening. "Richard? Why?" She needed the engagement. She was twenty-five, of the age to marry, and it was the only way she could leave her father's house.

Stew glistened on her father's reddish beard. He sighed. "He's changed his mind."

"You can hardly blame him," Norman muttered.

Hellen looked at the elder of her two younger brothers sharply. The beard he'd been trying to grow was patchy and thin. "What does that mean?"

"It means," Norman dragged out, "that now the lads are feart you'll do to them what Mother did to Da." Giles had testified that his wife had cast a cantrip to render him impotent.

Her father sighed. "Norman, stay out of this. Hellen, the

villagers are nervous. Give them time. I'm sure Richard will come around."

But Richard wouldn't come around. He'd only set to marry her because she was pretty and apprenticed to make money as a midwife. There was no love there. What would she do now? Hellen pushed her bowl away and Norman slid it toward himself, sopping up the remains.

"Father," she said, already regretting what the anger would make her say, "Did you ever consider it was your age that stole your manhood, rather than my mother?"

Giles's face went from weary to grim. "Watch your tongue, lass. I ken my own wife."

Norman chimed in, "The Guthrie men have never faced that struggle. We are a virile line. Only witchcraft could weave such a curse."

"Yeah," Duncan added. "We are a virile line."

"Duncan," Hellen snapped. "You aren't even old enough to ken what that means."

"Mother was a witch," he hissed. She drew back, struck. His big brown eyes gleamed as he added, "And you might be a witch too!"

Giles stood, putting a hand on his youngest son's shoulder. "Now lads, don't say such things in anger. Hellen is a good lass, a righteous lass, and you mustn't throw such words about. Especially not now, when the villagers are hot. Do you understand me?"

Duncan lowered his head. "Aye, Da."

Norman echoed, "Aye, Da," but he smirked.

"I'm sorry, Father," Hellen said, standing to clear the table. "In my grief I've let my tongue run away with me. Forgive me."

"Of course, lassie. 'Tis a hard time for us all, but it is well that the Meldrum lad has broken the betrothal. With your mother gone, we will need you more than ever, here, to tend the home."

***

Hellen stayed awake after her brothers and father had gone to bed, slowly adding peat blocks to the fire as she waited for Mery to return. She was drowsing with her head on the table when she heard a soft shift. The cat sat in the window, tail swishing. She stood, stretching, and circled herself on the sill, turning as if to lead Hellen away.

"Finally," Hellen whispered. She stood and pulled on her cloak, moving toward the door.

"Hellen," came a deep voice.

She whirled, swallowing a gasp. Her father stood in the shadows.

"What are you doing awake? I thought I heard your mother sneaking late-night bread as she used to."

The casualness with which he spoke of the memory pierced Hellen, and she could not breathe, much less answer.

Then Giles took in her cloak and shoes and stepped closer. "Why are you dressed to go out? Where are you going at this hour?"

"I… needed some fresh air. I felt stifled. I was going to walk for a bit in the cool."

"Tonight? Are you mad?"

She shook her head, unable to gather what he meant.

"Have you lost track of the days? The beginning of Allhallowtide is nearly upon us. The morn marks Hallowmass Eve."

She'd forgotten. She hadn't been out of the house in days, hadn't seen any of the villagers' traditional preparations. Aye, it was the thirtieth of October tonight. But Mery…

She looked for the cat, but she was nowhere to be seen.

"You cannot wander about, Hellen," he said, taking her by the arm and leading her toward her bed. "If anyone should see you, at a time like this…"

He didn't have to finish. All Hallows' was the time of witches, when they ventured out to dance with the Devil, and it was true she couldn't risk being seen out, not now.

"Aye, of course, Father."

"Good lass. Get some sleep now," he said, pulling back her covers for her as if she were a small child.

She wanted to find where Mery had dug up that thing—see what it might mean for mother, for herself—but now her father would be too watchful, and besides, he was right. It was good of him to look after her.

But as he pulled the covers and tucked them tightly under her chin, she wondered if that was actually the reason. Was he protecting her, or suspicious?

Had he been waiting up, keeping his eye on her?

Lying awake in the dark, listening to him make his way to his bed and climb inside, Hellen imagined this was how her mother had felt, turned upon by her own family, accused under the guise of salvation.

***

The nightmare came again. It began as the memory. When it reached the part where the magistrate lit the fagots and her mother was to say, *I love you*, Hellen was relieved the villagers were there. At least it wouldn't be the isolated, twisted version of last night. They crowded behind her in the mud as they really had, and her mother said it.

"I love you." The broken, fearful tone. She looked into Hellen's eyes with that brilliant green gaze. Murmurs from the crowd. "I love you," she repeated.

I love you too, Hellen mouthed, as she had.

"What's the matter?" Marjorie said.

Hellen looked around. Everyone stared.

"Aren't you going to say it back?" Marjorie asked, angry. "Aren't you going to tell your mother you love her before she burns to death?"

The crowd's murmuring grew into concerned discussion. If she said it, would they accuse Hellen of being a witch too? Would they call her loyalty allegiance?

The flames reached her mother's robe and she began to scream. Hellen felt sickly relieved at the return to the actual order of things. At least it wasn't that silence, that horrible silence of the night before.

When the screams grew frantic and ragged, just before her mother had tossed back her head and begun to thrash, the nature of the screaming changed. It was gradual at first. The screams slowed, grew false, and then Marjorie was pretending to scream, the way you would mock someone else who was screaming.

The crowd was silent now. The flames leapt towards Hellen's cloak. Her father didn't try to pull her back.

Marjorie's cruelly mocking screams morphed and bubbled into laughter. Rich, boisterous, atrocious laughter. She tossed back her head and laughed, her breasts jiggling with the motion, and the flames continued to climb, to eat her, and she laughed.

She laughed and laughed as her hair caught fire and the flames bit Hellen's cloak and the smoke slipped down her throat and smothered her, so heavy she couldn't breathe.

She woke with a start, hot, sweating and shivering, Mery's weight balled on her chest. It was well before dawn, pitch black, and the cat's eyes must have been closed for Hellen could see nothing, only feel the pressure of her, only taste bitter fear on her tongue, only hear the echoes inside her mind of mother's maniacal laughter as she burned.

**

Hellen rose with the dawn, cold and tired and heavy again, the men gone already to the fields. The harvest was largely over. Now they gathered the waste for burning in great heaped piles spread around the village. The air was distinctly colder and sharper, bordering on November.

She remembered to put on her shoes, so she didn't step on the pale gray thing left for her on the floor, but it still startled her. She bent, gripping it in the bottom of her skirt.

This time it was a foot.

It was larger but still tiny, chubby, with nails at the ends of the toes. It stopped cleanly below the ankle, cold and drained of blood. Hellen hurried to the outdoor fire, imagining the babe it'd come from. Had she been able to follow Mery last night, she might've found where the poor thing was buried. Probably behind the house of his or her wretched parents.

She tossed it into the flames, covering it with scraps.

As she turned to go inside, a wail rose from down the path between rows of dwellings. People clustered outside, a woman on her knees in the center of them. Who? Young Agnes, perhaps, with the newborn.

Hellen's stomach sank. Not again. Not another.

"Aye," came a scratchy voice from the side. Hellen jumped, peering into the shadows under Old Effy's front covering. The woman watched her with sharp gray eyes. "Another babe gone missing."

Jonet stood beside her, an unusually pretty woman of about her mother's age: one of those who had testified against her. She, too, watched Hellen rather than the small crowd gathering around Agnes.

Hellen's heart pounded. Maybe she wouldn't need to follow Mery to the bodies. "'Tis the first child since my mother was taken in. This proves her innocence! It cannot be her, for she is gone."

Euphemia laughed, the skin under her chin waddling. "Gone? Gone. Who's to say? There are those who will think someone else has taken up her wicked quest."

Blame. Aye, of course they would blame her. Unless she blamed someone else first. She imagined accusing Euphemia. *'Twas her*, she would shout out, righteous, *'twas Old Effy all along!* But she wouldn't do it. She couldn't do it. She could not stand the woman, but she did not believe she would kill babies. Probably Agnes's baby caught the cough like so many did now, and helpless, afraid of being accused herself, Agnes had buried the child.

Was that whose foot Mery had brought her? She had to stop her cat from continuing this. Should someone see Hellen with such a thing she'd be found guilty without explanation.

She looked into the women's eyes. "I was home all night," she whispered, voice cracking. "I never left the house. My father can attest to it."

Jonet spoke for the first time, her voice melodious and soft. "He can, aye, but will he?"

"I…"

"Have you been sleeping, child?" Jonet asked, crossing the straw-coated mud. In the gray light of dawn, her smooth skin looked radiant.

"Not well. I have this dream…"

"Poor thing. Have you tried valerian root? A tad in your stew will ease your slumber."

"I haven't any."

Jonet reached a wrinkled hand—so much older-looking than her face—into the apron tied over her dress. She pulled out a large, knotted mass of tubes that for a moment reminded Hellen of the baby's finger or a slow-worm tail, but then she saw the nest of them tangled over and upon each other and they looked exactly like the knotted veins pressing against the skin of Jonet's hand. The bunch was fibrous and earthy, the bottoms of the roots diminishing into thread-thin wisps.

Hellen did not want to touch it, but Jonet proffered it between them with the expectation that Hellen would accept it, so she did. They felt smoother than they looked, slick. Downhill, Agnes's cries had calmed to a muted sobbing.

"You need but a small bit of it," Jonet said. "'Tis effective in any brew. Just a pinch will ease your sleep, lass."

Then why did you give me so much? Hellen wanted to ask, but she kept her mouth shut and drew the tangle of roots toward her skirts.

"Aye," called Euphemia, still huddled in the shadows. "And don't mix it with ale, mind you, unless you wish to sleep like the dead."

Hellen stared at the hag. She never drank ale. What was such a caution? Through the dimness under the covering, Euphemia's wide, gray gaze caught hers, and she winked.

Shock ran through Hellen's tired body. She remembered her mother's green eyes in the dream, her wink, her stalwart, silent gaze as she burned. Hellen's hands trembled.

"Head inside now, lass," Jonet urged her. "I will come for a visit first thing tomorrow morn. Perhaps you miss a mother's ministrations." Fresh fear filled Hellen. What if Jonet found one of Mery-bell's leavings?

Euphemia's taunting call came next, following over Hellen's shoulder as she hurried toward the doorway to her family's small, squat hut. "Aye. Head inside now, Hellen Guthrie. Stay inside tonight, if'n you're a good lass, for Allhallowtide approaches, and the Devil's dues are due on Hallowe'en night!"

***

During dinner only a few lads came to the door begging firewood, and they stopped well before nightfall. Giles gave them each a bundle lest they bring any mischief on the house, but he cautioned them to go home and stay inside, and would not allow young Duncan to join in the old games. Fyvie was somber this year. If anyone told fortunes or tales of fairies, they did it quietly.

Hellen went to the window at dusk, where Mery sat flicking her tail against the stone. She stroked her, watching the neighbors light their bonfires before turning away. Mery jumped from the window and lay in the corner.

"No one is to leave this house tonight," their father said, closing the shutters. He looked at Hellen. "No one. Understood?"

All three of them nodded. Hellen bowed her head. "Aye, Da."

Giles and Norman both drank heavily at dinner, Giles even allowing young Duncan some ale. Hellen quietly refilled their wooden mugs before the bottom was dry. She kept the fire burning hot so the room would be warm, and she served them large portions of hearty stew, and by a couple hours after dark, Giles snored in his bed. Norman slept quietly, and Duncan fell asleep sitting at the table. Hellen carried him to bed and tucked him in.

If they'd tasted the valerian root, they showed no sign of it.

She changed into her darkest frock and took out her cloak. Mery twined in and out of her legs.

"Are you ready to take me on your hunt, wee one?"

A rich, hearty purr rose.

"Lead me to the same place you've gone the past two nights, alright? Let's dig up the proof my mother was no witch." Even if the villagers wouldn't believe, she could at least prevent Mery from bringing back the pieces and putting Hellen in danger. It would be safer on any other night, but Jonet had promised to pay her a visit first thing in the morning. Hellen couldn't chance the nosy woman finding Mery-bell's next gift. It must be tonight.

With the bouncing, hurried walk only a cat can make graceful, Mery darted out the front door, leaving Hellen no time to question her rightness of mind or the risk she was taking, and she was glad of it. Drawing her cloak over her hair, she followed.

***

When she was a lass, some of the braver villagers would take candles out onto the hills on Hallowmass Eve to leet the witches. Should the candle burn brightly the hour through, the village was said to be safe from evil, but should the flame go out it was taken as an omen of great woe. As she hurried now, hunched and silent, through the darkest space between two bonfires, beyond the village's bounds, Hellen wondered what it meant to have no candle at all.

Indeed, she longed for a light, but she couldn't risk it. Most people would be asleep by now, locked safely inside their homes, but a few may be out to keep the bonfires burning, and some may watch in dread of fetches approaching their home.

She was amazed by how quickly wee Mery-bell could run. She didn't get the impression her cat was trying to lose her, though, for she occasionally looked back as if to check Hellen followed. As they burst into the open hills, the air was cold and crisp.

Mery darted across the long grass, tail high, and Hellen followed. It wasn't until the bonfires were small behind them that she paused. The cat continued. Hellen whisper-called, "Mery-bell, where are you going?"

Two flashes of green as she looked at Hellen, but she did not stop.

Hellen pulled her cloak tighter. Surely the cat wouldn't lead her into the woods? She'd been so worried lest villagers think she was something to fear that she hadn't stopped to wonder if she should fear others. She was reminded of the jeer she and the other children used to yell at each other fleeing the bonfires on All Hallows' Night: "Every one for himself and the Devil take the hindmost!"

She glanced over her shoulder.

Swallowing, she quickened her pace, and Mery led her uncannily, relentlessly, into the dark, heavy shadows of the woods above the village.

***

Hellen had always known Mery prowled at night. She was the best mouser in the area, which was perhaps the only reason the villagers had not demanded her burned as a familiar, but had Hellen known how far and wide the cat traveled, she'd have marveled that she made it home alive.

They were deep into the woods, and although the air was less cold, Hellen kept her cloak wrapped tightly, for the very trees moved and shadows shifted and Mery led her through it— always quick enough that Hellen couldn't stop to rest, but never so fast she lost sight of her.

At first Hellen thought she heard her own panting, heavy and airy, underscored by the pounding of her heart, but as she continued deeper and deeper into the woods, the sounds separated and made themselves clear: chanting. Did she hear drums?

Her skin prickled. "Mery-bell," she whispered vehemently, "Stifle your pace, lass. Someone is afoot." Her throat was tight, mouth dry, eyes wide enough to burn in their attempt to see through the trees, but Mery did not stop. Hellen followed as quietly as she could.

The chanting grew louder, the distinct rhythm almost detectable as words, and Hellen grew less afraid of being heard over the din and more afraid of being seen. Ahead, striped by the ever-shifting trunks of trees, a fire burned. Shadows moved around it.

Mery headed directly toward it. Hellen was too frightened to call out to stop her.

Were there drums? Hellen couldn't tell. Perhaps it was the relentless chanting that gave the impression of drums. Perhaps it was her heart, pulsing in her ears, making her whole body feel warm. Or perhaps *that* was the nearness of the fire.

Hellen stopped, having come upon the outskirts of the gathering before she meant to. A single tree stood between her and the flames, and the mad figures that cavorted around them.

The words were clear now. Women's voices chanted:

Power, money, beauty, and prestige:

The Devil gives his gifts on Hallowmass Eve.

Murder, mayhem, sacrifice, and fright:

The Devil's dues are due on Hallowe'en Night!

Rich, gleeful laughter rose at will. Hellen stared, recognizing a face. The long, wavy white hair and the shriveled nose belonged to Euphemia Prat.

Hellen swallowed a gasp, searching the others. There was Jonet with her pretty face and old hands, and Mavis who was missing an ear, and even young Katherine, Hellen's childhood friend, large with child.

Mery-bell walked calmly into the middle of the revel.

I should have picked her up! In the center of the ring, hung over the fire, was a large bronze cauldron. Large enough to hold a cat. For a moment, Hellen felt certain the wild women would throw Mery into whatever foul concoction simmered there, and she should lose her only remaining tender companion on this Earth.

Mery stopped, sniffing low to the ground, and only then did Hellen spot the baby.

An infant child was bundled tightly, perched against one of the rocks that ringed the fire. Mery sat on her haunches beside it and licked the delicate hair on the top of its head, mothering it with long, efficient strokes of her pink tongue.

Hellen was so enraptured by this strange kindness, this unexpected familiarity, that it took her a moment to realize all movement had stopped except for the flames and Mery's tongue. The women stood still. When Hellen lifted her gaze, she gasped.

All four women stared at her.

"Hellen Guthrie," said Old Effy. "I warned you about this night."

Katherine, cradling her stomach, asked, "Do you come to join our Sabbat?"

"I—I didn't mean to—I'll go. I followed Mery..."

Jonet looked at the cat, who was still vigorously cleaning the baby, and said, "That isn't her name."

"Mery?" For a moment, confusion dulled Hellen's fear. "Aye, it is." She tilted her head to study her cat. The gesture she'd at first thought was tender now made her cringe. Mery's tongue was so rough, with its barbs, and a baby's skin so soft. She must be hurting the child.

"Perhaps when she was but a cat," Jonet said patiently, as if speaking to a child. "But you don't think a cat could find her way here, do you?"

The cat's furious licking did not cease. The baby's face scrunched in frustration. Still that black face hovered over the bundle, licking, licking... tasting?

Hellen shook herself, appalled. "That is my cat," she snapped, darting forward to shoo her from the babe. Then she realized she stood in the circle, beside the women. Her mouth dried.

Euphemia tilted back her head and cackled gleefully. "Aye, and what's more, your mother!"

A log on the fire broke in two, collapsing in a fresh shower of sparks. Hellen jumped, backing up, damp shoes shuffling through the dead leaves. "What?"

"Your mother's soul, anyway. For now," she added. "But not for long if she doesn't pay her dues before the dawn!"

Hellen's heel bumped the base of a tree and she stopped, pressing her hands into its rough bark. She stared at her wee black cat who now undulated sinuously in the air as if she were rubbing against the legs of someone who wasn't there, as if her spine were being stroked by invisible fingers. Around and around she circled, turning her head as if to better press it against something, but nothing was there.

"Mother?" Hellen asked, her voice small and high. She felt faint, but she could not pass out now.

The cat looked up, locking onto her with wide, piercing green eyes. They stared at each other for a long minute, and Hellen knew. Her mother's soul resided in this cat. Tears tightened her throat, threatened her eyes. "Mother." Her whisper cracked on the word. Then the cat blinked and continued sinewing back and forth as if about invisible legs.

The baby fussed, kicking in helpless lumps beneath its swaddling. Was it Agnes's child? Hellen's face felt painfully pale, drained of blood.

"You can't blame Marjorie, Hellen," Katherine said. "She had no way of knowing they would burn her before she paid."

"Before she paid?" Hellen echoed, looking at her old friend.

"Aye, before she paid the Devil his dues."

"The Devil," Hellen gasped, breathless.

Euphemia's jaw wobbled. "Marjorie owes Old Scratch a soul. If she doesn't pay up tonight, he'll take hers with him straight back to Hell." She tossed back her head and laughed.

Jonet eyed the cat, still rubbing itself against the air, and added, "No matter how much she tries to sweet-talk him. The Devil's dues are due."

All four of the women repeated it, chanting: "The Devil's dues are due on Hallowe'en Night!"

"My mother really is a witch?" Hellen whispered. Why had she brought her here? Her head spun with dizziness.

Katherine set a hand on Hellen's arm. She twitched. Katherine said, "Aye, but you can hardly blame her. What choice do we have, those of us with nothing?" She stroked her belly again. "We will do anything to protect what we hold dear."

"Did she—do you—?" Her balance wavered, fingers gripping the bark. "The babies?"

They turned to look at the infant propped by the fire, crying now in earnest.

Euphemia grinned, showing off her few remaining teeth. "The Devil deals in souls, lassie. 'Tis a small price to pay for all he can bring you."

Hellen's whole body trembled, but she raised her chin. "If she pays?"

"Then she'll keep her soul, as promised."

Jonet's smooth, pretty face folded in sympathy. "There are worse things, Hellen. At least you'd still have your mother."

The cat's black fur gleamed in the firelight. She paused to look at Hellen. Hellen's tears spilled over.

"It's up to you, lass," Jonet said. "There are three souls here tonight, and the Devil only needs one."

"Three?" She looked at the baby, at her mother. Revelation shocked her. "Me," she muttered. "I am a soul. I can give myself to save my mother?"

"If you wish."

Who'd spoken that? The voice sounded deeper than the women here.

Goose bumps rippled on her skin. "Will giving my soul to the Devil make me a witch?"

"No, not a pure soul. You have to sign the pact to gain the power of witchcraft."

"But won't the villagers think me a witch if they see the Devil's mark upon me?"

"If they see it, aye."

As if they wouldn't look. It was inevitable. The next person to be accused would accuse her in turn to save themselves.

Hellen pushed away from the tree, clenching her fists by her side. "I want assurance that the villagers won't turn against me." She pictured her mother screaming in the flames. "That my father won't betray me. I need out of his house." She thought of Richard breaking their betrothal so casually. "And not by marriage. I don't want to marry. I want to bide on my own."

Euphemia drew close, her neck skin waddling. "You'll need to pay something for all that, lass. You get no protection unless you sign a pact."

Jonet stepped forward as well, drawing a scroll from her apron. "Kneel, child. You can give yourself to save your mother, but you must pay to save yourself." *With what?* She placed the scroll on the dirt and Hellen unrolled it with shaky fingers. If she had to pay to save herself anyway, she could pay to save her mother instead, and then run, but that still left her powerless against the villagers. She lived in dread, every day. She knew how it would end.

Her mother wove through her arms, purring. "Mother,"

Hellen whispered, "how did you get yourself into this?" She closed her eyes as the soft top of the cat's head stroked the bottom of Hellen's neck. "I will save you. I will save your soul."

Eyes clenched, Hellen signed with the tip of her finger.

When she opened them, her name appeared in blood. For a moment her mother's tail wrapped her neck like a noose. Panic tightened her stomach, then her mother moved away in a silken caress, rubbing in and out again, but now it wasn't empty air she stroked herself against. No, it was strong, muscled calves balanced strangely atop two large, bird-like feet. Their thick, putrid claws dug into the leafy ground for balance. Hellen held her breath, gazing up. Bulging thighs, and, oh—her cheeks hollowed, burning—an atrocious manhood, grotesque in its prominence. An eerily luxurious torso, ruddy, dark skin, beastly shoulders, a thick neck, and... Hellen almost fainted.

A face so handsome and so horrid, topped by vicious, curved horns. He crossed his arms over his chest and two large wings shifted and flexed behind him, leathery as a bat.

"My child," he said, deep voice vibrating through the air like thunder.

She could see him. Hellen could see him.

Witch.

The other women began dancing, laughing and chanting as they circled the fire. Their comfort so near him told her more than she wanted to know. What had she let herself be backed into?

Hellen reached shaking arms to scoop her mother away from him, cradling her, the warm purrs vibrating against her chest. *Mother, what have I done?*

He knelt to look into her eyes, and Hellen's very spirit shrank, cringing away from him. His smile was profane, teeth thick and yellow as a horse, but his eyes fiercely human. The worst part was that he looked almost... familiar. Not someone she had met, but someone she should know, maybe. Like finally tasting a food she'd long smelled cooking from afar. Was this the presence she'd often felt when she was alone in the dark, hurrying through the village at night or afraid, as a child, to check for when she heard sounds across the room? How long had he been watching her?

"You owe me a soul," he said. His voice echoed with an almost bird-like chorus—like a flock of rooks taking flight—like the cries of the damned cawing up from Hell.

Her body shook, but it would not be her mother's soul. It would not be her own.

Hellen nodded, swallowing, and turned to the baby now screaming beside the fire.

THE GLAD STREET ANGEL

Ronald Malfi

We stop for lunch at the Harbor Grill, although neither of us are really very hungry.

"You gotta get your act together now, Gideon, gotta keep your nose clean," my father tells me. I watch as he arranges a mound of crumbs into a straight line with his pinkie. "There are no more second chances."

"Yeah," I say.

"For real, man. You're eighteen now. Ride's over."

"Yeah," I say again, "I know."

I watch him take two bites of a hefty club sandwich from across the table. He chews slow and methodically, as if the act itself requires much thought, and his eyes alternate between me and the throng of cars along Pratt Street. My father and I don't really get along. Throughout my childhood, I maintained the constant notion of him as some brooding, elusive cloud on the horizon, rattling the ground below with thunder. I can remember watching him shave before the bathroom mirror, the sink half-full with water and clogged with shaving cream icebergs. He seemed so big. Once, I held a ladder for him while he scooped gunk out of the gutters of our duplex. I remember looking up and seeing straight up his shorts. His genitals looked like snarled, graying fruit.

"What are you thinking about?" he says suddenly.

"Mom," I lie.

"Well," he says, exhaling with enough zeal to send the queue of crumbs scattering like fleeing troops, "your mother, she's not feeling well. She'll be glad to see you, Gideon, but she's not feeling well."

"What is it now?"

"Her headaches."

"I thought she was taking something for that."

"She is," my father says. "The pills, they don't work like they used to."

"Is there anything else she can take?"

"Sometimes she can't even get up," he continues without hearing me. "You remember what she was like when she first started getting them? Goddamn migraines."

Suddenly, I'm thinking about pills. One day out of the blue, when I was a freshman in high school, I was struck by these dull, throbbing stomach pains, but not really in my stomach—more like on either side of my stomach, and just below it. The groin area. It felt like someone had stuffed two billiard balls just below the lining of my belly. My plan was to wait it out and not worry about it—tough it out like a man—but the pain wound up lasting for several days, and I grew increasingly frightened. All I could think about was my junior high sex education class and if there was a possibility I'd contracted some venereal disease from Jenna Dawson, even though we'd never gone all the way. So I panicked and wound up passing out one morning in the school bathroom, cracking the side of my head against a grimy urinal. I'd imagined my urine coming out in thick, coagulated, snotty ropes (it didn't) and that sent me swooning. I awoke sometime later in a bed at U of M with my father at my side. His first words to me had something to do with how real men don't whimper like little girls, and just what did I think I was doing in that bathroom anyway? Was I on something, for Christ's sake? When the doctor recommended I take pills, my father scoffed and told him I didn't need any pills. The pains went away after about a week, anyway. The problem was never diagnosed.

I sip my Coke and don't touch my roast beef sandwich.

"Anyway," my father says, "things are gonna change. They

have to. You understand that, right? You understand that your mother can't handle your crap anymore?"

I tell him yes, I understand.

"And *I'm* through dealing with it, too."

I tell him I understand.

"I got you a job," he tells me, "doing some construction work for a friend of mine. This friend, he knows the deal—knows what you been through, I mean—and he's doin' me a favor by bringing you on. That means you don't embarrass me. I said it'd be okay if he gives you a monthly drug test or something. Told him I'd prefer it, really. I think that made him feel good about the situation. He's a good guy. Just don't screw shit up." He sighs and looks instantly miserable sitting out here on the verandah with me. Maybe he's thinking of my mom and her headaches. Or his construction worker buddy. Or whatever. "You start Monday," he says after too long a pause. "You better buckle down, Gideon."

I tell him thanks.

He is mulling something over in his mind. Caught in the throes of concentration, my father looks the way a washing machine might look if capable of thought, his brain all jumbled with faded chinos, polo shirts, worn house dresses stained with grease. "All right," he says finally, and there is some sort of resignation in his voice, "let's see 'em, Gideon. Up on the table." He says, "Let me see your hands."

I show him, holding them palms up, and there is no expression on his face. I feel I owe some sort of explanation. I say, "I haven't done it since I don't know when. A long time, anyway."

"Yeah, okay," he says, and only because he isn't quite sure *what* to say. He does not understand my hand thing. Neither do I, really.

A lumbering silence passes between us. I think of him shaving in the mirror again, his shirt off, his doughy paunch obtruding over the frayed band of his Fruit of the Looms, a wiry braid of black hair spilling out of his bellybutton.

"Can we stop at the gas station on the way home?" I ask. "I

need to grab some smokes."

My father sets his hands in his lap, anxious to leave. I am familiar with almost all of his idiosyncrasies. And I am familiar with his hands, too. I start to think about the way he rolled his handgun around in his hands that night, sitting on the edge of his bed, his head down. I am still thinking about this when he finally opens his mouth and says, "Anything you want to get off your chest before we get home?"

"Like what?"

Casually, he rolls his shoulders. He looks goofy doing it. Simple, somehow. "Anything," he says. "Anything. Whatever."

I think about my time in rehab, almost laugh, then shake my head.

We leave.

***

There is something frightening about my mother. And I realize I haven't seen her in five months.

She is sitting in a green recliner in front of the television set, her white hands pressed firmly in her lap, her eyes glazed over. Her hair is pulled back into a bun, gray and dull in the slivers of daylight that slide in through the partially-shaded windows, and her mouth is drawn tight as string. Seeing her, I am suddenly reminded of my grandmother's funeral and the way my mother had pressed rosary beads into the palm of my hand, insisting that I pray as we stood before the casket. She pressed hard, leaving behind tiny pea-shaped indentations. I cannot recall her words, cannot recall what Nona had looked like packaged in her satin-lined mahogany tube; I can only recall the brush of my mother's hair against my cheek, frizzled and damp with tears, and the stale-sweet smell of her breath in my face. Funeral breath. Mourning breath. Breath that cannot be masked by a million slabs of spearmint gum.

She looks up and sees me and smiles in her medicated way. Struggles to get up. I picture scarecrows swaying in a corn field and feel something hard and sick and moist roll over in my stomach.

"Ma," I say, and advance toward her before she has time to rise. Too much movement and her headaches start up.

I bend down and she hugs me, kisses the ink-spot birthmark just over my left eyebrow.

"Gideon," she whispers, squeezing me tight. I can feel the dull knobs of her fingertips pressing into my back. She is crying now. "Honey. You look too thin. Your father said you were being fed at that place…"

"I was fed," I tell her.

"Ralph," she continues, and her eyes—now wet and muddy in their sockets—shift beseechingly toward my father. She looks much older than I remember.

"They fed him," my father promises her from the tiny kitchen. He is searching through the refrigerator.

"How you feeling, Ma?" I ask.

She ignores me. "Are you angry with me for not coming to see you? I wanted to, I did, but your father, he said it would be too much, that I should stay home because it would be too much—"

"I'm not angry, Ma."

"I wanted to go and to bring you some food, some good food from home, and I can't image what…" She trails off. "My God, Ralph, they didn't feed the poor boy. Look at him, will you?"

"I've seen him," my father says back. "He's fine."

It's already too much. Five months at Crownsville and I've forgotten how easily people cry. Particularly mothers.

The apartment is smaller than I remember, too—much smaller than the old duplex. The carpet is an amber-colored shag, filthy and stiff with dried food and spilled cola, and the furniture looks cramped and uncomfortable against the paneled walls. There are only a few windows, the shades all half-drawn, and the room is musty and oppressive. I think of retirement homes and abandoned cars left on the side of the highway.

"I've been planning this all week," my mother says, finally pushing herself up from the recliner. She is all skin and bones, like a blouse and sweatpants threaded with pipe cleaners. "We'll sit down tonight, have dinner together like a family. I'll make something, cook it up. What would you like, Gideon?"

"You don't have to, Ma."

"It's your first day home. Tell me what you want."

I tell her hamburgers would be perfect, and that seems to make her happy.

While she busies herself in the kitchen, I move down the hallway and see my father staring without interest at some framed photographs on the wall.

"Look at these," he mutters.

"She doesn't look good," I tell my father.

"What are you talking about?"

"How long has she been this way?"

"What way?"

"So out of it," I say. "You can't tell?" I think maybe he's been around her too long to notice. "She needs to see a doctor."

My father finally looks up at me and his face is stern, his jaw set…yet his eyes seem hurt. I am not used to seeing him in this way. He says, "Your mother's fine." He says, "They're only headaches, for Christ's sake, Gideon. Just migraines." He says, "You worry about yourself, that's all you need to worry about."

Later, I go to the bathroom, urinate for what feels like an hour, then find myself standing before the bathroom mirror for a comparable amount of time. I have taken some of the clinic home with me, I notice: my face is pale like the walls, and peels like plaster. My cheeks are chapped and cracked and interrupted by a network of very faint blood vessels. My eyes look sucked into my skull, hollow like busted light fixtures. My skin is jaundiced, the color of the mashed potatoes served on Fridays. It is also the same color as my mother's skin.

Rinsing my hands at the sink, I scrutinize my palms. It used to amuse me the way my father would ask to see my hands, to hold them out for him. Yet today at the restaurant I found I only felt sorry for him. For whatever reason.

I stick my tongue out at my reflection, wag it back and forth, and go to the kitchen for dinner.

***

My bedroom seems alien to me, and I think it's only because we'd been living in the apartment just a few months before I was arrested. It's small and smells vaguely of turpentine. There are a few scattered comic books on the floor, some Star Wars figures still in their packages tacked to the drywall. A large poster of Jimi Hendrix covers the back of my door.

I lay on the bed in silence for a long while, thinking about my hands and that night on Glad Street. I remember thinking about my father the night I was arrested—sitting in the back of the police car, I had summoned the image of him on the edge of his bed, holding his handgun. It was odd to think of that then. Odd now, too.

Once my mom has gone to bed, I creep down the hallway and grab my jacket from the hall closet. It's been five months and I expect it not to fit, or to just feel strange, but it fits and doesn't feel any different than I remember. In the kitchen I load my pockets with matchbooks and stuff a pack of Marlboros into my jacket. Without having to look I can tell my father's watching me from the living room. He's seated in the recliner in front of the TV, but he's not watching television—he's watching *me.*

"What?" I say, not looking up. I pretend to busy myself with the zipper on my jacket. "What is it?"

"Where are you going?"

"Out for a while. That a problem?"

I can tell that it is, but he does not say so. Instead, he tells me not to stay out too late, that I need to keep my shit together and my head clear. He does not articulate his intentions very well, my father. What he really means is he doesn't trust me and that he's worried I'm going to fuck things up again. But what my father doesn't understand is that different people deal with things in different ways. My way had been to get caught up in shit, smoke dope, get laid, drink too much. Fine. Whatever. Everybody's got their own method of operation.

Not for the first time, I wonder what my father would say if he knew I saw him with his gun that night.

"Don't be home late," he calls after me, but I'm already out the door.

Outside, I am hit by a strong October wind. The air reeks of the harbor, even in the cold, and it is an unsettling chemical smell. The city streets are poorly lighted, surprisingly desolate, and uniquely Baltimore. There are a few Halloween decorations in some of the tenement windows. I walk and smoke, my destination premeditated.

When I get to Glad Street, I stop walking and just stand on the curb. I'm directly beneath a lamppost and my shadow is smeared across the empty street ahead of me. Someone has stolen a number of placards from the city's drug campaign—those ridiculous BELIEVE posters that do nothing but irritate property owners who remove them from their sidewalks whenever they appear—and a number of them now lay strewn in the street.

Shivering, I remain standing beneath the lamppost. Five months ago I was dragged across this street and slammed against the hood of a police car. My first offense, I had only to spend some time in rehab. So I was sent away and the city feels it's doing its job, getting punks like me off the street. Punks like me who pay no attention to BELIEVE posters. Whatever.

Something white flits through the darkness; I catch it from the corner of my eye. Turning, squinting down the blackened alleyway, I see nothing...but I suddenly feel much colder than I had just a moment ago.

No rest for the dead, I think, still trying to peer into the darkness. Looking for a shape, a visage...anything recognizable...

I see nothing. In the cold and the dark, I hang around Glad Street for forty-five minutes and still I see nothing.

***

Carter Johnson is my father's construction worker buddy, and he looks like someone stretched a pair of filthy coveralls over a city bus. His face resembles a burlap sack with eye-holes and his breath is an aromatic amalgamation of unfiltered cigarettes, peppered beef jerky, and steamed cabbage. He talks at an unnecessary volume and highlights every third sentence with profanity of a sexual nature. I immediately dislike him.

He's drinking beer with my father Saturday afternoon in our kitchen and my father introduces us.

"Good to meet you, Gideon," Carter Johnson says, rising and shaking my hand. It is like shaking a chain-saw. "Lookin' forward to havin' you come aboard Monday."

"I appreciate it," I say, and move down the hallway.

My mother is in her bedroom, propped up on the bed and staring blankly at the wall. It is the way my father sat that night while holding his gun. I enter the room quietly and pause at the foot of the bed, staring at my mother's profile. She doesn't turn to acknowledge me.

I say, "It's a nice day out, Ma. You should go out, get some sun."

She is slowly gnawing at her lower lip. I notice she isn't staring at the wall but peering out the window and down at the street below. She is watching a group of young black girls play hopscotch. My mother, she watches these girls like someone lost in a dream.

From the kitchen, I hear the dull boom of laughter.

"Ma…"

Without looking at me, she says, "You should eat something, Gideon. You look too thin. That's not a healthy thing for a boy your age."

"I been eating," I say. "I'm okay." I ask if her head hurts.

"No," she says.

But I can tell it does.

I spend the rest of the day hanging around Glad Street, but see nothing. People move by and it's like I'm invisible. Baltimore is good for that. I look homeless in my grimy sweatshirt and torn jeans, leaning against the PNC Bank with my head down and my hair in my face. I finish my final cigarette for the day and toss it in the street when I hear someone shout my name. I look up and see a girl rushing toward me from across the street, black hair streaming behind her, her right hand grappling with a shoulder bag that is slipping down her arm.

"It *is* you," she says, beaming, and hugs me awkwardly with one arm. "I thought I was seeing things."

The girl's name is Alicia Vance and we dated on and off prior to my arrest. She is thin, too thin, and her skin is so white you'd think if you held her up to a light you'd see her heart pumping through the wall of her chest.

She loops a bony arm around my neck. "When did you get back?"

"Yesterday."

"I've missed you." This is a lie. We were not really on speaking terms the night I was arrested. "What are you up to?"

"Nothing," I say.

"You should come by the loft sometime, see the guys. My God, Gideon, I feel like I haven't seen you in years."

"You still hang at the loft?"

"Sure. Come by whenever, we'll throw you a fucking party. It'll be like the old days. That's cool, isn't it? The old days, I mean. They didn't fuck with your mind too much in that place, did they? Crownsville, right? I hear it's real shitty, what they do to people there."

"It's cool," I say. "Wasn't too bad." I am looking past her and down Glad Street, only half-listening. She notices and mutters something. "What?" I say.

"I said, how 'bout a goddamn kiss?"

"Oh."

"What's the matter? They slip Soft Peter into your food or something?"

"I don't get it," I say.

"Never mind," she says. "Just kiss me."

***

Carter Johnson is excited about doing something important—in this case, contributing to the rehabilitation of a young urban drug abuser—so he personally shows up Monday morning to drive me to the construction site.

I sit in the passenger seat of his pickup in silence, watching the decrepit, ancient buildings of the city wash by the window in a blur. Carter Johnson, he is talking to me about nothing important, and I only pretend to fully listen.

"So you know," Carter Johnson says, "we give mandatory drug tests once a month."

This is bullshit but I don't say that. He's trying to play it simple, maybe save face, and I'll let him do it. I tell him that's fine, I have no problem with it.

"I mean, it's nothin' against you," he goes on anyway. "Just want you to understand that." Now he sounds like my father and it is suddenly very easy to comprehend their friendship. "All the guys—they all have to do it. It's a city regulation, Gideon."

"Sure," I say. Whatever.

Carter Johnson's men are erecting some office building on the outskirts of the city. The men, they all look like the construction worker cliché—burly, unshaven, flat faces with acne-pocked skin—but they are not. They work efficiently and mostly in silence. They take brief lunches and—surprisingly— are meticulous about washing their hands. A few attempt to engage me in friendly conversation, but something about my demeanor must blaze like an unwelcome torch, and they quickly relent.

I pay little attention to the work itself. Only when I taste grit and dirt do I remember I am sawing wood, am nailing nails, am carrying shit from trucks and whatever else.

Lunch, I slip away and find myself wandering closer to downtown. There are a number of people out at this hour—people in suits and people in cutoffs and other various people—and for the most part no one notices me. Hands in my pockets, my head down, I listen to my own respiration as I wander through the city.

And stop once I reach Glad Street.

There are people here, too. I recognize many of the buildings, have been inside many of them myself at one time (and not too long ago, either), but I hardly look at them now. I am more interested in the street itself. *Glad Street*. And the children. BELIEVE. The goddamn signs are everywhere now. It's like a plague. There are a number of residential tenements along Glad Street and there are a number of children playing in the street. It is a very different scene from the night before. I recall my mother sitting on her bed, half-gazing out the window at children playing hopscotch. I suddenly feel very angry. The BELIEVE signs—there's one so close to me, taped to the outside of a tenement door—I peel it off, getting my fingernails behind the placard, and hold it for a while at arm's length. Someone has punched two holes in the placard, each hole occupying the two enclosed bubbles of the B. I turn the placard on its side and hold it up to my face and wear it like a Halloween mask, peer through the holes at the children in the street. They are shouting and tossing a ball back and forth. They laugh and there is the *click-click* sound of a jump rope whipping the sidewalk.

BELIEVE. How can posters help if you don't know what they mean? And who wants to be preached at, anyway?

Looking through the B, I think I see an angel, a ghost.

I drop the placard and stare across the street, but there are only kids. No angel. No ghost.

And I am late returning to work.

***

The loft is really a basement. I don't know who named it or who actually owns it, but throughout high school it served as a private refuge where guys came to smoke dope and feel up their girlfriends. It is a large room, windowless and dark, lit only by the flickering illumination of a dozen or so candles. The floor is concrete, covered in places by mismatched rolls of carpet and fire-scarred furniture scavenged from various dumps. The walls are cinder-block and crowded with graffiti. Once, the loft had reeked strongly of mildew and animal feces. Now, only the acrid stink of marijuana exists.

Tonight Alicia is here, as are two other guys I don't recognize. I push through the loft's wooden double-doors and the two guys lethargically lift their heads from an arrangement of pillows on the floor, glance in my direction, then continue circulating a pipe. Alicia rises from a filthy-looking sofa and hugs me as I enter.

"You're soaking wet," she says, rubbing a hand through my hair. "Why did you walk in the rain?"

"I don't know," I say. I don't tell her that it wasn't raining when I left my building. I don't tell her that I hung around Glad Street for an hour before coming here, and that's when the rain had started. Anyway, Alicia wouldn't understand.

"Who is it?" one of the stoners shout.

Alicia takes me by the hand and introduces me to the two goons sprawled out like pharaohs on their pile of pillows. I immediately forget their names.

"You're the guy that got busted," mutters one of the pharaohs. "I heard about you. Some guy told me you got ass-raped in rehab."

"Someone told you that?"

"Yeah," he says. "That true?"

I shrug off my wet coat and fold it over the back of the filthy sofa. I say, "That's news to me."

"Yeah," the other guy says, "sure. I mean, that's what I figured." And he extends his little glass pipe. The inside of his arm is purple-black and covered in needle tracks. "Want a hit?"

"No," I say, shivering. I'm too cold and wet to think about smoking. Anyway, I'm still thinking of Glad Street.

"Come on," Alicia says, still holding my hand, and leads me down a narrow corridor that communicates with a basement-level apartment. Someone has spray-painted MIKE THE HEADLESS CHICKEN FOR PRESIDENT on the apartment door.

"Whose place is this?" I ask.

Alicia turns the knob and pushes the door open. "Mine," she says.

It is a small, one-bedroom job with worn carpeting and a toilet that runs continuous. It reeks of pot in here, too.

"Place is cool. You live by yourself?"

"Yeah," she says, but already I can see some guy's sneakers in the bathroom doorway, a couple pairs of unwashed boxer shorts lingering about the place. Beneath the pot smell is the undeniable smell of *male.* Yet I say nothing.

She takes me to her bedroom. It is as big as a closet, hardly large enough for the tiny bed that takes up most of the room, and the floorboards groan as if in pain when I walk across them. There is a window above the bed's headboard, facing Glad Street. I feel a chill rush through me—and then Alicia is there, peeling off my shirt.

"What?" I mutter.

"You're such an idiot," she whispers, and kisses my belly. I stare at the top of her head—at the pale white part down the middle of her hair—in the moonlight coming in from the window. "Come over to the bed."

I go to the bed. Alicia removes her shirt and stands in the semi-darkness half-naked. Her breasts are familiar to me. They are small and pale. Alicia's nipples won't appear until they're prodded and squeezed—and then they jut out like knots in bark.

She gathers me in her arms and pulls me toward the bed, down on top of her. We kiss and she tastes bad, like tonguing the bottom of an ashtray. I have difficulty getting aroused, mainly because I'm listening to the occasional car glide through the rain-swept street outside. Alicia works her way to the button on my jeans, tugs at the waistband, unzips the fly. She moans something but I'm not paying much attention. I feel her cold, thin-fingered hand slide into my pants and grip me forcefully. I am half-propped above her now, and I crane my neck to see out the window. But it's too dark and I'm positioned poorly, so I see nothing.

"What?" she says, irritated for the first time. "What? What is it, Gideon? You have to take a leak or something?"

"Yeah, I do," I say, which is not *completely* untrue.

"Get up, get up," she tells me, pushing against my bare chest with her hands. "Go use the goddamn bathroom, for God's sake."

I pull myself off her and stagger in the darkness beside the bed, my eyes still trained on the window. On the bed, Alicia scoots back against the headboard and props a pillow over her bare chest. As I move out of the room and into the darkened hallway I can hear her exhale with deliberate exaggeration. I do not turn and look in her direction, though that is what she wants.

Instead, I continue to the bathroom, click on the bathroom light—wincing—and close the door behind me. Standing shirtless before the mirror, I look like some peeled fruit. Sickly, the way my mother looks.

There is a small window between the shower stall and the toilet. I go to it and lift the moldy shade, peer out. There is a BELIEVE poster covering the glass. I feel around the sill for the latch, find it, unlock it. Sliding the window open, I push the poster away from the glass; the driving rain quickly drags it to the sidewalk.

This is a basement apartment; the window is at ground level and striped with wrought-iron bars. I see the lamppost on the corner of Glad Street. The rest of the street is dark and motionless, yet I cannot pull myself away from the view. My eyes run the length of the street, pausing longest in the darkened, shadowy alleyways between tenements. I think I see something, even through the rain, even through the runnels of water running down the pane of glass, but it is too dark to be sure. I consider opening the window farther—it is one of those windows that push up and out—when I hear the door creak open behind me. I'd forgotten to lock it.

"Gideon..."

I turn after some hesitation. Alicia Vance stands shirtless in the doorway, her thin arms propped over her breasts, her thin-fingered hands tucked beneath her armpits.

"Gideon, what the hell are you doing? You've been in here for twenty minutes."

I go to say something, but suddenly realize there is something in my mouth. I cannot form words.

"Jesus Christ, Gideon, you're bleeding," Alicia says, refusing to move from the doorway. "You're still doing that?"

I catch my reflection in the bathroom mirror and see the heel of my left hand pressed firmly in my mouth. A single teardrop of blood trickles down my wrist toward the bend in my elbow. I am suddenly aware of my teeth biting through the skin. There is no pain.

"Maybe," half-naked Alicia Vance says with little emotion,

"you should just leave."

A few minutes later and I'm back out in the rain. Hugging my sopping coat against my body, shivering, I stand outside Alicia Vance's apartment building for some time, unmoving, as a car passes slowly down Glad Street. I watch it turn at the intersection, its taillights glittering in the rain, before crossing the street.

And I catch movement off to my left.

I spin around, hair plastered to my forehead, rainwater coursing down my face, and catch the fleeting image of a small angel disappearing down one of the darkened alleyways. I see this and immediately cannot move. She is not a real angel—I know this—but, rather, she is a little girl dressed in a white satin gown with crepe paper wings and a pipe-cleaner halo above her head. It is fake; it is an illusion. I know this, too. She is just a little girl in costume.

Somehow, I am again able to move. I begin running in the direction of the angel, my Nikes crashing through puddles, my hair whipping my face, my heart slamming in my throat. Ahead, the angel has already vanished in the darkness and I can see nothing of her now. She is too fast. I have been waiting for her, expecting her since my return from rehab, but she continues to elude me.

I tear down the alley and crash into a wedge of metal trash cans. The sound is tremendous, rebounding off the brick alley walls. I spill to the ground, soaked, freezing…and think I almost hear laughter echoing from the other end of the alley. There is a street light at the other end—uninspired orange sodium—and its light falls across the mouth of the alley, but I cannot see the angel beneath the light. I hear her but cannot see her anywhere.

Catching my breath, my entire body suddenly sore and uncertain, I manage to pull myself to my feet and stagger back out onto Glad Street.

***

I am not sure where day stops and night begins. Things seem to be in a haze. In four days, the apartment has grown smaller and smaller. The air, it's like breathing motor oil. If I open a window my father comes around behind me and closes it. If I make too much noise in the kitchen my father stands with his arms folded in the small hallway and stares at me. I say nothing and try to do even less.

Carter Johnson calls the house on Friday and I answer the telephone. He asks me what's wrong and I tell him I'm sick and I'm sorry I didn't call this morning. He asks if I'll be in later and I tell him probably not.

"Is this about the drug tests, Gideon? You have to understand—"

I hang up.

My mother doesn't leave her bedroom. She sits there on the edge of the bed, mimicking the way my father sat that night with his handgun, and she stares silently out her bedroom window. Children play in the street. I, too, watch the children on occasion, but it just makes me angry. This whole city makes me angry. There is nothing to BELIEVE in this city, so who are they kidding? And these kids—there's no future here. So it just makes me angry, and although I'd lied to Carter Johnson about being sick, by Friday evening I am aware of a slight temperature working its way through my system. The result of moping around in the rain, no doubt.

Friday night, I move silently through the apartment toward the front door. I hear floorboards creak somewhere ahead of me and I freeze, imagining my father standing somewhere in the darkness. Down the hall I see shapes move.

"Dad," I whisper.

"Gideon." It is my mother. She steps into the living room, wrapped in a cloth robe, and her skin looks blue and translucent in the gloom. "Did you miss the bus?"

"What?"

"Will you be late for school?"

"I'm not going to school, Ma," I say. "I haven't been to school in a long time."

"I can pack you a lunch," she says. Her eyes are black and like two pits in the center of her head. Looking at her, I'm more conscious of my fever. "You don't eat properly."

"I'm going out," I say, and slip out the door. Hurrying down the stairs and out onto the street, I imagine my mother in the kitchen preparing me a bagged lunch to take to a school I no longer attend.

I make it to Glad Street in time to see the angel skipping down the sidewalk in the dark. I shout and feel something rupture deep in my throat. I pursue the little girl, my hands stuffed deep into the pockets of my jacket, my teeth rattling in my head. My body feels frozen and numb on the outside, aflame on the inside. I follow the angel toward the intersection of Glad and Charles. She pauses here and begins to spin with her arms straight out. The street is silent and dark and I can hear the scuff of her sneakers on the pavement. I shout again—I am shouting her name, although my brain hardly registers this at the moment—and I look around to see some tenement windows light up.

"Come here!" I shout, but the girl—the angel—does not come. Instead, she pauses and faces me, giggles…and vanishes into the night.

I am bad with time. I have no idea how long I have been out here shouting. But soon I hear police sirens tearing up the street. Like a thief, I hustle back down Glad Street and disappear down an alley. I run harder, faster, and break through to the cobblestone semicircle that is Water Street. My fever is rising and my lungs are fit to burst. I can't remember the last time I took a breath.

Two police cruisers sail past Water Street, their flashers on, their sirens blaring. I freeze in mid-stride. A sharp pain rips through my left hand and I taste blood. I am biting my hands again.

The little girl in the angel costume appears at the end of Water Street. She is staring right at me, waiting for me to see her, and when I do she turns and runs. I chase her, my legs pumping for all they're worth, my breath harsh and abrasive burning up through my throat.

I cross the street in pursuit of the little girl and I am suddenly aware of police sirens and flashing lights all around me. I am burning up with fever and am not all here. I feel I am floating somewhere just above myself. Turning down another alley I slam into a chain-link fence and quickly scale it, rat-style. I drop down on the other side into an alley swollen with garbage. This does not slow me down. I run faster, my heart about to burst from my chest.

The alley is a dead end. I come face to face with a brick wall, eye level with a BELIEVE poster. I tear the poster down, wrap it around my face, then hunker down in the swill. The poster pressed against my face, my breath strikes it and echoes in my ears. My eyes are pressed shut. I am thinking of our old duplex and my father scooping gunk out of the gutters. I am thinking of my mother's skin, brittle and yellow and like wax paper. I picture her now, at this very moment, searching for mayonnaise in the refrigerator.

I am suddenly aware of a presence beside me. I hear plastic trash bags shift and empty cans roll across the cement. I am not alone. Yet I do not remove the BELIEVE placard from my face. I hear the movement beside me and I feel my own hot breath against the cardboard. Mourning breath.

The girl, she giggles.

"What?" I whimper. And in my head I hear my father's booming voice: *Real men don't whimper like little girls, Gideon.*

More giggling. It's suddenly all around me.

"What?" I manage again. And think: *There's no rest for the dead.*

I tear the poster from my face and see the girl just a few feet from me, also hunkered down in the trash. She is forever young, her eyes wide and lost in innocence, and she is giggling behind a cupped hand.

"Stop," I tell her.

"Trick-or-treat," the angel whispers.

I reach out a hand to touch her but she quickly vanishes, and my hand goes right through the air, unobstructed. I touch the cold brick wall on the other side.

Police cars whiz by the mouth of the alley, and I pull the poster back over my face. My cheeks are burning. I can't tell if I'm breathing.

I wait for the sirens to die. When I remove the poster from my face and look around again, I see that I am alone. I remain crouched in garbage, unmoving, unthinking, until the first rust colors of dawn blossom between the cracks in the tenements across the street. Daylight, and I feel wiped out, exhausted. I toss the placard aside—had I really held onto it all night?—and stare down at my hands. My palms are covered in blood. There is a hunk of skin peeled away from one of my fingers, unrolled like a party favor.

I get up and start moving back toward home, feeling grimy and cold and sick. There is a dull pain on either side of my stomach, and just below the waist of my jeans. The groin area. By the time I reach our building, the pain is sufficient enough to cause me to pause halfway up the apartment stairs.

It is fully daylight now. I enter the apartment quietly. The place seems empty. I move down the hallway toward my parents' bedroom. I pause here and look at the framed pictures on the wall. There are two photographs in particular that attract my attention. One, it's my mother and sister and me at the kitchen table in our old home, a melting ice cream cake bristling with candles in the center of the table. The other photograph is from last Halloween. Having grown out of the tradition, I am standing against the railing of our home, looking slightly annoyed, slightly bored. My sister, dressed in her angel costume, smiles a gap-toothed smile at the camera. The sun must have been facing us that day because the shadow of my father, who is taking the picture, covers half my face. Only my sister is in full view.

I turn away and continue down the hall toward my parents' bedroom. My mother is there, sitting on the edge of the bed, staring out the window. My father is nowhere to be found.

"Ma," I say, "where's Dad?"

"Oh," she says, turning to see me in the doorway, "Gideon. Is it breakfast already? What would you like, dear?"

"Ma," I begin, but then say, "Eggs. Lots and lots of eggs. Do you think you can do that? I haven't been eating."

"Yes!" She says this with startling enthusiasm. "Yes, Gideon! I've been telling your father—that boy is not eating properly. That boy is getting too thin, just too thin, and he'll never make the football team. What did you say?"

"Eggs," I tell her.

She moves slowly off the bed and I stand in the doorway and watch. She pulls on her robe even though she is fully dressed and even though her skin is slick with sweat, then moves past me and out into the hall. When I hear pots and pans clanging from the kitchen, I cross the bedroom and open my father's top dresser drawer. His handgun is hidden beneath some socks. Beside the gun is a small box of bullets. I removed both the gun and the bullets and sit on the edge of the bed. It occurs to me that I must look just as my father had that night, sitting here with this gun in my hands. Last Halloween, a group of teenagers—most of them younger than me—were raising a commotion along Glad Street while I chaperoned my sister's trick-or-treating. City kids, they do things that even *they* can't fully comprehend, so how can I? And things just happened so fast. I heard gunshots before I even knew what they were. And when I went to grab my sister's hand, her hand was no longer there.

My sister. She was strewn across a pair of tenement steps, bleeding from the head.

Some many months later, after we'd moved from the duplex to this apartment, I walked in on my father sitting on the edge of this bed, turning this gun over and over in his hands. I watched in silence from the doorway, the heel of my right hand pressed firmly in my mouth, my teeth nervously biting down. I watched him without him knowing, and at one point I felt very certain he was going to do it—that he was going to put the gun to his head and end it.

But he didn't. He put the gun away and just cried for a long time.

I hear my mother humming from the kitchen. Her headaches started around the time of my sister's funeral. I think about that now as I load the gun. Before me, the single bedroom window looks out on a group of children playing in the street. Is there any hope for any of them?

Believe, I think. *Believe in what?*

I say nothing to my mother as I step out the front door. My belly cramping, my fever racing, it takes some effort to maneuver down the flights of stairs to the street. Outside, the sun is too bright and I wince. It hurts my eyes.

I carry the gun down the street, walking quickly for someone in such pain, and I think about my father shaving in his underwear. I think about his slow physical decline that started with my sister's death and continued throughout his visits with me at rehab. See, I was arrested one night on Glad Street with a bag full of weed in my back pocket. But the call didn't start out as a drug bust. The call started out as a disturbance. Apparently a number of people heard me shouting my sister's name from their apartments that night and called the cops. The dope—well, that was just an added bonus, I guess.

The sun is hot and I'm burning up. When my eyes adjust to the light, I manage to open them wide. It seems both sides of the city street are papered in BELIEVE posters.

I start to laugh. It hurts my belly, but I laugh anyway.

City kids—they're all a bunch of hopeless animals when you get right down to it. The good ones are gunned down, and the bad ones, well, the bad ones just grow weaker and weaker and smoke their lives away.

This is not a guilt thing.

Please don't think that.

I cross over to Glad Street and find it teeming with young children playing in the street. If their lives meant anything—anything at all—would they be so easy to end?

A ripping, agonizing pain tearing through my gut, I raise my father's handgun and begin shooting.

Made in the USA
Coppell, TX
26 September 2023